THE LAKE

By

N.G. JONES

ACKNOWLEDGEMENTS

Thanks to my lovely wife Sandi for her hard work
and assistance in editing this novel.

Thanks also to people who live around and near
Lake Lanier for inspiring me.

For David and Gun

Both dearly missed

PROLOGUE

800 AD

CHEROKEE MYTHOLOGY

In Cherokee mythology, and in that of Indian tribes generally, there is no essential difference between men and animals. In the primal genesis period they seem to be completely undifferentiated, and we find all creatures equal living and working together in harmony and mutual helpfulness until man, by his aggressiveness and disregard for the rights of others, provokes their hostility. When insects, birds, fishes, reptiles and four-footed beasts join forces against him.

Ela was excited because it was her wedding day. She had been a woman for one year and had loved Salonitah for as long as she could remember. The year had seemed like

1

an eternity and she thought this day would never come.

Ela was the most beautiful in Ani-kawi. Ani-Kawi was her mother's clan and her name, Ela, translated as earth. Salonitah meant flying squirrel and he was Ani-wayah, the wolf clan. When she was small Ela had been scared that she would not be allowed to marry Salonitah. She knew the clan system forbade marrying within the same clan. Salonitah had always been by her side so she assumed him to be in her clan. So scared was she to ask her mother that nine great moon ceremonies had passed before she had enough courage to face the possibility that they could not be married. When she finally plucked up enough courage to ask her mother she was surprised by her reaction. Her mother smiled compassionately at the angst in her beautiful daughter's eyes, then laughed. She held her close, stroking her long black hair. "Don't worry, little one. He has been yours from the moment he set eyes on you." Ela had cried with happiness.

From that day on there had been six more great moon ceremonies, six more years, during which time there had never been any doubt in Ela's mind. She would marry Salonitah.

The first day Salonitah had seen the beautiful baby girl, he grinned. He was three years old and had never stopped grinning since. It was obvious to the whole village their spirits were as one.

Ela stood by the river with her family and friends. The cool waters caressed the rocks and stroked the trout that swam gracefully around the natural pools that formed downstream of the boulders littered along the riverbed. She had fasted for four days, but the hunger pangs she felt the previous days had given way to butterflies as she excitedly waited for the Going to Water Ceremony to begin. She caught sight of her reflection in the water. Tall and slender, her naked body shimmered and her cascading locks rippled in the water as it flowed south towards the flatlands.

There would be a feast later that would fill her belly before Salonitah took her. But before that there would be the marriage ceremony. During the ceremony Salonitah's mother would give him to Ela's mother. Which meant, though born to another bloodline, he would now become part of Ani-kawi as Ela's partner. His blood would enrich the already illustrious Ani-kawi bloodline with new children. And it was Ela's firm intention that the first of this new dynasty would be conceived that very night. She grew excited at the thought of Salonitah mounting her. When he kissed her she had touched the part of him that would unite them as one being. That union would be consummated before the day was done and the thought of him entering her made her legs tremble. She made herself think about the marriage ceremony instead.

Salonitah would give her a blanket, which she would then tie to the one she gave him. Once that simple connubial act was completed he would always be hers and she his. A great feast would follow, stories would be told of the spirits and advice offered from the elders. Once all their bellies were satiated Salonitah would carry her down the ramp from the village Council House. It stood on the mound fifteen feet above the rest of the small village and overlooked the river. As they walked away the others would call upon the spirit world to bless their union and he would take her to the hut he had spent weeks preparing with his brothers and friends. It was in there that they would finally be alone and she could do all the things she had been imagining for the last year. It was here that she would pleasure the man she loved with her body as well as her heart.

Ela shivered with excitement as her thoughts turned once more to the imagined night ahead. In an attempt to calm the butterflies that swarmed within her she stared at the river. Bloated with its life's blood it swept along forested riverbanks, as the mountain streams converged and brought the Flower Moon's rains to inject new life into the flowers and seeds she and the other women had recently planted. Seven times she would be immersed in the cool cleansing waters of the river. Then she would emerge purified, ready for Salonitah.

Salonitah.

Once again she could feel her heart pounding hard beneath her breasts.

She sighed, and then squatted by the water and cupped her hands and gathered some of the cooling water to her lips and kissed it. The same water she imagined had caressed Salonitah's body further upstream where she knew he too was being bathed.

Salonitah splashed wit his friends in the pool beneath the waterfall. Mercilessly they ducked and teased him. But, joyously, he too cleansed and purified his soul in readiness for Ela.

Laughing, his best friend Atulya pushed him under the water for what was considerably more than the seventh time needed to cleanse his spirit. As Salonitah broke the surface again he flicked his long black mane at him. The soaking hair caught Atulya across the cheek. Salonitah turned to escape his friend's retribution for the assault. The retribution would undoubtedly be yet another ducking. As Atulya and two of his brothers grabbed him he heard a chilling scream that shattered the woodland idyll.

Alarmed, they all turned in the direction of the terrible noise. Without hesitation Salonitah struck out for the shore. He hauled himself out of the pool and onto the rocks. He grabbed his bow and arrows. Naked, he crashed through the forest to where he knew the sound had come from. Branches scratched and tore at his skin. He felt no pain as a two-inch thorn pierced his foot. As he ran, he could hear more screams and cries of bewilderment.

After what seemed like hours, but was little more than two minutes, he burst into the clearing by the river where he knew Ela would be.

What he saw wrenched his heart from within him. He ran towards her before his legs buckled and he fell at her side.

Ela's eyes were still open, but life had all but drained from her. He picked her near-lifeless body off the damp grass and pulled her against him. The arrow, which had penetrated her heart, ripped a gash in his side as he did so.

Her pale lips brushed his cheek. He strained to hear her whisper, "I love you, Salonitah," as her final breath squeezed agonisingly from her body.

Salonitah held her in his arms. In disbelief and bewilderment, he opened his mouth to scream but no sound came out.

ONE

"Come on, Thea, let's see if he is there yet."

Skye picked up the Frisbee that lay on the table by the patio door. She stepped out onto the deck. Thea bounced like a demented gazelle at her side, trying to the get the Frisbee in her mouth as Skye led her out.

In her mind Skye could hear Thea yell, 'Throw it! Throw it!' as she leapt, desperate to be reunited with her toy.

"Down, Thea. Wait until we are in the garden and on the beach."

It was always the same. Thea had a one-track mind, and that mind liked to chase Frisbees, balls, sticks or anything else that Skye would throw for her.

Skye had been joined at the hip with Thea for three years now, and Thea was just a larger version of the puppy that her dad her brought home after work one day. Skye was still a child in the dog's presence but physically she had developed into a young woman during that time.

"Hi, Mum. I'm just going down to the beach to throw the Frisbee for Thea," she said to the attractive woman who sat drinking iced tea by the pool, whilst reading a local news periodical, North Georgia Mountains (Fall Edition).

"Okay, honey. Dinner will be ready in an hour, and don't bring Thea back soaking wet." She smiled to herself. She always said it but knew it would never happen.

"Sure, Mum, we won't be late," Skye shouted back, as she released the Frisbee down the sloping lawn towards the beach that bordered the lake. Thea took off in pursuit of the flying delight and plucked it from the air with her mouth in a spectacular display of acrobatics that never ceased to thrill Skye. She squealed and clapped her hands as the dog landed on her rear paws, readjusted the Frisbee in her mouth before gently placing her front paws on the ground, and doing her lap of honour to the continued applause of her greatest admirer.

Skye's mother watched her fifteen-year-old daughter play with Thea. They made a striking couple. The bundle of fluff Tristan, her husband, had brought home that day had grown into the most striking leggy blonde she had ever seen, canine variety that is. Her daughter was the antithesis of her dog. She was just as beautiful, but dark. Her jet-black hair hung in natural curls the length of her long graceful back. She watched it swing from side to side brushing the top of her shorts as she walked across the grass. The summer sun had tanned her long legs the colour of mahogany, albeit only a few shades darker than her natural colouring.

Skye turned around and threw the Frisbee once again for the bouncing dog. Dark curtains of hair framed her face, and large almond shaped eyes the colour of agate smiled at her mother above the dimples that appeared beneath her high cheekbones.

She knew that Skye was not really taking Thea to the beach to throw the Frisbee. She was really hoping to find the boy. For three weeks she had gone to the beach every evening at about the same time, because it was that time of year again.

Skye picked up the Frisbee and peered out across the lake towards the island. The sun would set in about thirty minutes time. Would this be the day he appeared? She had been waiting for weeks and was growing impatient.

In previous years he had come by now, where was he? Surely he would be there soon.

Thea was going demented by her side, 'Throw it! Throw it!'

Skye smiled at her blonde, almost white Labrador. "I'm sorry, Thea. I was thinking about him. Go on, fetch."

She threw the Frisbee down the steep incline to the sandy beach some ten feet below. Thea took four steps, then launched herself from the lawn and flew horizontally before landing gracefully on the soft sand below with the Frisbee in her mouth. This time she did not return with it, but hurled herself towards the inviting cool of the lake where the Frisbee was deposited and promptly sank to the bottom.

"Thea, you daft dog. You know it doesn't float." Skye slipped off her sandals and waded into the almost calm water to retrieve Thea's favourite toy.

Thea was ready again, jumping in and out of the water, splashing Skye from head to toe.

"Hang on, I'm soaked." Skye was giggling.

'Throw it! Throw it!' Thea was paying no regard to Skye's half-hearted protestations.

Skye loved the mad hound. "Okay," she said, and she hurled it as far as she could along the beach, with Thea crashing through the water in hot pursuit.

Again Skye looked out across the still waters towards the lush green island with its beech, chestnut and ash trees towering above its narrow shoreline of sand and multi-coloured rocks. Iron pyrites, fool's gold, sparkled on the rocks in the evening sun. What if he did not come? Maybe she would never see him again. Why was he late this year?

The dog was back at her side and the Frisbee lay at Skye's feet, but she was not bouncing up and down anymore. Thea stood perfectly still, her ears were slightly pricked and her head and eyes stared at the island two hundred yards off shore in the lake. Slowly she raised one front paw and began to wag her tail. Her wagging accelerated until her tail thrashed frantically in a circular motion and her entire body gyrated from side to side.

Skye watched Thea get progressively more excited. She knew what it meant. The boy was coming. He would be there soon.

Slowly and expectantly she raised her eyes from watching her dog to scan the shore in the distance. Involuntarily, she breathed in. The intake of air was audible yards away. He was there.

He stood perfectly still. Even at two hundred yards Skye could see that his eyes were focused on her. Was he smiling? His long black hair contrasted against the near white sand. He looked magnificent.

For several seconds neither of them moved, and then slowly he raised his arm and waved to her. By his side, a black dog wagged its tail.

*

Phoenix bundled Shadow into his canoe.

Shadow looked rather indignant. He might be a Heinz variety of a dog, but he was clever and knew big black dogs were not really supposed to travel in small wooden canoes. He took his place in the bow of the hollowed-out log and waited for his master to throw in the rest of his gear. He would put up with it for now because he knew there would be rare treats at the end of their journey.

Phoenix eased the canoe that he had made away from the shore. He began to paddle between the dramatic, near-vertical, ragged, red rocks that edged the canyon lake in the Superstition Mountains of Arizona.

Everywhere was dusty and dry after a particularly hot summer, and even the usually succulent cacti looked weary as they clung desperately to the rock faces.

Phoenix knew exactly where he was going and where he would camp with Shadow. They would live mostly off the fish they caught and anything else that might find its way into his pot. They would remain on the same narrow beach until he saw the girl again.

The previous year he had waited for nearly two weeks before she appeared.

This was the third time he had come just to see her. The first time he had been camping and fishing with Shadow and she had appeared after just a couple of days. He had been fishing several times since and hoped she might be there but she never came. He'd concluded that if she came it was always at the same time of year, in the fall. That is what he hoped anyway, and if he were right she would come this time.

After forty minutes hard paddling he beached the canoe in a small inlet where a dried up stream entered the lake. The sheer rocks gave way to a narrow valley where the cacti grew more confidently.

Phoenix quickly made camp with the equipment he had packed into the canoe. He erected his small tent and placed inside the utensils and food he had brought with him. He would only sleep in the tent if it rained, but it rarely rained so he would sleep beneath the stars of the Arizona night sky.

He rigged two rods and reels, baited them and cast out into the lake, then rested the rods on tripods as he gathered scrub to light a fire for the charcoal he had brought with him.

In the days ahead he would scramble up the more gently sloping rock faces, which bordered the stream, to gather whatever else they may need. Occasionally he would use his bow to hunt for an alternative to fish.

From the narrow beach, where he had set up camp with Shadow, Phoenix could clearly see the delta of another, now dry, tributary on the far side of the lake where she would appear.

He thought back to the first time he had seen her. He had paddled the canoe to the other side of the lake to say hello. But as he approached within a hundred yards of the dark haired girl her image, and that of her near white dog, began to fade. Before he had beached the canoe, they had both disappeared.

During the following months he had returned several times and camped on both sides of the lake, the narrow beach where he was now and on the delta, hoping to see her but he was always disappointed. He had given up hope when almost to the day one year later he was camping with Shadow on the same beach when he'd looked over the lake. The girl and her dog had slowly reappeared. She had waved and her white dog wagged its tail furiously.

This time, Shadow decided the wagging dog was someone to befriend and had jumped into the lake and swum for the other shore. Phoenix pushed his canoe into the water to go and get him but, as before when Shadow and he approached, the waving girl had faded from view along with the white dog. Shadow had continued to the shore and franticly sniffed the entire region before giving up on his quest to find any scent or trace of the white dog. In frustration he peed twice on a rock and once on a log, and then climbed voluntarily back into the canoe and waited for Phoenix to row him back across the lake. Though inappropriate, it was easier than swimming.

Once on their own beach, Phoenix dragged the canoe out of the water and looked back across the lake. Once again the girl stood waving at him.

The girl's ability to appear, disappear and then reappear had perplexed him slightly, so he'd decided he would always wait on the beach for them to materialize across the lake and then just watch. Strangely, neither had Shadow tried to go back to them again. He had seen them, quite obviously, and had bounced in the water excited at what he saw, but with the extra sense that dogs somehow seemed to have he knew they only existed far away.

After this second sighting, he tried again to see her at the lake. In addition to his attempts to find her there he had tried to conjure up her image in other surroundings. He'd tried other lakes. He had studied a multitude of raven-haired beauties at school, and at home on the reservation, to find her likeness. Despite enjoying the quest none looked anything like her. That puzzled him too. How could he have seen a girl just twice, and at best from one hundred yards, yet know without any shadow of doubt exactly what she looked like?

He looked out across the water. In his mind's eye he could see every hair on her head; the colour of her eyes; every curve and crevice of her body and the dimples when she smiled.

Phoenix poked the fire he'd kindled and placed the fish on the cradle he'd erected. Shadow watched the prize and the brush surrounding it should any critter try and steal his master's, not to mention his own, dinner. When he had to be, he was a very vigilant dog.

Phoenix had kept his own vigil for just four days, four good days when man and dog bonded perfectly with their environment. Both enjoyed each other's company and their communion with nature. This idyll alone was enough, but when blended with expectation it was perfect.

On the fourth day of their camping trip she materialised. It was early evening and it was still hot. Before long the temperature would plummet, but there was still a light katabatic wind blowing down the rock face across the water towards the delta. Phoenix had just collected a second fish from the canoe, where he had left it in a cooler, when Shadow started to run up and down the beach barking at the expanse of water between them and the far shore. Phoenix dropped the fish back into the boat and turned to look expectantly across the lake.

The white dog appeared first. Initially it was still, and slowly it wound up into the frenzied pooch he remembered. Phoenix could see its head jerk as it barked, but he could hear nothing. His eyes were drawn away from the white dog to the slowly forming figure next to it. She was taller than last year, her body had more curves and her hair was longer. She was even more beautiful.

As in previous years she waved to them, and even from two hundred yards away Phoenix could see her smile. It was a smile he was familiar with, and one that haunted him whether he was awake or asleep.

*

The spirit of the boy she saw each year on the island similarly obsessed Skye.

She knew he was a spirit because on every occasion he'd appeared she had tried to go to him, but he would always fade away as she approached.

On the deck by the pool, Skye's mother, Missy, heard the 90hp Honda engine burst into life.

"He's here," she whispered to herself. She dropped the magazine on the table next to her and stood up to peer out towards the island, but all she could see was abundant deciduous trees that were changing colour and shedding their summer leaves. She hadn't expected to see anything. She had never seen the boy that her daughter waxed so lyrically about.

Below, Skye was untying the pontoon boat from the dock whilst Thea jumped and barked with excitement, the Frisbee temporarily forgotten.

Missy watched her daughter ease the boat from its mooring and open the throttle as she turned towards the island. She could feel the palpable excitement Skye was experiencing at seeing him again. At the same time she felt great compassion for her daughter. She was only fifteen years old and was besotted with a ghost.

Skye knew he would evaporate before she got to the island, but she had to be nearer to him. About a hundred yards from the shore she throttled back and allowed the pontoon boat to drift on the wind. From here she could see him clearly.

He was the most beautiful thing she had ever seen. His hair was the same colour as hers, but it was straight and was parted in the middle. It was held tight to his head by a decorated band. His eyes were kind and his smile endearing. She had once measured the height of the boulders he now stood next to, from that she knew him to be over six-feet tall. As always, all he wore was a loincloth made of animal skin, and strapped around his muscular torso was a wooden bow with a quiver of arrows on his back.

His black dog had once started to swim towards them, but as he approached he had slowly evaporated into thin air.

She called to the waving figure. As always she saw his lips move as he called back but no sound passed between them.

They watched each other for an eternity. The sun disappeared behind the trees, and half an hour later the last vestiges of daylight began to fade. Skye was struggling to see him as night fell, and with one last wave his image faded.

Thea whimpered at her side. Skye wiped the tear

from her cheek. "Goodbye, my love," she managed to half whisper.

She drifted along the shoreline not wanting the moment to end. Eventually she eased the outboard into forward and reluctantly crossed the short distance back to the boat dock at the bottom of their garden.

She moored the pontoon boat, as Thea bounced by her side looking expectantly at the Frisbee. Skye hardly noticed her excitement and readiness to play once again. After looking back at the island one last time she walked up the grass slope to the house.

Missy was waiting by the steps to the deck. There was no thought of chastising her for being late. She opened her arms and allowed her daughter to melt into them. Skye started to cry on her shoulder.

"Will I ever see him again, Mummy?" Skye managed to say through her tears.

"Of course, darling."

Despite her soothing encouragement, Skye's mother was not at all sure. In fact part of her hoped Skye would not see the boy again. Her beautiful daughter had a wonderful life ahead of her, and she was not sure she liked her being infatuated with a spirit. Even if she was part Cherokee Indian.

*

Phoenix knew he would have to wait another year to see her again. As he watched the sun disappear in the west, it struck him how easily and similarly the girl and her dog had evaporated.

Since they had gone he had been sitting thinking, with Shadow curled by his side on the beach. Phoenix had studied her from afar and although they could not talk, somehow they communicated.

He felt a bond with the girl that he could not explain and the emptiness he felt when she had gone bewildered him.

Phoenix had grown up on an Apache reservation with his grandmother and was not unfamiliar with the concept of the spirit world. Until he had seen the girl he had not attached much importance to the notion. And to be fair he still didn't, but this spirit undeniably existed and in some way was linked to him.

A year from now he knew he would be drawn to this place in the hope of seeing her again.

The next morning he baked the last of the fish he had caught and shared it with Shadow before packing all the kit away in the canoe. He paddled back to where he had left the old pick-up truck and he hoisted the heavy canoe into the back as if it were made of balsawood, along with the rest of the gear and his rods.

Shadow took his seat next to him in the cab and they drove back along the Apache Trail to the reservation. He had a great deal he wanted to ask his grandma.

TWO

The white haired lady stepped out of the cabin to greet her favourite grandson. She could hear his pick-up truck approach along the dirt road that led to their rickety wooden house. Plumes of dust followed the truck as he drew nearer. He braked hard and the truck slid to a halt in front of her. He grinned at the expression of exasperation on her smiling face. He always drove too fast as far as she was concerned, and he was happy to compound her opinion with a show of exaggerated bravado.

Shadow leapt through the open window of the truck and bounded up to Phoenix's grandma, or as they both knew her, Shichu, which was simply the Apache word for grandmother.

Pleased to see him again, she tickled the mutt behind his ears as three other dogs appeared from various parts of the homestead, all with similar parentage to Shadow. They greeted their large brother with wags and inquisitive sniffs.

She hugged Phoenix, who had also appeared by her side. "Did you see her?" she asked, anxious to hear the news.

"Yes, Shichu, I saw her." Phoenix began to untie the canoe from the wagon.

Shichu waited.

Phoenix smiled at the old lady who had raised him. "She was just as beautiful. No, she was more beautiful."

"Good. I have made a fresh stew. You must be sick

17

of fish. Come and tell me all about it." She turned, with Shadow by her side, and stepped onto the porch and past the rocker that still swayed from her standing when the pick-up had ground to a halt on the dry earth.

Shichu was not as old as she looked. After her husband had passed away in his forties she had farmed the meagre smallholding's chickens and vegetables on her own, whilst teaching first and second grade at the nearby Apache School. In recent years Phoenix had been a huge help, but a lifetime of hard labour had taken its toll. She was in her early sixties but her face was that of a seventy-five-year-old.

The Great Spirit had not been kind to her. Not only had he taken her husband, he had also taken her daughter and her own husband in a car accident just a few years later. In payment the Great Spirit had left her Phoenix, and she had cherished him ever since and raised him as if he were her own child. He was a fine boy and she had been blessed.

Phoenix took a shower while Shichu laid the simple wooden table. From the refreshing steam of the bathroom Phoenix could smell the enticing aromas of his grandmother's cooking.

Once he was seated at the table he could interrogate her about his musings, but not before three huge forks dripping with stew had passed his lips.

Before the fourth was placed in his mouth he managed to say, "Tell me again about the spirit world." Then he spooned another ladle of the piping hot stew into his bowl, before taking mouthful number five.

Shichu looked at Phoenix, the boy she had called Maba all his life. It was Apache for bear. As a child, he constantly clutched a tattered old teddy bear in his tiny hands. The bear went everywhere with him and it still sat by his bedside, even though he was now almost eighteen. The name Maba had stuck with him, and throughout the reservation he was called by his grandma's pet name rather than Phoenix.

"Maba, finish your dinner and we will sit and talk." Shichu gathered up her own dirty dishes and went to start the washing up, as Maba heaped yet another ladle into his bowl.

Fifteen minutes later they were sitting in two rockers on the porch drinking coffee. In a few weeks time it would probably be too cold to sit outside at eight o'clock in the evening, but tonight it was still warm enough as fall clung earnestly to its final vestiges of warmth.

Shichu knew it was time to tell Maba something she had kept from him for too long. She was not sure why she had not told him many years earlier, but the longer she had left it the harder it had become. At first she thought she was protecting him, thinking it would be easier for him to understand when he got older, but the passing years had somehow increased her reluctance to tell him. Now it was time, he must know. The spirits were calling him.

"You asked about the spirits, Maba." She watched him ease forward in the rocker. He sat perfectly still, all ears. She smiled to herself. "As you know, Native Americans have as many beliefs as there are tribes. The Apache believe in one Great Spirit, the creator, but we were not a fanatical religious people. We were nomadic and relied on our itinerancy for survival, all of which left little time for worship within a sophisticated belief system, so we kind of allowed people to form their own beliefs about the afterlife. We didn't even have formal burials, but we did gain a healthy respect for ghosts." She chuckled. "In fact, we were scared stiff of them because we believed they resented the living. The Navajo Indians were even more fearsome of the dead than us. If they even saw a corpse they would go through a long and costly ritual purification process."

Phoenix tried to wait patiently; he knew Shichu would tell him what he wanted to know, albeit at her own pace. He would try and accelerate the process though. "Is the girl a ghost?"

"Possibly."

"What do you mean? Is she real then?" Phoenix was getting excited.

Shichu ignored his questions and continued. "In essence we believed that our beings carried on in an afterlife as ghosts. Other tribes were more sophisticated. The Sioux peoples believed everything was spirit. They called it wakan, and their own being was just a manifestation of wakan and they only had the appearance of being real or natural. So everything was actually supernatural and beyond comprehension."

Phoenix smiled to himself. Shichu was a highly intelligent woman and remarkably well read, given the simple life she had led. There would be a point to all this.

"Some of the eastern tribes were probably the most sophisticated because they had rich fertile lands and had time to develop religions. The Iroquois beliefs were not that far removed from Christians with a slight Zen bias. Like us, they believed in one creator, but they believed that creator intended the world to be experienced only in the present. That's the Zen part. They were a pretty easy going lot." She scowled. "Unlike Christians, they had no desire to spread their beliefs or change the world."

Shichu laughed at the look on Maba's face. "I'm sorry. I have nearly finished."

Phoenix grinned at her. He was still trying to figure out how she knew so much about Zen and belief systems, as she put it.

"The Cherokee nation covered all the angles. They are extremely interesting, they believe in one Great Spirit, but also believed that every aspect and thing had its own spirit as well. Their one great spirit was called Yowa.

They also believed that all human disease and suffering originated with the killing of animals for improper purposes, and for each animal killed for pleasure or without proper ceremonies a new disease would enter the physical world from the spirit world." She paused, and studied Maba. "That is why they have such an affinity with animals. Just as you do, look at that dumb dog at your side." She smiled at Shadow. "As an aside, they believed that plants in response to witnessing the suffering made a medicine to cure each sickness that entered the world. They did it in order to restore the balance of forces between the two. That is, the physical and spiritual world. They were a cool bunch. The Cherokees liked their spirits."

Phoenix chuckled at Shichu's use of cool bunch. He waited in anticipation of her next surprise, but she didn't continue.

"What is the matter, Shichu?" He could see she looked perplexed.

"Nothing." She looked at him and added, "Well actually there is." She paused while she searched for the words. Eventually she just said, "I believe you may be Cherokee, Maba."

Phoenix opened his mouth, but nothing came out.

Shichu leant forward and took his hands. "I should have told you years ago." She saw the look on his face. "Let me explain. Your mother and I found you on a bus in Phoenix when you were just a few days old. Someone had left you on the back seat near the heater outlet. A note was pinned to the blanket you were wrapped in. It simply read, 'Please look after my son, I cannot.'"

She had decided that being blunt was the best way to tell him. She waited for her words to sink in, feeling wretched as she waited for Phoenix to adjust to the enormity of what she had said.

Phoenix had not quite reached two years old when

the woman he had assumed to be his mother had died in a motor accident. He had an older brother and sister who had never mentioned that he was not their real sibling.

"But...." He couldn't get any words out.

"I'm so sorry, Maba. I should have told you before, but it never seemed important until now."

Phoenix had gathered himself together and smiled at the woman he loved more than any other person in the world. He could see her anguish.

"It's okay, Shichu. Tell me now, it doesn't change anything." He had a sudden realization and laughed. "That's why I'm called Phoenix, because you found me there?"

His grandmother nodded.

"At least you didn't call me Bus! Come on, tell me all about it." He eased out of the rocker and hugged her.

Shichu managed a weak smile. "We took you to the police and they tried to find your real mother, but without any luck. You were quite obviously a Native American baby, and so we all naturally assumed you to be Apache. A huge effort was made to find your parents through all the contacts we have with our people, but there was nothing. At the age of six months we adopted you, and you actually lived with us since you were about one month old. After your mom died, I raised you and you attended the Apache School with your brother and sister." She smiled. "They do not even know you are adopted. Your sister was barely one and your brother was too young to be in the least bit interested about where babies come from."

Phoenix took it all in, whilst his head was spinning with images of his siblings and the photograph of the parents he kept by his bed. From nowhere he suddenly had a thought. "You said it was not important to tell me until now, why?"

"The girl you see by the lake."

Phoenix looked puzzled. "Go on."

"Remember, I only said that I think you may be Cherokee, but it is a strong feeling. If you had been Apache, I am sure we would have found your mother." She looked at him. "Our community is a small one, somebody would have known something. As you grew up it became apparent to me that there were facets of your personality that were quintessentially not Apache. Good facets. You are as one with the natural world; your empathy with animals from an early age astonished me. Every wounded or injured critter you found was nursed painstakingly back to health. Damn it, Maba, you won't even kill an ant. Sure, you will fish and hunt but with a reverence for your prey that is rare, and you will only do it for the pot. A reverence that a Cherokee would have." She touched his cheek. "You are the gentlest yet strongest boy I know."

She squeezed his hands. Phoenix laughed. "It's a big leap from being nice to animals to proclaiming I am probably a Cherokee Indian."

"Not so big, Maba." She waited and looked into the wise questioning eyes of the young man she had raised. "This girl you see, always has her dog with her doesn't she? They are not alone in thinking it, but the Cherokee have a particular affinity with the wolf and of course their modern day offspring. In Cherokee mythology there is no essential difference between men and animals. She is like you; she will not be parted from her dog. Shadow is always by your side." She looked down at the huge black fur ball at his feet

Phoenix was deep in thought, picturing the girl and her dog.

Shichu watched him. "From your eyes I can see that you love her." She squeezed his hands again.

"I don't know, Shichu. Maybe I do. But how can you love a spirit?"

Again Shichu thought there was only one way to explain what she believed, and that was bluntly. "It is easy, Maba. I love the spirits of your mother and father, and of course your grandpa. The girl is a spirit of someone you once loved and despite your reticence you still do."

Phoenix's mind was racing. He did not want to be in love with a ghost, yet despite himself he knew he probably was.

There was a minute or two's silence as Shichu allowed him to absorb what she had told him. And then from his deep pondering he vaguely heard Shichu ask, "Is she older each time you see her?"

"What?"

"Did she look a year older than the last time you saw her?" she asked.

"Yes, over the years she has grown from a small girl into a young woman."

"Then you are lucky."

"Why?"

"She is alive."

Phoenix looked dumbstruck. "What do you mean, Shichu?"

"I believe that the spirit you see is the spirit of a living person. Probably reincarnated many times. She will be your soul mate and it is very likely that she sees you too. If she were the spirit of a dead person she would not age but would look the same each time you saw her. The age she was when she passed and her journey was complete. Her journey, and by default yours, is not complete."

"Are you saying that the girl and I are meant to be together, and she exists?" Phoenix was almost dumbstruck.

"Yes, I believe you have unfinished business with her and judging by your demeanour, whenever she is mentioned, I suspect that business to be an affair of the heart. But it may be something else. She could be your enemy." Shichu looked a bit defensive. She did not want Maba to get his hopes up too high and it was a possibility, albeit a slight one. She carried on, trying to ease this last revelation. "There is one other thing that makes me think you are both Cherokee, and why I added that last bit."

"Carry on."

"Part of Cherokee legend suggests that every life, man or animal, has an assigned period that cannot be curtailed by violent means. If it is, then that life will be resurrected in its proper form until it has run its predetermined, assigned existence. When that is complete the body will finally be dissolved and its spirit free to join its kindred shades in the darkening land."

"So we may have been lovers or adversaries. Either way we met a violent death." Phoenix was almost thinking out loud.

Shichu raised her eyebrows and lifted her shoulders. "I fancy you were lovers. And all this assumes you believe in Cherokee legend. They are certainly better than our Apache ones." Her eyes twinkled.

THREE

Phoenix could not sleep. His mind was racing. Could the spirit of the girl he had seen for the first time years ago really exist in physical form? The idea excited him.

He eased himself out of bed and went to the window to close the shutters. It was cool outside and a breeze bent the branches on the Southern Magnolia tree Shichu had planted when he was tiny. She had always called it his tree. Arizona was not its natural habitat but she had nurtured and cared for it and it had somehow survived. It had always looked ill at ease surrounded by weaker cottonwoods, junipers, scrub and cacti. 'A rose amongst thorns,' Shichu had called it. He was now beginning to wonder if she had always seen him in a similar light. He put the thought out of his head and pictured the girl instead.

From the first time he had seen her he'd been drawn towards her, as if she possessed a magnetic field he could not resist. Each time he had seen her the attraction seemed stronger. Between each encounter he had thought of her many times, but since his last camping trip with Shadow her image haunted him constantly. It was not an image that he wanted to erase.

He closed the shutters, latched the window and sat on the edge of the bed and turned on the lamp.

Two months had passed since Shichu had revealed that he might not be Apache. After the initial shock of what she had told him wore off; the concept of his

26

forebears being from another tribe did not bother him. In fact it explained a number of things to him. Although he loved Shichu and his siblings dearly, he had never completely felt at ease with the rest of the people on the reservation. He respected and liked them, and he had a great number of good friends within the community. But at the same time he had always felt slightly different from them. Until Shichu's revelation he had never thought anything of it, but now there was possibly an explanation. 'A rose amongst thorns.' But he was no rose and they were not thorns. However, perhaps he was different.

It was a two-way-thing, his friends and neighbours almost revered him. Sure, he was extremely intelligent but with his intelligence came a prudence that gave him an aura others did not have. Despite his youth people gravitated towards him seeking advice and insight. Some said that Maba, the bear, could even talk to the animals. Of course he could not, but neither did any critter appear afraid of him and he undoubtedly had an affinity with all living things.

The net result of all of this was that at eighteen years of age Phoenix was considered charismatic. And many of his people held the boy, who had turned his Shichu's small barn into an animal hospital, in awe. Quite naturally, he was different.

Was he different because he was Cherokee? That was the question Phoenix had been asking himself for two months, and what he was now pondering at three o'clock in the morning. After school each day he had gone to the library and read dozens of books about the Cherokee Nation, their beliefs and their myths. He had felt a strange calm and a sense of belonging as he absorbed all he could about the people he now believed he was descended from. He had never been to Alabama, Tennessee, the Carolinas or Georgia where his people once lived, but as he read about their ancient lands he experienced a connection with the lush deciduous landscapes the photographs portrayed in the books.

When he read about the travesty and tragedy that forcedly moved his people from North Georgia west to Oklahoma along the Trail of Tears, he was deeply moved.

All his life he had been taught in the reservation school about the injustices the European settlers had dealt to the Native Americans. But he had never been moved by their disgraceful acts, until he read about the Cherokee struggle against their oppressors.

All of this had left him in little doubt that he was a Cherokee Indian, and he was descended from the people who suffered at the hands of the European settlers. He believed the spirit of the girl by the lake had played a part in his former life.

As he sat on the bed, more importantly, he now believed Shichu when she said that she was alive and would play a part in his destiny.

Therein lay the reason he could not sleep. If she existed, how on earth was he ever going to find her?

Something else troubled him. He had read the legend Shichu had mentioned that every life, man or animal, has an assigned period that cannot be curtailed by violent means and if it is, then that life will be resurrected in its proper form until it has run its predetermined assigned existence.

He found the idea that the girl could have met a violent death disturbing.

*

Skye had her own problems sleeping. She was well aware that her fifteen-year-old hormones would find boys attractive, but the boy on the island, the boy who did not really exist, was becoming an infatuation. She thought of him constantly to the point that she barely noticed other boys. Added to her hormonal desires it was a particularly close night for the time of year. Thunder was forecast and Thea was already aware of it in the vicinity, not that Skye could hear anything.

Thea stirred at the foot of her bed. Thunder always made her restless. Skye was restless for other reasons. She knew it was ridiculous and half-fought to purge him from her mind, with little success. She did not want to stop thinking about him.

She had bombarded her mother with questions about her feelings and that had helped, and she had also proven to be a fount of knowledge about her Cherokee ancestry. The ancestry that undoubtedly had given birth to the spirit by the lake that obsessed her.

Skye's bloodline was interesting, to say the least. When the exotic, raven-haired girl spoke her accent was pure Oxbridge English. Her father had been a lecturer at Oxford University. His own bloodline preceded Oliver Cromwell and he was English to his core. Skye had been born in Oxford and had a British passport. Her father, Tristan, had met her mother, Missy, whilst she had been a student at the university.

A First Class Honours Degree and a tiny baby called Skye later they married. Tristan continued to lecture on structural engineering, whilst Missy wrote books on American heritage interspersed with salacious novels about student life in one of the oldest seats of learning in the world. The American heritage books sold in hundreds to academia, the novels sold in hundreds of thousands to a public who devoured the scandalous exploits of the heroine.

When Skye was nine, Tristan was offered a professorship at Georgia Tech in Atlanta. With the appointment he was able to return Missy to her native Georgia. When Skye was eleven she read, unbeknown to anyone, the first of her mother's novels. By twelve she had read them all, and had her first and only fight with a girl in high school who called her mother a slut. Skye won the fight and the respect of her fellow students. And by fifteen both she and her mother were celebrated beauties within the teenage community at West Hall High.

They turned heads wherever they went. They looked like sisters, Skye looking older than her fifteen years and Missy much younger than her forty. It wasn't until you heard them speak that you would question their relationship, and whilst Missy had the most delightful husky Southern drawl, Skye had lost nothing of her crystal cut English accent despite six years of living in the South.

Genetically, though diluted with time, their Cherokee ancestry was still obvious to a trained eye.

She could now hear the thunderstorm approaching. If she had been asleep it may well have woken her. She counted the time off in seconds between lightening flash and the subsequent thunder. Twenty-four seconds, it was four miles away. The previous flash and crash had been thirty-six seconds apart. By North Georgia standards it was not much of a storm, but it would help to fill the lake whose water levels were still depleted after a dry summer. The last crash had persuaded Thea to jump onto the bottom of the bed. She could protect Skye more easily from there, and be nearer for a cuddle should the bangs get any louder. Skye leaned forward and tickled Thea behind her ears. Tickling always seemed to calm her down.

Skye was completely awake now, so she decided to read some passages from what had become her favourite book.

She was proud of her heritage, both English and Native American. But in recent times her Cherokee blood had seemed to hold sway over her being, thanks solely to the boy.

She pulled the book from the shelf. The cover had an artist's impression of Cherokee Indians by a river bathing and tending animals. Above the picture the words Cherokee Legends were embossed. She settled back onto the bed with Thea and started to read.

'There is no such thing as part Cherokee. Either you are Cherokee or you are not. It isn't the quantity of Cherokee blood that is important, but the quality of it and your pride in it. I have seen full bloods that have virtually no idea of the great legacy entrusted to their care. Yet I have seen people with as little as 1/500th blood who inspire the spirits of their ancestors because they make being Cherokee a proud part of their everyday life.'

She liked the words and had written them out and put them on the wall above her bed. Pride in her Cherokee blood. If she had ever doubted the strength of that blood, seeing the boy each year had confirmed its potency.

Her mother had been wonderful when Skye had cried over him. Missy understood the power of the spirits and their importance in their personal heritage. She believed in soul mates and in love. She believed the boy and her beautiful daughter had, in some way, been connected in a past life and that possibly they might be again, either in this or another existence. It was all part of Cherokee legend and they were Cherokee.

Skye picked up her book and read another of the legends.

'After Earthmaker created this island on which we live, he created all living things, man being the very last of these. The first and foremost animal that Earthmaker created was a bear of pure white colour, which he placed in the North. This is White Bear. The second bear that he created was Red Bear, whom he placed in the West. Earthmaker next created in the East a kind of grizzly bear, Blue Bear. Blue Bear was the colour of the sky, either blue, or as some say, grey. The last bear created by Earthmaker was Black Bear, who was placed in the South. These four kinds of bears were created as Island Weights to help stop the incessant spinning of the primordial earth.

Spiritually, they were not only bears, but the four cardinal winds as well. White Bear was chief over polar bears, Red Bear held hegemony over the brown bears of earth, Blue Bear ruled over grizzlies, and Black Bear was chief of the terrestrial black bears.'

Skye thought of the boy whenever she read this piece. She did not know why, but she thought Bear a very good name for him. She jumped off the bed and collected her Native American dictionary from the shelf and looked up the translation of bear. Her finger traced the suggestions on the page. Beneath the Apache word 'maba' was the Cherokee word 'yona.'

"I will call you Yona," she said out loud to any listening spirits.

On hearing the name Yona, Thea, who had been watching Skye with her chin on the bed covers between her front paws, suddenly looked up and stared at Skye.

The room lit up as the sheet lightening illuminated the sky. At the same instant the house shook with the cacophony of sound that announced the storm had arrived.

FOUR

Skye sat on the beach with Thea. Both watched the island waiting for any sign of life other than the Canadian Geese that had moved into the remote retreat. It was beginning to cool down and the night would be a cold one, but it was still warm enough for shorts and a T-shirt during the day. The sun still hovered high above the foothills of the Appalachians in the west. The trees still sported a thick, but fading, canopy that surrounded the lake, but a few weeks hence they would shed all their leaves and their colour. A sports boat flashed across her vision transporting its angler to a new site and fresh catch. Its loud engine and wake disturbed two of the geese.

Lake Lanier was increasingly becoming host to vast numbers of the migrating birds. Skye liked them, especially after they had hatched their goslings. Their own beach had been home to a family of seven, of which a miraculous six had survived the hot summer.

Yona had come on this exact date for the previous two years and each year he had been more handsome. This year Skye was sad and part of her did not want him to come, at least not yet. She was enjoying the anticipation of seeing him again.

She had celebrated her eighteenth birthday a month previously and a year from now she would not be by the lake. Soon she was going to college to start her training. She had realized a year ago that she would not be there when he appeared after she started college, and she'd spent an entire year trying to conjure him up at other times and in other places, all to no avail. It was obvious that Yona would only appear on his island, on Lake Lanier at a certain time of the year. That time was now. And for the foreseeable future she would not be there. It was not as if she could easily get back to see him either, she would be in England, at Oxford University studying structural engineering sciences. Even if she managed to fly home, she could not stay the three weeks he sometimes took to appear because it would be in term time.

It had all left her rather flat. She looked out over her beloved lake. Its beauty never ceased to uplift her, but even that seemed dulled this day.

She wanted to go to Oxford and realized what a wonderful opportunity it was. The entrance exam had been the hardest thing she had ever done and she was surprised when they offered her a place. Her father was thrilled that his beautiful daughter would follow in his footsteps at Oxford, as was her mother, but Missy realized the enormity of the move for Skye. She also realized why her daughter was so sad this day and what a momentous occasion it was in her short life.

Knowing it would be the last time Skye would see the boy for a few years, Missy agreed to wait with her for him to appear, even though she knew she would not see him herself. When Yona was gone she knew Skye would be distraught and need her. They also thought there may just be a way that Missy might sense his presence and at the very least could report to Skye that he had come in the years ahead when Skye would not be there.

It was the fifth evening the three of them had sat on the beach waiting for Yona to appear and the sun to set.

Missy was feeling for her lovely daughter, but at the same time was pleased that she was getting on with her life and not allowing the spirit world to dictate her actions. Three years ago she had thought it might not happen. Skye was headstrong and had threatened at the ripe age of fifteen to get a job in Flowery Branch, where they lived, and not go to university. The only reason being that she could be near the boy she now called Yona. Flowery Branch probably only had twenty jobs in the entire town, and none of them worthy of the intellect that was going to take their daughter to Oxford. Neither she, nor Tristan, had said anything. Their raised eyebrows conveyed their feelings; they suspected that she would see sense in good time. It had taken far longer than they expected. But it was that same single-mindedness and cussedness that had gained a coveted place at Oxford University, and made her the remarkable woman she was becoming.

Skye would shortly take up that place and her baby daughter would flee the nest far too soon. Missy was cherishing every moment she spent with her daughter and was thrilled when Skye had asked her to wait on the beach with her.

Each evening they had waited in companionable silence for the spirit to come. Each evening had been slightly cooler than the previous. Missy decided that if he did not show today, tomorrow she would wear a coat.

Thea suddenly stood up and took the few short steps into the lapping water's edge. Slowly her tail started to wag and, as on every previous occasion, within seconds her entire body was gyrating with her tail spinning like a propeller. Missy knew she would have no use for the coat.

Skye was on her feet instantly, her arms outstretched towards the island. She yelled, "Yona," as loud as she could and began to wave frantically at the empty beach two hundred yards away.

Missy could not see anything, but realized how she would be able to tell Skye that Yona had been in the years to come. Thea would tell her, Thea and her tail.

She watched the look of pure joy on Skye's face, a rapture that did not leave her for over an hour. She just walked up and down the beach staring and waving.

Skye did not speak again, until in an anguished half-whisper she said to Missy, "The sun is going. I won't see him for years."

She stepped into the lake and waded out until the water lapped around her waist. At first, Missy thought she would just keep on walking, but she stopped and said quite distinctly, "I love you, Yona."

As she exaggeratedly mouthed the words she held both hands to her breast and cupped them, symbolically taking out her heart and offering it to the spirit on the far shore. She then put her fingers to her lips and gently kissed them before blowing the kiss across the expanse of water to the waiting spirit.

"Thank you, Yona." Missy heard Skye say before she gave one last wave and turned towards the shore with tears rolling down her cheeks.

Missy met her at the water's edge. She had never seen her daughter look more beautiful.

"Did he speak to you? Why are you thanking him?" asked Missy.

"Yes, Mummy. His lips said that he loved me." She wiped the tears from her cheeks. "He's gone now. I guess those words will have to last me a long time."

Missy embraced Skye. She had definitely fallen in love with a ghost.

*

Phoenix watched her image fade

She had said that she loved him and he had replied

with the same words.

Was she crying? He could not be sure, but he could feel her anguish at leaving, and he felt an even greater loss than in previous years when her form finally faded from view.

He stood transfixed by the stillness and emptiness of the far shore that had just a few moments ago been both radiant and alive. Each year her presence seemed stronger and the area that surrounded her had gradually changed form. When he had first seen her she stood amid the arid scrub that filled the delta. In recent years lush forests appeared to engulf her when she waved at him, a rich green carpet and backdrop that he recognized as typical Appalachian foliage. The same foliage that covered the ancient lands of the Cherokee nation and still did cover vast tracts of those lands that now were called Tennessee, Georgia and the Carolinas.

After she had said 'I love you' she had used another word, perhaps a name that she called him, but he could not make it out. It did not matter. She had said it. Now he would have to wait a year to watch her say it again.

Shadow muzzled his hand and he was brought back to reality. He gathered up his gear and packed it all into the canoe. Luckily the girl had come at the same time as the previous year, because Phoenix had already skipped a few too many lectures at Arizona State University and he had an important exam in two weeks time.

As he paddled the canoe back to where he had left the pick-up, he was thinking about the halo of trees that increasingly seemed to surround her. Shichu had said that the spirit was of a girl who was alive. Was it a picture of where she now lived, or where she once lived? Each time she came to him, the forest area around her seemed to expand. Could he recognize the place from what he saw around her? There simply was not enough to go on. The vegetation offered little more than a vast region as a clue to her whereabouts.

On a number of occasions he thought of driving east to the Appalachians and searching for her. A lake surrounded by trees. He had poured over maps and identified thousands of such lakes that existed within the lands of the Cherokee. It would be hopeless.

Shichu had said it was destiny that he should meet the girl again. Destiny would find him. He did not know how or when. All he could do was live his life and wait for that moment. Now his life needed him to pass his exams if he was to stand a chance of becoming a veterinary physician and work with the animals he loved.

*

Missy was sitting with Thea on the sandy beach at the bottom of the garden. It was the third evening in a row she had taken her MacBook Pro to the beach and worked on her latest novel as she waited for the boy to appear.

Skye had telephoned each night to see if he had come. Missy could hear the disappointment in her voice when she reported that Thea had just sat calmly by her side and the boy had not made an appearance. More precisely he had not shown himself to Thea.

Skye had completed her second year at Oxford and loved her time there. Her being there had inspired Missy to start a trilogy about a young student who shook the bedrock of the establishment as she challenged, with overt sexuality, the misogynistic values that governed the world she inhabited. It was of course Skye, and Missy would regularly laugh whenever she thought what Skye's reaction would be to the femme fatale that was so obviously based on her. She could hear her say, "Mother, you are such an embarrassment."

It had been easy to write, especially as the heroine was essentially her own daughter. Missy had not even bothered to alter the appearance of her heroine; it was Skye from her toes through her long legs to the jet-black curls on her head. Writing about her had helped ease the feeling of emptiness she felt when Skye had gone to England, in part to follow in her own redoubtable footsteps. She was well aware of the effect Skye would be having on the academic world of Oxford. Like the heroine in her books, Skye would leave her mark on Oxford and Oxford would be better for having known her.

*

Skye was the first out of the door as the lecturer wound up his presentation on computational fluid dynamics. It had been over a week now, and her mother had told her that Yona had not appeared on the island. For the second time since she had come to Oxford she yearned to be back on Lake Lanier, just so she could see him for a few seconds. She knew she was being silly, but he had become part of her.

In James she had a perfectly nice boyfriend that most girls would fight for and some, to her amusement, had tried. But as much as she liked the Adonis who played in the centre for the Oxford University rugby team, he was not the spirit that haunted her thoughts. She'd had a marvellous time at Oxford, and for the majority of it the idea of Yona was fine. He did not affect the way she lived her life, but during the days running up to when he would appear she could not get his image out of her head.

She stepped out of the lecture hall into Market Street. She instinctively pulled up the collar of her jacket as a defence against the cool dank air that already invaded Oxford, even though summer had barely passed. She imagined her mother in her shorts sitting by the pool with Thea by her side soaking up any last vestiges of warmth the fall's sun may bring. It seemed most appealing as she put her rucksack over her shoulder, plunged her hands into the deep warm pockets of her jacket and braced against the cold wind that funnelled down the street.

She briskly walked the short distance to the sanctuary of her room, which overlooked the Old Quad of Brasenose College.

Even though she had been born in Oxford and had lived in the city as a small girl, the architecture and buildings that made up the university still thrilled her. Her own lodgings were nearly five hundred years old and had been home to men that had shaped history. Now those lodgings were home to Skye, a Cherokee girl who was in love with a spirit.

The old oak door creaked as she eased it open. Inside, she emptied her bag and put the books on an old desk, which looked out onto the manicured lawn in the Quad below. Cherokee artefacts hung on the walls and the legend of the bears took pride of place above her bed. She had never really explained to James why it was so important to her.

She made a cup of tea and looked at her watch. Shortly she would walk across the meadows to the River Thames, as she had each evening for the previous week. She knew it was stupid, and that he would not come, but it was by water and she could look across to the other bank and imagine him. She would wait for the sun to go down then come back and study until eleven o'clock. At eleven she would go there again and wait in the dark until the sun had set on Lake Lanier on the other side of the Atlantic. After that she would telephone her mother.

She loved the meadows that cradled the Thames as it

flowed east towards London. During the summer she had spent hours studying on its banks. She was drawn to the water, fascinated by it, just as the lake had captivated her during her childhood.

It would be cold and she would have to wrap up, but it was worth it if there was even the slightest chance of seeing him.

*

Phoenix was sporting a new haircut. For the first time in his life he had short hair. He brushed his hand over the alien scalp that did not feel like his own, the soft brush of hair tickled his palm.

He'd had it cut for Cameron, the girl he was currently dating, and to be fair the opposite sex appeared to find him even more attractive with his new appearance. Not that he ever lacked for attention before, but now his film star looks appealed to a far more eclectic mix of females.

Cameron was a dental nurse. Two months previously, he had a toothache for the first time in his life and had visited the dentist. A buxom blonde nurse had rested her right breast on his ear as she held the suction tube in his mouth for the dentist to work. Her eyes undressed him as her lips parted, and she mentally had sex with the poor boy pinned in the dentist chair. Later that day her hands and her body finished the job.

It all left Phoenix with mixed feelings about his first ever visit to the dentist. On balance he decided it was a good thing, and the toothache had stopped.

Cameron had so enjoyed the sex, both mental and physical that she had made it a regular occurrence. Phoenix had quietly acquiesced and played his role as the toy-boy to the best of his ability.

Cameron delighted in his being younger than her, albeit only four years, and had taken to mothering him when she was not seducing him, hence the haircut.

Phoenix was not sure about the haircut, as he was not sure about the dentist. And he was certainly not sure about Cameron.

The only thing he was sure of was that he enjoyed having sex with a large breasted, slightly older and seriously sexy woman. However, during these pleasurable and time-consuming sessions he would often find himself thinking about the girl by the lake. Which in no way detracted from his performance with Cameron. In fact it enhanced it.

Today Phoenix was happy on two counts. Firstly, he held in his hand his acceptance to the University of Georgia Veterinarian School in Athens. He had completed his pre-veterinarian degree at Arizona State with excellent grades and could have had his pick of veterinary schools. It was Shichu who had suggested he should use the opportunity to live closer to his spiritual home. An opportunity he was keen to embrace.

Secondly, it was fall and he was about to make his annual pilgrimage to the lake with Shadow in anticipation of seeing the girl.

He had mixed emotions about the visit. The previous year she had not appeared. The white dog materialized as usual, gleefully wagging its tail, but no girl. It had perplexed him and he wondered if anything had happened to her. Something about the dog's demeanour suggested that she was all right. He felt as if he would have sensed if something had been wrong. Shadow certainly would. None-the-less, it had troubled him for a year. The thought of not seeing her this time dampened his high spirits slightly.

Two days later, he was sitting on the beach by the canyon lake staring at the white dog as it performed its usual gymnastics on seeing Shadow, while Shadow bounced up and down for her delectation.

He waved at the dog and the emptiness around it. Where was she, the girl who'd said she loved him?

Her second non-appearance left him feeling anxious and deflated. What had happened to her? He could not wait to go east to Georgia and the ancient lands of his forebears. He could not wait for destiny any longer. He needed to find her and shape that destiny.

*

"I love you too, Mummy." Skye put the telephone down.

He had come again. Thea had seen him. Suddenly she felt guilty that she had not been there. A familiar feeling of emptiness consumed her, along with a yearning to be home by the lake.

She lay on the bed and thought about the Indian boy on the island; the boy who had grown into a man during their years together. Two years had passed, what did he look like now?

She spent three glorious hours allowing her mind to revel in thoughts of him before sleep took her.

The next day was Saturday. She studied in the morning then went to the rugby club to watch James play. That evening they had a simple meal in the middle of Oxford, and then returned to her room to watch an old movie on television. James wanted to watch a western, The Last of the Mohicans. She refused.

FIVE

.

Phoenix had been on the campus in Athens for a year. It had been a good year. Although not in the heart of the Cherokee lands, it was the closest university to them that he could choose with a good veterinary school.

At weekends and during breaks he had often taken the old truck, which somehow had managed the journey from Arizona, up into the Appalachian Mountains whose foothills stretched almost to Athens.

After a lifetime of dust, cacti and baking heat the lush vegetation and mountain streams seemed like paradise to him.

He walked the Appalachian Trail, rafted down wild tree-lined rivers and even skied for the first time in his life in a strange Swiss styled resort called Sky Valley.

As Shichu had suggested it might, it simply felt like home. Plus, he had grown his hair again.

He missed Shichu, but the cost of regular flights or the gas to drive back to Arizona was beyond his means. Anyway, the chance of the old pickup making another return journey was probably remote, so regular phone calls were all they had.

Just as big a wrench was leaving Shadow. He had wanted to take his beloved dog with him to Georgia but Shichu had, quite correctly, told him it was not fair on Shadow. With lectures and work he would not have time to care for him properly. Shichu had said, "This is his home, his brothers and sisters all live here. We will look after him, Maba. Maybe, one day, when you have finished studying he can be with you."

Phoenix had hated it, but he knew she was right. It was, in part, to see Shadow that he had taken three jobs. A little went by each month to pay for a cheap flight home.

The three jobs also provided the money to feed him, buy his books and generally pay his way. The first job was the traditional one of waiting tables in a diner, where both the food and tips were sub-standard. After the diner closed, he tended bar in a late night live music venue, mostly frequented by students supporting their local favourites from campus. To Phoenix's ears, none sounded like their illustrious predecessors in Athens, bands like The B52s and REM.

His third job was by far his favourite. It paid next to nothing and may even have cost him money, as he had to drive some distance to do it. During the summer months, on alternative weekends, he was a guide in a hick Cherokee Indian museum and village, situated fifty miles to the north near Tallulah Falls.

He had virtually stumbled across the museum shortly after he had started at UGA. On his second visit to the mountains, during one of his exploratory expeditions into the Cherokee lands, he saw a dilapidated sign to the Tallulah Falls Cherokee Village. He had spent the day walking in one of the National Parks, basking in the rich canopy of foliage the damp woodland was beginning to give up for the winter. It was almost dark and he was driving home when he saw the sign. He decided to investigate.

Four miles of forested roads later and three more decaying signs hanging at angles from gnarled trees, he drove into a gravel and dirt car park. He jumped out of the pickup and slammed the sun tarnished, multi-coloured door closed. He surveyed the scene. A sturdy wooden log-built structure, flanked by two huge boulders, was closed up and looked half way between down-at-heel and derelict. A sign invited people to 'Experience the Cherokee Nation and visit The Trail of Tears Museum,' all for the attractive price of eight dollars. A smaller sign said 'Open 1st April to 30th September.'

Phoenix was familiar with similar establishments back in Arizona. Indeed, the reservation he grew up on boasted an equally salubrious museum of learning. He also knew that if it was similar to home, the people or person who ran it would more than likely be passionate about their mediocre premises and humble museum.

A ramshackle entrance booth offered tours on the hour, and the exit was through a small gift shop. On peering through the cracked window he noticed that it had been stripped of its stock but had been left tidy, which led Phoenix to believe that the Cherokee village was still trading and had merely closed for the winter.

Ever since Shichu had told him her suspicions about his heritage he had read a great deal about the tribe of his possible forefathers. They were a fascinating people with a sophisticated culture. But if he were honest, he had never felt a connection to that culture, apart from when he saw the girl by the lake.

It was almost dark. He pulled up the collar of his jacket and took a couple of strides to the nearer of the two boulders. Figures and symbols were carved into the pitted surface. He stroked the symbols wondering what they portrayed. The cold stone was damp to his touch as it started to gather the evening dew. The fall trees discarded the last of their clinging summer leaves. Now tired of hanging on to the forest that had given them life, exhausted they fluttered to the damp carpet of browns and reds below.

Phoenix surveyed the woodland. He was intensely aware of the plethora of odours emanating from the tangled forest surrounding him.

He had a sudden thought. He had never really smelt trees before. His reservation had little more than scrub. A three-foot-tall bush was a tree in Arizona.

He closed his eyes and inhaled. The damp evening air acted as a conduit and magnified the aromas. Maples mixed with hickories and oaks. He could discern musty fungal and lichen smells from the sweet smell of rotting fruits nestling within the leaf carpet. Within it all there was another smell he was more familiar with. Wildlife. He had always been able to smell animals.

He sensed it was there. He opened his eyes and there, at his feet, a squirrel sat on its haunches staring up at him. Phoenix smiled at the tiny creature that made no effort to move. After nibbling for a while on a small acorn it scurried off between the tree trunks.

Phoenix experienced an overwhelming sense of belonging. It should have felt alien. But he was home. It was the moment he realised that he was indeed a Cherokee Indian and the forests, on these mountain slopes, were the home of his ancestors.

He took one last look around him. This is where he would start his quest to find the girl by the lake.

The following weekend he returned to Tallulah Falls and started to make enquiries about the Cherokee Village and Museum. He wanted to locate the proprietor.

Finding him proved easy. As he turned right off Historic Route 441 North, to wind his way up to the Cherokee Village, another dishevelled property's sign said, 'We buy junk and sell antiques.' Phoenix chuckled. Every half-mile there had been some form of antiques or scrap recyclers, but this was the first that made no pretence of its purpose.

He pulled the truck over to the side of the road. At the very least it deserved to be investigated and, if nothing else, it was a place to start his search.

He jumped out and took a look around. The yard was full of rusting mangles, truck fenders and assorted junk. He took the short walk to the porch, which was adorned with all manner of antique advertising hoardings for sodas, automobiles, beers, cigarettes and hundreds more. Oil lamps, wooden-handled hoes, cooking utensils and unidentifiable contraptions were scattered across the porch. A massive corn dolly, sitting in an old rocker, guarded the treasures with a rat-eared teddy bear on her lap. A rusty peanut boiler half blocked the entrance.

Phoenix loved it. It reminded him of the cabin back on the reservation. The only difference was that back home, they were not antiques, but state of the art and necessary home appliances!

He slipped past the peanut boiler and opened the door. An old bell announced his arrival. Inside, it was even more chaotic. There was hardly a square foot of free floor space. Antiques, or junk, were stacked from the floor to the roof rafters. It was impossible to see if there was anyone in the store.

"Hi," he called.

A muffled voice replied from somewhere in the rear, " Hey, neighbour. How can I help you?"

A burly figure shuffled through the artefacts towards him. He was quite obviously Native American, with broad features and a flat nose. His face exploded with lines as he smiled at his only customer of the week.

His smile demanded a reaction. Phoenix grinned at the man and offered his hand. "Hi, the name is Phoenix. Perhaps you can help me, I'm trying to find someone?"

The man took Phoenix's hand and shook it, and then laughed. "Figured you didn't wanna' buy nothing." As he laughed, his thick grey ponytail shook.

Phoenix felt a little guilty, as if he had let him down in some way.

The Indian could see his unease. "Just kiddin',

buddy. How can I help?"

Phoenix relaxed. He sensed this was a good man. "I'm looking for the proprietor of the Cherokee Village and Museum."

"You just found him, friend." He was still smiling.

"Well, sir, do you have time for a chat?"

"Sure, son, time I have plenty of. I'm intrigued." Then he added, "You're not from the IRS, are you? I'm all paid up."

"No, sir." Phoenix smiled. "I just want some information and a chat about the Cherokee Nation."

"Well now, that is something I know a bit about, Phoenix. Come on, you wan' a coffee? By the way, my name is Brad. Not very Cherokee I'm afraid."

Brad led the way to the rear of the store and into an office where a coffee machine, which actually was state of the art, emitted inviting smells of freshly brewed coffee.

"Take a seat, son." Brad cleared some junk off one of the chesterfield sofa that stood by a littered desk. "How do you take it?"

"Just black, thanks, Brad."

Brad poured two mugs of piping hot coffee and passed one to him. "So, ask your questions, son."

Phoenix did not quite know where to start, so just cut straight to it. "I was brought up on an Apache reservation in Nevada, hence my name Phoenix. Lived there all my life until a couple of months ago. I'm attending UGA, in Athens. One of the reasons I have come all this way is because I believe, and so does my grandma, that I may well be Cherokee."

Brad looked surprised. "Surely your grandma would know?"

"Actually, no, she doesn't. I was adopted and nobody knows where I came from."

Brad sipped his coffee, studying the young man.

"Why do you think you may be Cherokee?"

Here goes, thought Phoenix. "You may think what I am about to tell you a bit odd."

"Carry on, son."

He hesitated, but then he told Brad all about the spirit girl he saw once a year, and the deciduous foliage that always surrounded her apparition. He watched, looking for any sign that Brad thought he was mad. He saw none, so he continued with the story in more depth. He finished by telling him that his grandma thought the spirit of the girl to be alive because she aged each time he saw her. The only thing he didn't tell Brad was that he was in love with the spirit.

Brad listened to him intently and without interrupting. When Phoenix finished he didn't speak, but refilled his own coffee cup. Phoenix had not touched his. He'd been too busy talking. "You want that freshening, son?" Brad nodded at the cold coffee in Phoenix's hand.

Phoenix nodded back. "Thanks," he said, and offered the cup for a top up of hot coffee. He wondered if he had sounded a little manic with his monologue. He waited for a response.

Brad sat down again and studied the longhaired youth. He would not have looked out of place riding bareback with war paint and feathers flowing in a John Wayne movie. He looked Apache, but then again he could easily be a Cherokee.

Eventually Brad said, "When you are in the forests and in the mountains, what do you feel, Phoenix?"

Without thinking he replied, "I feel as if I am home."

The look on his face told Brad all he needed to know. "Then I believe you are Cherokee, son."

Phoenix grinned. He did not know why, but he was glad of this validation.

"So, what do you want to do about it?" asked Brad.

"Learn all there is to know about my people, and

their spirits. I have read a number of books, but I need to learn their ways from other Cherokee Indians. And preferably here in the Appalachians," replied Phoenix without hesitation.

He had taken to Brad. There was an intensity and power within his being, yet he exuded warmth that Phoenix related to. He was about to ask if he could work in the Cherokee village during the summer, but before he could, Brad offered, "If that is what you want, son, you'd better come and live with us weekends in the village. You will have to show a lot of fat tourists around during the day, but they will love you. You are what an Indian should look like, especially after we paint your face some and stick a peacock feather in your hair. The nights are fun, though. We actually stay in the village and live like our ancestors. We will show you all the old crafts and tell you the legends handed down through centuries. Just weekends mind, during the week most people actually have to earn a living. The pay is shit, but you may get the occasional tip."

Phoenix was grinning from ear to ear. It was far more than he had hoped for. "That would be fantastic, Brad. I don't know how to thank you."

"If you are willing to work, then that's thanks enough, son." He nodded at the young man. "What are you studying?

"I am studying to be a veterinary practitioner.

"Animals." Brad chuckled. "Yes, you are probably Cherokee then. But studying for that is real hard work, so come whichever weekends you can."

Phoenix stayed for the rest of the day and learnt a great deal about Brad. He was a Cherokee who had served his country in the Marine Corps in Vietnam, but one who had gravitated back to his roots once he was discharged. He had eked out a living for his wife and three children with the shop and Cherokee village that he had built with his own hands. Along with the help of friends and his kids, plus a grant from the Cherokee Preservation Foundation, which had bought the materials he required. Now the kids had grown up, he had more than he needed and was just happy to be at one with the land and the spirit world.

Phoenix left, uplifted and happy. He visited Brad on a number of occasions over the winter months and helped him with maintenance to the log cabins in the Cherokee village. On the first weekend in April, he left the campus after an afternoon lecture and moved into the village for the weekend. By the end of that weekend any slight lingering doubt that he was not Cherokee had evapourated.

*

If not quite the femme fatale Missy's trilogy would have her be, Skye was leaving an impression on Oxford University. James, the rugby player, was devoted to the exotic beauty that graced him with her attention. Her professors drooled, in a professorial way, over her intellect and obvious charms. And the Cherokee Indian Student Research Society, which she founded, now had three other members. All were male, and all were more interested in researching the society's founder member.

Their quest was to search the Bodleian Library for any hitherto unfound reference to the Cherokee. It met with little success, but made Skye feel closer to home, and her fellow members closer to her.

The more she read of the Europeans' treatment of her ancestors, the more at one she felt with her people. She did not harbour a resentment of that treatment. It had happened, she couldn't change any of it. In a modern

America it would not have happened. All that mattered was how her people were being treated now, and as a group they were probably a lot better off than a number in American society.

All that said, one day she couldn't help herself feeling a little triumphant when she read about the Spanish explorer and conquistador called Hernando De Soto, who led an expedition through her lands in 1540. By all the accounts she could find in the Bodleian, he had been less than caring in his treatment of the Native Indians he encountered. But he got his come-uppance. A Chief called Tuskaloosa attacked the Spaniards in a village called Mabila. 2500 warriors lay in wait for the conquistadores and, although taking huge losses themselves, over 200 Spaniards were killed and 150 were injured.

She punched the air and said, "Yes," before a voice in the reading room shushed her. She felt a little guilty at her reaction and pondered why this Pyrrhic victory should excite her. Other more devastating battles had been won, but they had not moved her in a similar way.

De Soto accounted for thousands of deaths on his travels. He died in 1542 from a disease, which he had acquired during his rape of the Cherokee lands. Skye thought about the Cherokee legend, which suggested that for each life wrongly taken a new disease is created.

She closed the text about Hernando De Soto, still wondering why she felt an antagonism towards a man who lived and died nearly five hundred years ago and had lent his name to the beautiful Gulf coastal city of Sarasota. It was a place she liked a great deal.

She put the thought behind her. Tomorrow she was going home to the lake and her family for the summer vacation. She went home at the end of every term, and was always greeted by a gyrating dog as she stepped through the front door. This time she was going to stay an extra two weeks. There would not be too many lectures, as two of her teachers were going to be away. She could study at home by the lake. And, if the spirits were willing and he came early, she may see Yona. She had missed him.

SIX

1540 AD

"They are looking for daloniga, Mai."

"Where have they come from, Elan?"

"From the flatlands towards the sun." Elan gestured towards the sun, which had traversed half of its daily arc. He looked flustered and anxious. "Some are not men. They have four legs like huge dogs and a man's body. I don't know what they are called, they are like sky beasts."

Mai was sitting on a rock with his best friend Elan by the side of the Chattahoochee River. Behind them were the fields the village women had cleared for planting crops.

Mai was trying to imagine such an animal, and what threat it might pose to the village. They had no daloniga, yellow rock, in the village or even nearby, but he knew of a place where the yellow stone could be found.

He idly tossed a pebble into the cool, life-giving water. It landed a foot from a large trout, which went to investigate the splash. What Elan was telling him was disturbing.

"How many men, without counting the beasts, Elan?

"Several hundred, and they have weapons I have never seen before. Some of the men have yellow hair and most have pale faces.

It was a threat that Mai knew they could not defend themselves against. Two moons ago word had reached them that an army was heading towards the forests and the mountains. Any who had opposed their advance had been cut down. Others had traded and survived. One female chief from the flatlands had turned over her tribe's pearls, food and treasures to the army and their sky beasts, in order to buy their favour. To a degree it had worked, but a number of the girls had still been taken and put to use by the invaders.

In fact the sky beasts were men on horseback, but no one had seen a horse before in the village. The army of pale-faced men were Spanish conquistadores, led by Hernando De Soto. They had set out from the Florida Panhandle towards the rising sun to find a passage to China and as much gold as they could en route. They had not found China and gold had proved elusive so far, so their disposition was becoming irritable.

More recently, word had come of another village being pillaged and levelled to the ground by fire, but not before hundreds of warriors had been slaughtered.

Mai, which meant deer, could see little reward in fighting the palefaces.

Theirs was a small village; any wealth had come from trading with the other tribes towards the sun, their brethren in the mountains and by the lakes. But mostly they were self-sufficient, the woods and the river were abundant with animals that they lived in harmony with and to their mutual benefit. They were equals in all respects since the primal genesis period.

The tribe had grown soft. Twenty Great Moon Ceremonies had passed since anyone in the village had to use their bow in anger. Not one of a warrior's age had seen combat. The only man to have fought in that battle was Elan, and although still fit he was getting old.

"How many days are they away, Elan? Mai asked.

"Six, maybe seven. What should we do?" Elan was still agitated.

"We will call a council meeting in the Townhouse. All will have their say. Come."

They stood up and walked across the fields where the women were planting the summer's crops.

Three hours later, over eighty squeezed into the round building built in the village centre on top of the mound. Another fifty stood outside the entrances, straining to hear the words spoken inside. The elders of the seven clans had gathered in the centre, sitting cross-legged on the floor.

Mai was sitting by their side listening to their analysis of the threat, the manner of which none of them could comprehend. Some were for the fight, others for total capitulation.

Elohi stood with Savita in her arms, looking at her husband Mai. Savita had been crying until she saw her father and then, as always, she had gurgled and grinned at him. She was just three moons old, and Elohi was the happiest she had ever been.

Mai threw them both a loving glance.

"Mai, you would lead our warriors if there is war. What do you think we should do?" asked one of the elders.

Mai was the strongest of all the hunters. He could draw his bow past his ear at arm's length. None of the others could get it past their chins. He was brave beyond belief and had risked his life many times to save others. But above all else he was wise, and although still young his word was heeded.

He looked across to his beautiful wife Elohi, which meant earth, and their baby Savita, fire. She gurgled at him again and the look of pride on her mother's face filled him with a longing that one Great Moon Ceremony of marriage had not satiated. Above all else they must be protected.

"We cannot fight them. We will lose. There are too many, and they have beasts and weapons we know nothing about. If we try to placate them, they will just take what they want. They will take the women we love and our families, whose hearts beat within us, and they will be destroyed."

There were murmurings around the Townhouse, some in agreement, many at odds with him.

He continued. "They are greedy. They want the yellow rock. I know where it can be found far away from our village and away from our families. It is in the hills where I have traded with the mountain tribes, but it is not near their villages so they should be safe from these people who come to our lands."

Some heads were beginning to nod in agreement.

"But first, we must make sure our women and children are safe." He looked up at Elohi and smiled. Five warriors should take them away from the river for five days. Some of the older women should stay, but only those who want to, so we can show a semblance of village life should they come here. Elan and I will intercept the invaders before they reach our village. They will approach along the river. I will fuel their lust for the yellow rock, so that in their greed to find it they will pass by the village."

"How far away is the gold?" a voice asked from the assembly.

"Three days. They will stay there until they have enough gold, and then move on towards the setting sun."

There was a general hum of concord now within the council meeting. The only face that looked less than happy was Elohi.

Back in their dwelling she flew into his arms, her long dark curls splayed over his shoulders. "I'm scared. It is too dangerous for you. You are a hunter, the best, but you cry for each animal you kill and put their bones to rest with a ceremony for each. You are a kindred spirit with the four-footed tribes. You are not a real warrior."

"I will be fine, Elohi. I am not going to fight the palefaces. And they will not hurt me because I know where the yellow rock is." He kissed her tenderly on her forehead and within minutes they were wrapped in each other's arms making love on a bed covered with the blankets they had tied together at their wedding ceremony. Each of them was praying to the spirits that their lovemaking would, in some way, protect the other.

Three days later all the preparations were complete and five warriors set off on foot with provisions for themselves and a small army of women and children. Elohi cradled Savita in her arms. An almost white dog trotted adoringly at her side. She looked back at Mai with a tear in her eye.

Mai was kneeling down by another dog. He was black, and obviously torn between staying with his master and going with his friend and the mistress he loved.

Mai was whispering in his ear, "Go and look after them, I will be back soon."

As if waiting for his command, the dog licked his master's face and ran to catch up with them. He caught up with the white dog and bowled her over in play.

Mai waved to the four living spirits he loved above all others, as they disappeared deeper into the dense deciduous forest.

The next day Mai and Elan set off downstream to intercept the Spanish conquistadores. Initially they took to their canoes, navigating the white water rapids with great skill. The late summer rains bloated the river and progress was swift. When they came to the waterfall they pulled their canoes from the water and left them to collect later. They followed a trail that hugged the meandering flow of the Chattahoochee River. Twelve hours later they could hear the approaching army.

They saw the sky beasts first, as they cut gingerly through the often-thick growth, churning up the red clay beneath their hooves. Other large dogs dragged wagons through the red earth, which left a path that hundreds of soldiers marched along. They carried small bows, the like of which Mai had never seen. Some wore metal tunics that clanked as they walked.

Mai stood and stared up at the first man on horseback as he cut a path towards him. Elan stood by his side. Both smiled unthreateningly at the sky beast, which spoke in a tongue they did not recognize.

The sky beast raised his crossbow to his shoulder and pointed it menacingly at Mai.

They both raised their arms in supplication, still smiling at the strange beast. By now, Mai realized it was a man on the back of a majestic animal, the like of which he had never seen before.

The horse whinnied and nodded a greeting to him, as it tapped a hoof in the mud. Instinctively, Mai stroked the beast's nose and looked into its kind eyes. He knew there was nothing to be feared from these animals.

The man on its back was different. He yelled at the two Indians that stood in his way. They stepped aside to allow him to pass.

As they did so another man on horseback approached with an Indian guide walking at his side. The guide spoke in a tongue they knew well, and the man on the horse greeted them courteously with a smile.

The column of wagons and men walked past them as they spoke. Towards the rear of the line were a number of Indians, not shackled but quite obviously prisoners. The majority were young women. Mai knew what their purpose would be and he knew he had been right to evacuate Elohi and the others.

The Spaniard on horseback asked questions that the Cherokee interpreter relayed to him. He wasted no time in asking the two Indians about the main purpose of the expedition, daloniga.

It was Mai's chance. He described the stream in the hills where he had seen the yellow rocks lying on the banks and beneath a small waterfall

The commander grew excited at his description of the chunks of gold that awaited them.

Mai wondered at his reaction. All things had spirits, even rocks, but they were not the spirits of the animal kingdom. What was it about daloniga that was so important? As an aside, he also thought the spirit of the sky beast far stronger than that of the man sitting on it.

A contract was soon forged. They would take them to the yellow rock in exchange for their lives. Mai was not scared. He knew that the palefaces needed them and, if they wanted, they could simply walk into the woods and the conquistadores would never be able to find them.

He and Elan led the column a safe distance around their village, offering a shortcut across a wide bend in the river that was not actually there. It worked, and by nightfall they were far beyond the village. The Indian guide may have known of its existence, but he said nothing.

In the evening they set up camp and Mai was able to study the strange tribe. In many ways they were like his people. They laughed and chatted animatedly, and they ate and drank a liquid that appeared to make them happy. Later, the laughter turned to anger and some fights broke out between them. Perhaps it was because they did not have their women with them, but there was no gentleness or reverence for the forests or the spirits that lived within it. Late in the evening a number of them took the Cherokee slaves into the woods. No affection was offered, and they were often brutal as they manhandled the women away from camp. Mai could hear their screams and sobs as the conquistadores abused them. He vowed that he would free them once they were in the hills.

Not all of the conquistadores were bad, some displayed decency more akin to his tribe. One such man rescued a young girl from the debauched attentions of one of the drunken soldiers. He struck the offending man across the face and put a protective arm around the girl who sobbed in his arms. Mai took him to be of rank, as the man accepted his treatment without retaliation.

Though he could not converse with the man, Mai offered a nod of appreciation, which was reciprocated.

Over the coming days the man continued to protect that one girl and eventually all others left her alone. Mai wondered if she reminded the man of his own daughter.

He befriended the man, who offered to show him his crossbow. They took turns with each other's weapon. The short arrows, and the devastation they could wreak, fascinated Mai. For his part, the Spaniard marvelled at the strength of Mai and his accuracy with the longbow. After three days of travelling they had forged a respect for each other.

During the gruelling journey the Chief, Hernando De Soto, never spoke to Mai. He remained within his small enclave of loyal officers.

They followed the river valley of the Chattahoochee, and later the course of the Chestatee. Each night they camped and left a trail of devastation through the forest, paying it little regard or respect. At times it was slow going, a wagon would get stuck or a stream would need to be crossed. The sky beasts, which Mai now knew to be called horses, were magnificent and worked tirelessly with the men to traverse the awkward terrain.

'What could I do with such an animal?' thought Mai.

Eventually they reached the hills where the gold

could be found.

Mai then led a small party along a tributary of the Chestatee River and just as he had described, chunks of the yellow rock nestled on the banks. They came to a waterfall that had polished the pebbles of gold beneath and around it.

The Spaniards gathered the rocks with glee, slapping each other on the back.

The next day hundreds of conquistadores trawled the river for the precious ore. They crated every piece they found. Mai sowed a seed in the invaders heads of even more gold, high in the Appalachian Mountains towards the setting sun. "It is there, other men have seen it," he said.

A few weeks later the expedition was ready to follow the sun to new riches and the Spaniards insisted the Indians go with them.

Mai realised the palefaces' greed would take them towards the sun, and they would not waste too much time pursuing them if they escaped. So that night he and Elan decided that they would free the women, and follow the Chestatee and the Chattahoochee Rivers home to their village.

However, first they had to escape. Perhaps they made too much noise or they were just unlucky, but a Spaniard's crossbow cut Mai down within yards of the waterfall where they had camped. The tiny arrow penetrated his heart and he fell at the hooves of one of the pursuing horses.

As he joined the spirit world Mai looked up into the horse's eyes and saw only sadness and compassion.

His death seemed to satiate the conquistadores, and the women who had stopped to help Mai were quickly corralled and punished for their impudence. They made little effort to continue their pursuit of Elan and the remaining girls. Their greed for wealth far outshone their need for whores.

Several days later Elan made it home along with the girls he had freed. Elohi was waiting as he walked into the village. She had tears in her eyes as he approached her. He could see that she already knew in her heart that Mai was dead. Without speaking he offered his arms for consolation. She did not move into the offered embrace, but fell to her knees. With her head bowed, tears soaked into the red clay beneath her. The damp clay turned the colour of blood.

It took several hours before she regained her composure. When she did, she was strong and determined. The next day she led a party to the stream of gold to recover his body, and to bring him back to the village.

He lay exactly where he had been murdered by the water's edge. She expected he would have been devoured by the animal kingdom. They had not touched his body, as if they had revered the man as much as he had them.

Normally, Cherokee spiritual law would have the body of the deceased returned and placed into Mother Earth before sundown of the same day. That could not be, but the forest spirits had watched over him. Two squirrels stood by, as they lifted his partly decomposed body onto the stretcher that would transport him to the village burial ground.

Elohi lovingly prepared his body, and four days later he was laid to rest

She wept for the spirit of the man she loved, the spirit whose path was incomplete. The spirit she knew in her heart that she would see again.

A black dog and a white one sat by his grave for several days, halting their vigil only to be fed. After about a week they got up and continued with their play, as if a spirit had released them.

Elohi visited his grave every day of her life and

would talk to the spirit she loved. As would Savita, daughter of the kindest spirit she knew.

SEVEN

The summer was glorious. Long hot dreamy days were spent with Thea walking the beaches of the islands and shoreline of Lake Lanier.

Skye got up each morning at about six o'clock and packed a cool box with juices and snacks. She had a cup of coffee, and then walked down the garden to the dock. Thea was spinning and wagging from the moment Skye got up, and all the way to the beach she was bouncing as she retrieved Frisbee whilst running towards the pontoon boat.

Skye fired up the engine, untied the boat and cast off. Her parents awoke each day to the outboard being throttled up as she sped away across the lake.

She spent most of the morning on the lake, swimming with Thea or walking along the beaches and through the woods that lined the shore. The beaches were constantly changing, appearing or disappearing depending on how much rainfall there had been. Or how much water had been let out of the lake at its southernmost end by Buford Dam to continue its flow down the Chattahoochee.

The dam had been built in 1956 by the US Army Corps of Engineers to supply the water to Atlanta. They had dammed the Chattahoochee, and over the next year the Chattahoochee slowly filled its own and surrounding valleys. Including the Chestatee River, which flowed into the Chattahoochee near the town of Gainesville, ten miles to the north of where Skye lived.

Hundreds of homesteads now lay beneath the lapping waters of the huge lake, which had well over 700 miles of shoreline. One or two small townships had to be cleared and the inhabitants relocated before the project began. Whole forests stood hundreds of feet below the surface. In the shallows, their stumps had claimed more than a few lives of swimmers and revellers whose limbs had got caught up in them. Its depths held a treasure trove of stories and history.

Throughout the lake small islands poked up, the tops of what had once been hills. Some still bore the remains of an old building, which reminded Skye of the follies English aristocrats built by their country piles to add a sense of mystery or romance to the view from the grand homes.

On this day Skye followed the line the Chattahoochee valley had once taken to the north.

The lake was at its most beautiful in the morning, and especially during the week, before the armada of boats created a swell and their engines penetrated the idyll.

Thea stood proudly on the bow, sniffing the morning air and allowing the wind to tickle her ears.

First stop was one of the largest islands on the lake. Here, she walked for half an hour with Thea, exploring the woods that thrived surrounded by the cool water. Occasionally they would stumble across some deer that could often be seen in the water swimming to the island. One inlet was home to a family of turtles who were basking on the rocks in the early morning sun. Thea had once picked one up, thinking it to be a Frisbee. Skye put her right, and returned the indignant looking animal to his rock. Thea had left them alone since that day.

From the island she continued north towards the Chestatee River. With over 700 miles of shoreline there was a lot of scope to explore, but for some reason she had always been drawn to the Chestatee. When she navigated the pontoon boat from the wide expanse of water that was the main lake into the river, the nature of the lake altered. More enclosed, the trees seemed taller, many reached out with their branches over the water as if they were stretching to reach the other shore. She continued west along the Chestatee towards Dahlonega, where Georgia had once seen its very own gold rush. Even now tourists could pan for gold in the mountains nearby.

A number of homes lined the river, usually hidden in the trees, but their boat docks stuck out into the water like fingers in a pie. A few were beginning to see some morning action, as people prepared to take their fishing boats out or play on their wave runners.

She continued for nearly an hour up the river. Slowly it narrowed even more and habitation became sparser. Tree stumps were beginning to poke out of the water so she stayed in mid channel to avoid them. She slowed the boat to about six knots and turned the boat hard right through a gap in the trees hardly any wider than the boat. She brushed off the foliage that was trying to sideswipe her, and ducked beneath a larger branch. Suddenly, she popped out into a small paradise.

She throttled back completely and dropped the anchor in the middle of a serene pool. It was about 100ft across, and at the far end a stream fed into it by means of a 10ft waterfall. Maples and oaks shaded the pool and it was perfect for Thea and her to swim in. Some large boulders broke the fall of the water as it entered the pool, intensifying the noise of the running water. The only other sound was that of a red cardinal calling for its mate.

Skye loved this place more than any she could think of on the lake. Apart from giving Thea shade from the glaring sun, it gave her a feeling of tranquillity, which somehow mingled with sadness. She viewed it as a spiritual place, but did not know why.

Quickly, she stripped down to her bikini and threw Thea's ball towards the small beach near the boulders. Thea launched herself off the bow of the boat towards the prize. Skye dived in after her.

For half-an-hour they swam and played. Then they showered beneath the waterfall and towelled dry on the boat.

The sun was getting high and was beginning to appear in the small patch of blue that the tree canopy allowed. It was time to go home, before the sun became too hot for Thea. Skye's mahogany skin did not seem to burn, but for a dog in a fur coat, albeit a white one, air-conditioning was preferable.

Skye raised the anchor, turned for the gap in the trees and eased the pontoon boat back into the main stream. She opened the throttle and set off for home.

Ninety minutes later she tied up the pontoon boat alongside the dock.

"Hello, honey. Where did you go today?" asked Missy, as Skye walked in with Thea.

"The pool."

Missy nodded. Her daughter was drawn to the spot regularly. Though Skye's Cherokee blood was even thinner than her own, Missy was sure her daughter had far more Cherokee spirit within her.

"Gramps is coming over this evening for dinner," said Missy.

"Great." Skye grinned.

She loved Gramps and visited him nearly every day she was home. Nearly eighty now, he was fiercely independent and lived in his own home surrounded by forests about two miles down the Chattahoochee below the dam towards Suwannee.

A property developer had been trying to buy his land for years, but he would not sell. It is where he and Grandma had raised Missy and two other children.

"It is where Grandma's spirit lives. When our spirits are reunited you can do what you want with it," he told the property developer, Missy, his sons and anyone else who suggested he live in more suitable accommodation for a near eighty-year-old.

Grandpa Donald had five grandchildren, and he made no bones about the fact that Skye was his favourite. The others didn't mind. If you had asked any of them who their favourite cousin was they would tell you Skye.

Dinner meant tales of legends, half of which he made up on the spur of the moment and half of which had a least their roots planted in truth. As a small child Skye had been bewitched by his stories, and she still loved to hear them, even though she now realized the tales often changed with their telling.

That evening, after dinner, Skye sat with him on the deck watching the sun set over the island where Yona would come. They talked about Oxford and her studies, her cousins and her mother. They chatted about thieving property developers and his new chainsaw, but not in the same conversation. How it was getting harder to look after the ten acres of forest that bordered the Chattahoochee, and how Grandma had cooked the finest Thanksgiving Dinner in the world. Followed by ruminating as to why his daughter had not inherited any of her mother's culinary skills.

"It's those books, you know," he said. "Lives her life in her head, making up stories. No time for preparing chow."

Skye giggled. "I wonder where she gets the storytelling from, Gramps?"

She decided to change the subject to give her mother a break.

"You doing much fishing?" Skye asked.

"Too hot for me, darlin'. When the lake turns, I'll get back out on the old Lund again."

"When is that?"

"Soon, maybe in a few weeks. It's different each year. It all depends on the water temperature."

"How does it work?" Skye was fascinated, she had never heard of such a phenomenon.

"Hell, darlin', you're the scientist."

"I'm still learning, Gramps." She gave him a sweet, little-girl smile.

"Okay, in its simplest form. After we get some cold nights and the surface-water cools to 39 degrees Fahrenheit it will contract and become denser. At that time it sinks to the bottom of the lake and pushes the warmer, less dense, water up from the depths. The lake flips. There is a whole lot more about thermocline levels, mixing and oxygenating that makes the water real healthy for the fish. But, to be honest, I don't know that much about it. Just know the fishing is better. But you can smell it when it flips."

Skye looked puzzled. "What do you mean?"

"When it turns, you can smell it. The water that has been at the bottom of the lake brings up decaying matter and sulphurous gases. For a short while you can smell it before it dissipates. You probably wouldn't notice it if you are not looking for it. But fishermen do. It's a real good time for the fish. It gets murky too."

"Does it only happen in the fall, Gramps?"

"On Lake Lanier, yes. But in other climates it can happen a few times a year. It is all about hitting the 39 degrees. Some years, if there is a cold spell, it can happen early fall. But I've known it happen as late as Christmas if it is real mild."

Skye's brain was racing. Had she ever smelt sulphur or noticed the waters become murky when he appeared? She couldn't consciously remember such a thing, but then again she only had eyes for Yona at the time. But it could explain why his spirit only appeared in the fall, released from the depths when the lake flipped.

That night she went to bed praying that fall would come early.

*

It was Phoenix's first weekend in the village. He had gone the previous weekend to see Brad's wife, Lucy, who measured him and had spent the week making his Cherokee clothing.

He was out of the door of the animal hospital that was situated on campus the second his lecturer finished the operation on the domestic cat. The cat had fallen down a well and broken its leg. Phoenix had set any number of animals' legs in his own makeshift hospital back in Shichu's barn, but never using the full paraphernalia available in the state-of-the-art facility they had available. A madcap drive north had followed to Tallulah Falls, his whole being enthused with anticipation.

The duds were presented to him with great ceremony before he went into one of the village huts to change. He stepped from the log cabin in his new finery to the applause of his newfound tribe. He was Cherokee Indian from the top of his head to his toes.

On his feet he wore beaded moccasins with a front seam. As it was summer, his legs were bare. He wore a breechcloth between his legs, folded over a cord around his waist. His muscled torso was left bare to titillate the paying public. It was his head and face that most startled Phoenix when he looked in the mirror Brad's wife had brought.

Though not going to fight, Brad had painted Phoenix's face with a menacing design of war paint. A single feather was tied to a lock of his hair at the crown of his head and hung jauntily to one side. Both of his ears felt heavy with earrings, not to mention a tad sore as they were clipped to his ears. Given the pain he was experiencing, he was seriously considering changing his position on body piercing.

Phoenix looked at Brad, who was resplendent in full medicine man regalia with a special feathered cape made of knotted twine and wild turkey feathers.

Brad could see him looking. "When you are Dr. Phoenix I may let you wear it," he said. "You look great, son, like a male stripper. Business should be good." He grinned at his protégé.

The others were all dressed in similar attire. One of Brad's sons, Pete, was in charge of the square ground, or dance ground. It was located in a flat area near the village entrance and consisted of a central rectangular space, which was used for dancing. Seven brush arbours surrounded it, one for each clan. The brush arbours were open structures with poles holding up a roof to provide shade for the clan members.

At two hourly intervals throughout the day Phoenix was to be part of the dance exhibition. It was the one part of his day he was not looking forward to.

Brad was going to give talks about traditional Cherokee medicine. When not doing that he would be recounting Cherokee legends in the townhouse. Phoenix was scheduled to be at the majority of these renditions. In time he would be allowed to conduct many of them himself, but first he had to learn them.

The townhouse was small with room for about fifty people, but it had been built to exacting specifications garnered from history books supplied by Brad and his family. It was Phoenix's favourite place in the village. He experienced a sense of belonging whenever he was inside.

Lucy was going to give regular demonstrations of basket weaving and beadwork. Others would demonstrate traditional artwork, and hopefully sell it. Lucy's friend, Brenda, demonstrated Cherokee cooking along with her daughter. To Phoenix the majority of it resembled typical fast food. Sales of traditional Cherokee hot dogs and burgers did, however, form the largest part of the revenue collected, so he could see why the ancient art had been slightly adapted to modern day America. Others read poetry from the ancients that luckily had been handed down from generation to generation and recorded in books and DVDs. All of which were available to purchase in the store by the exit. Plus, a host of other traditional skills were demonstrated, usually with an end product that could be sold. According to Brad enough sold to keep the village going and make a small profit.

On this, his first day, Phoenix's primary job was to watch and learn, dance when told to, and talk people through the woodland trail that meandered off into the forest. This was something that he had prepared for, having spent several months studying the flora and fauna of the region.

After the first few hours he was used to walking around half-naked and was warming to the gradual flow of tourists who found their way to the village. He only had to dance once, as the numbers attending hardly warranted the show. The one he did perform was worth it for its comedy content. He watched all the craft demos and listened to Brad's talks about village life and Cherokee legend, committing as much as he could to memory.

It was after the village closed to the public that it became alive to him. Seven of the staff stayed the night in the various cabins they had built over the years. Which included open summerhouses and more robust winter homes. Each represented typical construction from different periods in history. Being the most junior member, Phoenix bunked in a pretty basic shack reputedly representative of about 1000AD. Luckily there were modern bathroom facilities and a shower by the museum and shop.

Once all the paying public had left, they gathered around a fire pit near the townhouse and ate a meal they prepared over the fire. They ate out of bowls with utensils the Cherokee used 300 years previously, and they talked.

They talked about the old ways, modern day politics, sports and the ball games the Cherokee used to play. They talked about legends, and they talked about TV programmes. One conversation drifted naturally into another. The past and the present merged seamlessly into one. Occasionally one of them would slip into talking Cherokee, which was still taught in some of the local schools. They would quickly realise that Phoenix was being excluded and apologise, and then revert to English.

Brad told some of the stories his grandpa had told him from his youth. Slowly Phoenix began to tell the tales Shichu had told him when he was knee high to a grasshopper. He related tales of Apache warriors and cunning, of Apache legends, gods and spirits. Soon he was holding court, and they all sat transfixed.

Whenever he finished a story, Lucy encouraged him to tell another. "We have all heard the Cherokee stuff a thousand times. Your lot were so sexy, riding ponies along ridges looking down threateningly at the palefaces cowering below," she said.

"Don't listen to a word she says, son. Lucy is from Danish stock, damned European. Not an ounce of Cherokee in her, she just likes cookin' is all. Lucky we didn't get meatballs!" Brad teased his wife. "Before she had this mop of grey hair, she was blonde. We told the tourists we had kidnapped her, but her people would not pay the ransom, so I made her one of my wives!"

Lucy slapped his arm. "Actually, Phoenix, he did tell them I was just one of many wives. He didn't mention kidnapping me, well not often." She slapped Brad's arm again. "It made me laugh; their next question was usually, how many wives are you allowed? You could see them desperately trying not to use the word savages."

"One redneck offered to rescue her." Brad exploded with laughter.

"Not after you did a war dance in his face, honey." The two smiled affectionately at each other.

"Talking of war, who fancies a puff on the peace pipe?" Brad threw back his head and said mystically, "In the beginning of the world, when people and animals were all the same, there was only one tobacco plant, to which they all came for their tobacco until the Dagulku geese stole it and carried it far to the south."

They laughed. He pushed some tobacco into a clay pipe, lit it and took a couple of puffs, and then offered it to Phoenix."

"I've never smoked, sir," he said.

Brad instantly took it back. "Then don't start, son. It is our revenge on the palefaces." He took another drag on the pipe. "Unfortunately I did. It is my punishment for marrying one of them."

It turned out that Brad was the only one amongst them that did smoke. It was the final accessory to the dress and the face of a man that yelled Cherokee Indian at you.

During the next few months, Phoenix grew to love his time in the village and grew close to the people he worked and lived with on alternate weekends. Brad, in particular, became a close friend and almost a father figure. The ex-Marine sergeant was very similar to Phoenix. He had his own affinity with nature and the animal tribes. His gentleness was cut by the same raw power and strength his personality and body possessed.

They were both good men and would have been hunters and warriors in another era.

To a degree, Brad had been a warrior in Vietnam. By the fire, one evening, he confided to Phoenix his true thoughts about the struggle he was involved in.

"It was shit, son. I was drafted, and we should not have been there. They were not our lands. We were no better than the Europeans that made our people homeless. Worse than that, they cut off my hair!" He laughed. "You do realise the old Cherokees didn't really have long hair? Mine is long because I grew up in the sixties, and the tourists think all savages have long hair and feathers." He laughed again.

"Sixties eh! So you smoked things other than tobacco in your pipe then?" asked Phoenix, jokingly.

"Used to, man." He went hippy on Phoenix. "Actually, worse than that in 'Nam. They gave it to us, would you believe? Not official of course, but they knew it took the fear away. I only tried it once. It was not for me. I preferred to be shittin' myself!"

"It must have been hell, Brad. I've read all about it, not our finest moment."

"No. But that is enough about it. It's over. What about this girl you see by the lake? Tell me again."

Phoenix retold the story. This time he told it with his heart and let his feelings for the spirit be known.

"Sounds to me, you have a soul mate, son. It also sounds that you've got some powerful feelin's for her."

Phoenix nodded.

Brad continued, "Your Shichu, that the right pronunciation? She is right. The legend says that if your lives were taken violently and unjustly, you will be reincarnated until your preordained path is complete. Sounds like your path is the same as the girl. How far down that path you are? I don't know. I suspect quite a ways. Your spiritual awareness is strong, and you certainly have a deep connection with the animals. Those squir'ls just come to be fed by your hand. Ain't never seen that before. They run a country mile if anyone else goes near."

Phoenix was smiling. "All critters have just accepted me."

Brad was thoughtful as he puffed on his pipe again. "You say she only appears in the fall, and only by the lake? But you ain't seen her for a couple of years." He tapped the ash out from the pipe on a log by the fire.

"Yeah."

"Okay, son, what do you say we go do some fishin' up on Lake Burton this fall?"

Phoenix was excited. "That would be great, Brad."

"At least this time you will be on a lake a whole lot nearer. I'm sure she will appear, she was probably just not around for a while."

It was a simple explanation and one Phoenix wanted to believe.

Brad relit the pipe after packing a fresh charge of tobacco into it. Then he added, only half-jokingly, "Let's hope you two live long and peaceful lives this time, son."

EIGHT

The Escalade drove unhurriedly down Buford Dam Road heading west towards Cumming. The driver looked out through the tinted windows across the expanse of water to his right, with the islands stretching out like Florida Keys into the lake.

The air-conditioning felt cool inside the vehicle, belying the oppressive humid heat outside. The outside air temperature on the vehicle's computer said 106 degrees Fahrenheit. The temperature was nothing to the driver, he was well used to those numbers but it was not as humid where he came from.

He turned a corner and the dam appeared in front of him. The road ahead stretched across it in a gentle arc, and then disappeared into the forest again on the far side.

A Chevy Impala cop car was parked at the side of the road with Gwinnett Police emblazoned along the side. The cop sat inside, engine running, allowing the county's budget to keep him cool as he ate the sandwich he'd purchased at the gas station a half mile down the road. He glanced up, completely disinterested as the Escalade rolled by unthreateningly.

Inside, the driver looked to his left down into the valley below where the dam allowed the Chattahoochee to continue its temporarily interrupted flow towards Suwannee, and then on to Atlanta and the Southern States, which it would ultimately supply with their life's blood, water.

The guy in the passenger seat kept the video camera rolling through the blackened windows. He let it linger on the complacent cop, before filming the buildings and structure of the dam, along with the entrance and road that led down through a park to the powerhouse, which generated hydroelectric power from the dam's released water. They drove along the winding road, filming as they went. At the end they parked in a space intended for recreational park users. They had a great view of the gatehouse entrance used by the staff. The passenger pressed record again.

The film would be added to the one he had shot from the boat a day earlier, and the one he'd taken whilst hiking along the shore of the Chattahoochee River towards the powerhouse.

These images and videos would be stored in the computer that already held similar images of Fontana Dam in North Carolina, Shasta Dam in Nevada, Cougar Dam in Oregon, Grand Coulee Dam in Washington, Flaming Gorge Dam in Utah, plus eleven others already surveyed. Eventually there would be a list of fifty.

Six would be selected from that list and added to the one they had already chosen, the Hoover Dam near Las Vegas.

When the hand of Allah shattered the concrete walls that restrained the Colorado River, the ultimate symbol of Western decadence would literally be washed off the face of the Earth. Las Vegas would drown. The water Allah had used to create life would destroy the lives of those who did not believe.

The pair in the Escalade smiled at each other. They liked what they saw at Buford Dam. The structure was relatively small. It was a soft target, which would wreak havoc in one of the most flourishing cities in America. Metro Atlanta was a city that represented much of what the imperialists were trying to impose on the world. It hosted one of the most famous companies on Earth, Coca Cola, the company that had seduced their children with images of a profligate view of humanity. Another iconic company, UPS, had delivered and distributed the evil, subversive, capitalistic weapons of consumption the West had used to destroy their world. The world's largest airline, Delta, was based at Hartsfield Airport, and CNN, the purveyor of lies lay in the heart of the city. All would suffer when Lake Lanier's floodwaters crashed down upon the city.

Seven dams would blow simultaneously throughout the United States. Thousands would drown, or die of the disease that would ensue when their water supply was cut off. Crops would fail. Power would be lost to millions of people. The US economy would be in crisis.

It would be a glorious day, and one to rival the most magnificent day of their struggle, September 11th 2001.

*

Being an engineer and a scientist, Skye had taken a thermometer with her on her daily excursions across the lake with Thea.

The day after Gramps had told her about lake turnover, she dipped the thermometer into the water near the island where Yona would appear. It was 45 degrees Fahrenheit. Her heart sank. How long would it take? It was nowhere near cold enough yet.

She had never wanted the weather to be cold during the summer vacations in the past, but this year she prayed for it to cool down early. She had delayed her return to Oxford for as long as she could. It would mean her getting off the flight and getting on the bus to Oxford, which arrived eight minutes before her first lecture began.

It was brinkmanship, but two weeks before she had to return to university she was rewarded. An unseasonal icy blast blew down form the North. It lasted for the entire two weeks.

After the first week the water temperature had begun to fall rapidly. The previous evening it had dropped to 40.4 degrees.

It was close to the magic number she wanted. She had read all she could about lake turnover and discovered it happened at 39.2 degrees. She just wanted one more day of near freezing conditions. But it was forecast to warm up as the wind swung tantalisingly from the north towards the west.

After interrogating her grandpa she was further disheartened when he told her that if the lake flipped now it would be the earliest he could remember.

She studied the satellite images of the clouds and their likely path; she did her own analysis and concluded the forecasters were right. It would warm up. She studied the forecast again in the Atlanta Journal. According to her father, the chief meteorologist was the worst he had ever seen. He should know. 'He was used to terrible weather forecasting, he was from England.' She prayed her father's belief that all meteorologists were idiots put on Earth to cause havoc was correct. She had just two days left; she needed clear nights without cloud cover.

*

"Christ, it's cold up here," grumbled Brad.

It was the fifth day of their fishing trip, slash spirit vigil. The early mountain frosts had played havoc with the trees and they were parting company with their leaves far earlier than usual.

"Well it's fall, if not when we usually get it. Time to go fishing, son," Brad had said to Phoenix the previous weekend.

So each day Phoenix had driven from Athens in the late afternoon to pick up Brad and his rods en route to Lake Burton. Each day that had fished for the two hours before sundown from the rocks by the lake's shore.

It may have been cold but Phoenix didn't care. He looked around him at the stunning lake, its surface rippling in the light evening breeze. Heavily tree-clad mountain slopes rose steeply from the water, which lapped against the docks and gardens of quaint lake homes.

He pulled up his collar and cast again into the inky liquid and looked at his watch. Sunset was in an hour's time. Despite the desert temperatures that he had been used to all his life, he was not feeling the cold. He paid little attention to his rod or the fish he was supposedly trying to catch. His eyes never faltered from the far side of the lake.

*

Today was Skye's last chance. Tomorrow she was booked on the British Airways flight back to London.

Yesterday the thermometer had read 39 degrees. She checked at least twenty times all over the lake. None of the readings had been more than 40. All day she'd been taking new measurements from the pontoon. Some had registered beneath 39 degrees. Others still said 40.

There was nothing more she could do. The air definitely felt warmer. She was pretty sure there would be no further fall in temperature over the coming days. So that evening she waited with butterflies in her stomach, and Thea by her side, for him to come. Reluctantly, she was becoming resigned to the fact that he would probably not appear. But it was her last chance, and she could but hope.

She stood on the beach with the Frisbee in her hand and Thea bouncing by her side.

The butterflies had given way to emptiness inside and an intense feeling of loss that she would not see him. She must have come so close. Just a few more days, that is all she needed. For the first time ever she totally resented Oxford.

The sun was about to slip behind the island. A tear rolled down her cheek. Almost in anger, she threw the Frisbee at the dock and turned to walk away.

She had taken two steps before she realised Thea had not gone to retrieve the Frisbee. Instead, she heard her splashing in the water leaping towards the island.

Skye stopped in her tracks. Hardly daring to, she turned around. The tear had multiplied into a torrent as they streamed down her face. Without thinking she ran into the cold water towards him, shoes and jeans soaked to the thighs; the rest of her splashed wet by Thea's antics.

He was there, standing waving frantically at her, and he was mouthing the same words he had years ago. "I love you."

Skye held out her arms, imploring him to come to her. At that moment she would have willingly immersed herself beneath the water if it meant she could be with him. A maelstrom of emotions flooded through her. Need, love, resentment and anger were all there. Why should she be denied the person she wanted more than life itself?

"Oh, my God!" She cried out. "It's too soon. You are fading my darling. Don't go. Not yet. Please, I need more of you. I have always had you for longer."

She was panicking, which was something she had never done in her life. She needed to communicate with him. He was almost gone. She held up her index fingers high above her head, and repeated over and over, "Just one more year, darling. Just one more year."

Five minutes later she was still standing in the cold water with her arm held high above her head, repeating the words with tears flooding down her cheeks, when Missy put her arms around her and led her to the shore.

"Come on, darling. You will catch a chill. It's freezing in here." Missy was soaked herself. She had been calling for Skye from the shore for several minutes. But her calls had fallen on deaf ears. Eventually she had waded in to get her daughter. "He came, Skye. There, see, you were so worried he would not come. You will see him soon." She had her arm around Skye's shoulder leading her ashore.

At that Skye was inconsolable. Through her sobs, she managed to say, "Not for another year, Mummy. I can't bear it."

Once on the beach, Missy hugged her and led her towards the house. She helped Skye out of her wet clothes and wrapped her in a massive towel, before she went to run a hot bath for her.

By now Skye was calming down and managed a smile. "I suppose you think I'm silly?"

"No, Skye. You're just in love. It can get you that way."

"Thanks for being here, Mummy." Skye sniffed the final tear away. "His dog wasn't with him. I hope the dog is okay. And he was different this time. He had clothes on."

"What? He is normally naked?" Missy raised her eyebrows, teasing.

Skye managed a laugh. "You know what I mean. He

85

is usually dressed like an Indian brave." She became more serious, pensive. "They were modern clothes, a jacket and jeans. He was cold too." She furrowed her brow. What did that mean?

*

"Thank heavens that's over with. Now we can spend the night by a warm fire." Brad had his hand on Phoenix's back. He was jesting, trying to calm his young friend.

Five minutes previously, Phoenix had dropped his rod and started waving furiously to an unseen person across the lake. He had started yelling, "I love you. How are you? Where were you last year?"

Brad strained to see if anyone was there. It was a mere hundred yards to the other shore. If there had been anyone there he would have seen. The only movement he could see was a duck waddling along the shore.

Phoenix had started to give him a running commentary of what he could see.

"She is moving towards me, waving. She is crying. She looks even more beautiful when she is crying. She has opened her arms and is calling me to her."

At this, Phoenix had taken a step towards the water. Brad pulled him back.

"God! She is stunning. The white dog is there too, wagging. The girl looks inconsolable. I need to go to her." This time he didn't move towards the water.

"She's holding her arm up. One finger is raised. She wants me to know the number. Why? Oh, no! She is going, not yet. Please, stay longer."

After she had disappeared he sat down on a rock. He was staring across the lake to another time and another world.

Brad's words brought him back to the present. He felt the pressure of his hand on his back. He turned to look at his friend.

"You didn't see her did you?"

"No, son. But I know her spirit was there."

Phoenix smiled. "Thanks. Thanks for bringing me here and listening to me." He laughed. "I better get you back to your fire then, Old Man!"

"Yeah, and a beer, Young Crap Fisherman!" He offered the name in mock Indian dialect. "I hope my rod's okay." He bent down to retrieve the discarded rod.

NINE

Phoenix's studies were going well. He was not far off graduating as a Doctor of Veterinary Medicine. Shichu and his siblings had already booked their flight to Atlanta to attend the graduation ceremony. He had spent most of the previous year doing clinical medicine, delivering care to a large range of animals. He had worked with domestic animals at local practices, and with livestock on the farms of Georgia. But there was one rotation that thrilled him, and the one he had set his heart on doing after he graduated.

He had spent four months working with the Georgia Department of Natural Resources, caring for the wildlife in the State Parks. He was in seventh heaven, working with the animals he loved in the forests and by the lakes that had attracted him like a magnet from the other side of America.

It was not just caring for the sick; it was preserving their habitat and enhancing the environment for the present and future generations of man and animals to enjoy.

It is where he wanted to stay, in his spiritual home with the kindred spirits of shared centuries.

His commitment had not gone unnoticed by his boss within the veterinary department, which consisted of a small but dedicated team. They relied on student interns to make their limited budget work. There was a constant rotation of four at a time, which they used as slave labour

- the words the boss used on their induction day. Without them it would not have been anywhere near as successful. They cost nothing and the majority worked like men and women possessed.

Phoenix did all that, but there was more. The boss, Caroline, noticed that wild beasts changed when they came near him.

On one occasion a bear did something she had never seen before. The bear was lame. It was probably just a deep-seated thorn, but ordinarily they would have tranquilised him before they removed it.

This day, in the woods, Phoenix just walked up to the animal and said, "Hello, maba."

The bear offered his paw. Caroline had the tranquiliser gun to her shoulder, and when she saw the bear raise his paw she was expecting the worst. She gently squeezed her finger on the trigger, but before she could fire she heard Phoenix say, "Easy, big boy," and he touched the bear gently on the shoulder.

Phoenix inspected the paw and carefully removed the offending thorn with a pair of tweezers, calming the bear with soothing sounds as he did so. The thorn removed, the bear growled his thanks and padded off into the woods. He looked at Caroline and the gun before he left. She could have sworn he shook his head in disapproval.

Caroline was in shock. "Damn, Phoenix. That was incredible. It was like Androcles and the bloody Lion meets Dr DoBuggerall."

Caroline was English.

Phoenix looked at her, wondering why she was so surprised.

"What is maba?" she asked.

"Apache for bear, it is also my nickname back home."

Caroline nodded, still in shock. She knew she had to have him permanently in her team. She would do whatever it took to persuade him, and whatever it took to persuade the State of Georgia to increase her funding.

The first part was easy; all she had to do was ask. She was still working on the second part, and had even offered to take a pay cut to get him onboard. The suits were wilting under her barrage, entreating them to rubber stamp his appointment. It was going to work. She always got her way. It helped being an attractive forty-something imploring well-meaning fifty-something males.

Phoenix was still waiting to hear if the position was definitely his when he and Brad went to pick up Shichu and his siblings from the airport.

It was all an adventure for Shichu, she had never been on an aeroplane and had only once left Arizona. But she had not seen enough of Phoenix in the previous few years, and wanted to see her Cherokee boy in his homelands. She knew he would stay out East from his calls and short visits, and was happy for him, but she missed him.

She was going to stay with him for a month. After his graduation, both she and Phoenix were going to live with Brad and Lucy whilst Phoenix showed her Cherokee country, his new and old home.

After that he was going to fly back to Phoenix with her and stay a while, before returning with Shadow to Georgia and, he hoped, a new job.

Shichu could not have been prouder at the graduation ceremony. She sat with Brad, Lucy and a tribe of Indians, a Cherokee and Apache mix. Caroline was with her team and she was convinced that, if she had asked, half the deer, bears, possums, snakes and rabbits of Georgia would have attended as well.

They had a party afterwards for the graduating class of the Veterinary School. Half way through, Caroline approached Phoenix and asked, "When can you start, Mowgli?" She had taken to calling him after the Jungle

90

Book character because of his affinity with the animals and his appearance.

"I've got it?"

"Yes, Mowgli. Your jungle awaits."

Phoenix threw his arm around her in delight. "Thanks, Caroline, I don't know how to thank you."

"If you were twenty years older, I could think of a way." She was enjoying the embrace, thrilled at his excitement. "The pay's not brilliant, but you don't care, do you, Mowgli?"

"I wouldn't go that far, but I'm sure it is enough for a jungle boy."

Caroline smiled at him. He looked more like a rock star than a veterinary physician. Long jet-black hair and a body that girls would fight to get at, beneath a face that would make any woman's knees go weak. He would have been at home on the catwalks of Paris or London's fashion houses. All of it meant nothing when you saw him with the four-footed tribes, as he so charmingly called them. With them he was more. He was a god.

"You have no idea what just went through my mind, Mowgli. And I'm not going to tell you, before you ask, but welcome to the team. We will whip you into shape and one day you may be an asset."

" I will try my hardest, Miss!" He hugged her again and said, "Thanks."

She dismissed him, entreating him to go and talk to his fellow students. One in particular looked in need of his attention, a redhead with a welcoming bosom who had witnessed the embrace with more than a touch of jealousy in her eyes.

As he walked over and kissed the strawberry-blonde on the cheek, Caroline smiled to herself, he obviously didn't think about spirits and animals all the time.

Shichu and Phoenix then spent a wonderful month together in the Cherokee heartland. He drove her for miles through the Appalachian Mountains. They spent a weekend in the city of Cherokee, high in the Great Smokey Mountains. He drove her along the Blue Ridge Parkway and down through the gold mining town of Dahlonega to the biggest lake in the region, Lake Lanier. They stayed a night on the islands, just to the north of Buford Dam. Then he showed her some of the State Parks he would be working in, including Black Rock Mountain, the Chattahoochee National Forest, Unicoi Park and Lake Vogel State Park. The list was endless.

On a map he showed her the parks to the south around Savannah, Jekyll Island and dozens in between.

"I'll visit them all, Shichu, but it is around here I will enjoy the most." He gestured to the forests on the slopes of the hills and mountains.

Shichu kissed his cheek. He had found his paradise. All he needed now was the girl to share it with.

*

Skye had already graduated and had returned to Flowery Branch.

She did not have to; she had job offers in Europe. Good jobs, which she had turned down.

Her father was cross with her. "What is she playing at?" he asked Missy.

Of course Missy knew exactly why her daughter had come home. She also knew she had agonised over the decision to do so.

Oxford University had given Skye four good years. Years she would never forget, and years she was glad she had experienced. She had found a boy who had fallen madly in love with her, and had asked her to marry him.

She broke his heart and felt guilty. Not only guilty

for saying no, but for not giving him a truthful reason why she'd said no. She had never shared the spirit world with James, he would have laughed at her, so she just told him she wanted a career before she settled down. But then she promptly turned down two of the best jobs in the world, one in Berlin and one in London.

She was ashamed that she had left him so utterly bewildered.

Now her father was angry with her too. He was probably right to be.

Dumbfounded, he had said, "Damn it, Missy, the job in London was with Sir Norman Foster. He is iconic in building design; he designed the Gherkin and Hong Kong Airport. The man is a legend. What on earth was she thinking about?"

Missy didn't quite know what to say to her husband. If she was being honest with herself, she was also surprised at what Skye had done.

"I think it must be her Cherokee blood, darlin'. You know we get over attached." She stroked Tristan's arm in an attempt to placate him, whilst giving him a lustful look that she hoped might defuse his frustration.

It worked, and he smiled. "Bloody Cherokees, bane of my life, but sexy as hell. Come here, squaw." He pulled Missy to him and planted a kiss firmly on her redskin lips. It tasted good. His papoose was forgotten for the time being.

Skye did realize she had to get a job, if for no other reason than to appease her father. Unfortunately, there were not too many international structural design engineers based in Flowery Branch who were interested in the obvious flair she had shown at Oxford for avant-garde bridge construction. There was a filling station, a café and a curiosity shop. The closest to grand design was a lumberyard.

Atlanta might offer more, and probably would, but it

was not home. And for some reason she knew she needed to be near home. It was not just to see Yona. Her rational side, which she was rapidly deciding hardly existed, had told her that she could not base her whole life around seeing a ghost once a year. But deep inside her a force field told her to be in this place.

Flowery Branch was unique. No other town in the world had the same name. Every State in the US had a Paris, an Athens and a Rome, but nowhere had a Flowery Branch. Its name was a direct translation of the Cherokee name Anaguluskee, a Cherokee village that had nestled for centuries on the banks of the Chattahoochee.

After all she had read Skye had come to the conclusion that her soul was, in some way, tied to Anaguluskee. When she had been studying in the country of her birth, there had always been a yearning within her to return to the place where her Cherokee bloodline had begun.

She looked at the words she had posted above her bed when she was a girl and read them out loud, "There is no such thing as part Cherokee. Either you are Cherokee or you are not. It isn't the quantity of Cherokee blood that is important, but the quality of it and your pride in it. I have seen full bloods that have virtually no idea of the great legacy entrusted to their care. Yet I have seen people with as little as 1/500th blood who inspire the spirits of their ancestors because they make being Cherokee a proud part of their everyday life."

She could not put a finger on why she was so proud to be Cherokee. Was it seeing the spirit Yona? Or would she have been the same without seeing him?

It did not matter. She was not pure blood, but the part of her that was Cherokee told her to be in Anaguluskee. There was no other choice she could have made. She would find a job and her doting, although temporarily angry, father would eventually calm down.

As it turned out job hunting didn't prove that difficult. In the interim she served coffee and muffins in the café.

One day some guys from the world's largest public engineering, design and construction company came in for coffee. They were in uniform, the letters USACE on their badges.

"Hi, Guys, what can I get the United States Army Corps of Engineers?" Skye smiled sweetly at them.

"Coffee, a blueberry muffin and another of those smiles, honey."

Skye giggled, served the coffee and flirted with them a little.

"A pretty girl like you oughta be in the Army," the cheekiest one said.

"I'm trained to build things, not kill people," she replied.

"What do think we do, honey? The answers on the badge."

"I know, but I like it round here, and I don't look good in a uniform," she said.

"Beg to differ, ma'am. As for liking it round here, we're doing some work on Buford Dam. There's stuff all round here we work with. Hell, we built that goddam lake over there. You don't have to wear a uniform anyway. The Corps employs over 38000 civilians. Only a small percentage is actually in the Army. We are it." He laughed as he gestured to his three colleagues.

The seed was sown. Skye made enquiries and was given an interview with the Corps. They snapped her up and she worked in the department with responsibilities for planning, design and construction of dams for flood plain management, and the supply of hydroelectric power throughout the South Eastern States.

Daddy was happier, which made Mummy happy, and Skye was thrilled. She would be doing something useful, using her skills and, most importantly, could still live at home by the lake in Anaguluskee, as Flowery Branch had now become in her head.

TEN

Fifty dams had been researched, photographed and the necessary reconnaissance completed by the team. Soon their report and recommendations would be sent for consideration to the highest level of command within the network.

There were well over sixty sleeper cells established within the United States. Most had yet to strike a blow against the Zionist puppet masters. Even before the great day in 2001 there had been successes. A bomb in the World Trade Centre had killed 6 people and injured 1,040. For that Ramzi Yousef was convicted, but he showed the way and others had tried since.

Even after 9/11, despite an increase in homeland security, others had struck. In 2009, Abdulhakim Muhammed, a Muslim convert from Memphis, Tennessee, gloriously shot two soldiers outside a military recruiting centre. He pleaded guilty and called the shooting, 'A jihadi attack to fight those who wage war on Islam and Muslims.'

More recently in New York, Faisal Shahzad set a car bomb in Times Square. It did not explode, but he was a brave man who would inspire others.

Most had been small attacks, but now they were ready to shock the world again. The cells were deeply entrenched within respectable communities. Many of the jihadists attended the infidel's blasphemous Churches and were trusted within their communities.

The team had spent three years preparing dossiers for the attacks that would strike fear into the heartland of America. Attacks that would teach the infidels that no one would be safe from the wrath of Allah. From the bankers on Wall Street to the chicken farmers of Georgia, all would feel his vengeance.

The pair had selected the dams using a simple formula. For six of the dams it was the maximum devastation for the least amount of effort. For the Hoover Dam extra resources would be used.

They did not know who, or where the sleeper cells were. All they had been told was that resources were available in the vast majority of US states.

After the Hoover Dam, their first choice had been Buford Dam. It was small but with a high profile contagion. To spread the pain geographically, Dallas was chosen with Lake Grapevine the intended target. In California there were hundreds to choose from, but they had ruled most of them out as those near the major conurbations had too many earthquake precautions and contingency plans in place to deal with structural failures of their dams. However, the Shasta Dam on the Sacramento River was selected because it was the biggest reservoir in the States and it was vulnerable.

To demonstrate that farmers were not safe, Grand Coulee Dam in Washington would destroy irrigation to over half a million acres, whilst knocking out 500 million dollars of revenue per annum through its hydroelectric generating capability being destroyed.

Boston would take a double hit. Both the Winsor Dam and Goodnough Dike would be destroyed, turning the Quabbin Resevoir and hundreds of square miles around into a shallow sea. Boston would be become the New Orleans of the North.

The final choice was hard. They opted for a symbolic target, the city that had already felt the wrath of Allah,

New York. The water supply system was a complicated system of reservoirs, aqueducts and tunnels, but was gravity fed. The vast majority of the drinking water filtered through Hillview Reservoir, the last in a chain. It was close to the city. When its dam was blown up, gravity and panic would do the rest.

These seven were simply their suggestions. Others would choose the eventual targets, the men who had conceived the plan. They were great heroes. Heroes like the men who had plunged a knife deep into the imperialist's complacency with 9/11, and others who had humiliated America in Mogadishu and Kenya. And there were heroes who had terrorized the populations of London, Paris and Bombay.

They would not know the heroes who would commit the attacks, or whether they would be transported to paradise in honour of their deeds and their service to Allah. Their job was done, the research complete.

Insha'Allah, Allah willing, another magnificent chapter in their jihad would terrorise their enemies.

He uploaded the seven files in turn; along with those of the ones they had rejected and pressed send.

In a large walled detached home in a suburb of Islamabad, the files were downloaded and then printed for further consideration.

*

Phoenix had been working for six months with Caroline and the rest of the team. Although occasionally visiting the coastal parks and those in the flatlands, it was the Mountain parks and forests of North Georgia that he was primarily seconded to, where the majority of wildlife lived.

The Georgia Department of Natural Resources had a new employee, albeit unpaid. Shadow had returned with Phoenix from Arizona and was now a mountain dog and fully paid up member of one of the Cherokee four-footed tribes.

When Phoenix had returned with Shichu to get him he had gone berserk and leapt on top of Phoenix, who just about managed to catch the deranged dog. They had been inseparable ever since.

The Cherokee Shadow had a new seat in the cab of a green Department of Natural Resources Ford F-150 pick-up, a blanket in the back and his own bed in the corner of the office Caroline and the other physicians used in the field hospital.

Caroline's husband had set up the animal hospital sixteen years ago just outside the Unicoi State Park. It had started as a charitable hospital, caring for wildlife in the region, and being partly funded by locals bringing their cats and dogs. Needless to say it had always struggled. Unfortunately Neil, her husband, died three years later from cancer. Caroline kept it going for as long as she could, but struggled. Eventually she donated it to the Department, who accepted it on the condition that she continued to work with them. It was perfect, funding increased and she got paid. Within a few years she headed the Veterinary Section and had increased its staff and scope.

She could never bring herself to move the centre of her expanding operation away from the hospital. Mowgli had suggested to her why, he'd said, "This is where Neil's spirit is." It was certainly where she was the happiest.

The hospital had grown too. There were now five permanent veterinary nurses and three physicians. Throughout Georgia another four practices and two hospitals served the four-footed tribes, as all were now calling them since Phoenix's arrival. Not to mention the abundant birdlife, reptiles and dinosaurs in the shape of alligators in the south of the state.

They did more than just tend to the pastoral care of sick animals; they worked with the rest of the Natural Resources Division to improve the environment in which they lived, for everyone's mutual benefit, man and animal.

Phoenix was in heaven. He and Shadow rented a small cabin near the park just outside a town called Helen, which was quite the most bizarre place that Phoenix had ever seen. It had once been a logging town but had resurrected itself as a replica of a Bavarian Alpine village, a slice of the Tyrol in the middle of North East Georgia. It both fascinated and horrified him, but it did make him smile.

Since his last sighting of the girl, Phoenix had given a great deal of thought to the painfully short encounter. Although being the shortest by far it had left him with the greatest hope.

Why he had not realised it before, he could not imagine. It had been so obvious. He should have seen it when she first offered him her heart in her hands and blown him a kiss. When she held her arm up with one finger extended, she had done it again. He was annoyed with himself that it had been so obvious and he had not seen it, but now there was hope and he would find her.

With these gestures he had finally realised that they could communicate. She could see him too because she responded to his own actions. It was simple, with gestures and hand signals she could simply tell him where she was. He was praying their next meeting would be far longer than the few seconds the spirit world had allowed them last time. The process would take a while, and she would need to work out what he was asking of her.

After the freezing evening fishing on Lake Burton he had agonised about what the single finger had meant and he and Brad had discussed it at some length. They had concluded that it was a promise to be there again in one year's time. It may have been a thousand other things, but given her obvious anguish at not being there for the previous two years it seemed the most probable explanation. It was at that point that he realised she was talking to him.

He had given a great deal of thought as to how they were going to communicate. He wondered if she could sign, but realised they were probably too far apart to be able to see the small gestures required to talk to each other. The same applied to lip-reading, other than obvious mouthed words like 'I love you.' They would have to be grander gestures, whole arms, or body movements. He chuckled as he thought about it. A long-distance game of charades that any onlooker would think akin to madness, or at best assume them doing Tai Chi on the beach.

But there was a chance. Now it was early summer and autumn was not far away, especially if it came early again as it had the previous year

Not only had he been thinking about how they would communicate but he had done other research as well. Why was it always in the fall when she appeared? She would have to be by a lake when it happened, and he knew that lake had to be somewhere in the Cherokee heartland, here in the Appalachians or their foothills. It was his spiritual home, so it had to be hers.

There was never a clear image of her immediate surroundings, other than it was quite obviously a wooded lake. Unfortunately, they all were. But there would be something about the lake that made it special, a special lake in the fall to which they both had a spiritual connection.

*

If she could have communicated with Yona, Skye would have told him that the lake water's flipped in the fall and released their spirits from the depths to give them a short window through which they could see each other from afar.

She had been wondering why he appeared just before sunset? Why not at the point the water turned over? It was a gradual process, and certainly would not happen at sunset each year.

She was well aware of the spirit legend about wrongful deaths and reincarnation, and concluded that the sunset must have played a part in one or either of their deaths in a previous life and that is why the spirits were released at that time.

She had been wondering if he'd understood her sign saying she would be here this year, and not abandon him as she had before? He had not really reacted to it, but there had been no time, he was gone too soon. This year, if the spirits were willing, she could tell him more.

She was now convinced that those spirits were released from Anaguluskee, the ancient Cherokee village that must lie beneath the lake just a few hundred yards from her home. Why else would she have been called back?

She shared these beliefs with Missy and Gramps, but others, less spiritual, would not have understood. Her father's anger had softened with her working in structural engineering once again. In reality, just having his daughter home again had been sufficient. She was hard to stay cross with and impossible not to love.

Skye had started her new job with the Corps of Engineers and was enjoying it. She was working for the South Atlantic Division whose headquarters were in

Atlanta. It was just an hour's drive from her home, but she rarely visited the offices. Within her remit were water supply and storage, flood protection, and the provision of hydroelectric power. In short, dams and anything else that was required to cover her mandate.

With that in mind, she travelled around the Southeast. But a lot of her work could be done from home where she had set up an office in the ground level of the house, which overlooked the lake and the island.

She was currently working on two projects. The first was Nickajack Lock and Dam on the Tennessee River near Jasper, Tennessee. As part of that project, she had been asked to design a new dam and lock to completely replace the aging structures. The second was far closer to home. Buford Dam.

She had fought to be given the job of conducting a structural survey on the old dam, and putting forward recommendations for safety enhancement and modernisation. She didn't have to fight hard, she lived closest and it was not the most exciting of projects on offer, but she could not wait to get started.

The dam had played an important part in her life and her growing up. She had known about it from a very small age when she had first gone to Grams and Gramps house on a visit from England. Their home was, and still is, just a couple of miles below the dam on the banks of the Chattahoochee River.

She used to delight in the siren blowing, like a train's whistle, fifteen minutes before four hundred million gallons of water was released each day by, what appeared to a tiny girl, a monster.

The siren was to warn people downstream that a sudden rush of water would be coming their way. She would rush down to the rivers edge with Gramps to wait for the powerful wave to arrive, and always marvelled at the ferocity of its surge.

Later in life, when she was older, she would ride the wave through the rapids in a kayak and had become quite proficient in the skills required to manoeuvre the canoe.

She now considered it a privilege to work with the Goliath she had held in awe for so many years. Of course, as dams go, it was not so big. At less than two hundred feet tall it was a quarter of the size of the Hoover Dam, but to a five-year-old it was the biggest thing in the world.

Her first visit was scheduled for the morning, when for the first time she would see into the heart and workings of the giant she had looked up to all her life.

*

Amir received the email he had been waiting seven years to get. And it was seven years since he had spent six months in an Al Qaeda training camp in Pakistan.

The subject line of the email was the codeword that he had been given all those years ago. He had almost forgotten what the word was. The message was also coded. He knew the code, but both that code and the email address would never be used again. He had a handbook of codes with a pre-arranged order to use them, which had lived beneath his bed. He currently used a hotmail address and had done for seven years. He would never use it again. From here on a new address would accompany every message. All would be Internet based, Gmail, Yahoo, Outlook. All would be untraceable after their contrived and random routings through the dark web.

He'd had mixed feelings when he opened the email. He still harboured the same ideals he had before he went to Pakistan with two colleagues on an idealistic quest to find adventure and jihad. And after the six months of indoctrination and religious instruction he would willingly have died for Allah and the cause. But now he had a family that he loved, two small girls and a boy on the way. He already had a paradise here in Lawrenceville, a good job and friends, friends who were infidels. Regardless of how many virgins would be waiting for him in Paradise, he did not want to die.

He was still in touch with the two colleagues he had gone to Pakistan with and they lived close, they were his brothers. By contrast, they had not lost anything of their fervour, still unmarried and both out of work; they hated America and its decadence. They were happy to live off the Al Qaeda handouts and he knew they would not share his qualms at crushing the infidels in their homes.

A man was coming to brief them on their mission in one week's time. He acknowledged the email, and then deleted it.

ELEVEN

'A special lake in the fall.' The same thought kept repeating itself to Phoenix. What happened by lakes in the fall? Leaves dropped, the sun set earlier. Was it a particular month? He thought back over the years, no, he had seen her in different months.

He had spent some time next to every lake he had visited or worked near hoping he would feel a connection, but there hadn't been any seminal moments. He had closely watched Shadow's reaction to each of them, but other than his usual excitement at being taken for a walk there was nothing in his behaviour to indicate that he had found the location for which he was searching.

One evening he was fishing with Brad by Tallulah Falls Lake discussing his plans for finding the girl. They were joking about what signing he could do to communicate, and how virtually anything he did could be misconstrued as sexual innuendo. Shadow was exploring an interesting looking clump of trees and claiming it for interesting looking black dogs.

For well over two hours they had enthusiastically cast out into the lake using all manner of bait with little success.

"Nothing biting today, Brad," offered Phoenix.

"No, son, the lakes dead, there's no oxygen. We will have to wait for the fall," he replied.

Phoenix turned to him. He couldn't believe he had

been so stupid, why hadn't he seen it before? Damn it, he was a fisherman. "When the lake turns."

"Yeah, that'll get 'em excited."

"I'm so stupid, Brad. That's it."

"What is?" Brad was wondering at his young friend's sudden outburst.

"What is special about lakes in the fall?" he asked his friend.

Brad was still none the wiser.

Phoenix could see the bemused look on his face. "The reason why she only appears in the fall." He looked to see if Brad had twigged. "And why it is a different day each year." He was not getting a reaction. "It's when the lake turns. Hell, I should have seen it years ago." He was quite angry with himself now.

"Calm down, son. You've figured it out. How does it help, anyway?"

"The spirits are released from beneath the water when the lake flips over. So the spirits are beneath the lake. I don't know, perhaps they drowned or," he paused, "they are buried down there." He was suddenly excited. "Which could mean the lake was once not a lake. A reservoir made by man."

"I'm afraid it doesn't help you that much, ninety-five percent of the lakes in these parts are man made. The one we are fishing on is. I can't think of one that isn't."

Phoenix laughed. "Your positivity is encouraging."

"I'm sorry, son." Brad chuckled, he realised he had sounded a bit grumpy. "It's because the fish aint bitin'."

Phoenix still felt happy. It was falling into place. When he could communicate with her again, he would fill in the gaps.

Meanwhile, he could prepare for that meeting. There was a good museum in Gainesville, part of Brenau University, which hosted a wealth of local Cherokee history. He would start there, and find out if they had a record of known Cherokee burial grounds.

*

Skye drove the short distance to Buford Dam in her convertible Mini with the top down, turning off McEver Highway and taking a left down Buford Dam Road, it took seventeen minutes. She pulled up outside the restricted access barrier and reported to the gatehouse, where she was expected. The old man who had worked the gates for fifty years inspected and swiped her USACE identity card and welcomed her to Buford Powerhouse, as it was known locally.

The huge barrier swung open, she drove through and parked by the main building. The first thing that greeted her, and delighted her, was a herd of about ten goats chomping happily on the grass that formed a U-shaped outcropping around the powerhouse. "Cheaper than a grass trimmer and mower," she muttered to herself.

She looked around; it was like walking into a history museum, or the set of an old science fiction movie.

She opened the main door and stepped inside and called out, "Hi, anyone there?"

She heard a door open along a corridor and a grey haired man appeared, beaming a smile at her. "Ms. Clifford, welcome. My name is Brian, I run this old junk yard."

Skye smiled at the welcoming manager. He was at least an average stiletto heel shorter than her. What he lacked in height he more than made up for in width. He scurried along the short corridor and offered his hand.

"Nice to meet you, Brian, I'm Skye." She took his hand, which was surprisingly cold. In fact the whole place was cold, given the extreme heat outside.

"Coffee first, and then I will give you the tour." He turned and scurried back to the office he had come from.

Skye followed him, looking at the antique treasures around her. "This floor is beautiful."

"Oh, yes." He turned to admire the floor he had taken for granted for so long. "It's white pine, it's original," he said, pointing to the cubes of intricate wood that were separated into grids. "I've been told it's one of the few left in Georgia.

Skye glanced into a small room, and asked, "What's that?

"It's a welding station, just in case any lil' ol' piece breaks," he said with an exaggerated accent.

Skye looked at the plaque that said 1945 on the anvil.

They took a seat in his office, which to Skye appeared to be straight out of a Dickens novel, and discussed what she was going to do.

"Well, Skye, it sure needs a lil' freshinin' up round here," agreed Brian, again in his Southern drawl.

"I love it, well, what I've seen. All I want to do is make sure it is safe and efficient. I don't see why we would need to change the character of the powerhouse."

Brian liked what he heard. "I'll show you the rest then, lil' lady."

Brian took her to an old iron elevator. "You like old? Look up there."

He pointed to a hole carved out around the light structure where she could see the ropes and pulleys, surrounded by stone, slowly pulling the cart up the four-storey shaft.

After the whirring and grinding had finished he pulled back the iron access gate and ushered her in. He closed the gates behind them and pressed a button, then pulled a lever. The noise started again and they were lowered to the generator and turbines that produced the electricity in the powerhouse. The rooms were diverse down at these levels. The exteriors of the water driven turbines were accessible in a small room. The generators were situated in much larger rooms.

Brian continued the tour on the other levels, using the old elevator to climb back up through the building. On one of the floors he opened a door that led into a long dark tunnel created by blasting through the granite. The walls were damp and the floor was wet and muddy from the water seeping through the rock. Skye wished she had worn a more suitable pair of shoes. It was even cooler in here. She couldn't stop a slight shiver.

Brian noticed. "It's because the water outside is so cold and we are deep inside the rock now. We use this cold air to cool the whole plant, built in air-con," Brian smiled, as he explained. "This tunnel leads to the pressure doors so we can gain access the penstocks. We need to get in there for maintenance work. I am sure you will become well acquainted with them, lil' lady. That is where the real work needs doin'."

The penstocks were five metre wide tubes that allowed gravity to feed the water from the reservoir through the turbines and into the river below. Sluice gates would open and close to regulate the flow of water. One of Skye's jobs would be to check these penstocks. They were an old construction of concrete; it was almost certain that after her stress testing new steel penstocks would be installed.

She spent the whole day at the dam, meeting the workforce and seeing how easy her job would be. At three o'clock in the afternoon the siren began to sound. She noticed that virtually everyone stopped work to go and watch the foaming water gush from the concrete outlets and create another tidal wave for the waiting kayakers downstream. Suddenly she was a small child again holding her grandpa's hand.

Like everyone else, she decided that every day

whenever the siren sounded, she would stop whatever she was doing to watch the rushing water and relive the excitement she'd experienced when she was little.

*

The muezzins called out adhan from the mosques. Outside people drifted towards the call to prayers coming from the minarets. It was hot. The mosques would offer a blessed respite from the clawing heat of Islamabad.

Inside the simply furnished residence three bearded men studied the files. They liked what they read. The research had been thorough and well considered. They were in agreement. The time was right. The high command would approve it. Others, the four men who'd had the idea, would now make a decision on the definitive process of its execution.

The youngest of the three terrorists called to an armed guard, standing near the door, to take the files and their recommendations to the camp. He put all the plans into a leather case and handed it to the man waiting by the front door. He slipped the case into the pannier on the motorbike and started its 700-cc engine. It would be a long ride to the training camp. He would take it easy, he did not want to be stopped. He had no desire to shoot any more Pakistani soldiers because he too was Pakistani, however, most in the camp were not. But there were great minds there, people who would take jihad to the West and kill his enemies.

The great minds were waiting for him, anxious to see the report and its recommendations, but there had already been some discord within the group of planners as to how best to proceed. For thirty minutes they evaluated the recognisance. In general they liked what they saw.

"It will be a magnificent day," the first said.

"Yes it will, but it is a massive operation with huge potential for failure," a second added.

"But it would be a day to rival 9/11," a third offered.

"Yes, I agree, but it must succeed; we have had too many failures in recent years. The idiot in Times Square forgot the keys to his getaway car, and some of the others in America are fools also. We are all agreed that to wash Las Vegas of the face off the Earth would rival even 9/11, but it has to work and I doubt the ability of some of our people in America to deliver."

"I take your point," the third man said. "Bojinka failed because it was too big and too many people knew about it."

"But without it, 9/11 would never have worked. We learnt so much from Bojinka." It was the first man speaking again.

"Yes we did, we learnt to keep things small. Like the bombing of the World Trade Centre, that was a glorious day." The fourth man at the table was speaking now, and he had their attention. He looked at each of the others in turn, before he continued, "9/11 was a small team. We know that is the way it works best, friends and family. We must learn from history, and the most effective hero we've had is Imad Mughniyeh. He used friends and family only. The TWA hijacking in 1985 that freed over seven hundred Hezbollah fighters, The Beirut bombings at the embassy and barracks in 1983 that killed over three hundred American and French soldiers, the Israeli Embassy in Argentina. All this he did with a small team and his family." He looked around the table again. "Bojinka should have been less ambitious. To assassinate the Pope, blow up thirteen airliners and attack seven airports at the same time was foolhardy. It was never going to work. But you are right, we learnt from it."

"So, what are you suggesting, Said?" asked one of

the more junior planners.

"To take all seven dams at the same time is too complicated and needs resources we would be pushed to supply. It was a fine master plan, but on reading the research it would be difficult to achieve. Remember, our real goal is the Hoover Dam. Destroying it would match if not surpass 9/11."

"Are you saying we only go for the Hoover Dam?"

"No, I am saying we have a trial run, like Bojinka was for 9/11, so that when we strike at the infidels in their den of vice we will be triumphant."

The other three heads were nodding in agreement.

Said continued, "There is one target in the list of seven that could cause devastation. It looks soft. If we can hit that we can monitor the infidels responses, and get a clear picture of the kind of damage we can achieve. Then we can adapt the plan for maximum effect in Nevada. There is even a family at the core of a cell near there, which could help."

"Which target, Said?"

"Atlanta. It is a small target and according to the reports it is poorly guarded. One large bomb could be devastating. To maximise its effect, as the report suggests, there is a minor target that will need to be taken care of as well, but that should be a simple task."

"I agree, Said. It is the softest target and it will wreak havoc in one of the most important cities in America."

"Then we are all agreed? Buford Dam will be the dummy run."

Said looked to the other three for an affirmation. They all nodded.

*

Caroline lifted the raccoon onto the operating table. Shadow had found him cowering in the hollow of an old tree trunk.

Shadow had gone to find Phoenix and, by the age old method used by dogs, barked and ran towards what he had found until Phoenix followed.

Mr. Raccoon had a broken leg, they assumed sustained by an altercation with a passing car. Phoenix was about to set the leg and the raccoon would stay with them in the hospital until he could walk properly again. It was something he had first done at the age of seven back in the barn at Shichu's cabin.

As they worked together on the raccoon, Caroline asked, "How is the research going, Mowgli?"

"Okay, I guess. It's interesting anyway."

"Any breakthroughs?" she enquired, as another layer of plaster was applied to the leg.

"No, not yet. There were settlements everywhere and they all had burial grounds. One of the larger ones was a place called Anaguluskee. It is roughly where Flowery Branch is now, down on Lake Lanier. It appears there was a big bust up there about the Trail of Tears era. That's all I know so far."

He continued to work on the not so small furry animal that, judging by his size, had found a wealth of food in the garbage cans around Helen. "This fella is going to eat us out of house and home when he comes round," he muttered to Caroline.

"Probably." She handed Phoenix the last plaster to wrap around the poor mite's leg.

"So, when you find this dark sultry maiden, do we all get an invitation to the wedding?"

Phoenix laughed, but added perfectly seriously, "Of course."

Caroline had sat riveted when he had told her about the girl by the lake. At first, she had believed it to be complete nonsense and thought he was winding her up. After a short while she realised he was serious and there really was a spirit by the lake, at least in his world. Such was the steadfastness of Phoenix's commitment to his belief that it now seemed completely plausible to her, and she was pretty sure that she had become a believer in Cherokee spirits.

Rather she wanted to believe in spirits, and she wanted to believe for two reasons. Firstly, she loved Mowgli. Along with her ex-husband he was the noblest of men, and she wanted him to be happy. Although, she noted, he quite obviously did not allow the spirit girl to stop his enjoyment of life and other girls. The strawberry-blonde she had recently seen him with had given way to a buxom brunette. She idly mused that chest size seemed important to him. However, he never really talked about any of his admirers or girlfriends; he was quite obviously in love with the girl by the lake and that was the only girl he ever mentioned.

The second reason was that she still loved her husband, and the idea of his spirit waiting for her was one she found attractive.

"Can you join up to be a Cherokee?" she asked, not realising that Phoenix would not have heard her thought processes.

Phoenix chuckled. He actually did know what she had been thinking. Her preoccupation with the spirit world had not gone unnoticed and he knew why.

"Have sex with one and then have his baby, that's as close as you'll get." He grinned at her. They enjoyed flirting, it made the days fun, but they both knew it was just a game.

"You offering, Mowgli? Because this cougar might just take you up on it," she threw back at him, trying not to imagine the scenario.

"If the spirit girl doesn't exist then you're on, Aunt

116

Caroline!"

She threw a dollop of wet plaster at his face, which stuck to the end of his nose. A short plaster ball fight ensued before a nurse came into the room to see what the commotion was.

"You two are like children," she said affectionately to the physicians. "How is the patient?"

They stopped laughing and throwing lumps of plaster around the room and lifted the anaesthetised raccoon onto a gurney so the nurse could wheel him to his new home.

"He's a big son of gun, Caroline," the nurse said, as she wheeled him away.

Still giggling, Caroline said, "We better clean up this mess. What are you doing this afternoon?" she added.

"I'm driving down to the Chattahoochee River Recreation Park. We have a report of some clown setting turkey traps in the forest. The park ranger has found two and thinks there are probably more. Let's hope the turkeys are wise to them."

"Why do people do it? They know it's illegal." Caroline was angry.

"They're assholes," Phoenix added. "Anyway, the ranger wants to see if any other critters have stumbled into them. He already has one injured bird. I'll see to him, and bring him back if necessary. Hopefully it's superficial. Then Shadow and I will go for a walk and search for more. Shadow is partial to turkey; he can sniff them out a mile away. So if there are any in traps he'll find them."

"Sounds like an excuse for taking Shadow for a walk in the forest." She smiled at him.

"Purely work, Boss." He grinned back at her.

Changing the subject, Caroline asked, "Are we still on for Saturday evening?"

"Sure, I'll pick you up about six o'clock."

Although Phoenix did not work in the Cherokee

village any longer - he simply did not have the time - he still went regularly and spent the evening with his friends by the fire pit after it closed.

Caroline had taken to going with him on a number of occasions. With her newfound belief in the spirit world, these evenings spent by the fire with Cherokee Indians were the best she could remember since her husband's passing. They gave her serenity and a profound sense of belonging.

*

Skye was standing by the side of the Chattahoochee with her grandpa. The siren had just sounded and they'd walked down the hundred or so yards to the river's edge waiting for the torrent to begin.

"I'm working up at the dam, Gramps. It's brilliant in there. Like a world that time forgot. I'm not too sure how safe it is though. There are small fissures all over the dam and I'm not sure what's lurking deep within the concrete. What do you think would happen here if the dam burst?" She looked around his smallholding by the river.

"The whole lot would be swept away, honey. Depending on how catastrophic the burst was, a wall of water would come down here fifty feet high. The house, everything would go. Anyone in the parks or on the trail by the river would drown. The whole of Suwannee would be under water within minutes. Thousands of people would at best be homeless and at worst be dead." He gestured to the hillsides around them. "This whole valley would fill up and anything in it would be gone."

"What about below Suwannee?" she enquired.

"That depends, honey, on how Morgan Falls Dam stands up to the rush of water. If it is breached, there is nothing to stop it. All the wealthy suburbs of Vinings, Buckhead, Sandy Springs, Roswell, Dunwoody and Peachtree would be under water."

"Morgan Falls is pretty old, isn't it?"

"Yeah, over a hundred years old."

Skye made a mental note to find out when a structural survey was last done on the aging dam.

She could hear the water roar as it came downstream towards them. She looked up and watched four hundred million gallons of water sweep past. It was just a small splash down a narrow river. She shuddered at the thought of what a thirty-eight thousand acre lake, which was over a thousand feet deep, could do if its pent up power was suddenly released. She doubted if Morgan Falls Dam could stand in its way.

TWELVE

Amir drove his old blue Honda Odyssey minivan to pick up his two brothers. They lived close by in a condo. He was to pick them up and take them to the pre-arranged meeting point in the Food Hall of the Mall of Georgia in Buford.

Amir had often thought it would be the target of an attack, and assumed that was to be their target. When it was built it was the fourth largest in the United States. It was undefended and just asking to be destroyed. He thought it a little ironic that they would actually get their briefing there. Paradoxically, he thought, its roof looked like the roof of a Mosque.

Nawaz and Jamal were younger than him by three and four years respectively. The passion for jihad still burnt deep within them. They were excited when Amir had called and told them that they had become operative.

As they drove to the mall they fired questions at him about their mission.

"I don't know. That is why we are meeting our contact," he retorted, a little annoyed at their cross-examination.

Amir parked the vehicle in the parking lot in front of Barnes and Noble and they walked the short distance to the Food Hall. They each ordered something from McDonalds and took a quiet table in the centre of the vast seating area.

Two minutes later a white man joined them. He was

American. He shook hands with each of them in turn and sat down without speaking.

They looked expectantly at him, waiting for him to begin.

Chillingly, he asked, "Are you still willing to die for Allah?"

Nawaz and Jamal solemnly nodded. Amir said nothing. The American noted his silence.

"It may not come to that, but in jihad it is always a possibility. What we are asking you to do will result in a glorious day in our fight. Are you willing to take the fight to our enemies?"

This time all three nodded.

"Good. You will be heroes, and will inspire others to embrace jihad."

Amir remembered similar lines of incitement that had been used to indoctrinate him in Pakistan. His brothers had given up talking to Amir in this way; they knew he still believed but not as passionately as they did. Talk of jihad and glory had slowly been eliminated from Amir's vocabulary.

"Is it here?" Amir looked around at the mall.

"No." The American opened a briefcase and handed them three files. "Read these, they explain everything."

The three brothers took the files he offered. The American then handed Amir a prepaid cell phone. "I will call on this cell in two days time with instructions for our next meeting. After that, destroy the phone. I will bring you new ones."

The American stood up. "Gentlemen, you can call me Mohammed. Read, mark and learn everything in those files. Till next time." He turned and left.

The three looked at each other, and then down at the files on the table in front of them. Two were thinking of virgins in Paradise. The other was thinking about his little girls.

In between oppressively hot days, it had been a wet summer with more than the average amount of rainfall. The lake levels were high and the rising water had reclaimed a lot of the beaches it had previously given up.

Thea had not minded shrinking beaches because her Frisbee thrower was home. At weekends they made their daily pilgrimage to various parts of the lake, and regularly visited the pool further up the Chestatee River. When it was possible, she would accompany Skye to work. Buford Powerhouse was Thea's favourite because Brian, the manager, loved dogs and all the staff at the dam and powerhouse pampered her. Some could even throw a pretty good Frisbee.

The survey was progressing well and Skye was beginning to think that the State of Georgia would get away with a bill of less than three million dollars to repair the decaying dam, as long as it was done soon. The biggest expense would be the penstocks, which were in a terrible state and if not fixed soon the crumbling concrete would irreparably damage the turbines.

Today was a powerhouse day and Thea was going to work too.

Amir watched the Mini pull out of the driveway of the big house by the lake. The white dog was with her again. The girl would be the key that would get them into the compound. He pulled away from the curb and followed the car the short distance to the dam.

He had kept the dam under observation for about a week from the nearby wood. He had hiking gear, a stick and binoculars. No one would have suspected him of being anything other than a rambler with an interest in birds. Regardless, he was sure that nobody had seen him, he had been careful. During the week he had seen the girl come with her dog each day, and he had followed her home the previous evening. She fascinated him.

After he'd read the file that Mohammed had given him the despond he'd felt when called to jihad had been replaced by hope. He was not going to be just another suicide bomber. He had options. He had immediately set about finding a method whereby he could gain access to the plant that did not involve him going to Paradise. All he needed was to get the explosives inside, set them, and he could be long gone before they unleashed their destruction.

Allah had been kind to him.

To develop his plan he needed to know what the girl did in the powerhouse and decided the easiest and most obvious way was to ask her. He observed that she took her white dog for a walk each day about lunchtime, usually downstream to a house by the river where she would go inside and stay about twenty minutes before returning.

He timed his approach to her carefully, making sure other walkers were near so he would not frighten her; other walkers were plentiful through the park and along the river path at lunchtime, as others returned to walk their animals.

"Nice dog, ma'am," he casually said as he passed by. He smiled warmly at the beauty he had now seen at close quarters for the first time, "What breed is she?"

Skye returned his smile. "A Labrador, yellow." Then she added, "Hi," to her grandpa's neighbours who were walking their Spaniel in the other direction. She turned back to the stranger. "I'm taking her back to work."

He smiled again. "Where does the lady work?"

"At the old powerhouse. We are doing a structural survey there. Well, I am, she's just helping." Skye nodded toward Thea who was staring less than benevolently at the stranger.

"Then I mustn't keep you any longer. You have important work to do." He addressed the last part to Thea. "Have a great day, ma'am." Then he carried on his way. Thea watched him go as Skye continued towards the powerhouse.

The man didn't look back. He smiled to himself. One short conversation, knowledge gained and trust established. Next time it would be easier. Yes, she was the best option. It would be easy to get the slip of a girl to comply with his demands.

The previous evening he had shared his plan to use the girl with Mohammed. The cell leader liked Amir's plan. It was clean and uncomplicated and they would dispose of her afterwards, or leave her in the dam when it exploded.

After a short walk he doubled back to follow her again. He watched the girl as she waved to the old man in the gatehouse who raised the barrier to let them in. He did not even look at her ID. It would be a shame; she was extremely pretty and reminded him of his cousin in Hyderabad with her long black curls. But she was a woman, an infidel and so she was expendable.

Some of Amir's old passion for jihad had been rekindled when he realised that he would not have to die.

His brothers, Nawaz and Jamal, had been given the task of weakening or destroying the second line of Atlanta's defence, Morgan Falls Dam. It was unclear whether it would actually be of any significance in protecting Atlanta from Allah's fury, but any helping hand to weaken its resolve to do so would be advantageous.

Mohammed was an explosives expert and had trained with Hezbollah in Lebanon. In fact, he was Lebanese, but had come to university in the United States fourteen years previously. He had acquired an American accent that he could turn on or off at will. But most importantly he had blond hair and did not look like an Arab. He blended in well with Middle America.

Amir loaded his rucksack into the rear of his Honda. He drove out of the car park and past the gates of the powerhouse towards Buford. He was ready. His plan was formed. He was just waiting for Mohammed to tell him when he should implement it.

*

Phoenix said, "Hi," to Iris, one of the volunteer guides, as she waved goodbye to the small children she had been taking around the museum.

"Hello, dear, any luck with your search?" Iris asked the handsome young Indian boy who, at times, had been almost camped in the reading room of the museum.

"Not yet, but Anaguluskee looks promising, Iris."

He continued into the small library and retrieved the most likely source of information from the bookshelf where he had left it the previous week.

He had become sidetracked with the whole Trail of Tears thing and was not really reading about what he had originally come to research.

If he had the time, and was passing Gainesville, he would pop into the museum to read about his heritage. The staff all knew him and welcomed their very own Cherokee warrior with open arms - literally in the case of the younger female staff.

This day he spent an hour, with Shadow by his feet, reading one particular text over and over again.

Eventually he closed the book and tapped its cover. Could that be what had happened to them? Why their path was incomplete? And why he loved her so much?

He chuckled to himself; Caroline was going to love

125

this. He couldn't wait to tell her what he had just read.

He stood up. "Come on, Shadow, we have got to go somewhere."

Shadow leapt to his feet, still very agile for an aging mutt, and charged towards the door. He almost knocked Iris over as she came through the door in the opposite direction.

"Sorry, Iris, he seems in a bit of a hurry.

"That's okay, dear. Have a nice day."

Within minutes they were driving down Interstate 985 towards Anaguluskee, Flowery Branch.

He pulled off the Interstate and drove towards the old town. He crossed Atlanta Highway and over the railway line into the Town Square, past the old railway depot that was now a museum, up the hill, past the café and on towards the lake.

He thought Aqualand Marina as good a place as any to start his search. It was on a promontory that thrust out into the lake, he would surely get a feel for the location here.

In the Marina, he parked by a lunchtime diner and walked out onto one of the pontoons, which stretched out into the water and was lined with dozens of boats of all shapes and sizes, bobbing benignly on the tranquil lake.

Shadow trotted by his side. As they made their way further along the pontoon, Shadow gathered pace and galloped on ahead. When Phoenix caught up with him, Shadow was standing with his eyes transfixed on the horizon, His ears were as vertical as they could get and he was wagging excitedly.

"They are here, boy, aren't they?" Phoenix squatted down and put his arm around the dog.

They remained on the pontoon until the sun set, wondering if the girl and her dog might miraculously appear from across the water.

Before the last vestiges of light disappeared, Phoenix

walked back along the timbered quay with Shadow, who kept stopping to look behind him.

Back at the pick-up, Phoenix noticed that the wind had got up and he brushed the first leaves of fall from the hood.

"Just a few more weeks, my darling," he said to any listening spirit.

THIRTEEN

1838 AD

The medicine woman had spent five years in Anaguluskee. She was no ordinary medicine woman and no ordinary Cherokee.

The rest of the village called her Dahlonega, because she had hair the colour of the gold the palefaces had discovered in the hills. She too was a white woman, but not like the others. She was gentle and kind.

Seven years previously she had set out from Charleston with four men and a Cherokee guide to research and find Cherokee medicines.

She had been inspired by an ancient Cherokee legend that one of the gardeners at Middleton Place Plantation had told her.

She had been staying with her aunt on the plantation, with a view to immigrating permanently to America. It was a country where, she hoped, there would be fewer prejudices to her practising as a doctor. She had fought with her family to train in the profession, and had met with nothing but chauvinism and bigotry throughout. Finding work in her native England had proven hard. But Lady Katherine Stanley, youngest daughter of the Earl of Abingdon, was fiercely independent and refused to let English society stand in the way of what she wanted to do. Though short of being completely disinherited by her family, it was thought that emigration to the New World was the most suitable method of dealing with the problem their youngest daughter posed.

Lady Katherine was actually quite happy about her deportation and her original plan was to set up a practice in the thriving colonial town of Charleston. That was until she met the gardener, John, on the plantation.

John was actually the first Cherokee Indian she had met. His features and colouring were different to anyone she had seen before, but not unpleasant. They had become friends and he would often walk her around the formal gardens where he worked. It was during these walks that she first learned about Cherokee medicines.

It had started when a rattlesnake in the field had bitten one of the young slaves. John had quickly picked a fern from the hedgerow, boiled the root down to syrup and applied it to the bite. The boy had lived.

Lady Katherine was amazed and started to ask John about other Cherokee plant remedies.

"I am not a medicine man, Lady Katherine. I just know a few tricks. Others much more knowledgeable than me, who live in the mountains to the west, have the real knowledge. However, I will tell you the legend of how our medicine began. It is a good one." John's eyes twinkled

"Please, go ahead." She held his hands encouragingly, as they sat on a seat by the rose garden. She liked John; he was a good man, a man at ease with the world around him. She wondered if all Cherokee people were like him.

John began, "The Ancients say that at one time all of Creation spoke the same language. The Plants could communicate with the Fish, the Four-footed ones could speak to the Trees, the Stones could talk to the Wind, and even the most pitiful part of Creation, the Two-leggeds," he chuckled, "that's us, could speak to the other parts of Creation. All existed in harmony, Plants, Animals and the Elements, but they knew that for the pathetic Two-leggeds to survive they would need their help."

Lady Katherine was grinning at the pictures he was painting with his words.

"The Animals gave of themselves, willingly sacrificing, so that the humans could have food. They knew that their skins were much better suited to survival than that of the humans, so they allowed their skins to be taken and used for clothing and shelter. The Finned ones, The Fliers, and the Crawlers also allowed themselves to be used by the humans to ensure their survival.

The Plant People, the Standing People, that's the trees, and the Stone People freely gave of themselves too, so that the humans had what they needed for food, clothing and shelter. An agreement was forged that the Two-leggeds would ask permission for these gifts, give thanks for the sacrifice, and take no more than they needed. And so, it was good.

But then, the Two-leggeds started growing in numbers, and began to feel more important than the rest of Creation. They began to believe that the Web of Life revolved around them, ignoring the fact that they were just one small part of the Circle.

The Two-leggeds began to kill without asking for permission. They began to take more than they needed. They ceased to give thanks. All parts of the agreement were broken.

The great Animal Councils banded together to determine what they should do to right these wrongs. They needed to protect themselves from destruction and eradication. And so the council decreed that if one of their clan was killed by the Two-leggeds and thanks was not given for the sacrifice, the Chief Animal Spirit would afflict the disrespectful killer with a devastating disease.

The Plants were distressed and said to the Animals, 'They wrong us, too. They dig us up, trample us, burn us out, and don't even listen when we try to tell them what we can do to help them. Yet we feel compassion for the Two-leggeds. Man struggles to realize his place in the Web of Creation and he cannot learn if he is wiped out by disease. Man needs our help, so for every disease you animals bring to them, we the Plant People will give them a cure.' So from that day the Plant People have provided a cure for every disease."

"It is a wonderful legend, John."

Lady Katherine had been spellbound throughout. What she had heard, though just a story, seemed to hold countless possibilities.

"What other cures did the Plant People give to the Two-leggeds?"

John was thrilled at her reaction to the legend. "Well, we use boneset tea as a remedy for colds. Wild cherry bark is used for coughs and sore throats. It is good for diarrhoea as well. To ease the pain during childbirth and speed the delivery process, Blue Cohosh root is used in a tea. Fevers are soothed with teas made from Dogwood, Feverwort, and Willow bark."

"Can you show me some of these plants, John?"

Lady Katherine was excited. Something that would ease the pain during childbirth and speed the delivery would be a breakthrough in European medicine. She had none of the blinkered attitudes held in the London teaching hospitals. She realized that medicine was a constantly evolving science battling to find new cures for diseases that were being discovered daily.

"Of course, Lady Katherine."

Within minutes he had located a number of them growing within the garden.

Over the next month he showed Lady Katherine how to prepare the teas and potions, and by the end of the month she knew what her mission would be. She was not destined for life in a comfortable Georgian home in the Battery tending to the rich and privileged. No, she would scour the lands of the Cherokee for cures of diseases the wretched Two-leggeds brought upon themselves.

Three months later she set off towards the mountains in the west with a wealth of her own medical knowledge and an open mind.

Her travels had taken her inland to Charlotte and on to the Appalachian Mountains of North Carolina. She spent some time with a medicine man near Asheville, and later travelled on to Georgia and through the high mountains. Wherever she went she sought out the healers and learnt from them. Everyone she met gave her something new. She had followed the mountain streams to small settlements near Qualachee on the headwaters of the Chattahoochee, and then turned south along the Tallulah River. Here she was told of a great healer who lived further to the south in a Cherokee village called Anaguluskee.

She pressed on, following the Chattahoochee until she came to the settlement. She was not disappointed. In Anaguluskee she had met a medicine man whose knowledge had surpassed any she had met in the previous two years.

Within months her own European medicine had combined with his to create a powerful combination and Anaguluskee had become known as a place of great healing. People would travel vast distances to consult with the healers, and they ran a small hospital to accommodate those who needed to stay.

She had also fallen in love with the medicine man, and Lady Katherine Stanley, once of Abingdon Manor, now lived in a log cabin with Adahy. To the authorities that ran the State of Georgia his name was Peter Woodman, but to Dahlonega and the entire village he was

Adahy.

Five wonderful years passed. Her knowledge grew and she grew to love the people she lived with, and they loved her.

The village was a good size. Thirty homesteads formed the centre of the settlement where craftsmen and traders operated near the water's edge. The healer's cabin acted as a surgery and the hospital had been built nearby. Another fifty small farms were all within a few hours walk of the village. Three hundred acres had been cleared for corn and other crops. Orchards of peaches and apples grew abundantly in the river valley.

It was still remote, but in more recent years the government was beginning to sell lots of land in the region to European settlers using a lottery system that had been established in 1832. In reality they were simply giving away land that was not theirs, and some of that land contained gold. It had been discovered in 1829 not far from Anaguluskee. Since then, what had been a trickle of settlers had increased to a flood of travellers on their way to the mountains to pan for gold so they could get rich quick. After the gold had been discovered any land within fifty miles became subject to a feeding frenzy of greedy prospectors, clamouring for leases to the land. Anaguluskee was on the edge of that feeding frenzy.

With this rush of people came other things, things that did not add to their quality of life. Goods were often taken from the Cherokee Indians without any payment being offered or made. They showed little or no respect for the Indians or their way of life. They damaged their property, physically and verbally abused any 'savage' that got in their way.

When the Indians complained to the authorities, little was done. Their complaints just increased the white man's interference in their lives, with a level of autocracy that only Dahlonega amongst them could understand

133

having witnessed the growth of an empire from within.

But even with the increasing numbers of English and Europeans invading their Cherokee land, Dahlonega was happier than at any time in her life. She fitted in perfectly with the Cherokee way of life and shared in its values.

Not all the foreigners were bad; a number of perfectly decent settlers had begun to farm some land nearby. They had lived in harmony with these people for three years.

She had become close friends with the family who had emigrated from Ireland, enjoying their company on a number of occasions. They were happy to have food on their table and be free from English oppression that had starved so many of their fellow countrymen.

During this time, Dahlonega's greatest friend was a Cherokee girl called Newadi. She was younger than Dahlonega and she had tended to the teenage girl shortly after she had arrived in the village. Newadi had badly fractured a leg near her hipbone. Dahlonega, with her knowledge of anatomy, was able to set the awkward fracture and nurse her back to health.

It cemented an already growing respect and love for the two healers. It also started a bond between the two girls.

Newadi was the most delightful creature Dahlonega her ever met, sweet, innocent and quite beautiful. She was convinced that Newadi did not possess a bad bone in her body or wicked thought in her head.

To Newadi, Dahlonega was a goddess, wise and clever with long golden hair and sky-blue eyes.

"Your eyes are like my name," Newadi said to her one day.

"What do you mean?"

"They are the colour of the sky, and that is what Newadi means."

The delightful Newadi had a man she loved. He was twenty-two years old, her childhood sweetheart and she was about to marry him. His name was Yona.

Dahlonega loved Yona too, he was strong yet gentle. He was everything John's derogatory description of the Two-leggeds was not. He lived in perfect harmony with all of Creation and in total contrast to the ugly world the settlers were bringing to their lands.

Dahlonega thought it a great shame that the Cherokee Indians were having their heritage diluted by the white men. For the most part they had taken English names and now wore European clothes. Their cabins were slowly filling with the white man's artefacts. Some were good and brought quality of life, others merely removed their own identity. She prayed that the white men, the people of her birth, did not bring the bigotry, which had poisoned everything they touched throughout the world. She knew her prayers would be in vain.

It was the eve of Yona and Newadi's wedding and Yona was watching Atul smoke his pipe. He had come to his uncle's cabin for advice about marriage. Atul had prepared them a simple meal of fresh trout and corn, which in deference to his guest they had eaten before he lit the pipe that dangled permanently from his mouth.

"Will I make a good husband?" Yona asked Atul.

"Probably not. None of us do. But they need us to have babies, and I'm sure you will be adequate at that." Atul puffed on the old clay pipe.

Atul was also the elder of Yona's clan, which he would shortly be leaving to join that of Newadi's mother.

"As you know, son, we live in a matriarchal society. If you do as you are told, you will have no problems. Marriage is fine, just remember who wears the loin cloth." He laughed at his own joke.

Yona joined in. He had known Newadi since she had been born. He appreciated his uncle's somewhat cynical view of marriage, but he knew that his union with Newadi would be a marriage of equals. "We will both wear them, or nothing at all," he replied.

Atul smiled at the young man he respected above all others in the village. "I will put that thought out of my head." He refilled the pipe. "Is everything ready?"

"I think so. I was just told to turn up suitably cleansed. Are you coming to my drowning in the morning?"

"I wouldn't miss it, son." He took another puff. "Will you have babies straight away?"

"That's what she wants."

"So you will."

"Yes." They both laughed

"Well I hope these damned politicians don't make your life a misery with their talk of relocating our people out West." Atul was more serious now.

"How are the discussions going?"

Atul grunted. "Not well. As you probably know we signed treaties with the United States Government years ago, in which they promised to leave us alone in our own lands. But still the settlers come, more and more of them greedy for our land. Now, this gold rush in the mountains has made it even worse. We are in the way; they do not know what to do with us. The government was not supposed to let this happen. They have broken the treaties." Atul was angry.

"What will happen?" asked Yona.

"The government has bought all the lands to the west of the Mississippi beyond the mountains. They want us all to move there. They have already started to move the Choctaw, Chickasaw, Creek, and Seminole. The Seminole are fighting, but losing many warriors. They are the only tribe that never signed any treaties with the palefaces."

"Should we fight, Atul?"

"Ha! It is a good question. We could fight and we would lose. Or we could do as we are told and we will live, but not in our ancestral lands. There will be many more council meetings yet and much discussion, but eventually we will go and we will live. They say it is good fertile land to the west, but so far they have lied about everything, so I think it is safe to assume it is not. My worry is where they will move us next after they have found more gold to the west." Atul sounded defeated.

"You don't paint a rosy future."

"It's not, son." He suddenly smiled. "But life is what you make it, and you have the most beautiful wife the tribe has to offer and I am sure you will have a long and fruitful life with her."

The next day Yona went through the cleansing ceremony in the waters of the Chattahoochee with his friends and uncles. As always, during the ceremony he was ducked far more than the seven times required. That afternoon he tied his blanket to Newadi's and lay with her that night in their new home.

Eight weeks later Dahlonega declared Newadi pregnant.

The first six months of her pregnancy were the happiest days of Newadi's life. She spent six joyous months with her husband sowing the crops and preparing for their baby to be born.

Dahlonega attended her best friend weekly and reported that all was well with the baby. Four months into the pregnancy she declared that all was well with the babies. She had heard two foetal heartbeats. It just magnified their joy, and Yona built a second cot.

Three months before the birth of the twins two men came to the village on horseback. They asked to speak to the village elders.

A meeting was called in the townhouse. Seven clan leaders, the two men and a few others were present. Yona, Adahy and Dahlonega, in her official capacity of Lady Katherine Stanley, attended in an attempt to add some gravitas to the Indians' cause.

The two officials were courteous but insistent about the message they had been told to deliver.

"I'm sorry, Lady Stanley, there can be no exceptions. Let me read to you again the letter sent to the Cherokee people from President Jackson."

He opened a piece of paper and began to read:

"My Friends: I have long viewed your condition with great interest. For many years I have been acquainted with your people, and under all variety of circumstances in peace and war. You are now placed in the midst of a white population. Your peculiar customs, which regulated your intercourse with one another, have been abrogated by the great political community among which you live; and you are now subject to the same laws, which govern the other citizens of Georgia and Alabama.

I have no motive, my friends, to deceive you. I am sincerely desirous to promote your welfare. Listen to me, therefore, while I tell you that you cannot remain where you now are. Circumstances that cannot be controlled, and which are beyond the reach of human laws, render it impossible that you can flourish in the midst of a civilized community. You have but one remedy within your reach. And that is to remove to the West and join your countrymen who are already established there. And the sooner you do this the sooner you will commence your career of improvement and prosperity."

He handed the letter to Lady Stanley. "Surely you can see it is for their own good, Lady Stanley."

Dahlonega was fuming, "Civilized! He dares to use the word civilized. These people are far more civilized than the barbarians who seek to remove them from their homes." She leapt to her feet. "Many of these

UNCIVILIZED people are old and sick, there are small children and heavily pregnant women. They can't be expected to just get up and leave their homes and travel over a thousand miles on your whim." She spat out the word uncivilized.

"It is not a whim, Lady Stanley. The Cherokee leadership has agreed to it. In three months time my men will come and escort everyone to the holding stocks. When everyone is there they will be escorted to their new lands using the route I have given you on the other document."

Not once had the official made an assumption that Lady Stanley would go with them.

"You make an assumption that is without merit, my man. THEY will include me, for I am as Cherokee as any man or woman in this village." She shot him a look that was intended to wither. All it garnered was a smirk. She would have struck him if Adahy had not taken her hand.

She swung around to look at the hand that had restrained her; her fury instantly dissipated when she saw the man she loved. She looked compassionately at him and wanted to cry. Instead she turned to the official and said, "History will damn you and your government for your actions in this matter."

She did not wait for any odious reply he might give her. She stormed out of the townhouse, as the tears began to cascade down her cheeks.

She continued to lobby against the forced removal right up until the day the soldiers came for them, but it was an unstoppable force. Her pleas fell on deaf ears. The men who ignored the 'mad English witch' could only see value in wealth and none in compassion or charity.

To make matters worse, Newadi became sick about a week before they came. She was running a high fever and Dahlonega feared for the babies. She and Yona nursed her round the clock, but the fever was not reducing.

Adahy tried a number of remedies, whilst Dahlonega bathed her in the cool mountain waters of the Chattahoochee to keep her temperature down.

The one who had smirked at her rode into the village with fifty soldiers to march the Indians, and Lady Stanley, to the temporary forts, or stocks, which had been built to accommodate them before the exodus began.

Word had already reached them of the inadequacy of these shantytowns, and disease was already rife within them.

Dahlonega was livid when she saw the loathsome little man who had delighted in destroying their village.

She strode up to him and looked down at the man who was now the sole target of her anger and frustration. "You cannot do this. Some of these people are too sick to travel. I have one girl in my care who is very ill and pregnant, she will lose her babies." She shouted at him.

"Then you can bury them en route." The first sign of the smirk was appearing on his repugnant face when Lady Katherine Stanley punched him in the eye.

The full smirk never appeared; instead his face turned puce as the anger rose within him.

"Damn you, woman!" He drew his sword and was about to run Dahlonega through when the arrow hit him in the chest and penetrated his heart.

Fifty yards away Yona had watched the argument develop. On seeing the man about to kill Dahlonega, he swung his bow from his shoulder and with one swift and well-practised movement delivered the arrow to its intended target.

The charged atmosphere was heightened by the sound of musket shot.

Yona lived no longer than three seconds from shooting his arrow at the man who was about to kill his friend.

A bloody battle ensued in which seventeen Cherokee

were cut down and two of the soldiers died. Amongst the dead was Adahy.

The second in command of the soldiers was less arrogant than his, now dead, superior. Already having enough to explain away to his commanders, he agreed to allow Lady Stanley and Atul to bury the Cherokee dead.

He marched the remaining villagers away form their homes and the land their ancestors had farmed for nearly two thousand years. Most did not look back as they took their first steps on the Trail of Tears.

That day life stopped for Dahlonega. Without Adahy she was merely Lady Katherine Stanley.

She had managed to persuade the soldiers to allow Newadi to remain with her. She would have been just one more burden for them to carry.

Tragically, despite Lady Katherine's best efforts Newadi died too. Her fever passed shortly after the slayings and she was becoming well once again, but the news of Yona's death broke her heart. It seemed to Lady Katherine that she simply lost the will to live. She gave birth to two beautiful little girls, but weakened from the fever and all that had happened, she passed away shortly afterwards.

When they were old enough, Lady Stanley took the children and her knowledge of Cherokee medicine back to the undeserving world of the Two-leggeds in Charleston.

FOURTEEN

Phoenix did not sleep much the night after he had left Lake Lanier. His mind was racing with the implications of what he had read, in the museum library, about Lady Katherine Stanley and the slaughter at Anagaluskee.

He was strangely quiet the next morning at the animal hospital too.

"Are you okay, Mowgli?" asked Caroline. "You are as quiet as a church mouse."

"Sorry, Caroline. Got a few things on my mind. Do you mind if I bunk off early today?"

Caroline had never known him ask for, or do, such a thing. She assumed it must be important. "Of course, is there anything I can do to help?" She was concerned.

He smiled at her. It was not a worried smile. She felt better.

"Not yet, but I fancy in the near future you will be able to."

"What?" She was intrigued.

"I need to do a bit more research. By Saturday, I may well have enough information. So let's go over and see Brad and the guys at the village. I will tell you all about it then."

"A mystery, how exciting. Sure, bugger off when you are ready. It is a quiet day anyway."

"Thanks, Caroline."

At three o'clock he drove back to Gainesville, the self-styled chicken capital of the world, and grabbed a coffee and a doughnut from Starbucks. Actually he grabbed two doughnuts, a custard cream for himself and a ring for Shadow.

He gave his customary greeting to Iris, and took his seat at his usual reading desk.

Within minutes he was lost in the text. The same text he had read at least four times the day before. Eventually he closed the book. Then he selected another book from the shelves and flicked through the pages until he came to the part he wanted.

Half an hour later he went over to the reception to see Iris. He had a favour to ask.

"Hello, Iris, would it be awful if I asked to borrow these books over the weekend? I will return them first thing on Monday morning." He gave her his most charming smile.

"Of course, dear. You are the only person who ever reads them anyway," she said.

"Thanks, I promise I will look after them." He tucked the books under his arm and led Shadow to the truck.

It was still only four o'clock, so he drove the short distance across town to Gainesville Marina where the Georgia Department of Natural Resources kept a boat. Part of the department's remit was to look after the wildlife around, and in, the lake. He was hoping the boat would be available as it was late in the day.

It was, and it was already fuelled for the following day. Within minutes he and Shadow were speeding south towards the main archipelago of islands and Buford Dam. He spread out a map of the lake on the seat next to him and deliberately followed the course the Chattahoochee had taken before it had been dammed and flooded.

It was quiet on the water; the majority of summer's revellers now shunned the cooler waters and shortening days. A few anglers trolled off promontories in their sports boats hoping for a late catch.

The powerboat was fast, he was up to thirty knots within seconds and within minutes he was passing Aqualand Marina, where he had visited the previous evening with Shadow. He continued along the river's path towards the point Shadow had been staring at from the dock. The same point his eyes had naturally been drawn to.

Shadow was getting excited again. They must be close.

He scanned the shore to see if anyone was walking, perhaps with a white dog. There was nobody there.

He saw an island a few hundred yards off the shore and steered the boat towards it. It was roughly the direction they had stared towards the previous evening. Shadow grew more excited. He slowed the vessel and circled the island. He looked into the trees for any sign of life. It was quiet, just an occasional bird disturbed the foliage.

He throttled back further, and before he could stop him Shadow jumped into the water and swam the short distance to the shore.

Phoenix eased the boat towards a narrow beach and checked for rocks. It looked sandy, so he gently eased her bow first onto the beach, raising the outboard as he did so. He removed his shoes and socks and jumped into the shallow water.

Shadow was charging around sniffing anything in sight, with his tail in constant motion, pausing occasionally to leave his scent on an obvious stump or rock.

This had to be it. He looked out to the lake that surrounded him; a burial ground or the place they had died in a previous life had to be beneath these waters. Shadow knew it and Phoenix could feel it, they had to be near.

He walked around the island, clambering across

144

rocks and around trees that hung out into the water. It was not a huge island; perhaps eight hundred yards all the way round.

He half expected to get a sudden feeling of belonging at some point as he stepped over his own bones. He chuckled at the thought, but there was nothing that obvious.

The trees that covered the bulk of the island were healthy and played host to a number of nesting birds. The beaches were liberally covered with goose droppings, though none of the birds were in evidence at the time.

As he made his way around the southern end of the island, the mainland came into view. About two hundred yards away four lovely homes stood proudly facing the setting sun in the west. Each home had its own dock. One dock had a powerful Donzi and three small wave runners on hydraulic platforms tied up to it. The second was completely empty, its occupant either out on the lake in their boat or the boat had been hauled out early for the winter. The third dock had an expensive twin inboard motor yacht moored beneath a raised deck area, which was adorned with multi-coloured chairs and matching parasols. The last, and most northerly house had a less ostentatious pontoon boat tied up to its dock.

He studied each of the homes in turn to see if there was anything that looked familiar. They were impressive, with sweeping lawns that led down to narrow beaches and the water. But there was nothing he recognised; it had always just been the girl with generic trees behind her. No boats or houses. A couple of times she had somehow floated over the water towards him, but then disappeared when she came too close. Other times she had come closer but had always remained just far enough away that they could still see each other. Had she come on a boat or swum out to see him? He did not know, but he was convinced he would soon be able to ask her.

Shadow was standing still at the water's edge, as it gently lapped over his paws. He too was looking towards the four homes. Could he sense something? Or was he just looking there because Phoenix was?

It felt right, but not overwhelming. Was he even on the right lake? He began to doubt what his gut instinct was telling him.

He glanced at his watch and it was getting late. Phoenix wanted to return the boat before sunset, and take Charlie for a beer as a thank you for letting him use the boat at such short notice. He still felt sure that he would want it again in the near future and he wanted to keep Charlie onside.

Before he got back into the truck he called Brad on his cell phone. "Hi, buddy. Can Caroline and I come up to the village tomorrow evening, have a couple of beers and something to eat with you guys?"

"Of course, son, you know you're always welcome. Both of you," replied Brad.

"I have something I want you both to see. I think it might be best if you see it in the village, especially Caroline."

"Can't wait, son, see you tomorrow."

*

"So, if we take the girl," Mohammed referred to the notes Amir had given him for her name, "Skye, you think we can force her to take us in and show us how to get to the penstocks?

"Yes, Mo."

"What if she wants to be a heroine, and refuses to betray her country?" asked Mohammed.

Amir had assumed that threats and violence would be

146

sufficient. She was just a girl. "You don't think fear will be enough?" he asked, raising his eyebrows.

"No, my friend. We have found that under interrogation women are often stronger than men. But they have a weakness men do not." Amir waited for him to continue. "They do not fear pain and most will not crack when being tortured. But they are nurturers and they fear for the ones they love."

Amir could see where Mohammed was going. "Are you saying we don't threaten her, we threaten the people she loves?"

"Yes, but your report does not really tell us who those people are. Husband, children, parents, siblings, what do we know of them?" Mo looked at Amir.

Amir suddenly realised how inadequate his report had been. "Okay, I will gather more information on her. I don't think she is married. I know she lives with her parents and she always has her dog with her. I don't know about a boyfriend. Give me a few days."

"You have all the time you need. We do not want to strike yet." Mo looked at the man he believed to be the weakest link in the plan.

His brothers were perfect, fanatical, intolerant and dull of mind. Ideal cannon fodder. Amir was reasonably clever, and Mo could see that he had lost some of the idealism the Imams and camps had planted in him. However, he could still be a potent weapon, especially if he was not asked to personally mete out physical violence.

"It will be better this way, Amir. She will be compliant if she fears for the people she loves."

Amir nodded. He had not been looking forward to beating the girl.

*

Skye was showing her father the plans of Nickajack Dam. The new dam she had been commissioned to design for the Corps on the Tennessee River.

"It looks pretty good to me, darling."

He studied the water volumes and depth of the river again. "Yeah, it will work. But you haven't scrimped on the design. Your first problem will be when they say they can't afford it." He smiled proudly at his daughter.

"I know, Daddy. That's why I did these as well."

She dramatically opened the wide drawer in the architect's desk and removed another set of plans.

"Ha! Let me see those."

He eagerly studied the design whilst Skye made a pot of English tea for them both.

"Now, these are clever, darling. This could be built on half the budget of the others and it is a beautiful structure."

He took the cup of tea Skye was offering and put it down by the plans. He hugged her and kissed the top of her head.

"I can see why Sir Norman Foster wanted you. They really are good. Sir Norman's loss is our gain."

Skye could hear the emotion in her father's voice. It felt good.

He released her and picked up the cup. "How's your day job going?" He nodded south towards Buford Dam.

"Fine. It is all a bit old and in need of a little tender loving care and attention, but she will scrub up well and hold back the floodwaters for decades to come. I love it down there; the siren reminds me of when I was little. Nice people work there too." She giggled. "They use a herd of goats to cut the grass, it's brill'."

"That's what we need, I'm fed up of cutting that grass." He nodded towards the lawn that ran down to the lake.

Skye looked out through the patio doors at the lush

green grass that he moaned about regularly, but watered passionately.

There was someone on the island, easing their way beneath the branches of the forest. Had Thea been with her or she had seen the black dog, who was currently inspecting some treasure deep in the woods, she would have run the length of the lawn in question to the pontoon boat.

But no dogs were present or in view. There were often people exploring the island and the man was probably about to do some fishing. She dismissed what she'd seen. And then turned to her father, and asked, "Have you forgiven me, Daddy?"

"Of course, darling. Mum has been trying to explain to an old paleface how much your Cherokee blood means. I'm just an old inbred Saxon, bigoted and foolish. You are happy. That is all that matters to me."

She hugged her dad. Yes, she was happy. She knew he would come soon.

*

Caroline picked up the cool box with beer and steaks inside and walked to the green Georgia Department of Natural Resources pick-up truck that had just pulled up outside her house.

Shadow was already thundering up the path towards the front porch. He was anxious to see her for two reasons. Firstly, he wanted to get his cuddle, but more importantly he needed to inspect the cool box. Experience had taught him that cool boxes contained good things.

"Okay, Mowgli. What's the mystery all about?" she said to Phoenix as he opened the door for her.

Grinning, he replied mysteriously, "I will reveal all later, when we get to the village."

He had to bite his tongue on the drive. He was excited about what he'd discovered. Instead he managed to keep the conversation to work matters. He parked in the lot by the entrance to the village and carried two boxes to the source of the enticing aromas coming from the fire pit.

The group chatted whilst the steaks cooked and the corn boiled in the old iron pan. Brad puffed on his pipe and they drank beer. Phoenix dexterously avoided the topic they all wanted to hear about until after they had eaten.

Replete from her meal, Caroline could wait no longer. "Come on, you have to tell me now, Mowgli. What is this all about?"

The others laughed. "Okay, I have something I want you both to read." He nodded to Caroline and Brad in turn. "Or I could read it to you."

"Is it Indian stuff?" Caroline asked.

"You bet, this is Indian stuff alright."

"Then you read it to us. You do the Indian stuff so well, Mowgli."

He picked up the first of the two books and was about to open it when he asked, "Caroline, did your late husband have any Cherokee blood in his ancestry?"

"Not that I am aware of?" She shook her head.

Phoenix nodded. "Listen to this first. It is a piece of history, or legend, I have never heard before. Then I will ask you again."

Caroline looked bemused and looked around the group for some sort of an explanation. All she got were blank looks and then a shrug of the shoulders from Brad.

Phoenix opened the book to the page he had marked and began to read:

"Long ago, when the troubles of the Cherokee began,

the ordinary Cherokee did not understand that anything was really wrong. All they knew was that their tribal chiefs travelled back and forth to the white man's place called Washington a lot more often than they used to. They also knew that upon the chiefs' return there were many quarrels in the tribal council.

Now, up in the hills, where the Ani Kituhwah - the True Cherokees - lived, word of the changes came slowly. Many of those living in the hills never left their farms, and when they did they just travelled to the trading post and right back. Few travellers ever ventured into the hills, into the uplands, where the mists of the mountains shut out the encroaching world. So when the news arrived that some of the chiefs had touched the pen, and put their names and marks on a paper, thus agreeing by doing so that this was no longer Cherokee country, the Ani Kituhwah could not believe their ears.

Surely, they told each other, the news must be false. No Cherokee, not even one of mixed blood, would sign away his own and his people's lands. But that was what the chiefs had done! The word came that the chiefs were now even more divided amongst themselves. Not all of them had touched the pen. Some were not willing to move across the Mississippi, to settle around Fort Gibson in Oklahoma.

'Perhaps we should stay,' thought the Ani Kituhwah. 'Perhaps we will not really have to move.' But they knew in their hearts that false hope was the cruellest curse of mankind.

Within the Ani Kituhwah was a medicine man called Adahy. He was pure blood, 100% Ani Kituhwah. He was wise with many powerful medicines. At all times his wife stood at his side, a spirited woman with hair the colour of gold. She was not Ani Kituhwah, but had come from the land of the rising sun. Like Adahy she possessed great medicine and people would travel many days to seek their healing powers.

The people called the woman Dahlonega. Dahlonega and her husband Adahy were not rich and did not farm, but they never lacked for food, shelter, clothing or their love for each other. They gathered at the great dance ground where the seven clans met each month at the full moon. There they danced their prayers in time to the beating of the women's terrapin-shell rattles, around and around the mound of packed white ashes on top of which bloomed the eternal fire that was the life of all Cherokees. They danced with people who loved them.

The occasional missionary would visit the village and fuss over the children, giving them white men's names. The Cherokee listened politely to the missionaries, for the missionaries were great gossips, and by listening they would learn their news while ignoring the rest. They told the Cherokee that this time there was no hope. Everyone would have to move, the Georgia troopers were moving in and all would have to go west.

'Never,' Adahy answered. 'This is our land and we belong to it. Who could take it from us? Who could even want it? Even we have a hard time farming here. Surely only the land in the lower valleys is of any use to the white man?'

'They want these hills more than anywhere else,' answered the missionary. 'Don't you see you poor ignorant Indian? They are finding gold, here in Kituhwah country.'

Yona, Adahy and Dahlonega's great friend spoke and said, 'But it is worthless, just yellow dust. Who would want it?'

Yona's wife, Newadi, was with child when the soldiers came to take them away. The spirited one with the yellow hair fought with the soldiers to leave them in peace and allow them to live in Kituhwah country.

Yona saw a soldier strike Adahy's woman, his friend

Dahlonega. Yona was a great hunter and he drew his bow and shot the soldier.

A great battle ensued, which took the lives of a number of Ani Kituhwah. Amongst the dead were Adahy and Yona, and Newadi, who was with child, died of a broken heart when she learned of her husband's death.

The spirited one, whose hair was turned gold by the rising sun, was restored to the spirit world. But she left the Ani Kituhwah with the spirit to fight for their land... So speaks Spirit Hawk."

Phoenix put the book down and studied the faces around him. Each was wrapped deep in thought but there was silence. Caroline was in shock.

Phoenix picked up the other, more historical ledger, opened it at the page he had left a bookmark and began to read:

"In 1838 reports of a skirmish between soldiers and rebel Cherokee fighters was alleged to have taken place on the banks of the Chattahoochee River in the native settlement called Anaguluskee.

Eyewitness reports stated that a number of savages attacked a column of soldiers sent to escort them to the New Lands handed to them by the Federal Government.

The rebels were subdued and the uprising crushed due to the bravery of the soldiers.

They continued their mission to re-locate the Indians to the stockades."

He closed the book. "It is the only official reference I have found so far about the massacre. But as you know, Anaguluskee means flower of the branch and it was near where Flowery Branch is now."

There was more silence.

Eventually Caroline said, in little more than a whisper, "Are you saying that I was some warmongering bitch who incited a massacre?"

"Yeah, kind of." Phoenix was grinning.

Brad burst out laughing. "No, Caroline, you were sent from the spirit world to show the toothless Cherokee Nation how to fight."

Caroline was smiling now. "And, are you saying that I was Adahy's woman?'

"Yeah, in as much as your spirit once lived within the woman who lived with him, and…"

She cut him off, "And Adahy's spirit lived within Neil. And we were meant to be together, here in the lands where we were cruelly ripped apart," she paused, and then added, "just as we were in this life." There was sadness in her voice now.

"Yes, Caroline. I believe all that, but I believe more," Phoenix was serious now.

She looked pleadingly at him.

He continued, "I believe my spirit to be one with Yona, and I believe the woman I see on the lake to be Newadi. I believe all of our destinies to be travelling a similar path. And I believe we are being brought together again for a reason."

"But, if all this is true my destiny must lie with Neil, and he is already gone," Caroline mused.

"His body is gone, Caroline, but his spirit is still here. He brought you here and you stayed for a reason. In the legend you disappeared. I don't believe you were sent by the spirits to get the Cherokee to fight. I think that after you lost Adahy you probably went back to wherever you came from, maybe England."

Caroline's mind was racing. Was Neil's spirit all around her? Did he bring her back to Georgia for a reason? Would all this mean that she would see him again in another life?

Phoenix watched her, then leaned forward and took her hand. "I was drawn across America for the same reason. I don't know what it is yet, but we will find out. It was love that brought us both here again, Caroline."

"Why were you so insistent I was here, son?" Brad interjected. He had been listening, fascinated by everything Phoenix had been saying.

Phoenix turned to his great friend. "Because I think you are part of it, Brad. Sure, there is no straight reference to a character in the legend that is obviously you, unlike Caroline. Hell, man, look at her golden hair. But when I came east, nearly the first goddam thing I did was drive straight to your front door. Something led me there, Brad. You feel it too. I know you do."

Brad was nodding.

Phoenix continued, "Our spirits go way back, you can't feel as comfortable with someone as we did the day we met if you've never encountered them before."

"Okay, son. I am Cherokee, I'll go with it."

Phoenix turned back to Caroline and waited for her to speak.

She looked across at him, deep into his soulful eyes. "I want to believe, Phoenix. It is just such a huge leap for a Home Counties English girl to take."

"Okay, let see if we can help you with it. Was Neil spiritual?"

"Yes. Not overtly, as in hey man, make love not war." She did a good impression of a seventies hippie. "He was like you, Mowgli. He thought more about the four-footeds than his fellow man, and they had a similar trust in him. Not as strong as it is with you, but yes, if what you have is spiritual then he was intensely spiritual."

"So are you, Caroline. I know you don't think you are and you joke about it, but you are a spiritual person, and you are not a young spirit."

"Cheeky bugger!" Caroline was smiling; she liked what he was saying.

155

He laughed. "You know what I mean, your spirit is wise and has travelled a long way but its path is not complete."

"So, are you implying that had my spirit been older and wiser back then, I may not have got everyone killed?" Caroline was only half-joking.

"Probably not." Phoenix was grinning.

"I will bear it in mind next time I am about to start a fight," she added flippantly.

"I'll bet you have never been in a fight in this lifetime, have you?" Phoenix was serious.

Caroline thought for a moment. "No, I haven't."

"There you are, you are spiritual, you learnt from your previous mistakes." Phoenix was still holding her hand.

Caroline was still in shock, but she was happy. She wanted to believe it all, why not?

"Okay, son, why do you think we are all here then?" asked Brad.

"I don't know. I believe it has to do with the girl mentioned in the legend, Newadi. And as so many injustices were committed back then, I think it may be to right some of them, or deal with another injustice."

"Any leads on her?" asked Brad.

"I've been to Anaguluskee with Shadow. At least where we think it probably was near Flowery Branch. Shadow and I followed the course of the old river, where it once flowed beneath the lake, and it feels right. I think Newadi's spirit and the girl she now lives within are close to Anaguluskee."

"So when do we go look for her?"

"Fall has begun. I will see her soon. I will be with her soon."

Caroline looked at the remarkable young man who had given her life new meaning from the day he had walked into it. She saw the look of utter devotion on his face, and prayed that he would find his soul mate soon.

FIFTEEN

Caroline was enthralled with the possibilities Phoenix's revelations had offered. The deep feeling of loss she had felt during the years since Neil had passed had been lifted. Somehow his spirit now appeared to be in everything she saw and heard.

In particular, each day spent in the animal hospital that they had built together became magical. The things she saw there, which had once made her sad, now gave her great happiness. Neil's spirit was around her in everything she touched.

Phoenix was right, she was spiritual; she had just never given it any thought or credence before. But now it was different, she felt completely at one with the world in which she lived. She could look at the forests and lakes and they were now part of her.

She had always loved the North Georgia Mountains from the day Neil had brought her here, but now she could feel a connection with everything that lived and existed there. They were part of her and she was part of them.

It would not have mattered, because it could not have changed the way she felt, but her inquisitiveness wondered about the golden haired woman who had brought her spirit here nearly two hundred years previously and had met and married Adahy, a healer like herself. There had to be some record of the woman. Her journey, to say the least, had been an unusual one.

She thought that if she could find out more about what had happened that day in Anaguluskee, there might be a clearer picture as to why they had all been reunited here and now.

From the history book that Phoenix had brought she knew the slaying in Anaguluskee had taken place in 1838. The woman was quite obviously a white woman with blonde hair living with a Cherokee man, and if the legend were true she had come from the East. So she started with the United States Census of 1830. The 1840 census would have been too late. She had disappeared by then. But was she there as early as 1830?

The Internet gave her some of the information she required, if not the answers she sought. She found a list of all those living in the region of Anaguluskee, which included the names of the heads of families, addresses and a demographic of households. One of the questions asked in the census was the number of free white males and females, along with their ages. There were only twelve reported in the census, but they were either small children living in all white households or they were too old. All the other households were Cherokee, which is who she assumed *free coloured persons* to be, but none had a white female declared. Another group she hoped might reveal something in the census was *non-naturalized foreigners*. This also drew a blank.

By the 1840 census it had completely changed. No Cherokee was recorded at all; any that had remained were off the radar living in the dense forests of the Appalachian Mountains.

She returned her attention to the Cherokee included in the 1830 census, they had an interesting mix of English and Indian names, and some had a profession attached. This is where she got her first break. A man listed as Peter Woodman, in a Cherokee household, was listed as being a doctor. He had to be Adahy.

Again, online she was able to get access to a marriage registry of the period hoping Cherokee weddings would be recorded. There was nothing.

She was beginning to think her quest to be futile, when she had an idea. The woman with golden hair possessed great medicine; she too was a healer like Adahy. Was she a registered doctor? Firstly, if she were registered there would be very few female doctors in the whole of America at the time. And what if she had taken the surname Woodman after she had married Adahy?

For three days she searched later censuses for the entire country. The 1840 census had 12,000 people claiming to be doctors and the1850 census had 24,000. But there was only one Dr Katherine Woodman practising in Charleston, Georgia in 1850.

After that it became easy. She just Googled the name and it turned out that Katherine Woodman was something of a cause célèbre in her day. She pioneered the inclusion of a number of Native American medicines into traditional Western medicine. She was English by birth, and her full title was Lady Katherine Caroline Stanley, the youngest daughter of the Earl of Abingdon. She had married a Peter Woodman and taken his surname. She had become revered in the City of Charleston; some said she had mystical powers and could heal by merely touching the sick. She died in 1881, age 73. She had two daughters who also became celebrated doctors, Margaret Woodman and Victoria Woodman.

Caroline thought about this last fact. There had been no mention of children in the legend. Neither was there mention of her remarrying in anything she could find on the Internet. Were the children Adahy's and Lady Katherine's?

The idea of the children preoccupied her for days. Given her newfound belief in spirituality she felt sure that her being would have identified with them in some way, but she felt nothing. Lady Katherine had obviously brought them up and they had followed in her footsteps and bore the family name.

Caroline had returned to the museum in Gainesville and reread the legend. 'Newadi was with child,' and, 'She had died of a broken heart.' It was purely a gut feeling, but Caroline was convinced that Newadi was the mother of the children and Yona the father.

*

It was getting cooler. The past couple of days had seen the first signs of breeze blowing in from the north and Phoenix had witnessed the occasional leaf part company with its branch.

He was getting impatient. Barely six weeks had passed since he had formed his conclusions about Anaguluskee and the girl, but it seemed like an eternity.

He visited lake Lanier whenever work commitments would allow him. At least twice a week he had borrowed the boat from Gainesville and visited the island. He visited other parts of the lake to see if he felt any sense of belonging. Alarmingly there were a number of places that he was drawn to. Was he imagining the whole thing? Had he allowed his overactive mind to create scenarios that had no basis in reality? Whenever he found a place that pulled him, he would immediately return to the island, where he best guessed Anaguluskee to be, to compare its aura. The island near the houses usually won, but it was marginal and there were a couple of places he actually felt more attracted too.

If it were not for Shadow he would have doubted his assumptions. But Shadow would always get excited whenever they went to the island.

Each time they were on the lake, Phoenix would constantly be scanning the shore for a white dog and the girl. On more than one occasion he had steered the boat towards a figure or to investigate a light coloured dog, but none proved to be the correct animal or girl.

Caroline and Brad had come with him on a couple of occasions. This had helped his faltering beliefs; both said they felt an affinity with the island and the general area.

Needless to say, Caroline had become known as Lady Caroline after her discovery that it was Lady Stanley's middle name.

Phoenix had asked her, "What do you think, Lady Caroline?"

"They are here, Mowgli. The spirit that was Newadi is here and I think Adahy's is too." She sounded so convinced that Phoenix took heart.

"Brad?"

"Yeah, son. I'm on board, it feels right." Brad replied, somewhat less enthusiastically thought Phoenix.

Phoenix watched another brace of leaves tumble haphazardly to the red earth below. He needed the lake to turn. He would come to the island every evening from now on. He had convinced himself that she might actually be there. But if she were not, her spirit would be able to tell him where to find her.

Unfortunately it was still too mild and the leaves he watched nestle on the ground were from a tired and weak trees; fall would be late this year. The trees would cling to their leaves much later than the previous year. He had heard a tale that one year it had almost been Christmas before the lake flipped.

*

Amir had been closely watching Skye's movements, along with the movements of her parents and grandfather. They would be the levers they used to make her cooperate. He reported his findings to Mohammed and his brothers in their condo in Lawrenceville.

"And the dog, Amir," added Mohammed, "some of the infidels think more of their animals than people. The dog will be a good persuader."

Then Mohammed turned to Jamal and asked, "How are your preparations going?"

"Well, Morgan Falls Dam is poorly guarded. We will use a boat to gain access and set the explosives. One charge at either end will breach the dam, and when Allah rains down his wrath from above, in the form of Lake Lanier, the weakened dam will crumble," replied Jamal.

"Good, I have your explosives ready, Semtex courtesy of a thief in Czechoslovakia. It came in by boat last year. Two kilos will level a two-storey building. You are getting twenty kilos, ten for each end with detonators and simple timers," Mohammed said.

"How much are you using for Buford?" asked Nawaz.

"One hundred kilos. I don't want any of it standing after the explosion," answered Mohammed.

Nawaz was grinning, he high-fived his brother in an unintentional, ironic display of American celebration. "When will the great day be, Mohammed?" he asked.

It was Mohammed's turn to smile. "Christmas Day, of course."

*

Thea was particularly restless and sat whining by the patio door. Skye was working on the plans for the

Tennessee River at her desk in her office at home.

"What's the matter with you, girl? Do you want out?" she asked her restless dog.

By way of reply Thea whined again.

"Okay, I hear you."

Skye stood up and walked across the office to the door. She pulled the handle to slide it open, but it was locked and the key was not in the lock. She glanced out and saw a blonde-haired woman on the island opposite with an older man walking along the beach.

"Where has Daddy put the key this time, Thea?"

She spent five minutes searching for the elusive key, which she eventually located in an antique silver cigarette box that sat on top of a filing cabinet. The box had housed everything other than cigarettes all her life.

"I should have looked here first, Thea, he is like a squirrel."

She took the key out of the box and went to open the door. She watched a boat race away from the island heading towards Gainesville. She expected Thea to go out into the garden to relieve herself and then trot back in. Instead, she flew down towards the beach with her barks drowning the noise of the retreating boat.

Skye followed her out and crossed the grass to the water's edge. Was Yona coming? Surely not, it was too early. She looked at Thea. "Have you seen him?"

Thea was beginning to calm down. She whimpered a couple of times and looked up at Skye, then to the boat that was little more than a speck in the distance.

Skye's eyes alternated between the white dog and the boat. Something was different, Thea had never barked at a boat in her entire life.

She decided to go and investigate the island where she had seen the man and woman walking earlier.

She walked back to get the keys for the pontoon boat. Thea was reluctant to leave the shore and stayed, trotting up and down the beach. When Skye returned and went to the boat she became excited again.

Skye made the short crossing to the island, where Thea leapt ashore before she could beach the boat. She then proceeded to run around sniffing every tree stump and rock, like a dog possessed, her whole body gyrating with excitement.

Skye peered over the expanse of water in the direction the boat had gone. Butterflies swarmed in her stomach and her heart involuntarily missed a beat. They were here. Either their spirits or the man and dog that hosted their spirits had been to the island. She had not seen a dog, but Thea had. Neither had she seen the boy, just two other people, but he had been here. She was sure.

She almost felt panic stricken.

*

Amir watched the girl and her dog get back onto the pontoon boat. It had not been a long walk, just once around the island and they had returned to their home.

He had been watching her for several weeks. There was no real need to anymore. Their plan was made and he had all the information about her and her family that they needed. But she had become something of an obsession. He thought she was the most exquisite looking woman he had ever seen. Seeing her in her bikini during the summer had aroused him to a point where he was uncomfortable with the fact that he fixated on her so much. He was married with children. The American girl must be a whore to bewitch him so. His lust for her was exacerbated by an emergent disgust that she could have such an effect on him. The more he watched her, the more he desired her. But it was a desire mixed with anger. The angrier he got the more aroused he became. It had started when she smiled at him by the river and his obsession had grown. Now he needed to possess her, but not in a loving way. He wanted to degrade, dominate and punish her for the effect she had on him.

He made himself take his hand away from where he had been stroking himself. "Damn you, bitch. You and your fucking infidel family will pay for this."

He put the binoculars back into their case. It would be Christmas before too long. All his frustrations would be taken care of. He would strike a blow for Allah and jihad, and teach the whore a lesson.

When it was over, he could be a good husband and father again and get on with his normal and comfortable life. He would be able to live the American dream once more. There would just be fewer of them to live it with and the bitch would be gone from his life.

With his loathing for the bitch and the thought of her came another erection. He got the binoculars out of their case and trained them on the house. He would watch her a little longer.

SIXTEEN

Christmas was a week away. Phoenix would normally have gone back to Arizona to be with Shichu, but the lake had still not turned. He was expecting it any day now and had started to visit the lake each evening, making up for the lost time at work by starting well before sunrise at the animal hospital.

The last forty-eight hours had felt particularly cold after the preceding mild weather. He had a feeling that the lake would turn today, so he left the hospital even earlier than usual.

His visits had become such a regular occurrence that Charlie had the boat refuelled and waiting for him when he and Shadow arrived.

"Coffee, Phoenix?" asked Charlie.

Phoenix looked at his watch. He was far too early. She only appeared an hour or so before sunset at best.

"Sure, thanks," he replied.

"How is the search going?" Charlie knew all about the mad bunch from the hospital and their theories about Anaguluskee and reincarnation. But they were good people and extremely likable so he accepted their idiosyncrasies with good humour.

They settled into the chairs in his office near the dock. Charlie threw Shadow a biscuit, which he devoured with two rapid crunches. He passed Phoenix a mug of coffee and said, "This could be your day, Phoenix. The lake flipped this morning."

Phoenix never even sipped the coffee. He was on his feet and on his way to the door. "Sorry, Charlie, I've got to go."

Charlie was laughing. "Good luck, buddy."

As Phoenix ran to the boat, Charlie called after him, "Can you still smell it? Sulphur. It definitely flipped."

Shadow, bolstered by Phoenix's excitement, jumped into the boat as Phoenix untied her. He started the engine and flicked the last slipknot from the cleat on the dock and opened the throttle.

Shadow stood on the bow of the boat sniffing the air. It was becoming a warm evening. The chill of the previous days had just given way to a southerly breeze blowing up the lake from the Gulf of Mexico six hundred miles away, but not before the cold air mass blowing down from Canada had done its work.

*

Skye was taking iced-tea with her mother on the deck, constantly looking at her watch.

"What time do you make it, Mummy?" she asked anxiously.

"Four-thirty, darlin'. You sure it will be today?"

"Yes, it has turned. Can't you smell it?"

Missy couldn't smell anything other than tea. "Why don't you wait on the beach? You know that is where you want to be."

"Do you mind?"

"Of course not, darlin'. I will watch from here, just like I did when you were little." Missy touched Skye's cheek. "Now go." She shooed her away with her hand.

Skye picked up Thea's Frisbee and walked with the bouncing dog the short distance to the lake. Once there, she started to pace up and down throwing the toy for Thea, who had never tired of her favourite pastime.

She knew he would not come yet, it was too early, but there was so much she needed to tell him that she could not afford to lose a second of precious time with him. She suspected he was close and he may even have been on the island. She had to tell him exactly where to find her. For weeks she practised how she would do it.

*

Amir was sitting in his usual voyeuristic position on the headland to the south of Skye's home. As usual he was dressed in camouflaged fatigues to blend into the foliage around him. He raised the binoculars to his eyes and watched her pacing the sandy beach with her white dog. She looked anxious, but she still looked desirable in her tight jeans and figure-hugging sweater. He allowed the lenses to trace the line of her long legs to her slim waist, and then he allowed them to linger on her full breasts before moving up to her provocatively wanton face with its huge eyes and red lips.

He was almost salivating at the thought of ripping the clothes from her and squeezing her breasts, before his fingers explored her groin.

It would be soon. The whore would be his. Involuntarily, his hand slipped inside his pants.

*

The powerful outboard growled as it ate up the water. It seemed to be taking forever. He could see the island but it didn't seem to be getting any closer.

Shadow's ears were flapping in the wind. His eyes were trained on the island ahead, his head erect and unmoving.

Phoenix pushed the throttle lever, but there was nothing more that the engine could give.

*

Skye was totally lost in thought and anticipation. If she did it right she might be reunited with Yona today. The butterflies in her tummy were unbearable. She had never been as nervous or as scared in her life. She felt physically sick.

Absent-mindedly, she picked up the Frisbee and flicked it along the beach. Thea took off after it for what must have been the hundredth time. Skye peered at the island for what must have been the thousandth time. Where was he?

"Yona, where are you?" she whispered plaintively.

She began to panic. What if he didn't come? Like she hadn't done for two years running. "Oh my God, Yona, please come to me, my darling."

She was staring at the island and hadn't realized that Thea had not retrieved the Frisbee. She heard a whine and then a half-bark. Was he coming?

Thea's tail started to wag and then her body. Skye watched her beloved dog. She knew what it meant.

Skye stepped into the water and waited, her eyes trained on the island two hundred yards away. She was so wrapped up in concentration that she did not hear the boat approaching behind the island.

She was up to her waist in the water, oblivious to its cold temperature, standing motionless.

On the far shore the black dog appeared.

"Oh my God! They're here, Thea," said Skye involuntarily.

She raised her arms as the spirit began to appear from the trees.

*

Phoenix beached the boat on the narrow sandy strip on the far side of the island, paying little attention to any rocks or obstructions as he normally did.

Shadow was already off and running through the trees. He looped the anchor rope around a rock and set off after his dog.

In his head he was rehearsing the signs he was going to use with Newadi so he could find her. As he did so, he dared to believe that she might actually be on the island or nearby.

The trees seemed thicker than usual, he was getting abrasions as he ran and a branch slapped him across the face. He could hear Shadow barking. Was she there?

*

He was a faint outline at first, but soon his whole form was apparent. He was dressed in jeans and a white T. Like the previous year he was not in his loincloth and there was no bow slung across his broad shoulders. But his long jet-black hair framed the handsome face, the face that she knew so well.

She began, as she did each year, holding her hands to her chest and offering her heart to Yona.

Thea was going berserk by her side, splashing and barking as she spun around in circles.

Slowly Skye became aware of another dog barking in the distance. It was the black dog, going as crazy as Thea.

She had never heard the black dog make a sound before. As she was trying to work out the ramifications of what she was hearing the boy fell to his knees.

*

As Phoenix fought his way through the woods he could hear two dogs barking. Was the white dog there?

He stumbled out of the trees onto the sand to see Shadow running in and out of the water towards the houses.

Phoenix looked up, almost scared in case she was not there.

He saw the beautiful girl holding her heart out towards him. In astonishment he dropped to his knees and stared at the sight before him, almost paralysed.

The white dog pirouetted and barked. It was the most beautiful sound he could imagine. There was no generic background framing her image. There was a beach, a dock and a house with a garden and trees. The same house and garden he had seen several times before.

He realised at exactly the same time as the girl what the cacophony of barking from the dogs meant.

The girl stood staring in shock at what she saw. Tentatively, she raised her arm and waved to him.

His face broke into a smile of such happiness he began to laugh. He waved back at the girl and the dog that was barking almost as loudly as Shadow.

They were there. They were really there.

He was afraid to speak in case he was imagining it.

What should he do?

He got to his feet and copied her gesture of offering his heart, and whispered, "Newadi," scared to shout out to her.

Newadi stood completely still for several seconds. And then took off like an Olympic sprinter towards the pontoon boat. The white dog followed, overtaking her before leaping into the boat.

It was going to happen. She was going to come to him. Not an apparition on the water that would disappear as soon as it got close, but a girl, a real girl, on a boat that would reach the shore on which he stood.

Two souls that had been violently ripped apart nearly two hundred years ago were about to be united once again.

Phoenix stood and waited.

*

It had taken a few seconds for Skye to realize what had happened.

The spirit she had loved since she was a small girl, and knew she must have loved in another life, had finally taken the form of a real man.

The second she comprehended the significance of what she had just seen she ran as fast as she could to the pontoon boat. She had waited long enough. Every extra second would be unbearable.

As she ran to the boat her eyes never left Yona. She was scared if she stopped watching him he would disappear as quickly as he had come.

She fumbled with the ropes that moored the boat to the dock, and pushed her adrift before jumping aboard and clambering clumsily into the captain's seat. She turned the ignition. "Damn!" It would not start. She turned the key again. "Thank God!" The engine fired up. She slammed it into gear and sped towards the island.

Two hundred yards, he was still there.

One hundred and fifty, he was bigger, smiling and holding his arms out.

One hundred yards, would he begin to fade?

Fifty yards, no, he was laughing and walking towards the water.

Twenty-five yards, he was running and Skye was crying.

Twenty yards, she throttled back to slow the boat, but it would still beach at a good speed.

Ten yards, Thea was in the water and swimming to Shadow.

Five yards, Skye was in the water and running through the lapping waves towards him.

Two yards, the boat beached and ground to a halt in the sand. Skye stopped running a yard in front of him.

Tears were rolling down her cheeks. Still, neither had spoken. They stood and looked at each other. Scared to take the final step that would close the gulf of centuries. Phoenix lifted his arm and gently wiped a tear from Skye's cheek just as a tear appeared in his own eye.

She was real. He could feel her skin. Skin he already knew as he knew his own.

It was Skye who finally spoke. "Yona, my love."

She knew his name.

Phoenix finally closed the gap between them and took her in his arms.

As he did so she raised her head, inviting the kiss she had waited for so long.

Their lips touched, gently at first, but within seconds they were consumed with a longing nurtured over centuries of forced separation. But it was a kiss and an embrace they knew well.

Missy had watched the whole thing from the deck. Thea's barking had warned her that the boy was coming.

As in previous years she had expected to see nothing, just her daughter and her dog performing a pantomime on the beach. She looked over to the island expecting to see an empty beach and had been shocked when a black dog appeared, followed by the boy a few seconds later.

Missy held her breath in astonishment. Though over two hundred yards away, she could see he was the boy her daughter had been infatuated with since she was small.

"Oh my, darlin', I don't believe it," she whispered.

She brought her hands to her mouth in shock and delight. "He really came for you."

When the boy took Skye in his arms, Missy burst into tears of joy.

She had to sit down, her knees felt so weak. "Oh, Tristan darlin', you are goin' to have to believe your Cherokee daughter now, honey."

*

Amir did not like what he was watching. "Who the hell is that?" he said to himself.

He raised the binoculars again and watched them kissing. "Fuck!" She was his, and there were things he wanted to do to her.

An irrational hatred surged up within him. Whoever the man was, Amir wanted to kill him. A few months ago he did not want jihad, or death. It was different now. Allah had given him strength once again. The lamb had

175

finally become a lion.

"She can watch while I pull out your entrails, infidel pig," he spat out at no one in particular.

SEVENTEEN

Skye and Phoenix stayed on the island until the sun had set.

After they parted from the first embrace, without speaking, they both turned to see what Thea and Shadow were doing.

It was comical. The hitherto mad dogs were lying on the sand. Shadow had his head over Thea's neck and both were just staring up at Skye and Phoenix. They both had a look of total contentment on their canine faces. Occasionally Thea would lick Shadow's muzzle and he would close his eyes.

They laughed at the aging dogs they loved so much, finally reunited just as they had been.

Phoenix suddenly realized that he had been with her for several minutes and had not spoken a word. It had not been necessary, but he thought perhaps he should at least introduce the twenty-first century Yona and learn Newadi's real name. He was also fascinated to find out how she knew about Yona.

"Other than knowing that was the best kiss I have had for well over a hundred years, there are a number of other things we have to reacquaint ourselves with and a great deal we need to learn about each other." He smiled at the girl he'd waited for so long.

"Where do you want to start, Yona?" She threw her arms around his neck and stole another kiss.

After they parted he chuckled and asked, "That's as

good a place as any. Why do you call me Yona? And what is your name? I know you as Newadi."

"I call you Yona because of the legend of the bears. It was my favourite when I was little, and I have always thought of you as bear. Yona is Cherokee for bear."

Phoenix was shaking his head in disbelief. "I have so much to tell you, but my grandma calls me Maba, which is Apache for bear. And Yona was my name when we were married back in 1838."

"We were married?" Skye was suddenly excited.

"Yes, but it is a long story and one we can explore later. What is your name now?" He couldn't resist the temptation of kissing her once again.

When she came up for air, she said, "We've done that before a few times, haven't we?"

"Yep, I suspect we have."

Resisting the temptation to repay his offering of a kiss, she said, "Skye, my name is Skye."

Phoenix was laughing again. "That is what Newadi means, blue sky. It's unbelievable."

"It's only unbelievable if you are not Cherokee," offered Skye, and then asked, "What is your real name, Yona?"

"Phoenix. That is where the name connection ends, but believe me another story begins." Skye looked puzzled. "I'll explain all that later too."

They talked at some length about their spiritual encounters and how they had each perceived them. During this conversation Phoenix gave Skye the bones of his Apache upbringing and talked with great affection about Shichu.

"I can't wait to meet her, she sounds wonderful," said Skye.

Within minutes they were already talking about the life they were going to have with each other, their future taken for granted.

"There are two people you have to meet, Yona." Skye, despite knowing his real name never made any effort to use it and still called him Yona. "My parents, Missy and Tristan, have lived with your ghost for too long. I must introduce the spectre to them. Mummy will be going mad, she will have witnessed our whole reunion and will be dying with anticipation." She giggled.

"It is dark, perhaps we should go now before Mummy thinks some stranger has kidnapped you." He emphasized the mummy. "I can't wait to hear why a Cherokee Indian has an English accent."

"It is another long story, and one we will have in the days to come. But first, before we go, I want one more kiss, Yona. We have a lot of catching up to do."

Skye took his head in her hands. The kiss she gave him was different to the others, it was sensual and erotic and promised a myriad of delights to follow.

When she let him go, he said, "Do we have to go just yet?"

"Yes, darling, Mummy is waiting."

She looked at Thea and Shadow who had remained quiet and were now asleep spooning each other. She nodded towards them. "They have always been with us in the past, haven't they?" she asked.

"Yes, and they have brought us together now. The four-footeds have powerful spirits."

Skye looked at Yona and saw the admiration and love in his eyes for his dog. She sensed his compassion and respect for animals and inwardly smiled at his quaint reference to them as four-footeds from Cherokee legend. Any other person using the term she would have thought it peculiar, but from Yona it was simply the correct thing for him to call them.

"Come on, you two," Phoenix said to the dogs.

Thea got to her feet and stretched. She walked over to Phoenix and licked his hand. "It is nice to meet you too."

He looked to Skye for the dog's name.

"Thea," she said.

"Thank you, Thea, for bringing Skye back to me."

Thea gave him a frenzied lick.

Skye watched them. She had never seen Thea go up to any other person outside of her family, let alone lick a stranger. But Yona was not a stranger, and Thea understood everything he had said to her. There was so much she needed to learn about the man she loved, or was it just stuff she had forgotten?

"What is Thea's boyfriend called?" she asked.

"Shadow."

"It is a wonderful name, and you are a wonderful dog." She tickled Shadow behind his ears, just the way he liked it. "Thank you too, Shadow. I have some steak for your dinner. You must be starving after all that searching. We will give you both a treat."

Shadow was going to like this lady.

They sailed the pontoon boat across the bay to the dock and walked up to the house. Thea led the way and bounded through the patio door with her beau, Shadow, to introduce him to Missy.

Shadow and Thea were already munching on extra large dog chews when Skye walked in with Phoenix.

Phoenix looked assured but shy, and smiled warmly at Skye's mother.

"Mummy, this is Phoenix. I've told you about him."

The look on her daughter's face melted Missy's heart. It was pride, mixed with adoration.

Missy suddenly felt a little protective towards her. The thing she had feared the most for her daughter had not happened. The object of her fixation, all these years, had actually materialized just as Skye always believed he would. Now he was here, Missy realized she did not know anything about him. The one thing she did know was that he was handsome to the point of distraction.

"Hello, Phoenix, welcome to our home. Call me Missy." She offered Phoenix her hand.

He stepped forward and took it and smiled at her. "It is a pleasure to meet you, Missy. To say the least, this must all seem a bit confusing to you. I apologize for any...."

"No need to apologize, Phoenix. I am Cherokee too. But we do need to get to know each other if you are going to marry my daughter."

"Mother! Who said anything about marriage?" Skye was not shocked at her mother's statement, it was Missy and she spoke her mind. But she did feel the need to show some mock surprise at least.

Phoenix laughed. "We will, Missy." He turned towards Skye. "Don't sound so shocked, Skye. You said yes to me at least once before. I can prove it."

Missy was already won over. The man was gorgeous and obviously in love with her daughter. 'I hope you are everything Skye thinks you are, and not some drug dealer off the streets,' she thought.

Missy had prepared for this moment. She had put a couple of bottles of Champagne in the fridge when she saw the dog and the boy on the island. It would have had time to cool. "So, let's get started." Missy stepped over to the fridge and removed one of the bottles, leaving the other for when Tristan returned home. She collected four glasses from behind the bar and handed three of them to Phoenix.

"Open this and let's have our first toast to your future," Missy said.

Phoenix took the bottle and the three flutes, popped the cork and handed a glass each to the ladies.

"To your beautiful daughter Skye. I promise that I will always love her and guard her with my life against all evils." He raised his glass.

'You'll do, Phoenix,' thought Missy. "To Skye." She

raised her own glass.

"Apart from bewitching my daughter, what do you do, Phoenix?" asked Missy. It was time to learn something about her future son-in-law.

"I am a veterinary physician."

Skye made a little leap and clapped her hands together in delight. She saw the look her mother gave her and shrugged her shoulders. "We are all on a voyage of discovery, Mummy."

"You didn't know, did you?" Missy looked at Skye and then a smile invaded her lovely face. "Well I never, this sure is different, darlin'. It's like winning a son-in-law in the lottery."

Missy secretly loved it all. It made her novels seem like nursery stories. "What else don't you know about this handsome young man?" She raised her eyebrows questioning her daughter.

"I don't know anything, Mummy, except that I love him."

She stood on her toes, raised one leg backwards and kissed Phoenix on the cheek. It made Missy smile. She had never seen Skye do it before. Not to Tristan, Gramps or any of her boyfriends. Not even the rugby player who had pursued her fervently in Oxford. It was something she had always done to Tristan and something she had only seen her own mother do to her father.

As if reading her thoughts, Skye asked, "When will Daddy be home?"

"Any minute, darlin'. Come on, Skye. Give me a hand in the kitchen. Looks like we are feeding four this evening. You stay and keep the dogs company, Phoenix." He had been dismissed. "I need to interrogate my daughter whilst she helps me prepare dinner."

They looked at the two dogs. They were once again curled up together in front of the gas log-fire. Missy shook her head. It was all too much. She appeared to have acquired a dog-in-law as well.

Phoenix sat on the floor with the animals, adjusted his position and appeared to melt into the general melee of legs, paws, tails and ears where he was unconditionally accepted.

Skye and Missy turned and watched him settle with his pack as they left the room.

Skye was grinning like a cat that got the cream. Missy giggled quietly to herself as she dragged Skye away. Her plan was not just to have a talk to her daughter, she wanted Tristan to meet Phoenix on his own and he was due back any second.

Ten minutes later all three were asleep when Tristan walked in through the patio doors. A black dog, which he had never seen before, had its head on the shoulder of a longhaired youth that looked half way between being a Colombian cartel member and the lead singer in a heavy metal band. A white dog, which he had seen before, lay sprawled across the black dog and the youth's broad chest.

He coughed. The youth was suddenly alert. The dogs glanced up disinterestedly at him.

Phoenix was soon on his feet. The dogs, mildly perturbed at having been interrupted, settled back into an easy companionship.

"Excuse me, sir. My name is Phoenix. I am a friend of your daughter." Phoenix was straightening himself and his attire after his slumber with the dogs.

Tristan was mildly amused at the youth's fluster. "You wouldn't be the boy from the lake, would you?" He knew the answer before he asked. Who else would be allowed to walk into his home with a strange dog, and then curl up and go to sleep on his floor? The youth was obviously a Cherokee Indian, and after twenty-two years of marriage to a descendant of the tribe he was no longer surprised at anything they said or did.

He had come to terms with the ghost's existence a long time ago. Part of him was happy for his daughter that the ghost now had a form. Another part wished the form did not look like the lead in Hair.

"Yes, I am, sir." Phoenix was trying to give Skye's father his most disarming smile, but suspected he was grinning like a maniac at his prospective father-in-law.

Tristan nodded. He was well aware of what yes implied. "Well, I suppose that I should introduce myself and welcome you to our home. My name is Tristan, and I am Skye's father." He didn't offer his hand to shake.

"It is a pleasure to meet you, sir." Phoenix was nervous. He wanted this man to like him.

Tristan was appraising the young man in front of him. If he were being honest, he had never expected to see the spirit Missy had been defending for several years. He still hoped that Skye, in contradiction to her name, would come back down to earth and get a regular shorthaired boyfriend who had a job. He doubted the youth in front of him was gainfully employed. He sighed audibly. That was not going to happen now.

There was an embarrassing silence between them. Phoenix knew what Tristan must be thinking, but did not really know what to say. Eventually to break the silence he simply said, "I love your daughter, sir, and I will never hurt her. I promise you."

"You had better not, Phoenix. You start with a blank sheet and I will not judge you. So let's get to know each other, and you can try and convince me that you are worthy of my daughter."

Tristan surprised himself with the severity of his tone, and the words he had used. He was known as an easy going man, laid back, relaxed. It was not his usual persona to be as threatening.

"I hope that I can do that, sir. If I can't, you may ask me to leave her alone."

Tristan noted that Phoenix did not say he WOULD leave her alone. That was good. Whatever else this man was, he was serious about Skye.

Tristan studied Phoenix some more. Not threateningly, just trying to get the measure of him. Phoenix returned his look with openness and friendliness, but there was steel in his eyes.

Skye entered the room and broke the silence, "Daddy, you're home and you've met."

She walked over to Phoenix and put her arm around his waist, as he pulled her into a protective embrace beneath is own arm. She looked up at the man whose face she was still reacquainting herself with.

Tristan watched his daughter move to Phoenix's side and saw the look of devotion on her face. At that point he knew his only option was to accept the spirit from her past and make him welcome.

"Yes, we have introduced ourselves, darling. Now we have to get to know each other." He finally held out his hand for Phoenix to shake. Phoenix took the offered hand and gave Tristan a firm handshake, always important to an Englishman. Tristan gave him a genuine smile. "Can I get you a drink, Phoenix?"

"We have some Champagne, Daddy."

Phoenix returned the smile. "That would be great, thank you, sir." He understood Tristan's reservations; he would have been the same if Skye were his daughter, probably worse. He hoped one day to find out.

The rest of the evening went well. With each hour that passed, Tristan grew to like the young man more. The majority of the conversation covered their present lives, jobs, pastimes, friends and family. It was just as much a voyage of discovery to Phoenix and Skye, as it was to her parents.

By the end of the evening, Missy loved her prospective son-in-law almost as much as she loved her daughter. Her father was more than a little impressed by him as well.

"You had better stay the night, Phoenix." Tristan said. He had absolutely no idea how Phoenix had arrived. There was no vehicle in the driveway or boat by the dock. "How did you get here? You didn't appear out of the lake did you?" he said, jokingly

Phoenix laughed, knowing that part of him had. "No, I have a boat, it's on the other side of the island."

"It's late. Get it tomorrow. I'll make up the spare room," said Missy.

"Thank you, it's kind of you." The last thing that Phoenix wanted to do was leave Skye now that he had finally found her.

Skye intervened, "Let's take a walk, Yona. I want you to myself for a while."

Skye kissed her mother and father goodnight. Missy kissed Phoenix on his cheek and Tristan said, "Good night, Phoenix," and then added, "welcome home."

It was more than Phoenix could have hoped for. Tristan had acknowledged his right to be there, his Cherokee ancestry and the destiny of his daughter with just two words.

"Thank you, sir." He nodded his appreciation of Tristan's gesture.

Skye took his hand and led him through the patio doors to the garden. A black and a white dog leapt to their feet and followed.

They strolled through the garden and along the shore, their path lit by a full moon.

For the first time ever Thea was not bouncing at Skye's side waiting for the Frisbee. She walked at Shadow's side.

After a while, Skye asked, "Earlier, you said we were married. Why were we torn apart, Yona?"

Phoenix explained the legend of the golden haired

woman and its reference to Newadi and Yona. He remembered, almost verbatim, every word he had read because he had read it a hundred times.

Skye listened intently, transfixed by his words. "So you were killed by the soldiers and I died of a broken heart. I wonder if we had the baby before I died?"

"I don't know? But I know a woman who is trying to find out."

"Who?"

"The golden haired woman is here too. I believe that we have all been reincarnated together."

"What? Why? I must meet her, darling." Skye was excited.

"You will. Her name is Caroline. You will like her. Hell, you already do." He chuckled. "You were great friends and her story is, in part, our story. But her story did not end that day in Anaguluskee. She was a fascinating woman and there is lots more to learn about her."

"Skye had stopped and was pulling his arm. "When? When can I meet her?"

"Tomorrow. Are you free in the morning? I can take you to the animal hospital with me. She will be there. She is a physician too."

"Yes, of course. I've taken a week's holiday for Christmas. I can't wait to meet her and, anyway, there is no way I would let you out of my sight."

They strolled for nearly an hour before returning to the house. Inside, Skye prepared a pot of herbal tea and they sat by the log-fire with the dogs at their feet.

They lay in each other's arms into the early hours of the morning. Chatting between kisses, which becoming increasingly passionate.

"I want you so much, Yona." Skye's voice was rasping with animal intensity.

"And I want you, darling." He kissed her again, his

tongue exploring hers. He came up for air and chuckled. "Your dad might be a bit miffed if he knew what we were doing. He seems like the type that would expect me to be married to you before I had my evil way with you."

She laughed. "We are married." Her tongue attempted to make her point. "But you are right. We should give him a bit more time to get used to it." She kissed him again. "You are not going to bed though. You can sleep with me here on the sofa. As I said, I am not letting you out of my sight."

EIGHTEEN

The next morning Missy came downstairs to find them asleep in each other's arms. She left them in their slumber and took the dogs to the kitchen to feed them. Replete, Shadow and Thea retired to the garden to explore.

Tristan appeared in the kitchen and poured himself a cup of coffee. "At least he had the decency not to take our daughter to bed with him." He was almost smiling as he gestured to the couple on the sofa in the lounge.

"Yes, darlin', but as much as it will pain you to hear it, I suspect she begged him too."

"Enough, woman. Not my little girl, she is not like her wanton mother." He kissed Missy on the lips. "I'll take them over to his boat before I go into the city. I assume she will bugger off with him?"

"She sure will. Pancakes, darlin'?"

Phoenix awoke to the smell of bacon and eggs. A mixture of longing and contentedness enveloped him as he became aware of the girl in his arms.

Skye stirred, and half-turned towards him. She opened her eyes and squealed with delight when she saw him there. Her lips continued where they had left off the night before.

"Good morning, Yona," she said when she had finished the re-arousal of her soul mate.

"Uhhuh!" Tristan coughed as he entered the room. "Mum has cooked breakfast. Then I will run you over to

189

your boat, Phoenix. I assume Skye will be going with you?" He was smiling.

"Yes, Daddy. And we will call you with our plans later," replied Skye.

Tristan was pretty sure what those plans would be.

One hour later, showered and fed, two Cherokee Indians and two dogs were in the Department's boat heading towards Gainesville.

Charlie was the first to see the spirit from the lake. He was rendered nigh on speechless. He caught the line Phoenix threw to him and stepped to the cleat to tie off. Staring at Skye, he kept on walking and nearly fell in.

"Wow! Buddy, spirit, mermaid, whatever, you're hot, lady," he finally managed to get out.

Skye laughed. "Thank you, kind sir." She offered her hand to Charlie to help her off the boat. He gleefully took it.

Forty minutes later, Phoenix brought the pick-up to a halt outside the animal hospital.

"This will sound daft, but I'm nervous, Yona," said Skye, before she got out of the pick-up.

"Not half as nervous as I was meeting your dad," he replied. "Come on. She's here, that's her car over there."

Skye climbed down from the cab and was quickly by his side again, slipping her fingers into his.

Caroline heard his truck pull up. Would she be with him? She decided to sit by her desk without peeking out and wait for the door to open. Fifteen seconds later it did.

Phoenix gently rested his hand on Skye's back and eased her through the door into Caroline's office.

"Lady Caroline, I would like to present an old and dear friend," he said in the best English accent he could muster.

Caroline stood up, she did not know what she would feel when Phoenix finally introduced her to Newadi. What she actually experienced shocked her. A lump in her throat appeared from nowhere and she wanted to cry. A tear ran down her cheek.

On seeing it, Skye flew across the floor and took her in her arms. She knew this woman, almost as well as her spirit had known Yona. Her nervousness evaporated the second she saw her golden hair. She even knew her name without asking.

"I've missed you, Dahlonega."

They were both crying and laughing at the same time, aware of the absurdity of the situation.

Phoenix watched, enthralled by the reunion. It had completely taken him by surprise. He began to laugh.

"What's the matter with you, Mowgli?" Caroline asked, seeing his reaction.

"If the world could only see this. Not only would they think us complete nut-jobs for believing in spirits, but it beggars belief that two of those Cherokee spirits are actually English roses."

"Yes, I suppose it is a little outlandish," said Skye, still holding onto Caroline's hands.

Caroline was smiling at her oldest friend. "We have some catching up to do, young lady."

"Yes we do."

"And I have a sick snake, and a heavily pregnant deer to check on. So I will let you catch up," said Phoenix as he left the office.

The two dogs tried to follow him. "You guys stay with Skye," he said.

*

Amir accepted the fresh coffee from the waitress. Mohammed declined by holding his hand over the cup.

"I don't know who he is, Mo. He just appeared from

nowhere and they went off in his boat this morning. It is definitely her boyfriend, they never stop kissing," said Amir.

Mohammed was thinking. "It may complicate things. The mother and father will be easy to take, the old man too if we wish. But this guy is young and big, you say. He may put up a fight. I think we should only take the family and the dog. They will be enough leverage; we don't need the boyfriend as well. If he gets in the way, we kill him."

The idea appealed to Amir. He wanted the girl to himself for a while before he killed her too. But there was a problem.

"I don't know where they have gone, Mo."

"It doesn't matter. They will be back. I say we take her parents whenever there is an opportunity. Now would be a good time, she is away and so is her boyfriend. The dog is with her, so we get that when we take her. Once we have the parents, we will have the girl's cell number. When she finds out they have been kidnapped she will soon come back and do as we say. Get your brothers. We still have three days."

Amir stood up and took his check for breakfast to the cashier. He returned to the table and left two bucks tip for the waitress.

As Mohammed finished the last pancake with hot maple syrup, he was staring with his face a mixture of disgust and loathing at the obese man at the table next to them, as he stuffed yet another pork sausage into his mouth. He hoped the gross infidel lived downstream of Buford dam.

Without sitting down again, Amir said, "I'll call you as soon as there is an opportunity to take them." Mohammed nodded as he picked up his own check.

Amir left Cracker Barrel and got into his minivan. He pulled out of the lot and onto Lanier Island's Parkway, then headed back towards Skye's home near Flowery Branch.

*

Caroline and Skye began with questions about their present lives. Where they lived, their jobs, their parents and England.

It transpired that they had both attended Oxford University and had frequented the same pubs, walked through the same meadows and spent hours in the same libraries. They even found a professor they both knew. He had not taught either of them, but he had lusted after them both.

"He was actually quite handsome when I knew him," Caroline offered.

"He was still distinguished looking, but unfortunately he still thought he was Brad Pitt. I'm being unfair, he was fun and amusing, but thank God he found someone who didn't mind his beer belly," added Skye. They both laughed.

Caroline changed the subject. "So, you turned down a job with the world's most famous architect to design dams for the Corps of Engineers?" She had a questioning look on her face.

"I know, Daddy thinks I'm mad too, or he used to. He's coming round now. But I had to be here, Caroline. I knew he would come for me. I didn't have to think about my decision for more than a nanosecond. And I was right, he came, didn't he?" Skye had a smile of complete contentment and satisfaction on her beautiful face.

Caroline studied her. She had only been with her for half-an-hour, yet she felt as Phoenix had with Brad when they had first met. She knew this girl inside and out. Like

193

a couple who had lived together for a lifetime, she knew what she would say next, what her reaction would be to things she said. Her expressions and mannerisms were all familiar. But there was one thing that fascinated Caroline. It was Skye's smile.

Caroline knew Skye's smile like she knew the back of her hand. Some people have a smile that is so unique it is only associated with them, like Goldie Hawn or Cameron Diaz, Simon Baker or Clark Gable. Skye had one of those smiles.

Caroline was not fascinated by it because it was so captivating or because it was so distinctive, but because she knew she had seen it before on two small girls.

Phoenix had insisted she had a spiritual side, and seeing Skye's smile made her realize how right he was. Her smile had transcended generations and Caroline's spirit could see it on Newadi's face and the faces of her twin daughters. The girls she was now convinced she had raised as her own children in another life, and whose smiles were engraved on her being.

"There is something I want you to see, Skye. But before I show you, can I assume Phoenix has told you the story and legend about Dahlonega, Newadi and Yona?"

"Yes, last night. It's so sad."

"So you know you died after you had given birth? The legend says of a broken heart, but the physician in me suspects there was a far more rational reason."

"Yes."

"Here is the thing. I have done a lot of research into Dahlonega and the children. Dahlonega was actually Lady Katherine Stanley. She married Peter Woodman, Adahy. After Adahy and Yona died in the massacre, followed by her best friend Newadi dying in childbirth, she returned to Charleston and practised as a doctor. She raised two girls who took her husband's name Woodman. But they were not his; neither was Dahlonega their natural mother. You were, Skye, or rather Newadi was."

Skye looked shocked. "How do you know?"

"I have done the genealogy from Lady Katherine onwards. Actually, from her parents onwards. Because she was of noble birth it was quite easy, and her two daughters became noted doctors in their own right. Margaret married and stayed in the US and continued to work in Charleston. The other daughter, Victoria, returned to England in 1868, she was thirty and began to work at Great Ormond Street Hospital for Sick Children. I am sure you have heard of it."

"Yes, I had a friend who ended up there when I was quite small. My mother took me to visit her."

"You asked me how I know. This is how. Come over here."

Caroline pressed a button and her computer woke up from its sleep mode. Her fingers played the keyboard and a family tree appeared. At the top was the Earl of Abingdon. "We will come back to this." A few more taps later a sepia photograph appeared on the screen.

Caroline began to explain, "It's the staff of the hospital in 1875. Victoria would have been thirty-seven." A classical group photograph showed the doctors and nurses with the Director of Medicine in the middle. She pointed to a female form three to the left of the director. "That's her."

Skye strained to get a better look at the woman, but the quality was not good.

"Luckily each of the doctors had their portraits taken separately," said Caroline, as she watched Skye straining to get the likeness of the woman she had pointed out.

She punched a few more keys and a series of unsmiling sombre faces filled the screen. She was deliberately building up to the crescendo of her presentation. "Miserable looking bunch, aren't they? All apart from this one." With aplomb she hit enter.

"Oh, my God!" Exclaimed Skye. Her hands involuntarily moved to her mouth.

"Recognize that smile?" asked Caroline.

Skye was speechless. She was staring at a photograph of herself. Her hair pulled back and a little older, but it could have been her.

"Yep, Victoria Woodman, your daughter or great-great-great-great grandmother. It all gets a little confusing," joked Caroline.

Skye was beginning to come to terms with the revelation. "I had two daughters."

"Twins actually. The records show the same date of birth. I don't have a photo of Margaret, but I think we know what she looked like."

Skye suddenly felt sad. "I never lived to see them grow up, Caroline. I would never have just abandoned them, not even if Yona was killed." She was half-muttering to herself.

Caroline took Skye in her arms. "I know. That is why I know you didn't die of a broken heart."

"Thank you, Caroline. Thank you for looking after them."

"This spiritual stuff is all a bit new to me, Skye, but I am pretty damned sure that it was more than my pleasure. They were my delight."

They embraced for a while, each of them wrapped in thoughts of the past, with their present day bond now cemented. Eventually Skye asked, "What happened to Victoria?"

"She devoted her life to caring for sick children. She married, but had none of her own. She died at the age of seventy-six in London."

"What about Margaret?"

"That's different. She bred like a rabbit, twelve in all, six boys and six girls. They all lived and they all married. They provided Margaret with over thirty grandchildren, and I'm still working on the family tree. If they were all as prolific as Margaret, half of Georgia must have Cherokee blood by now." Caroline giggled. "What is your mother's smile like?"

"No. You don't think so, do you?"

Caroline tilted her head questioningly

Skye laughed. "It's a bit like mine, actually."

"What goes around comes around!"

"Oh God! It's a bit incestuous."

Caroline laughed. "Not really, with your ancestors' sexual prowess the blood line will be somewhat depleted. You will have married in and out of hundreds of different clans, nationalities and races by now."

They continued to talk about ancestry and studied Caroline's family tree, trying to see if Skye could connect back to it with her own knowledge of family. They could not.

Phoenix could hear them laughing as he approached the office. He opened the door and said, "You two caught up yet?"

Skye answered, "Yes, and I want twelve children, but two of them have to be twin girls."

Caroline laughed. Phoenix did not have a clue what she was talking about.

During the afternoon the three of them walked Shadow and Thea through the forest and trails of the Unicoi National Park, via some of the prettiest waterfalls Skye had ever seen. The girls filled Phoenix in on why he was required to sire so many children.

"I don't mind the siring part, but that's a whole lot of hunting to feed all those mouths," he said.

"You are a great warrior and hunter, Yona," Skye said encouragingly. "We won't starve."

"I'm not sure about the warrior part. The last I time a fired my bow at a man, I died shortly afterwards," he snorted.

"You're much better now, Mowgli, and I promise I won't start a fight," declared Caroline.

Their next stop was to introduce Skye to Brad. He was expecting them and a fresh pot of coffee was brewing when they arrived at the antique/junk store.

Each time Phoenix visited the quantity of junk seemed to have increased, whilst the sale of antiques appeared to have decreased. "It's a bit of an unofficial pawn shop for folks who are a bit short of cash." Brad had once offered by way of an explanation.

They fought their way to the front door, moving several items to gain access. As the bell rang out, Brad called, "Coffee's brewing, come on through, folks."

Phoenix led the way with the dogs, followed by the amused girls who were stopping to look at every other artefact. At the office door Brad stood with his arms wide. "You two later. Let me first hug the elusive girl from the lake." He grinned at Skye.

Quite naturally she stepped into his embrace and folded her own arms around him.

"Let me see you, young lady." He held Skye at arms' length. "Yeah, you'll do. You're as advertised. Pretty as a picture."

Skye was beaming. She liked the junk/antique dealer. He had the kindest face she seen since visiting Santa when she was tiny. And like everyone else she had met since finding Yona he seemed familiar, in some way a part of her past.

Brad embraced Phoenix and hugged Caroline. "Lady Caroline, how nice of you to visit my antique store. I hope you can find something that will suit your ancestral pile," he said with a passable English accent, and then bowed.

"I doubt it, my man. Do you have any Wedgwood, or pieces by Chippendale?"

"Being delivered tomorrow, milady."

"Very good, I will send my man to collect them." They both laughed. "Seriously, Brad. Do you even know what you have in here?"

"Not really. I remember for a year or two, but then I forget. Never kept any records. Doesn't matter though, it's all going up in value. Find a seat, folks. There are plenty in the store if we haven't got enough in here." He grinned.

Phoenix looked at the two stacks of dining chairs in the corner and the three-seat Chesterfield, now occupied by two dogs, along with the three rockers that were all crammed into the office. Phoenix moved some books from one of the rocking chairs whilst the girls settled into the Chesterfield and melted into the dogs that squeezed together to accommodate them.

"Tell me all about the long-awaited reunion while I pour the coffee," said Brad.

Skye told the story as it had unfolded the previous evening, and hardly paused for breath as she continued with everything Caroline had told her about the twins and the photograph.

When she had finished, she asked Brad, "Where did you fit in to all this?"

"Don't know, young lady. Just know I was there."

Phoenix added, "None of us know, but I do know he was part of it and part of why we are all back together."

Brad chuckled. "Ah, yes. Phoenix thinks there is a reason why we have all come back again now. And he thinks that reason is more than just continuing his courtship of you, young lady."

Skye looked at Yona. He had not mentioned anything, but to be fair only nineteen hours had passed since he had come to her. "What could it be, darling?" she asked.

"I don't know, Skye. I really don't know. It is just a feeling."

NINETEEN

Amir had observed Skye's home from afar. She had not returned. Her father had obviously gone to work, only her mother could be seen inside the house.

His cell phone rang; it was Mohammed asking for a report. Amir told him the situation.

"Okay, we take them this evening when the father returns from work, the girl too if she is there. If the boyfriend is there we kill him. Go back to your brothers' now, there are other things we need to prepare." Mohammed hung up.

Amir parked the Honda minivan outside the condo. It was a perfect place for his brothers to blend into American society. The development was run down and littered with tatty vehicles. Some of the inhabitants had jobs but the majority lived hand to mouth, many of them illegal immigrants from south of the border. If not a ghetto, it was a united nations of alien residents. The predominant language was Spanish, but Urdu was spoken by more than a few of the inhabitants along with Arabic and Amir had noticed, more recently, a variety of Eastern European accents. A slowly decreasing black minority generally spoke any English that could be heard.

He locked the doors of the vehicle and double-checked the lock on the rear door. More than a couple of his tools had disappeared from the van in the past. He looked at the kids playing soccer nearby and decided they were too young to be interested in pilfering his gear.

He walked the short distance to his brothers' door and knocked. Nawaz opened it without talking and beckoned him in. Jamal handed him a beer from the well-stocked fridge. He did not speak either, but he did nod at his older brother. Amir couldn't help but wonder why their fanaticism stopped short of being teetotal. But then again, their fanaticism generally only embraced the facets of Islam that suited them. They attended prayers when it was convenient and ate whatever they felt like in private. In public only halal meat passed their lips and their piousness astounded him. The one thing that was consistent was their hatred of Americans, but bizarrely not American things. He picked up the empty McDonalds bags that littered the kitchen table and put them in the trashcan.

There was a knock on the door. It would be Mohammed. Amir let him in. He declined the offered beer as his eyes surveyed the room. 'Cannon fodder.' The words kept echoing in his head. He did not care if the brothers lived or died. Neither did he really care if there would be a place in Paradise for them. He hoped there would not be, especially if he was destined to be there himself one day.

He was carrying a box. It was reasonably heavy.

"Nawaz, Jamal, come here. I have something for you," he said, as he set it on the table.

He lifted the top flap and removed a slab of greyish matter wrapped in greaseproof paper and set it down gently. Then he removed two detonators, each the size of a little finger. Next, he lifted out two small LCD stopwatches. From his pocket he produced two 9-volt batteries.

"There, soldiers of Allah, enough Semtex to remove Morgan Falls Dam off the face of the Earth. Along with all you need to initiate its passing."

Nawaz and Jamal's faces lit up.

"Pick it up. It's inert. Won't harm you unless you detonate it."

Jamal lifted the block off the table. It was much heavier than he thought it would be. He was grinning.

"Nawaz, get a knife. Cut it in half. It's just like putty, one half for each end of the dam. Do you guys remember how to assemble an IED?" He looked at the cannon fodder. The look in their dull eyes told him the answer. "Don't worry, I'll assemble the first one. Watch. We just won't attach the wires to the detonator."

It took Mohammed exactly one minute to assemble the first harbinger of death. He handed it to Jamal. "There, all you do now is clip these two wires together and press the button on the clock. I have preset the time on this one to thirty minutes, but you can set it to anything up to twenty-four hours. Have a go." He passed the rest of the gear to the brothers. "Just don't clip the wires together."

Their first attempt took ten minutes. The fifth, three minutes. 'It is as good as it was going to get,' thought Mohammed. The only reason they were still alive was because he had not given them the batteries. The clowns had even connected the detonator on the second attempt despite his instructions not to.

"Okay, happy?" he asked. They nodded. He was not convinced. "Give me the parts." He held out his hand.

He built the second bomb inside thirty seconds and preset each of the clocks to sixty minutes. "That should give you plenty of time to clear the area. If you want more time change the setting. Remember, all you have to do is attach the wires and then press the buttons on the clocks." He looked up at them for affirmation that they understood.

Not too sure whether he got the affirmation, he put the two bombs inside wooden boxes and then the boxes into two Macy's shopping bags. He then handed one to each of the brothers.

Amir watched the pantomime and sensed Mohammed's frustration with his brothers. Despite his own opinion of them he heard himself say, "They will be okay, Mohammed."

The blond haired Arab did not reply. He did not really care. Cannon fodder. It was Buford Dam that would do all the damage. Instead, he turned his attention to Amir. "I will work with you. I'll build our bomb. First we must take the hostages. Where are we going to keep them?"

"Here, I thought." Amir wondered if he had said the right thing.

Mohammed looked around. It was not a bad choice. People were invisible in neighbourhoods like this. He walked around the small condo, and selected one of the two bedrooms. "We lock them in here. Put some locks on the door. Bolts as well. All on the outside." He walked to the window and looked outside. It was good, not overlooked. "Board up the outside of the window, but first paint the glass black." He stepped into the bathroom that served the bedroom. It was perfect, there were no windows, just an extractor fan.

Amir was pleased that Mohammed did not deride his choice. He was more than a little afraid of the man. Tentatively, he said, "The girl and her dog have not yet returned. She has been gone for thirty-six hours." In an attempt to put Mohammed's mind at rest, he added, "But she didn't take any bags when she left with the man."

Mohammed nodded. He too was afraid of his own bosses. The girl was essential to their plan. He did not want to rely on firepower alone to gain access to the dam's inner workings. Such a plan would be doomed to failure, or rather it may well succeed but ultimately they would be doomed. Sure they could get in and blow up their target, but they would not get out alive. He did not consider himself cannon fodder. That said; if he failed in his mission he might as well be dead. They still had three days to go. It was time he got more involved in the implementation of the terrorist act. Amir was better than his idiotic brothers and far brighter, but he still could not trust him with his own future.

"Okay. She will be back. It's nearly Christmas, the infidels spend Christmas with their families. But to be sure, we will take the parents and hopefully the girl too if she has returned. You two, do what I've told you with the window and doors," he said to Nawaz and Jamal. To Amir, he said, "We will go and get the parents. We can wait a while for the girl to return first, it would be easier."

He handed them all a new prepaid phone. The fourth they'd each had. "Destroy the old ones."

*

The evening was drawing to a close. Skye's reunion with her friends had been magical, but there was something else she needed and she did not want her friends around for that.

They dropped Caroline back at her home. As she got out of the vehicle, she said, "Take some time off, Mowgli. You two need to catch up. We will manage till after Christmas. If I really need you, I have your number."

"Are you sure?" Phoenix asked, but not too convincingly. Time with Skye was exactly what he wanted.

Caroline had sensed the pent up sexuality between them all evening. It was like a pressure cooker about to explode. There were certain things they needed to attend to, and quickly. She figured a few days of lovemaking might help relieve some of the tension. Something from her past told her Skye would not easily be satiated, despite her profound love for Phoenix. He would have busy nights and days ahead. It was probably a good job that Christmas and family would intervene to give him a rest. Then again, she knew her man; he would be a willing and, she suspected, an able partner.

She smiled mischievously at Skye, whose eyes were dilated in anticipation. "Thank you, Caroline. I promise I'll send him back in one piece."

Caroline noticed Skye's hand resting perilously close to his groin, which was quite obviously aware of its proximity. She giggled. "Okay, you two. Twelve, remember, Mowgli, and twin girls."

"I'll try my hardest, Lady Caroline." He was grinning from ear to ear. "Catch you soon."

It was a short five-minute ride to Phoenix's place. Skye left her hand on his thigh the whole way there. "Are we nervous about this?" she asked.

"Ha! You bet your ass we're nervous, at least I am," he offered.

"Me too." She allowed her hand to travel the short distance to his penis. "Feel familiar, Indian boy?"

Phoenix could have exploded in his pants. "Yeah, it feels familiar." He heard the zip open and felt her fingers search and caress him.

"What about this?" Her hand wrapped around his hard penis.

"Oh yeah, that feels familiar." He was trying not to press his foot hard on the accelerator.

Suddenly her head ducked down to his lap and her lips took over the job her hand had been doing. After thirty seconds of bliss her head appeared again with an impish grin on her perfect lips.

"Are we still nervous, Indian boy?"

"No, Indian girl, not any more. And by the way, that

did not feel familiar. You've learnt some stuff since we last did this." He chuckled.

"You have no idea. And from what Caroline has told me you have not exactly been dormant!" She raised her eyebrows and tilted her head.

"Just practising for you, Skye." He grinned at the girl who had left him on the verge of the orgasm he had waited nearly two hundred years to have.

"Then we better go inside and find out what the other has learned." She pulled his zip up and patted the bulge in his pants. Then she turned to Thea and Shadow, who had witnessed the entire encounter. "And that is all you two are going to see. From here on in, it's private."

The dogs did not care. They were already half way to the front door. Phoenix let them in and handed the dogs a biscuit from the barrel he kept by the fridge. Then he opened a cupboard and produced a second dog's bed. He placed it next to Shadow's. It was almost white and contrasted the black one on which Shadow was already curled up. "Got this in for you, Thea. I hoped we would get to use it before Christmas."

Skye was by his side. She was close to tears.

"Unfortunately, I didn't get you one, Newadi. You're in mine."

"I wouldn't want to be anywhere else, Yona."

He took her hand and led her to the bedroom. "Do you want to call your folks and tell them you are staying?"

"No, Mum knows already. She'll break the news gently to Dad."

"Okay. Let's finish what you started in the car."

"That may take a while, Indian boy."

"I hope so."

He took her in his arms. "So, are YOU scared?"

"Petrified. I have imagined this every day for ten years," she answered, as the butterflies swarmed once again in her stomach.

"No, my darling. You have remembered it every day."

"Yes, I know. Kiss me."

*

"So, I suppose he is having his evil way with my little girl?"

"I would imagine so." Missy looked at her watch. "Probably for the umpteenth time by now." She teasingly smiled at Tristan.

"Why is it always easier for mothers?" Tristan was not actually angry. More resigned.

"It probably would not be, but this boy is different. I'm afraid you got a little more than you bargained for when you married your squaw, darlin'. I am so happy for her, and he is drop dead gorgeous."

"It doesn't make it any easier."

"What do you think she has been up to in Oxford with that lovely James?"

"That was different, he was British." He was grinning when he said it.

"Well that's okay then, old chap." Missy slapped him playfully on the arm as she delivered her retort with her English accent.

"When did she say she would be home?" he asked.

"When she has finished, darlin'. You know how we Cherokee women are."

It was the final straw. He visibly winced. "The thought of my baby girl behaving like her strumpet mother is too much. I'm off to the mall. I need some new shoes for work."

Missy cuddled her man. "Okay, darlin'. Can you stop

in at Publix and get me some more herbal teas. You know the ones I like."

He shuffled out of the front door and got into his BMW. He headed south to the nearest Publix store on Holiday before driving to the mall. He did not notice the Honda Odyssey parked along the street from his home. It was just like every other minivan parked outside the millions of suburban homes across America.

Inside, Missy was making last minute preparations for Christmas. There was at least one more mouth to feed and possibly more if Phoenix had any nearby family. Not for the first time she realised how little she knew about the man who was undoubtedly seducing her daughter at that very moment.

The doorbell rang. Usually Thea would have given her due warning of anyone approaching the house, but she was not there. She had a sudden vision of Thea being seduced by Shadow in whatever ménage they were all living. She giggled at the thought.

She put down the list she was making and went to answer the door.

A tall blond haired man stood on the porch next to the bougainvillea she'd put in the pot. "Hi, can I help you?" she asked.

He smiled, an open smile on a not-unattractive face. Thirty-something, a family man, thought Missy. He was casually dressed, but smart, an office worker.

"Sorry to bother you, ma'am. My name is Danny; I've done some work with your daughter for the Corps. I wonder, is she at home? I have a few questions I need to ask her about the survey at Buford Dam." He smiled again, and then he lied, "I don't seem to able to get her on her cell."

The last part did not surprise Missy. She doubted if she would have answered her own phone under similar circumstances.

She smiled back at the man. "Sorry, Danny, she is away at the moment. Perhaps her cell battery is flat."

"It's not that important. Just a couple of things I may need to order before Christmas for the renovation. Do you know when she will be back, ma'am?"

"Almost certainly later today. Shall I get her to call you?"

"No, it's fine. I'll call her again tomorrow. Phone's probably charged by then. Sorry to bother you."

Mohammed knew all he needed to. The girl would be home later. She had not gone away for Christmas. He felt relieved. The plan would still work. Why Amir could not have asked the simple question himself, he was not sure. Perhaps all three brothers may meet their maker on December 25th. It would make his life far easier. Other than a few meetings he had never had anything to do with them before. It would be difficult for the authorities to make any connection between them, especially if they were all dead.

*

Skye awoke with her head on Phoenix's chest. She had to pinch herself to make sure it was real. She slowly twisted her head so she could see his face. A lock of his long black hair caught on her eyelash and rested on her lips. It was cool. She gently blew the hair away.

"You are awake," he said without opening his eyes.

"Um, awake enough."

Within seconds they were making love again. Each time seemed to get better and each time was different. They took turns in taking the lead; both seemed able to time their orgasms to coincide with the other. This time, once they had climaxed, Phoenix said, "Enough squaw. I need to eat and so, I'm sure, do the four-footeds." He playfully slapped her bottom and got out of bed.

Shadow and Thea went wild when they both appeared in the lounge where they had spent the night. Phoenix prepared the dogs breakfast, as Skye grilled some eggs and bacon for the two-leggeds. Once replete, they fought the desire to take to their bed again and decided to take the patient dogs for a long walk in the forest.

"Wrap up warm, Skye. It's chilly out there this morning," Phoenix said, when he came in from the small yard by his cabin.

"I don't really have anything. Remember, we departed rapidly from home."

"Good point. Take one of my jackets from the closet."

Skye opened the closet door. She was not surprised to find few clothes inside. She did find, hanging proudly on a hanger, the loincloth she had seen him wear the first few times he had appeared. She pulled it out with glee.

"When we get back, you wear this when you shag me." She held it up and looked at him with seductive eyes.

Phoenix burst out laughing. "Shag! You are kidding me. That's brilliant. I'm not sure a Cherokee warrior ever had a shag before."

"They had about eight last night alone." She grabbed his groin again. "Perhaps you could wear that feather thing too and strap your bow across your back next time?" As an after thought she added, "Where is it?"

"In the back of the truck."

"Do you ever use it?"

"Not so much these days. I used to when I was a kid. When I first saw you I was out camping with Shadow. I'd use it occasionally to hunt the odd thing for the pot. These days all my food comes from Publix, which suits me just fine. Now I use it for protection."

"Don't you have a gun for that?"

"No. I don't like guns. But there is a stun gun in the truck for anaesthetising any frisky patients."

"So you hate guns. How wonderfully British." She leaned up and kissed him on the cheek. As she did so her right leg kicked up. "You must be pretty good with the bow, if you are prepared to stake your life on it."

"I'm okay."

"Show me. Bring it with us. Shame you can't wear the loincloth and feather too."

"It's too cold. It's summer gear. Anyway, we'd never get out the door."

Skye considered that option, and then looked at the expectant dogs. "Good point."

She slipped on the jacket she'd chosen and snuggled into the aroma of the man who'd worn it. She took his offered hand and they stepped out into the yard. Phoenix grabbed the bow from the pick-up and strapped it across his back, and then they walked into the forest. It was a glorious morning with dappled sunlight shining through the near bare branches. They followed a trail he and Shadow knew well. Shadow led the way showing Thea all of his favourite haunts.

As they walked, they added some more strokes to the pictures they painted of their separate lives to date. In particular, Skye was fascinated about his Apache upbringing and the woman he was obviously devoted to, Shichu.

"I can't wait to meet her, Maba. That's what she called you wasn't it?"

"Yes."

Shadow spooked a squirrel that had been tempted out by the sunshine. Skye expected it to disappear up the nearest tree. Instead it scurried along the trail and hid behind Phoenix's legs. Shadow paid no attention to it, so

Thea followed his lead and chased him to the next place of interest.

"I've walked these trails for years and I have never seen so much wild life as I have today," Skye observed idly. "Look there are three more deer over there. I've seen chipmunks, raccoons, weasels, shrews and look, that is the third snake I've seen. There are birds everywhere. Usually you walk for hours and see nothing."

"They are always there. They just choose not to be seen," said Phoenix.

"But they don't hide from you, do they?"

"They certainly aren't afraid of me and I do seem to have an affinity with the animal kingdom. We've always kind of been there for each other."

Every moment she spent with him was a voyage of rediscovery. Skye could never have imagined how complete and happy she could feel. She stopped and pulled his arm. "Kiss me here, Yona," She gestured around her. "Kiss me surrounded by your four-footeds in your kingdom, no our kingdom. This is our land. All these animals are our people. Each and every one of their spirits is connected to our spirits."

She would not have said something like that forty-eight hours ago. She would have thought it a bit cranky. But the bond she now felt with Yona and the spirit world had been fused.

Phoenix said nothing. He just took her in his arms and did as she asked. Skye could have sworn the forest's chorus grew louder.

The kiss left her weak at the knees. She considered ripping his clothes off and having her way with him again on the damp forest floor. She resisted the temptation, but needed to move out of the moment. With her arms still around him she managed to say, albeit with a sexually aroused rasp to her voice, "How good are you with this weapon?" She pulled one end of the bow.

He exploded with laughter at the unintended innuendo. "I've never had any complaints."

Skye beat his chest. "You horror. You know I didn't mean that."

"I'll show you, if you like?"

Phoenix released the bow from his back and dexterously withdrew an arrow from the quiver. He looked around quickly and settled on a large gnarl of wood on a tree trunk about thirty yards away. "There, see that lump on the tree?" He pointed to the tree trunk.

"It's tiny, my hand is bigger."

Phoenix shrugged. It was a still morning. There was no wind to affect the flight. It would be an easy shot. He loaded the arrow against the knocking point. Raised it to head height and drew the bowstring back past his ear. The bow's limbs creaked as they strained beneath his strength. He took aim and flicked his fingers away to release the arrow at its intended target. There was a twang, a whoosh of air and a thwack as the arrowhead embedded in the lump of wood.

"Wow! That's impressive."

"Actually, not really. It gets interesting when the wind is blowing. At that distance the wind would barely affect the flight. A bit further, on a windy day, I might miss."

" I don't think you've ever missed."

They walked over to retrieve the arrow. "I've spent a lot of time making these little babies. They are proper Apache warheads!" He cut the arrowhead out of the tree with a small knife he had in his pocket. Cleaned it off and slipped it back into his quiver.

"Used to kill murdering, raping palefaces." She giggled. "Can you do it riding bareback on a great white stallion, whilst galloping along the crest of a hill?"

"Of course."

"Damn you, Yona! Now I feel all horny again. Take

me back to your tepee."

TWENTY

They had all returned. The father had come back and the man with long hair had driven into the drive in his green pick-up truck with the girl. The dogs had jumped out of the back and bounded up to the front door, which opened to let them in. The girl's mother stood and watched them run past. She then embraced her daughter and her boyfriend.

Twenty minutes later the boyfriend had left again with his dog.

Amir was suddenly afraid. He knew he was finally going to have to be proactive. Finally, he would have to threaten people instead of simply imagining his role as one of Allah's foot soldiers. At the same time he became sexually aroused at the idea of controlling the girl, who was now defenceless without her boyfriend.

Mohammed had been prepared to kill the longhaired man, when his sudden departure had taken him by surprise. It was a break he could not have hoped for. He had been a potential problem.

"Okay, we take them now before he returns," Mohammed said to Amir.

Initially Amir did not respond. Mohammed prodded him with a 9-mm handgun. "Come on, we are on." He handed Amir the weapon. Amir nodded and took it.

Mohammed put the assault rifle that he had been cleaning on the rear seat. He removed a second 9-mm handgun from inside his coat. He double checked it for ammunition and slipped it back inside. "Go, park in the drive outside the house," he said to Amir.

Amir nervously started the Honda's engine and eased it into drive. He gently rolled the two hundred yards to the house, drove through the gates and parked in front of the steps that led to the front door.

*

"I'm sorry, darling, Caroline said it should only take a couple of hours. She needs me at the operation." For the first time in his life Phoenix did not want to go and help an animal. Rather, he did not want to leave Skye at that precise moment.

"Don't be silly. I will still be here later. Anyway, I need to tell Mum everything you have done to me." She had a wicked grin on her face.

Phoenix looked at her. He was pretty sure she was joking but, on the other hand, Skye had told him about Missy's novels and he had read a few pages of her latest book. It was a modern world and he was sure Skye's mom was at the cutting edge of the new epoch. He would not have been at all surprised if Skye were to share all her secrets with her mother. Skye and Missy's relationship was nothing like the one he enjoyed with Shichu.

"It's okay, I'm only kidding you." Skye loved that she could shock him so easily. "Now go. The sick deer needs you. Just call before you leave and I'll have some food ready for you when get back."

Skye leaned up and kissed him.

Shadow looked at Thea and then at Phoenix. He looked once again at Thea and then followed him out the door and jumped into the cab.

Missy stepped out of the house with Thea and waved

them goodbye with Skye at her side. Shadow peered out of the rear window at the three girls.

He whimpered by Phoenix's side. It was not really a noise he'd heard him make before. Puzzled, he looked across at the dog. Shadow returned his stare and then looked out once more and barked.

Phoenix took the display to mean he was lovesick. Something he later regretted.

*

The doorbell rang.

"I'll get it," Skye called to her mother. Her father did not answer the doorbell. She had no idea why, but he never did.

As always Thea accompanied her to the front door, curious to see who or what had made the noise. She could see two figures distorted by the frosted glass in the imposing entrance. She did not check who was there through the peephole provided. She never did, there had not been a crime registered in their immediate neighbourhood since they had arrived from England. A second later she wished she had.

Before she could speak to the two men standing before her, the blond haired one raised a gun to her face and calmly said, "Not a word." His voice was not threatening. In fact he was smiling.

By his side a slightly shorter, dark haired man looked less relaxed.

Skye was not afraid. Her chin rose defiantly. Without being asked she raised her hands in the air. Bizarrely she wondered why, had she watched too much cop TV? The man gestured with the gun for her to go into the house.

"Where are your parents?" he asked, again smiling

and unthreateningly.

Thea looked at the gun. It meant nothing to her. She had never seen such a thing before, and the man sounded friendly. So as Skye turned, she followed.

Walking to the kitchen, with Thea by her side, a sudden shiver worked down Skye's spine as she realised why she had been reunited with Yona and the others. How had the legend put it? The taking of their lives had been violent, an inappropriate end to life on their spirits' preordained paths. For the first time she was apprehensive. But it was not for her safety. The apprehension slowly turned to panic as she realised that she might be ripped apart from him after such a short time. As quickly as this dread had taken her it too was replaced by another emotion, something she had never experienced before. A confidence and serenity flooded through her. These men could not hurt her. Her spirit had survived centuries along with that of her soul mate. Death could only interrupt their journey.

It was a fine and noble thought that was instantly dispelled when the smiling one pistol-whipped Missy across the face as they entered the kitchen. Thea growled. He kicked her. She whimpered and ran out of the room.

Skye flew at the grinning bastard. She received the same treatment. Then she held her mother in her arms. Missy was in total shock. She had seen none of it coming. Blood was running down her cheek from where the gun had broken the skin.

"You bastard. What the hell do you think you are doing?" Skye's dark eyes bore into the man she knew to be her enemy. Hatred and anger had taken over every other emotion. At the same time she was profoundly aware that the equanimity her spirit gave her may not be sufficient to protect her mother. A little of her resentment became tinged with fear for Missy and Thea.

At that point her father walked into the room with

Thea trailing behind him. He had heard the commotion from his office, and then Thea had scurried in with her tail between her legs.

"What's going on?" he asked sternly.

Then he saw his wife and daughter embracing along with the blood, which was now on both their faces.

"Bloody hell! What do you think...?"

His protestation was interrupted and greeted by a punch to the gut that knocked the wind out of him. Despite that, he went to attack the man who had delivered the blow. At which point he put the gun to Missy's temple.

"Stay there or I shoot her." He was no longer smiling.

Thea was growling again but not advancing on the intruder.

"And shut that dog up or I'll shoot it."

Alarmed, Skye leapt to Thea's side and calmed her. "It's okay, girl. Don't worry. It's okay." She stroked her near white fur. It had the desired affect.

Skye looked up at the one that spoke all the time. She wanted to rip his throat out for what he had done to her family.

"What do you want with us?" she hissed in a voice she hardly recognised.

"You'll find out. You are coming with us. All of you, including that fucking mutt." He gestured towards the door with his gun.

"What if we refuse?" she hissed at him again.

"I'll shoot your dog. Now, get a fucking move on!" He yelled. "Hang on. Whose bag is this?" He held up a handbag, which was sitting on the kitchen table.

"It's mine," said Skye.

He emptied the contents onto the table and rummaged through them. Satisfied, he removed the cell phone, repacked the rest and threw it at Skye. "Bring it."

Amir watched the proceedings without uttering a

word. The violence towards the girls had given him an erection. He grabbed Missy by the hair and with a gun to her head led her outside to the waiting minivan. Skye followed, leading Thea. Tristan brought up the rear with the pistol in his back propelling him forward.

*

It had been a tricky operation. Some damned hunter had hit the deer with a crossbow bolt. It was a bad shot, close to the heart but not lethal. He was a young fit buck and managed to escape. The hunter, or hunters, had not bothered to pursue their prey, but left it to wander with an injury that they knew would have been fatal before too long. Luckily, a park ranger had happened across the distressed animal. He tranquilised him and called for the services of Caroline and her team.

It was not the hunting that angered Phoenix, though he no longer indulged in it, it was the disregard for the deer's welfare.

"Why don't the buggers do the job properly? If they are going to eat the poor thing, fine. But this is just fucking target practice." He used the word bugger a great deal now. It was Lady Caroline's favourite word.

"I know. But at least this fine chap is going to be okay." She pulled off the bloodstained gown and threw it in the bin. "Thanks for coming, Mowgli. It needed the two of us on this one."

"No problem." He removed his own gown and began to wash his hands and arms clean.

"So, how'd it go with my best friend?" Caroline had been dying to ask for the last three hours, but had been too busy saving the four-footed's life.

Phoenix grinned but didn't answer.

"Come on, you bugger, tell me. Is she pregnant yet?"

"Not through lack of trying." The grin grew even wider.

"Good boy."

"I'm not a dog."

"Yes you are. All men are, and I've been watching you for a long time, remember."

He shrugged. "Well, I'm a one woman dog now."

"Seriously, was it worth the wait?" She looked more imploringly into his eyes.

"Every second, every hour, day, month, year and century."

Caroline wanted to cry. It was the happiest she had ever felt for another person. Instead, she slapped him on the back. "You are a lucky bugger. Don't lose her this time. Now, get off back to her and both of you have a lovely Christmas."

Phoenix hugged her. "Thanks, you too. Let's all hook up straight after."

Caroline watched Phoenix and Shadow jump into the pick-up and drive away. She had no idea why, but she felt uneasy about something.

*

Shadow jumped out of the cab and flew towards the front door. Skye's Mini was parked in the driveway with Tristan's BMW next to it. The lights were on in the house and the front door was wide open.

As he walked through the door he shouted, "Hi, y'all," in the manner he'd become accustomed to in the South. There was no response. "Hi, anyone home?" he shouted again. But there was still nothing.

Shadow was scampering from room to room in

search of Thea getting progressively more perplexed.

Phoenix began a similar search of the premises. The stove was still on with some enticing aromas emanating from it. Papers lay strewn across Tristan's desk. He went to the garage to see if Missy's car was there. It was. He walked down to the dock to see if they had gone out on the pontoon boat. It was still there.

He dialled Skye's number on his cell phone. It went straight to answer phone. He listened to the voice that was both known and new to him and replied to the message, "Hi, Skye. Where are you guys? Anyway, I'm back. Hope to see you in a minute or two. Love you."

He pressed End Call. He looked up at the house in the distance, lit up, warm and inviting. A shiver went down his spine. He began to run towards it.

This time his search was more frantic but no more productive. He tried to be analytical. Had they taken anything with them, or packed any bags? He didn't have a clue what bags they had. Winter coats? He'd seen them. Damn, they were still hanging on the coat-stand by the front door. He searched for a message on tables, desks and in Skye's studio. Nothing. He went to the kitchen for the third time, surely, something. There was. Three drops of fresh blood on the worktop and two on the floor. He walked towards the front door. There was a drop by the coat stand he'd looked at earlier and another on the porch.

At that moment Phoenix knew why they had been brought together again. Skye's life, Newadi's life was in danger once more. But he also knew that she was not dead. He would have sensed it, as if his own heart had stopped beating. He knew that he had to save her. Surely they could not be ripped apart again?

He tried Sky's phone for a second time. He got the same pre-recorded message. 'Skye could not come to the phone at the moment.' He called Caroline, and then he called Brad.

Thea was locked in the luggage space. Amir drove and Mohammed sat in the front with the gun trained on his prisoners. He didn't speak. He took Skye's cell out of his pocket, looked at the contacts and then he turned it off before putting it back in his pocket.

Amir pulled up outside the condominium. He scanned the street. It was quiet. He removed his own gun from his jacket pocket and then got out of the vehicle, opened the rear door and grabbed a handful of Skye's hair and dragged her out.

"You too, whore," he whispered to Missy.

Mohammed kept his handgun trained on Tristan.

Missy eased herself out of the van and stood next to Skye. Both were taller than Amir. Both looked at him malevolently.

He transferred his attention to Missy, grabbing her arm and then her hair, inflicting as much pain as he could. "You, get the dog out of the back. Anything funny and I'll shoot it, and your fucking mother."

Skye opened the tailgate and allowed Thea to jump out. "It's okay, Thea. Come on, old girl." The dog reluctantly went to her side.

"Inside." He dragged Missy as he pointed his gun at Thea.

The door opened as they approached the condo. Two more men, both swarthy in complexion, grabbed the girls and hauled them towards a room at the rear of the condo. They pushed them and the dog inside, and then locked the door.

Mohammed followed them into the condo with

223

Tristan. He sat him in a chair by the front door, as one of the brothers locked it.

"Your job is to make sure those two do as we ask." He punched Tristan hard on the nose. "Didn't I mention to nod when you understand?" He laughed and hit him again.

Inside the girls could hear every word and the sound of fist on crunching bone as Tristan's nose shattered.

Mohammed rained a few more blows on him to make his point and increase the sound effects for the listening women.

"Do you understand?"

Tristan nodded.

"Good. You can stay with them but you cannot talk. Any of you." He raised his voice so the others could hear. "If I hear a sound, both of your women will get seriously abused. Do you understand?" Mohammed's delivery left now doubt in Tristan's mind what abused meant.

"Yes."

The girls heard another crack as Tristan was struck.

"I said nod, you fucking imbecile."

He dragged him to his feet as one of the others unlocked the bedroom door. And then he shoved him in with the rest of his family. "Not a sound, remember?" A malicious smirk appeared on his face.

Missy jumped up to catch her husband as he fell, bloodied, to the floor. She was about to protest when Tristan covered her mouth with his hand and shook his head.

Mohammed looked straight at Skye expecting to see fear in her eyes. Her chin raised an inch and he could have sworn she was half-smiling. He did not know what the expression in her eyes was, but it was not fear.

He closed the door, locked and bolted it. He looked at the brothers, then back at the door. The girl alone would outwit them. He knew he would have to keep a very tight

224

rein on the operation from here on. He also knew that if he were to stand any chance of walking away from this without being caught, his fellow jihadists would have to be martyred.

He looked at his watch. It would be Christmas Day soon. It would all be over inside twenty-four hours and he would be on his way home to New York. Paradise would have to wait.

*

It took less that an hour for both Caroline and Brad to arrive at Skye's home. Phoenix was waiting for them at the door.

"How long do you think they have been gone?" Brad asked.

"All the lights were on when I arrived. It had been dark about an hour, so I would say less than two hours."

"What else have you found?" enquired Caroline.

"Not much. Skye's bag is gone, but nothing much else. But what do I know? I hardly know this house and its contents. Valuables, papers, they may have taken something, who knows?"

"If they wanted to take stuff, valuables and other things, why take the people? I reckon that whoever it was, they only wanted the people." Brad was thinking out loud.

"You can't find Thea either?" It was Caroline.

"No. They took her too. If they hadn't, Shadow would have found her scent and tracked her down. I'm sure of that," offered Phoenix.

"We should call the police," said Caroline.

Brad replied, "Yeah, we could call, but it's pointless. They won't start a missing persons search after just two hours, especially for three adults with no real evidence of kidnapping. And why would they? They'd just suggest that they had gone for a walk with Thea."

Phoenix took it up, "Brad's right. They won't do anything on the hunch of a few Cherokee Indians who claim they know they've been abducted because they are old spirits."

Caroline understood their point, but said, "You are probably right, but I am going to call anyway. I'll do it now. I'll try and make it sound more believable." She took her cell from her pocket and dialled. When someone answered she left the room to talk.

Brad and Phoenix stood in silence for a while. Eventually Brad spoke, "So this is it. Why we are all here. We have to stop it happening again, son"

Phoenix nodded.

Caroline heard what Brad said as she walked in. "We will get her back, Mowgli. I want to see those twelve kids."

Phoenix had to smile. "What about the cops?"

"Terribly polite. Call back in forty-eight hours."

Phoenix shrugged.

"Okay, put the coffee on, Caroline. This is going to be a long night. We need to figure out why this is happening now? What the nature of the threat to Skye and her family is? And where she might be?" said Brad.

Caroline was eager to be doing something. She quickly found her way around the kitchen and soon had a pot of coffee brewing.

They sat around the kitchen table warming their hands on mugs of freshly brewed coffee.

Brad started. "Why now? After nearly two hundred years."

Phoenix replied, "Because Skye's in danger."

"Agreed, but it's really her spirit that is being threatened. All of our spirits have come back for some reason. That is what Phoenix believes," said Caroline.

"Yeah, but believe and know are two different things. We are making a number of assumptions here based on little known fact. We have convinced ourselves that on the basis of one recorded event at Anaguluskee we are all old reincarnated spirits. Maybe the Trail of Tears incident was just another event on her journey, our journey," Brad said.

"Are you saying you are not convinced?" Caroline was surprised at what she heard.

"No, no, not at all, Caroline. You know I'm a believer. But to anyone who doesn't see it our way, Phoenix just met some hot chick by the lake and then she disappeared. If we are right, there is a reason why she disappeared that is fundamental to why we have come back here." Brad was trying hard to explain himself to Caroline.

Phoenix interjected, "I think what Brad means is that however many times we have existed in physical form, for us all to be together again now there is a threat that our spirits need to deal with. And, as with the Trail of Tears, we face a violent and an inappropriate end to our lives unless we can figure out what our spirits are destined to do."

"Okay, but what could that be?" Caroline asked.

"Fuck knows!" Phoenix was getting frustrated.

"Let's attack it a different way, son." Brad put a hand on Phoenix's shoulder. "Your spirits live here, beneath the lake in the ancient burial grounds. We know it is here that you were murdered before. These are Cherokee lands and the threat back then was to our lands and the Cherokee nation. We have come back to the exact same spot. The first time history recorded these lands being threatened by infiltrators was when the Spanish conquistadores came in the sixteenth century. There will have been times before that. You can rest assured. The

Spanish raped and pillaged. The other night, when we first met Skye, she told us about places on the lake she was drawn to that she couldn't explain. One was towards Dahlonega, on the Chestatee River, wasn't it? Dahlonega, gold, the Spanish found it there. Perhaps the place Skye is drawn to could be linked to something the Spanish did in the sixteenth century. Other places she has a strong affinity with may have witnessed different threats before modern history began to record it. Things that have only been passed down through our own legends or have been forgotten about. If so, it is all happening around this lake and the rivers that flow through it."

"You mentioned Dahlonega. Could it be anything to do with gold?" wondered Caroline.

Phoenix pondered the idea. "I can't see why. There's no real gold in these parts anymore, and there hasn't been for hundreds of years. Not only that, it has never had any value to the Cherokee. Why would we want to protect it?"

"No. It's the lake." Brad stood up and started pacing. "The Cherokee nation no longer really exists in these parts. Sure, up in the Great Smoky Mountains there is a reservation, but not down here anymore. But these are Cherokee lands and have been Cherokee lands for thousands of years. No matter who inhabits this countryside, it is Cherokee." He stopped pacing and stared at Phoenix and Caroline. "Don't you see? It is our lands that are threatened. They were threatened before and some of us died for them. Who knows? Maybe we died on a number of occasions protecting our lands."

Phoenix took up the thread. "The Lake, the Chattahoochee, the Chestatee and all the land surrounding them. How would you threaten them?"

"You would blow up Buford Dam," Caroline interjected.

"Atlanta was built on Cherokee lands. It would

drown beneath the torrent that would be unleashed when the dam burst," Brad finally said.

"Terrorism," Phoenix finished their thought process.

All three sat in silence working out the ramifications of what they had concluded. Finally, Caroline said, "It would be catastrophic."

"Hell!" A sudden realisation hit Phoenix. "Skye did not tell you where she has been working, did she?"

"No, but she told me what she did. Let me guess. She has been working at Buford Dam," said Brad.

"She's been doing a structural survey there." Phoenix looked into the eyes of the others. "Is that it?"

Brad nodded.

"We should call the police again, Homeland Security, whoever," Caroline said.

"And tell them what? A bunch of old Cherokees believe that they have been reincarnated to stop an act of terrorism," Brad added in frustration.

"We must at least warn them, guys."

"You're right, both of you. Caroline, call the cops anyway," said Phoenix.

She was on her feet and out of the door, dialling as she left.

"They are going to laugh in her face, aren't they?" Phoenix asked Brad.

"Yeah, son, and that's why we are here."

"We haven't succeeded before, have we? The lands were taken from us," said Phoenix.

"No, we haven't. But the land never moved, we were taken from it and we allowed our lands to be disfigured and pillaged by others, but they are still Cherokee lands and always will be. What these terrorists propose to do to them is abhorrent, not to mention what they want to do to the people living here."

Caroline came back in. She looked crestfallen.

"Well?" asked Phoenix.

"They were polite."

*

"What about the old man?" Nawaz asked Mohammed.

"I don't think we need him. The parents and the dog should be enough to persuade her," replied Mohammed. He took another sip of his coffee and a bite from his Egg McMuffin.

"What if he comes looking for them or he calls the cops?" It was Jamal.

"They won't care. They haven't been gone long enough and it will be over before they take any notice." He took another bite from the Egg McMuffin as Nawaz slurped the last vestiges of Coke from his own waxed paper cup.

Without wiping the dribble of the sugary soda from his chin, he asked, "What time do we blow the dam?"

"Midday, 12:00 exactly. Do you have everything you need ready?" asked Mohammed.

"Yeah." Jamal smirked.

"Okay. We will try and take out Buford at exactly the same time. By the time the waters reach Morgan's the inertia will be catastrophic," said Mohammed.

"When do we kill the parents?" Jamal whispered as a customer walked nearby on their way back to their car carrying bags of fast food and a tray of coffees and soda.

Mohammed grinned. "I thought you boys could take them to the old man's house by the Chattahoochee, en route to Morgan's Dam. Make sure they can't get out, including the old man, and they will all drown. Just a few more tragic victims of Allah's will." He was grinning, amused that their daughter's actions in attempting to save their lives would actually directly cause them. He though

230

he might mention it to her just before he killed her.

"Afterwards, do we meet up again?" enquired Nawaz.

Mohammed looked at him. There would be no afterwards for them. If they ever met again it would be in Paradise. "Yeah, back at your condo for a debriefing and a celebration."

"Won't it be under water?"

Mohammed tried not to stare in disbelief at the imbecile. He had pored over maps of the entire area with them all and discussed, with reference to relief maps, the areas of Metro Atlanta that would be affected. Lawrenceville was nowhere near the flood plain. "No, Jamal," he said patiently, "it will be fine."

He needed Christmas to come and go, so he could be free of these idiots. With that thought he remembered brother Amir, whom they had left guarding the prisoners whilst they went out to get some breakfast before their day's work began. It had been forty minutes and, though more trustworthy than the cretins he was talking to, there was something about his more recent behaviour that worried him. He had become fixated on the girl. His eyes never left her and they were filled with pure lust. Depending on how stupid he was, it was not beyond the bounds of possibilities that he had either fucked her by now or let her go.

"Come on, we need to get back," Mohammed said.

When he got back he intended to tie up the prisoners and cover their heads with sacks or bags. Purely so Amir could not see the girl's face. He should have done it earlier. After all, that is what terrorists did. He'd seen the movies and watched Homeland. He was angry with himself that he had not. He hadn't even tied them up.

As soon as the others had left the condo to go to McDonalds Amir opened the door to check on the girl. He had positioned himself near the door from the second

Mohammed had issued the implied threat to rape the girls if they made a sound. There he had sat, willing one of them to whisper or make a noise. There had been nothing but silence.

He stood in the doorway with three bottles of water in one hand and an Uzi submachine gun in the other. The girls were sitting on the bed. At the sight of the gun they eased back against the headboard. Tristan was standing near the boarded window. He had been looking for a weakness in the barricade.

Amir tossed the bottles on the bed as he stared at Skye. She was casually dressed in jeans and a sweater, but all he could see were her curves beneath. A picture of her in a bikini filled his head.

Suddenly he was aware of movement in the corner of his eye. He swung the Uzi to cover the imagined attack. It was only Tristan stepping to the bed to retrieve a bottle of water. At the sudden movement of the gun he stopped in his tracks and raised his hands.

"Sorry," he said without thinking.

"You were told to be quiet. You were told what would happen." Amir's pulse was racing. This was his chance. Demons deep within him said it was all right. She was an infidel whore. He would not be committing a sin. Allah would not care. His wife would not know. Soon the bitches would be dead anyway.

"You, come here." He gestured to Skye.

"Fuck off!" She fired back at him. Her tone was defiant and full of confidence.

Skye's mind had not been idle. The two men gave them no reason why they had been abducted. Several hours had passed and Skye had been through the same thought processes that Phoenix and the others had. She knew why their Cherokee spirits had returned and been reunited. She knew that it was their lands that were under threat; she knew that she was the one who was being specifically targeted and not her parents. However, she knew they would be used to persuade her to bend to their will. She knew what her value to these men was. She knew that until they had destroyed the Cherokee lands they would not kill her. She knew that once that had been achieved, her death, the death of her parents and beautiful dog was inevitable. The legends had prepared her for this moment. She was part of those legends, but she was not living in the past. She was living now. The spirits of her past had merely prepared her for this moment. She had watched a movie entitled I am Legend. For some reason the title came to her at that moment. I am, it was in the present tense, not the future or the past. The legends she had read about still existed in the here and now, and they were all part of it. I am legend rang in her ears. She was not afraid of death. She knew Phoenix and the others would have figured it out too. If necessary they would also die defending their Cherokee lands.

"Didn't you hear me? Fuck off, I said." There was venom in her voice this time. "I know what you bastards want and you need me. So fuck off and leave us alone." She stood up and walked towards Amir, almost threateningly.

Amir was taken aback. He had not expected such a reaction. His arousal was instantly deflated. Fifteen seconds earlier he was about to rape the girl. He may even have raped her mother as well, but now his resolve disappeared.

He backed out of the door and slammed it shut, anxious to relock it before she said anything else.

"And what's more, we are going to talk to each other, you shit." The words faded as he closed the door.

He stepped back, astonished at the attack. He could hear them whispering. He put his ear close to the door and strained to hear what they were saying. It was too muted. He wanted to stop them but he was scared to open

233

the door. He stepped away to the far side of the room.

Inside, Skye explained what was going on to her folks and the inevitable conclusion she had come to about the terrorist's intention to destroy the dam.

"You won't do it, will you, darlin'?" Missy said, after listening to everything Skye had said. She was Skye's mother and she was Cherokee. It was more of an instruction than a question.

"I can't, Mummy. You know that. I will do everything in my power to stop them. Phoenix and the others will too."

"We are here purely to coerce you, then," stated Tristan.

"And Thea, they will use her too." Skye stroked the faithful dog that lay at her side. "You know I can't, Daddy. What they propose to do will kill thousands of people," then she added, "and animals too."

Missy held her husband's hand. He embraced her and she sank her face into his shoulder and began to weep. Skye touched her arm. She did not know what to say.

Her dad broke the silence. "Bloody Cherokee Indians. You'll be the death of me."

Missy's tears turned to a smile. She raised her head and kissed him passionately on the lips. "Oh heck, honey. I love you. You don't deserve all this."

He pulled his daughter into the embrace. "No, I don't deserve either of you. But if I am about to die for the cause, tell me I get to come back in another life and be with you all again."

"Yes, Daddy, you will. But we haven't finished with this life yet, any of us. We need to be brave. I've got a lot of living to do with that long haired youth, as you called him to Mum behind my back the other night." She smiled affectionately at her father.

"You will get to live with him, if we have anything to do with it, Skye. Do what you need to do. All those people must live. We are not part of the equation. We can look after ourselves."

Skye loved her father. His strength at this moment made her adore him. He had offered his life unequivocally for others. He was a good man. She crushed herself against him and hugged him.

"Thank you, Daddy. When we get out of this we are going to delve into your family history. There is Cherokee blood in there somewhere."

Tristan smiled. "Who knows? Perhaps there is, Skye."

She could hear the others returning and their raised voices. The leader, the blond man, was angry.

She could hear the locks being turned and the bolts pulled back. He stepped inside with Amir, looking sheepish, behind him.

"It appears you can't do something as simple as keeping quiet."

He was holding ropes, duct tape and canvas bags in his hand. He bent down and put them on the bed. As he came up he struck Missy hard across the face.

"Don't think we won't hurt you. It was not an idle threat." Looking at Skye, he added, "We will degrade your mother later, but we have things to do first. Seeing that you won't be quiet, we will have to shut you up."

He grabbed Missy. She tensed against his touch, but Skye saw the steel in her eyes. No matter what, she knew that her wonderful mother would accept whatever terrible things these obnoxious creatures did to her. As she knew she would herself.

They tied Missy's hands and legs brutally with rope and slapped a strip of duct tape across her mouth. The blond one then placed the bag over her head. He squeezed her breasts hard as he stared into Skye's eyes. A muffled squeal of pain came from beneath the sack. He smirked maliciously at Skye.

Skye watched her father's reaction. He tensed and took one step towards his wife's abuser. Jamal intercepted his movement by putting an assault rifle to his temple.

"One more step and I'll do her right here in front of you," Mohammed said.

Tristan stopped. Skye could see a vein pulse above his eyebrow as he seethed with anger.

To add insult to injury Mohammed punched Missy hard in the stomach. She doubled and fell to her knees. The muffled expulsion of breath was accompanied by the crack of the rifle butt hitting Tristan's chin as he advanced on her attacker.

It was a hard blow that temporarily stunned him, and then he fell to the floor unconscious.

Skye's resolve waned momentarily. She had to remind herself what was at stake. Their lives were insignificant compared to potential slaughter these people proposed to inflict. If she was going to stop them she needed to bide her time and pick the right moment.

She watched anxiously as her father came round. Still disorientated, he was also bound and gagged with a sack over his head.

Skye sensed Thea trembling by her side. She stroked her reassuringly. "It's okay, girl. These nasty men won't harm you."

Amir grabbed her arm and pulled her away from Thea. He kicked out at the dog that deftly avoided the blow. Her whimpers turned to snarls as she watched her mistress being dragged from the room.

The door slammed closed. Thea scratched ferociously at the barrier between her and Skye. She barked and howled again.

Soothing sounds issued from beneath one of the sacks. After several more attacks on the door the calming sounds finally eased her anxiety. With a final whimper she investigated the noise from beneath the sack with her nose. Three sniffs later she had pulled the sack off Missy's head. Three licks later, she had calmed down. She wondered why the licks had not generated their usual cuddle, so she licked some more.

Despite their desperate situation, the maniacal basting Thea was giving her made her giggle. After a while Thea nestled next to her with her head on her lap. When Skye was not there, Missy always took her place.

Missy wondered if she could get Thea to take off Tristan's sack. She made gestures and noises towards him, but Thea was happy on Missy's lap and appeared in no hurry to move.

Instead, she listened to hear what was happening outside the room. All she could hear was talking, and then a loud slap followed by even louder vehement expletives.

Thea was instantly on her feet, barking at the door once again. Missy smiled inwardly. What spirit her daughter possessed. And what an eclectic mix of profanities she possessed!

TWENTY-ONE

"So, where do we start? Where could they have taken them?" asked Caroline.

"The dam. That is their target. They must have gone there, or will be going there when they are ready," replied Phoenix.

"If they went straight to the dam, we have to get over there and try and stop them," added Brad.

"What weapons do we have?" It was Phoenix again.

"I've brought my hunting rifle. It's old and so am I, but I was good with it once, and my knife. I always have my knife. Oh, and this." Brad removed a 9-mm handgun from his waistband. "I know," he held up his hands, "it's not very Cherokee, but I am ex-military."

"I don't have anything. I'm British, we don't do guns," said Caroline.

Phoenix nodded. Skye had said something similar to him. "I've only got the stun gun, but I have my bow."

"Anything in the house?" asked Brad.

"No, it's a British household, they keep their weapons in the military. There won't be anything."

"So we have what we have and we don't know what the hell we are going up against." Brad sounded a tad frustrated.

"But they don't know we are coming. An invisible foe is the most dangerous." Shadow licked his hand as he spoke. "We've got Shadow too." He smiled.

"Okay, let's get going. It's still dark, but there is

enough moonlight to see by. If we want stealth to be our ally, I suggest we park away from the dam and approach on foot." Brad looked at the other two. "What do we know about the dam and its surroundings?"

Phoenix began, "Not a hell of a lot. I've been into the park a couple of times. I can remember the approach to the powerhouse, which is what they will have to blow up to get maximum effect. It will channel the water down through a canyon they've cut below the powerhouse. The canyon will give a Venturi effect that will accelerate the initial flow to cause mayhem."

"Are we sure they will hit the powerhouse. Why not just put charges against the dam from the lake side?" Brad enquired.

"They may do that too. But I think they want to blow the dam up from the inside. That is why they want Skye. She can get them into the places their explosives will be most effective," explained Phoenix.

"The powerhouse it is then." Brad turned to Caroline. "Can you use this?" He passed her the handgun.

"No, I haven't got a clue." She looked aghast at the weapon being offered to her. "All I've ever used is the stun gun. If I have to put an animal down I use an injection."

"Come with me."

Brad led her out to the front yard. In the driveway he handed the 9-mm to Caroline. She took it hesitatingly. "Stand in front of the garage door and pick a small area to hit. Aim at the handle."

"What about the noise? The neighbours," she asked.

"Fuck the neighbours. They hear some gunshots; we may get the damned cops attention. And they may give some credence to your phone calls. Go on squeeze the trigger, real slow now."

Caroline did as she was asked. She missed the handle by two yards.

"Okay give it to me. Like this." He stood, legs apart, and held the weapon in both hands in front of his face and aimed at the door handle. "It has two pressures. Squeeze and pull. It hardly kicks at all. It shouldn't feel much different to the stun gun."

He squeezed to take the slack out of the mechanism then fired once. A hole appeared two inches to the right of the handle.

"You try." He passed the gun back to her.

This time Caroline was more relaxed. She put a hole through the garage door eighteen inches from her intended target.

"Good. Now empty the magazine into the door and your training is over."

Caroline was smiling when she had finished. She walked up to the ruined garage door. "Skye's parents won't be too pleased."

"I can assure you they won't care, if they are still alive."

They turned to see Phoenix loading some gear into the rear of the pick-up. "Come on. We have work to do," he called over to them.

Fifteen minutes later they parked the pick-up in the woods half a mile form the dam. Shadow leapt from the rear of the truck and instantly started to sniff the surrounding countryside. Phoenix slung his bow and quiver across his back as he watched Shadow, not expecting but hoping that he might pick up Thea's scent.

Shadow tried his best, but there was nothing. He knew from the Frisbee that Phoenix had asked him to sniff what his job was to be. Frustrated, he spread his search wider until Phoenix called him to heel.

"Come on, boy, we will find her, you have done just fine," he said to the frustrated hound as he stroked his fur. It was slightly damp. A drizzle had started to penetrate the cover of the forest.

They made their way through the trees towards the park that bordered the powerhouse. As usual a menagerie of wildlife came to watch the spirits that walked amongst them. Unafraid, some followed curious about their purpose.

Ten minutes later they were on the edge of the grassed area that looked up to the dam and down to the Chattahoochee River. There were no cars in the car park or any other sign of life. Phoenix circumnavigated the park towards the gatehouse. He knew it was manned 24/7. He held up the night-vision binoculars he had brought from the pick-up, which had been hanging from his neck, and trained them on the hut by the entrance. The old guard sat watching a TV. He raised a cup of coffee to his lips and took a bite from the sandwich by his side. Phoenix scanned the compound. The goats Skye had told him about were lying down unperturbed on the grass near the main building. Nothing looked out of place. Nothing felt wrong with the scene. Phoenix knew they were not here. He felt sure that Shadow would have been more excited if Thea was anywhere in the vicinity. He lowered the glasses from his eyes.

"They're not here yet, are they?" he said to Shadow.

As if given a direct order, Shadow trotted over to the entrance and began to sniff every last inch of the area. The old man just watched TV and ate his snack. After a few minutes Shadow returned, a little hangdog and obviously disappointed.

"Okay, boy. We just wait. She'll be here soon," he whispered.

They made their way back to the others.

"Nothing, not yet," he said in answer to their enquiring looks.

"Could they have approached from the lake, son? Come in the back door, so to speak," suggested Brad.

"Possible. Shadow and I will check the fence that

241

borders the compound on the lakeside. In fact we will check all the way around. You guys watch the entrance. Call my cell if anyone comes near."

Phoenix estimated it would take about forty-five minutes for Shadow to check the entire perimeter. He was confident he would pick up Thea's scent if she had been anywhere near the compound's fence.

Forty minutes later he rejoined his friends. "No. They are definitely not here yet."

"What's the time?" asked Caroline.

Phoenix glanced at his watch. "Three twenty-four," he said.

"Happy Christmas," she said. "I'd forgotten with all this," she added.

Phoenix looked at Brad. They both realised at the same time the significance of the two words. Since 9/11, December 25th had held another significance to the Western World. It had become a day to fear as well as rejoice. A day that certain factions had promised to turn into a day of destruction. It had not happened yet, but each year threats and implied threats dampened the spirit of millions throughout the world.

"It will be today," Brad said.

Phoenix nodded agreement. "Yeah, makes sense."

Caroline shuddered at their thought process, but found it hard to disagree with their reasoning. "I'm going to call the police again."

"Sure, what is there to lose?" Brad shrugged.

The others listened to her conversation. This time she refused to be fobbed off by the cops.

"Happy Christmas to you too. This is a real threat. You need to take this seriously. I know it's Christmas Day and you have fewer crimes this day than any other in the year, but this is going to happen and it is going to happen today. No, listen you idiot. Sorry I didn't mean to be offensive. Christ, just send a fucking squad car to the

242

dam to keep an extra watch, that's all I'm asking. Thank you. I'm sorry I swore at you. Yes, I know it was wrong. I will not do it again. Thank you." She hung up.

"Well?"

"The clown said he'd send a vehicle out as soon as the next guy came on duty, and no, he wasn't polite. But neither was I."

Phoenix smiled. "Did he say what time they would send a car?"

"Nine o'clock, maybe. He wasn't exactly committing."

Brad was not surprised. "Even when, or if, they come they probably won't stay. They will be understaffed, take a cursory look and go away again. We've got this, son. Nobody else is going to be interested," said Brad. "Should we get nearer? Maybe park up in the car park? The pick-up has officialdom printed all over it. It won't look out of place."

Phoenix nodded. It would look perfectly natural parked near the front gates. "It would make us an obvious target. We don't know how many people we are dealing with here. An army might drive up to those gates, take us out as easy as pie and just drive through them."

"If there is an army, why do they need Skye? No, it's a small operation," said Brad. "Just a few guys and probably not suicide bombers. They want to walk away from this. Skye gives them that opportunity. If they go in all guns blazing they may blow the dam but they don't walk out."

"Okay, agreed, but we don't want to commit our resources in one place. I say we park it there and leave it empty. Skye will see it and it will tell her we are here. She knows the vehicle well now. I'll drape Shadow's blanket over the side so she is in no doubt that it's our truck. The one he lies on in the back. She knows that too and commented on the Apache design. It will give her

243

hope knowing we are nearby. She will be expecting us, but to see we are here will lift her spirits."

"Okay, makes sense," agreed Brad.

Caroline opened her mouth to speak, but nothing came out.

Phoenix noticed. "What is it, Caroline?"

"What exactly are we going to do when they come?" she asked.

Brad replied, "You, nothing. Last time you got involved it all went pear shaped. You use the gun only if you have to, and it will be obvious when that is. We..." Brad touched Phoenix's arm, "we will kill the cocksuckers."

Phoenix chuckled. "You asked weeks ago why Brad's spirit had come back with us. I think he just answered you."

*

Skye knew what they wanted, but she needed to hear them tell her. She needed to know exactly what the threat was and exactly the role they expected of her.

"Is this crunch time? When you tell me what this is all about?" She addressed the question to Mohammed.

"Yes. It is simple. You take us into the dam and the penstocks," the blond man said.

"Where you will set explosives?"

"Yes."

"You intend to slaughter thousands?"

"Yes."

"And this is in the name of Allah, I assume. Why do you think I will help you?"

"Because if you do not, we will kill your parents and your dog."

Skye looked into his intelligent eyes. He did not appear to be the archetypal fanatical terrorist, which the media would have you believe was hell-bent on destroying America. Damn it, he looked American and sounded American. Skye realised there was little point in trying to reason with him, or ask him to question his beliefs, or engage him in any rational conversation. She had already seen enough abuse of her parents to know he was beyond that.

Mohammed half-sensed what she was thinking. "We will do it anyway. If you help us, we will do it and you can all live."

"What makes you think we will be able to live with ourselves after we have been complicit in your diabolical slaughter?"

"I don't care if you can live with yourselves. But you can live. It's a simple choice. Live or die. If you choose to live, you can deal with your conscience later."

Skye knew that both she and her parents had already made the choice. She was also pretty sure that they would be killed regardless of whether she helped them or not. Alive she might be able to thwart their plans. She knew it was her destiny to at least try. She also knew that it was the destiny of her lover and their friends to attempt to halt this abomination. She knew they would be willing to die to stop this happening. She wondered about Thea and Shadow. The four-footeds were as much a part of this as they were. Strangely, her heart went out to them. They were dogs, but were their spirits aware of the threat that awaited them?

"What guarantee do I have that you will not harm my parents?"

"None."

"You piece of shit!"

Mohammed slapped her across the cheek. The blow drew blood from her lip and inside her mouth where her teeth had cut into the soft tissue. She spat out the blood, making sure it went on his shoe. He raised his hand to strike again.

"Stop. I will help you, but if you hurt my mother or my father you can go and fuck yourself."

Mohammed looked at the striking woman in front of him. She was worth ten of the fools he was about to commit this atrocity with. He looked over at Amir and saw the excitement in his usually dull eyes. She did not deserve the abuse Amir was imagining, even if she was an infidel. He suspected that her parents did not either. Not that he could care one way or the other, but he did want his mission to be successful. Mohammed was more driven by glory in this life than in the afterlife.

He laughed malignly at the girl who'd just spat on his shoe. He was not sure if he respected her or despised her, but he wanted her help. It just made it easier.

"Okay, we'll leave them alone. But if you try to double-cross me they will experience long, slow and agonising deaths."

Amir listened, disappointed at the words of placation he heard. He knew the parents and their daughter would all die. Before the girl died he would make sure he had something to remember her by, despite Mohammed's hollow words.

Skye knew they would be safe for the time being. She had bought some time. "What exactly do you want me to do?"

"Easy. You get us into the powerhouse and show us how to get into the penstocks."

"Then you blow up the dam?"

"Yes."

"How do I know you will let us go?"

"You don't. You have to trust me."

"Where will my parents be?"

"With two of my men."

"Will they be away from the floods?"

"Yes."

"What about Thea, my dog?"

"She will be with us. One final persuader should you change your mind."

"Afterwards, you will let us go?"

"Yes."

"When will all this happen?"

Mohammed looked at his watch. "Four hours time."

Skye nodded. She was not sure what she could do to stop them, but she would die trying. She prayed the others would be there to help her.

*

"Hey, Bert, Merry Christmas."

"Same to you, Jack. Anything happening this fine Christmas Day?"

Bert dropped his rucksack on the desk in Flowery Branch Police Station and went to the coffee machine to pour a brew.

"Not a lot. Some Brit nut-job keeps calling about some missing folks. Then she called saying they were hostages in a goddam terror plot. Bangin' on about blowing the dam. Pour me one of those. Just enough to keep me awake for a bit longer."

"Heard it all before," replied Bert. "Ever since 9/11 there is a terrorist on every other corner; on Christmas Day every corner. What did you say?"

"Said you'd swing by when you came on duty. Just go check it out. I had to log the calls. If you go, we've covered our asses."

"Okay, buddy. You off home now?"

"Will call in at my son's for breakfast. Then home, a

couple of hours horizontal and we are off to my daughter's." He quickly slurped the coffee and made his way to the door.

"Have a great day. My turn next year," Bert said.

"Ciao, and Bill will be in shortly. He called, he is running a bit late, if you could hold the fort till then. Harry has already left. He refuelled the car before he went. His only call out was to investigate some shots near the lake. He found nothing. Hunters I guess. "

"Sure, no problomo. Enjoy your day," Bert said, as Jack stepped through the front door.

*

Phoenix drove the pick-up into the car park and left it in full view of any approaching vehicle. This time Shadow rode in the cab with him. The others kept watch, one on the road and one on the lake. It was still quiet.

Phoenix laid his blanket over the side of the rear storage bed. He walked up to the gatehouse with Shadow still sniffing enthusiastically at his side. He tapped on the window.

The guard opened the door to his post. Smiling, he said, "Merry Christmas." It was his first of the day. He always enjoyed the first. By the end of the day he would be bored with Merry Christmases. "You're up good'n early, partner. How can I help?"

"Merry Christmas to you too, sir." Phoenix flashed his Georgia Department of Natural Resources ID card. "We've had a report of an injured deer in these parts. Have you seen or heard anything during the night, sir?"

"Been quiet as a morgue all night."

It gave the answer to what Phoenix's next question would be. Instead he asked, "Many folks in working today?"

"Minimum staff, but there will be a few to make sure the sluices open properly when the peak demand goes up later today. Till then it will be real quiet."

"What about you? You on all day?" Phoenix enquired.

"Nope. My partner takes over at ten o'clock."

Phoenix was in two minds as to what to tell the guard. He didn't want to alarm him. He was so old that any stress looked as if it might be terminal.

"Do you guys go on high alert round Christmas, for terrorists and the like?"

"Hell no, not these days. Ain't much happens round here."

Phoenix nodded. The white-haired old man would be totally ineffective in stopping any attack. There seemed little point in voicing his fears.

"Okay. I'll be leaving the vehicle there whilst Shadow and I search for the deer on foot. Have a great day, sir. Are you spending it with your family?"

"Yeah, going to my daughter's place this evening, and Merry Christmas once again."

The old boy went back into his hut. Phoenix hoped he would be off duty before anything happened, he had a kind face. He looked at his watch. The sky was turning a lighter shade of grey. The sun would be up within thirty minutes. He suddenly felt very tired and wondered how the others must be feeling. He had spent two magnificent sleepless nights making love with Skye, then a day in the operating theatre followed by a stressful night awake preparing for a terrorist attack. He steeled himself to remain alert.

*

Mohammed decided to separate the girl from her parents. She was resourceful. He did not trust her to bend easily to his will. It would be better to keep her in sight at all times. It did provide him with some logistical problems. There were things he wanted to do that would be better unobserved.

He tied her to a wooden chair with her hands behind her back and placed a strip of duct tape across her mouth. He was pretty sure she would try and use her tongue to undermine him. Lastly, he blindfolded her. Lack of sight was the most distressing of senses to lose when under stress. He had been taught that in the training camp in Somalia. Fear of impending attack was terrifying. He had spent a day similarly bound and blind, awaiting the next strike. Never knowing which sound would precede the blow. Each blow was painful, but not as painful as the wait for it.

He looked at the girl. "You make a sound and I will hit you."

"Hmm!"

He hit her.

Skye hated the blindfold. She felt completely vulnerable. But she knew it was only for a few hours. She listened intently to every sound she could hear. Imagining what they were doing. Things were being moved. The front door to the condo opened and closed. She heard a squeaking sound move past her and out of the door. Was it a wheel perhaps?

They did not talk much. Just the odd phrase interrupted the silence. "Pass me that, no, that one. Don't need those, the other ones. Shit!" Occasionally, the blond one got angry with his cohorts.

It was apparent to Skye that he held them in low regard, if not contempt. 'They were not the sharpest tools in the box,' she concluded. Was that something she could use?

After about an hour, the blond one said, "You three go and get us some more breakfast from McDonalds. I'm starving still. I'll finish this off."

Skye heard shuffling as the men put on jackets. "What do you want?"

"Coffee and two Bacon and Egg McMuffins, maybe a couple of those potato things."

She heard the door close. The blond man moved over to the window. She heard their vehicle take off with a screech of spinning rubber. 'Not the sharpest tools in the box,' she thought again. Why draw attention to yourselves when you are about to commit the worst terrorist attack on American soil since 9/11?

She heard the blond one sigh. His opinion obviously matched her own.

When they were gone he walked across the room and into another. A few seconds later she heard him return. He put two objects on the table. The next sounds were not obvious to her. Shuffling, and then quiet, he was working with something intricate with small movements. Finally she heard a series of bleeps, like setting the clock on an oven. There was a pause, and then another series of bleeps, the exact same series as before. There was more shuffling, the scraping of a chair as he got up and walked again to the other room.

A few seconds later he returned and continued to do what he had been doing before the men had left. The sounds emanating from his general direction were similar to what she'd just heard.

Fifteen minutes later the men returned. Bags were placed on the table, rustling as their contents were removed. It smelt good, fresh coffee and fast food aromas reached her nose.

She was angry that she could think of food at a time like this, but a Bacon and Egg McMuffin would have been great.

They ate in silence. Skye could sense the apprehension in the room. Nobody spoke. Throughout, there had not been one sound coming from the room where she knew her parents and Thea were being held. She hoped they were not too scared. Strangely, she knew that Thea would be a calming influence on them both. Happiness always surrounded her lovely white dog.

That is exactly what was happening in the room next door. Missy had managed to get over to Tristan and lay against him with her head on his shoulder. His head lay on hers. Thea had somehow managed to lay across her lap with her chin on Tristan's thigh. Without the restraints and gags, it would have made a touching scene.

The enforced idyll was shattered by an outburst of loud conversation from their captives in the room next door.

It was the blond man's voice and it was in a foreign language.

Skye was not sure, but it could have been an Arabic dialect. It didn't mean a thing to her other than the words Allahu akbar, God is great. However, its tone did mean something. It was time. Her heart missed a beat. She expected someone to come over to her and get her out of the chair. Nothing happened.

Instead she heard the locks being released on the door where her parents were. The next thing she heard was the patter of Thea's paws shortly followed by her full weight landing in her lap and a wet tongue basting her face. Her heart leapt. The proximity of her wonderful four-footed made her want to cry. She desperately wanted to cuddle her.

"Get that fucking dog off her," the blond man yelled.

Thea was summarily dragged from Skye's lap. She whimpered. Anger rose inside Skye. Were they hurting her? Then she heard something else that made her heart soar again.

"Come here, Thea, good girl."

It was Missy. She heard Thea scamper over to her mother. She imagined her tail wagging ferociously as she anticipated a walk.

"Take them. Remember timing is everything," the blond man said.

Missy was obviously free to speak. Her father remained silent. "Don't worry, darling. We will be fine. Don't worry about us," she said to Skye as she was ushered out of the door.

Skye could hear a car door close. It was not the minivan they had been brought in. No sliding doors and a different click to the door closing. Neither was there a patter of paws. Thea was still there. As if to confirm the fact she barked once.

"Shut that fucking thing up."

The man had forgotten Skye was still gagged. He stepped towards her and ripped the tape off her mouth.

"It's okay, Thea. It's okay," she said quickly before anyone could threaten or hurt her if she reacted to the violent move.

"Get her up and bring the mutt," he said to Amir, gesturing towards Skye.

Amir untied Skye from the chair, leaving her hands bound and removed the blindfold. His hands were remarkably free and anxious to explore her curves for such a simple task.

"Leave the bitch alone, you pervert. We have business to attend to," Mohammed yelled at him. Then he turned to Skye. "We want to take the vehicle into the compound. Can you make that happen?"

"Probably, but I don't know. Any cars going in should have a sticker. I guess deliveries are allowed in. But it's Christmas Day, they won't be expecting anything," she replied.

"Figure something out. I'm your brother or

253

something. If you can't get us in easily we will shoot the guard on the gate. Your choice."

Skye nodded. She knew they wouldn't hesitate to kill whoever was there. She loved all three of the gatemen. Together they had a combined age of two hundred and seventeen, and all three still had a twinkle in their eye. She would get them in. Could she get a message to whoever was on duty at the gate though? That is what she was wondering, and if she could how could she do it in a way that would keep them alive?

She looked around the room. A number of boxes that had been stacked near the wall earlier had gone. Some sort of device lay on the table. It was obvious to her what it was. The explosives must have been in the boxes. She remembered the wheels coming and going three times. She was familiar with explosive devices with her work. If it were any of the modern materials used for exothermic reaction, three loads that needed a trolley to move them amounted to one hell of an explosive charge. Once inside the compound, moving and setting the device would take time. It was time she could use if she was still alive. And it was time that Phoenix might be able to use.

Mohammed passed a dog's lead to Skye. Thea was excited again. A lead meant only one thing.

"This gun will be pointing at you all the time. One move and you are both dead." Mohammed pointed the gun at Thea.

"You," he nodded at Amir, "put that in the back with the rest."

Amir gently picked up the detonator and timer. He still could not get his head around the fact that without an electric charge it was harmless. He took it to the van and placed it as far from the explosives as he could.

Amir looked at his watch. It was nine o'clock. "Move."

"Where have they taken my parents?" Skye made no

effort to move.

"Somewhere safe. Now get in the van or I shoot your fucking dog now."

With her hands still bound, Skye led Thea to the van that she knew contained enough explosives to flatten a small town.

TWENTY-TWO

"Have we got this right? What if we have just imagined the whole thing? And there is no terrorist plot and we aren't reincarnated," Caroline said. She needed more affirmation. She was new to this spirit thing.

She was talking into her cell phone. They had no sophisticated communication devices, just phones. She had staked out the approaches from the lake and had seen nothing. Only one lone fisherman had ventured within eight hundred yards of the dam in his sports boat. He dropped a line for five minutes; decided nothing would bite and sped off again.

Caroline was beginning to wonder if they were going to get a bite. Part of her hoped they wouldn't.

Hearing the doubt in her voice, Phoenix answered, "We have it right. It will happen, Caroline. Hang on in there. They will come. This is real; you are not living a fantasy. I promise you."

"I know, Mowgli, it just seems so unreal somehow. I'm usually opening my presents about now, sitting by a warm fire with a cup of tea in my hand with White Christmas playing on the stereo and mince pies warming in the oven. By the way, nothing is happening out on the lake and the fence is clear all the way along." She decided she should get back to the task in hand.

"Good, all we've had are two dog walkers. Both have gone again. You are doing a great job, Caroline. But remember, you only get involved as a last resort. You are our back up."

"Okay, okay, I hear you. I'll call again in fifteen minutes. You get anything, just dial and let it ring. I will call the cops first before I do anything else, just as you instructed."

Caroline had enjoyed the contact with the others; it had made it feel less surreal. She hung up and pulled the collar of her jacket tight around her neck. It seemed to be getting colder and the misty drizzle seemed more persistent than before. She looked up. The grey clouds were giving way to a threateningly dark sky.

*

The traffic was good and the roads were almost deserted. It had only taken thirty-eight minutes to get to the old man's house. Missy and Tristan had remained quiet, as they had been instructed. But Missy had an unpleasant feeling in her stomach as she realised they were driving down increasingly familiar roads. Each turn they took angled closer to the home she had grown up in. With less than a mile to go there was no doubt left as to their final destination.

The battered Dodge turned into the rough gravel and stone driveway that led to the old wooden structure. The grounds needed some attention, but her aging father had managed to keep the house in a good state of repair. He had even repainted it top to bottom during the summer, refusing any offer of help, fiscal or physical. "It keeps me young," he'd said.

The car came to a crunching halt in front of the wooden steps that led to the veranda and front door.

Skye's grandpa heard the car approach. He had been worried, as nobody had returned any of the calls he'd made the previous evening and again this morning. He didn't recognise the sound of the car, but hoped it might be his daughter, Tristan or Skye. Perhaps it was the boy Missy had told him about. He was looking forward to meeting his prospective grandson-in-law.

He opened the door. First he saw Missy, but then he saw the man with a gun to her head. Tristan got out of the other door; a second man with an assault rifle was threatening him.

Missy held up her bound hands. "Merry Christmas, Pops." She tried to smile.

Missy's father had seen most things in his life but he never expected to see this. He was temporarily speechless. The realisation that the assault rifle was now pointing at him loosened his tongue.

"What the hell is going on here?" he shouted at the intruders.

"Just do as you are told and nobody gets hurt," Nawaz bawled back. "On your hands and knees, old man."

He considered dashing back in for his own shotgun but, whether it was old age or not, he couldn't remember where he had last seen it. He did as he was told and struggled to the floor, as best his old limbs would allow.

A minute later he was dragged back to his feet and marched into his own home with his hands bound behind his back.

"You keep them covered, Jamal. I'll take a look around."

Nawaz started a systematic search of the premises. It did not take long to find the perfect place for them to drown. The basement.

Jamal prodded Tristan in the ribs with the rifle, it was an indication he should move towards the doorway where his brother stood. In the entrance hall a door was ajar, through it stone steps descended into an already damp cellar.

Tristan looked into the dark void. If there were to be an escape it would have to be now. Once in the cellar, there was no way out. He had been down there many times. Missy's father used it as a storeroom and with every year that passed he seemed to have more to store. There may even be stuff down there that they could use to extricate themselves, but he knew they would be bound if not just executed once they were in the cellar.

He looked at Missy. He knew she had come to exactly the same conclusion. If the dam burst they would drown.

He felt the rifle prod him again in the back, urging him to take the first step down. It was now or never.

He swung around; his momentum pushed the rifle barrel away from him as he had hoped. Jamal was surprised at the sudden movement, but he managed to pull the trigger anyway. The woodwork by the door shattered. Tristan kicked out at him, catching him in the groin. Jamal doubled up in agony. Tristan heard a scream and caught a glimpse of Missy falling to her knees. He hesitated. The next thing he felt was the rifle butt in his own guts and he was toppling backwards. He felt every stone step as he tumbled into the basement. He heard his leg snap like a twig half way down. His shoulders dislocated as they took the full force of the fall with his hands and arms tied tightly behind his back.

He briefly lost consciousness, awaking to excruciating pain. His leg was doubled at an impossible angle. He was totally immobile. But his only thought was for Missy, his beautiful Cherokee wife.

Next, he felt hands drag him to his feet as if he were a rag doll. A punch to the face followed. "You fucking prick," the angry voice said. "I should fucking kill you now. But that would be too kind. You can drown with your damned wife and the rats with this old fool."

Tristan was slammed against a wooden support. His arms were released from their bonds and promptly retied behind him and around the support. Once again Tristan passed out with the pain. When he awoke he had slumped to the floor like a discarded toy. One leg was splayed out; the other was doubled up beneath him. He was completely helpless.

"Oh God, Tristan," he vaguely heard the words Missy was saying to him. "Tristan, my poor darling, how bad is it?"

"Broken, leg, shoulders. I don't know what else," he half whispered in agony. "But you, how are you?" He suddenly became more alert with the realisation that she might be harmed.

"He stabbed me."

"Oh no, where?" Tristan was coming round fast. As he did so the pain increased.

"The side."

Tristan noticed weariness in Missy's voice. Sudden dread filled him. It was pitch dark in the cellar. He needed to see her. He needed to find out how badly she was injured, and how much blood she was losing, but he was totally incapable of movement.

"I watched it happen." It was Missy's father. Tristan had forgotten in his haze that he was there. "I couldn't stop it. I'm sorry, Missy."

"Don't, Pops. I'm sorry this has happened in your home." Missy winced as she spoke.

"How bad did Missy's wound look, Pops?" asked Tristan.

Her father couldn't tell the truth. He couldn't get to his daughter to help her but he had seen the blood oozing from her wound, as they tied each of them to separate wooden supports. Once they had closed the door it had gone dark. The only thread of hope he took from what he'd seen was that the blade was short and it was only one stab.

"Not too bad, Tristan. Short blade. One strike, not too much blood." He prayed his last lie would not come back to haunt him.

His mind was racing. He was the only fit one there. It was his home, his cellar. He knew every last piece of junk that was down there and he knew where every piece of that junk was stored. There were things that could get them out, but he had to be able to reach them.

He also had to try and keep his daughter and Tristan alive. He needed to get free and he needed them to stay conscious. He had a bad feeling that if they lapsed into a coma it might be the end for them.

"Why the hell are we here?" he asked.

*

Caroline's phone was ringing. She slid the accept call bar across. All she could hear was heavy breathing and what sounded like people running across rough terrain.

"It's started," she whispered to herself.

She felt for the 9-mm gun in her pocket, took it out and released the safety as Brad had shown her. She was angry; all feeling of apprehension had receded. She idly thought that the reaction and anger she was feeling must be exactly the same as Lady Katherine had experienced. She started to run to the point the boys had briefed her to go if she got the call. With every step she took her anger rose.

*

Skye sat in the passenger seat with Thea between her and the blond man. The oldest of the others, the one she now knew was called Amir, sat in the rear with a gun held low but trained on Thea.

Whether it was intentional or not, Skye knew the terrorists had picked the perfect day for their massacre. It was more than just symbolic that they should strike on the holiest of Christian days. The only person on duty would be one of the old guys who worked the gate. Christmas Eve and the morning of Christmas Day were effectively a holiday. Two staff would probably pitch up just before lunchtime but she did not know who they would be. She assumed, and hoped, they would be ones without kids.

It had begun to drizzle and the wipers were set to intermittent to clear the annoying spray. Their rhythm was interrupting Skye's thought processes. She desperately wanted a plan, but nothing came to her. She kept thinking about her parents and what had happened to them. She knew the terrorists had no need of them anymore. Their abduction had purely been to bend her to their will. She prayed that they had not been harmed and that they were still alive.

The minivan pulled off the road and into the park that led to the powerhouse. It swung around the one hundred and eighty degree turn back past the park gates. In front of her and slightly off to the left she saw a green pick-up. Could it be?

As the minivan got nearer, she could see an Apache blanket hanging over the pick-up tailgate. She had joked with Phoenix that Shadow must give her the blanket so he could join her clan and marry Thea. Phoenix had suggested that it was a nice thought but Shadow would find his own way of consummating his relationship with Thea. She smiled, thinking about the conversation and what happened shortly afterwards.

Next to her, Thea's ears suddenly twitched, as alert as they ever became, and she stared at the Georgia Department of Natural Resources vehicle.

They were here. Just as she had expected, Phoenix had figured out what had happened and that they had been reunited to protect the Cherokee lands once more. At that moment, life or death seemed irrelevant to her. She looked at Thea who was staring straight back at her. She wanted to cry. Man and animal, equal spirits. On the verge of what she suspected might be their death, she had never felt so alive. She was about to go into battle with her four-footed soul mate. Thea knew it too. Every fibre of her being would stay that way until it was over, one way or another. Any opportunity that came her way, she would seize and she would kill any person that threatened them.

The first opportunity she seized came far sooner than she thought it would.

*

Phoenix watched the van drive into the park. It was the seventh vehicle to drive in since the sun had risen. Two were still there and both of them were empty. Every vehicle that had come had a minimum of one kid inside. Usually they were there to play with recently opened presents. Toys that needed the open spaces of the grassed park, or the newly laid blacktop to test new roller blades and skateboards. Each arriving vehicle had pulled into one of the clearly marked parking spaces. It was quiet now. The occupants of the two remaining cars were taking walks by the river.

One car had arrived about ten minutes earlier. It had driven up to the gates, and parked next to the gatehouse.

Its occupant had on the same uniform as the old man Phoenix had talked to, but the new guard looked another five years older. After a brief chat the night watchman left in his own vehicle and his older colleague took up residence in the hut.

The Honda Odyssey minivan did not pull into the first group of parking spaces it passed. It drove slowly past the two empty parked vehicles. It looked just like any other family vehicle. Phoenix raised the binoculars to his eyes. He expected to see another group of excited kids anxious to play with their new possessions. The windows were tinted. He could see figures inside but he couldn't make out whether they were male, female, large or small.

Next to him, Shadow stirred. He had been lying beneath some branches in an attempt to keep the ever-increasing rain off his black fur. He looked at the van in the distance, then stood up, alert.

Phoenix quickly raised the glasses again. "Is it them, boy?"

The van slowly drove past the remaining parking spaces and on towards the gatehouse. It was in no hurry. Could it just be staff arriving for the Christmas Day shift?

On his other side, Brad was now giving the vehicle his full attention. It was the first real, possible target to approach the gate.

"Damn tinted windows. I can't see who is inside," said Phoenix.

He hoped they would get out of the van. Unfortunately, the new gateman came out of his hut and approached the driver's side window. He seemed happy, revelling in his festive greetings. He touched his brow in a half salute, just as his younger colleague had to Phoenix when they parted company. He stood back and pressed the button that raised the gate. It was obvious to Phoenix that the gateman knew the occupants of the vehicle.

The van eased slowly through the gates and turned

left and out of sight. Phoenix had hoped to see who was sitting in the passenger seat. If it were Skye, he was sure she would have left the window down. All he saw was a raised tinted window.

"We have to find out who was in that van, Brad. I'll go and have another word with the old boy on the gate."

As he stepped out of the trees, where they had concealed themselves, a white dog suddenly flew around the corner heading towards the barrier. From behind him, a black dog took off towards the same barrier as fast as its legs would take him.

"Shit! It's them," Yelled Phoenix.

"How many?"

"I couldn't see, man. I don't know."

Shadow was already fifty yards ahead of him. Phoenix started to run after him. Shadow was getting away; a shower of water droplets were expelled from his wet fur as he ran.

Brad followed, but more circumspectly with his rifle locked into his shoulder, ready to cover any attack on Phoenix or the dogs.

Phoenix had his phone in his hand pre-dialled to Caroline's number. He pressed call. He was still hundreds of yards from the barrier when a blond man appeared in pursuit of Thea. He had a gun in his hand, raised and ready to fire. He stopped, planted his feet and took aim at the white dog.

Phoenix screamed, "No!"

It distracted him. Through the now heavy rain Phoenix heard two dulled pops as the silenced weapon spat out its death. They missed. Thea continued beneath the barrier towards her soul mate. Pop, pop, two more. She was sixty yards clear. Pop, pop, eighty yards and she was getting further away. It would be a lucky shot if he hit her now. Pop, pop, two more misses. Phoenix was sure she was safe.

Behind him a more resounding crack accompanied Brad's first shot. A second and a third followed. Phoenix kept running. He was two hundred yards from the dogs. Shadow had nearly reached her. There was one last pop.

"No!"

*

Al didn't mind the Christmas Day shift. He had no family. He had eaten with his neighbours the previous evening and it had been nice, but now he was looking forward to a peaceful day reading his latest Jack Reacher novel.

The gatehouse was a bit too warm for him. The first thing he did was turn down the electric heater. Then he took the trash out to the can behind the hut. When he came back in he set his Thermos on the desk and removed the sandwiches, which he had made with the beef his neighbour had sent him home with, from his bag. He took the novel out and placed it next to the flask.

He looked at his watch. Nobody was due in for another two hours; he would be well into the book by then. He opened the pristine paperback and began to read. He had only read two pages when an unfamiliar minivan approached the barrier.

The window wound down. He was thrilled to see Skye sitting in the passenger seat. She was a delight, the best thing to have happened to Buford Dam Powerhouse in years. He was quick to put down the book and go to see how he could help her.

"Hi, Al. Happy Christmas to you," she said, whilst leaning across the driver.

"Hello, Miss Skye, and the same to you. What brings you this way on this wet Christmas morning?"

"Two things, Al. My cousins are staying with us for the holidays and I've been telling them how wonderful the old powerhouse is. They asked if they could come and see the white pine floor and the old pulley lift."

Mohammed smiled and waved at the gateman. "Howdy, would that be okay? It sounds fantastic," he said.

"I also asked if they could help me to carry in some heavy equipment that arrived yesterday. It's gear I need for the survey." She smiled sweetly at him, afraid at what they may do to him if they suspected she was trying to double-cross them.

"Sure, l'il lady, y'all go right ahead." He leaned through the window and tickled Thea's neck. "Hi, Thea, did Santa bring you some nice bones?"

He liked dogs and Thea had been to the powerhouse a number of times with Skye.

"You should see them," Mohammed smiled, and shook his head, "could be from a dinosaur."

Al laughed. "Okay, Miss Skye, the place is all yours." He saluted, stepped back and raised the barrier.

He watched them drive around the corner and stepped back into the hut. Perhaps it wasn't too hot. He turned up the heater again.

As he straightened from adjusting the temperature he saw Thea bolting towards the barrier. Skye's cousin was chasing her. He chuckled to himself. He'd always figured Thea would be spirited. She had sure been a little restless in the van. Skye had to restrain her all the time.

He was watching the dog and not the man when he heard the first pop, pop.

"Christ!" He exclaimed. He was shooting at Thea. What in hell's name was he doing that for?

He tapped on the window. "Hey!" He shouted. "Stop that!"

He had a gun strapped to his belt that he had never

used. He never even thought to get it out. He could hear more shots and then another sound, as a round was fired from a different gun further away.

He pulled open the door and marched out. "Hey, stop that. You can't shoot the poor dog." Two more pops rang out. "Hell no! Stop it now!"

He took three more steps towards the blond man before a 9-mm bullet pierced his skull right between his eyes.

*

Skye had been holding Thea back from the second they had driven past the pick-up. She knew Shadow was nearby.

Her mind was racing. If she let her go Skye was sure Thea would bolt and go to find Shadow. If she got away she would be safe with Shadow and Phoenix. At the same time she did not want Al to be hurt, and if she tried to jump through the cab window the psycho in the rear might well shoot her. And God knows what they would then do to Al.

If she let her go when they were away from the gatehouse, the bastards would probably do nothing. What could they do about it?

A few seconds later, she found out.

It seemed a risk worth taking. As she got out of the van she unclipped the lead from Thea's collar. Thea took off.

Skye was horrified at what happened next.

"You stupid bitch!" Yelled Mohammed.

He slapped her and pushed her into the waiting clutches of Amir, who still had the gun in his hand.

Amir gratefully accepted the bundle of sexuality that

had been forced upon him.

Mohammed ran after Thea, and then he pulled a gun from inside his jacket and started to fire at the fleeing dog.

"No! Stop it, you bastard, not Thea. Leave her. No!" Skye screamed, as she squirmed trying to free herself from Amir's vice-like grip.

For her troubles she received the butt of his pistol across her face. It did not stop her struggling. All Skye cared about were the silenced pops she could hear, as Mohammed fired round after round at her beautiful dog. And all she could think about was the fact that each bullet fired must mean he had missed, and Thea was escaping. She could run like the wind.

She could hear Al shouting, and further away the voice of the man she loved bellowing, 'No!' The voice was getting louder. Phoenix was getting nearer. There was another gun somewhere too.

Then, there was one last sinister shot. Followed by one last agonised cry of 'No!' It went quiet. What had she done?

TWENTY-THREE

The daughter he loved was quite probably bleeding out just a few feet away from him, and he felt helpless. He struggled with the electrical ties that had been pulled tight around his wrists and ankles. The more he tried to prise them apart the more they cut into his wrists. He could feel the warm blood trickling down his hands. The pain did not bother him. He would have willingly cut through his wrists if it meant he could free himself and help Missy.

Quite obviously, Tristan was less able to free himself.

"From what you've told me, they will blow up the dam?" he asked.

Both Tristan and Missy had explained to him why they had been abducted and that it was Skye who was the terrorists' main prize. They believed themselves to be little more than leverage to make Skye do as the terrorists demanded.

"She won't let them, Pops." Missy's voice was barely more than a whisper.

"If she can't stop them, we will drown down here. What on earth do they think they can achieve by such an act? Surely, Skye cannot know what they have done to you. I don't get it." Gramps was thinking out loud.

Even talking was painful for Tristan, but he managed to say, "They have to kill us anyway. We can identify them. They are just sick bastards and enjoy mental cruelty as well as inflicting physical pain. They will have told Skye that we are safe as long as she does as they ask.

Once she has no value to them they will kill her too."

Pops worked his bleeding wrists against the plastic straps again. He had to get free. If the dam burst they would have twenty minutes at best before the water filled the basement.

Gramps was sitting facing a wooden support with his arms and legs wrapped around it as if he was hugging it. He couldn't stand up, but he could swivel around if he embraced it harder and pulled his full weight off his backside. He tried the manoeuvre. It worked, but what had he achieved? He was further away from Missy and no nearer to any of the tools he had stored in the cellar. It was painful too, but he didn't care.

However, he did notice that as he hugged the timber support the ninety-degree corner pressed against the plastic strap. It added more pressure to his cut wrists. The wood was also sharp at that point. He pulled his hands hard back against the wood and began to rub up and down. It was not sharp enough to cut into the plastic. In fact the opposite happened and the wood splintered. A shard of the splintered timber entered the open wound in his wrist. He winced. In anger he rubbed even harder. Nothing gave way. Clenching his teeth he went at it again. Nothing but pain, but the plastic was getting warmer.

If the plastic would not cut perhaps it would stretch, as it got hotter. If it stretched it would become weaker. There may be a chance. Frantically he worked the plastic against the wood. He closed his mind to the pain as the splinter drove deeper into his wrist. But there was hope.

"Tristan, talk to Missy, don't let her fall into a coma."

Gramps knew what his job was. He was their only chance if the dam burst, and he had to give them hope even if he knew there was very little.

"I can get free. I just need a few minutes. Till then you keep Missy talking," he said to Tristan.

Tristan knew exactly what Gramps was saying to him. He was completely immobile, but as the body sometimes does it was shutting out the pain. He might be immobile but he was not helpless.

"Tell me again what our lovely daughter did in that last bit of smut you wrote."

Gramps heard Missy giggle weakly. It gave him renewed vigour.

*

Caroline held the phone to her ear, listening to the dissonance of noise that emitted from the speaker. She tried to make sense of what she could hear. Running, panting, then it went quieter. She heard a shout of 'No!' It was Phoenix's voice; faint, but it was definitely his voice and it was her signal to start running too.

Wet branches crashed against her. Huge water drops fell from sodden trees. She heard rifle shot, one, two and then a third. It was loud. Was it Brad? Or was it a terrorist shooting at her friends?

The shock of the gunfire made her raise her head, when before she had been running with her head ducked down to avoid the overhanging branches. A substantial bow caught her across her face. At the same time her feet slipped on the rotting, soaking wet leaves beneath her. She fell; the cell phone in her hand went flying. She scrambled amongst the leaves in an attempt to locate it.

There were more shots. "Bugger it!" She exclaimed. "Damn the fucking phone."

She was up and running again, the cell phone was left in the tangled undergrowth.

"No!"

She could hear Phoenix yell again. This time it was

272

not through the cell's earpiece.

Suddenly she broke clear of the forest. She had dreaded what spectacle would greet her. She stopped dead in her tracks and wiped her wet face hoping to get a better view.

Two hundred yards away, Brad lay prone on the wet grass. His rifle was tucked into his shoulder with his chin resting on the stock. He was the model of a Marine sniper. Her eyes followed the line of his aim. A blond man stood by the gate with what looked like a gun in his hand. At his feet a man was lying on the ground.

Half way between Brad and the group by the gate, Phoenix was kneeling by what looked like a large black bag. Next to him, Thea was sniffing the bag.

"No, not Shadow," she whispered to herself. Then the anger swelled inside her. It was an uncontrollable wave that took hold of her. She began to run towards Phoenix and the four-footeds.

Before she reached Brad he fired one last measured round at the man by the gate. It knocked him off his feet. Caroline stopped briefly.

Another two hundred yards away, Phoenix was inspecting the black bag that was now quite obviously Shadow. Shadow had raised his head in response to both Phoenix and Thea's attentions.

"Thank God," she said to herself.

Even though she felt relieved that Shadow was alive, deep within her the rage found new fuel as she began to run again.

The man by the gate tried to get to his feet. She increased her pace, furious with the bastard that dared hurt a four-footed.

As she passed Brad without stopping, he shouted, "Hey, Caroline, be careful, he has a gun."

Brad watched the blond man get to his feet. He knew he had hit him somewhere in his midriff but he had no idea where or how effective his shot had been. He raised the old rifle to his shoulder again and sighted his target.

"Bloody hell, Caroline. Get out the fucking way," he yelled. But he knew she couldn't hear. She was completely blocking his line of sight.

Caroline paused briefly by Phoenix and looked down at Shadow. She did not say a word, but continued her charge towards the man.

"Caroline. Christ! Come back you lunatic. Caroline, don't he's armed," Phoenix screamed after her.

There were no words that could stop her. She was a hundred yards from the bastard. He looked dazed, staggering as he grabbed the barrier for support. She kept coming. When she was forty yards away he saw her.

He raised the 9-mm handgun and pulled the trigger. It missed. He fired again, but he was not seeing straight.

Twenty yards away Caroline pulled her own gun from her waistband. She pointed it at the cowardly shit that dared to shoot Shadow. Still running, with the weapon out in front of her she squeezed the trigger slowly, just as Brad had instructed.

The first round hit him in his gun-arm shoulder. The 9-mm fell from his grasp. The second round hit him in the stomach. It was delivered from ten yards. The next four hit him in the head on the ground where he lay.

If there had been more than six bullets in the gun they would also have been in his anatomy.

She stood over the very dead body of Mohammed; her pulse was beginning to slow when a short burst of bullets shattered the wooden barrier next to her. She looked up to see another man holding Skye in front of him as a shield. He had a lightweight Uzi trained on her. As she dived for cover behind the gatehouse another burst splintered the wood of the hut.

She looked back towards Phoenix. Brad had reached the group and was helping.

If she'd had any more bullets in her gun she would have charged the next bastard too, but as her anger receded she realised that discretion was the better part of valour. She leaned back against the hut and took several deep breaths.

They needed to regroup and Phoenix might well need her help with Shadow. She peeped out from the side of the hut. Skye and her captor had disappeared.

She made her way back to the others, making sure she kept the hut as cover for as long as she could. Finally, she ran the last fifty yards to them.

"How does he look, Mowgli?" she enquired, as she knelt by their side.

"He'll live," Phoenix kissed the dog's head, "the daft bugger," he looked up at the wild woman, "but not as daft as you," he added. "What the fuck was all that about?"

"Sorry, I got a bit angry."

Despite the gravity of the situation, Brad laughed. "Thought you might. It's in your genes." More seriously, he added, "But that's it, Caroline. This is not over yet. There is only one down and we have not got a clue how many there are. We don't think many, but there are bound to be more. You do that again, you'll get yourself killed."

"I know, I'm sorry. I saw one more man. He has Skye, but I don't know where they went. They just disappeared."

Caroline started to inspect Shadow. Phoenix had packed the bullet wound, which had entered his right shoulder.

"Muscle and bone, I reckon. But that bullet needs to come out, and we have to see if there is any internal damage," proffered Phoenix.

"Is your kit in the pick-up, Mowgli?"

"Yeah, everything you need."

"From that, am I to assume I have been sent back from the front line?" she asked.

"Yeah. You've done your bit. We all walk away from this, right?" He looked at Caroline. "Any of us get killed, then we will only have to do it all again in a couple of hundred years. So, from here on you are running the field hospital and Shadow is your first patient. He needs fixing quick. Okay, Lady Caroline?" He smiled at her.

She nodded.

Phoenix was already carrying Shadow to the rear of the pick-up. "Drugs, scalpels, everything is in the box." He gently lowered Shadow into the covered flatbed. "Caroline will mend you, Shadow." He looked deep into the eyes of the four-footed he had shared an eternity with. They were bright and alert. Phoenix was sure he would be fine. "See you soon, boy."

Caroline was already busying herself with the supplies she would need to remove the bullet. Every bullet she had ever removed from a four-footed had made her cross. She steeled herself to remain completely calm whilst she operated on Shadow.

Phoenix patted his dog and gathered his bow. "Call the cops again, Caroline. Two dead bodies might actually get their attention," Phoenix said, before he and Brad used the cover of the hut to approach the powerhouse.

Caroline squeezed a roll of furry flesh with her fingers and eased the syringe full of anaesthetic into Shadow. "Sure," she answered, engrossed in the work at hand.

*

Amir got out of the rear of the van. It had all gone smoothly. The girl had done everything they'd asked. They were inside and would be unobserved from here on. According to Mohammed, once the girl had shown them the entrance to the penstocks, they could set the charge in under thirty minutes. The only other problem was transporting the explosives. For that task he had brought the trolley they'd used at the condo. For the first time his level of anxiety decreased. He heaved a sigh of relief as he got out of the van.

He leaned back inside to get the holdall in which he had brought a miscellaneous selection of weaponry. As he did so, all hell was let loose.

First, he heard Mohammed shout, "Fucking dog," and then, "Grab the bitch."

Amir did as he was told and grabbed Skye's arm. The whore was smiling. He watched as the white dog fled away towards the gate. Mohammed gave chase, shouting at the animal. Then, to Amir's horror, he drew a pistol and started shooting at the dog. Whatever possessed him to do such a thing, he could not imagine. It was only a dog and they were in, almost home free.

The whore shouted, "Run, Thea, run," and then began to squirm in an attempt to get free from his grip. He struck her with an Uzi he had removed from the bag. As Mohammed's shots rang out, she stopped squirming in his grip and was now easy to restrain. She stood and watched in dismay at what was happening.

"Run, darling," she whispered as the dog turned the corner and darted beneath the barrier.

Still Mohammed pursued the animal, firing repeatedly at the hound. Then Amir heard a man shouting and a different gun. This one was much louder than the silenced handgun of Mohammed.

After that he too became transfixed. The guard came out from his hut, only to be summarily executed by Mohammed. He fell face first to the ground like a sack of potatoes being dropped from a height.

As Amir stared in bewilderment, Mohammed dropped to the ground too. A nanosecond later the resonance of the shot that put him there reached his ears.

Both he and the girl stared at the scene in front of them, each trying to compute what had just happened.

He watched as Mohammed got slowly to his feet again, only to be cut down by more gunfire. The girl, whose arm he had released, started to move slowly away from his side.

He raised the Uzi and pointed it at her. He would have fired had she made any further attempt to escape. But she had stopped and was standing perfectly still. She whispered a name, "Dahlonega."

There was more gunfire and he turned to the gate again. A golden haired woman was standing over Mohammed and was emptying a magazine of bullets into his head, which was disintegrating as each round found its target and splattered the brain matter and blood that had once been his life's force.

Amir grabbed the girl and pulled her in front of him as protection from the mad woman who had slain Mohammed.

He raised his Uzi and fired. Bullets slammed into the barrier by the woman's side. As she darted for the cover of the gatehouse he squeezed off another volley.

Almost incapable of thought, he dragged the girl through the door behind him. With his gun trained on her, he ordered her to close and bolt the entrance.

"What the fuck am I going to do?" he said to himself, but perfectly audibly to Skye.

"You're going to die," she answered for him.

"Shut up, bitch." He slapped her hard across the face. Skye hardly flinched. "Sit there while I think." He dragged her to a wooden chair that sat on one side of the entrance hall they found themselves in. He pulled the plastic ties even tighter around her wrists.

He anxiously paced around on the intricate white pine inlaid floor that had been used as the pretext for their visit. He was alone and he was scared. The explosives were all in the van and there were people out there with guns. It may even be the police.

He gave no thought to completing his mission and becoming a martyr to the cause. He just wanted to escape. He looked at the girl whom he had hoped to rape before she died. Now he looked at her and he was afraid. If she died, so would he. It was a simple equation; if she was alive, as his hostage, he stood a chance.

He stepped to the door and listened. There was nothing but silence. His mind returned to the training camp. "Silence is a weapon. It breeds fear," they had told them.

Amir was very afraid.

*

Phoenix knelt down and felt for a pulse in the gateman's neck. There was nothing. There was no point in bothering with the terrorist; Caroline had taken care of that.

He quickly stepped back behind the hut where Brad had already taken cover. "How do you see our options, son?" he asked Phoenix.

"Time, it's about time. How much time do we have?"

"You mean, are the explosives still in that van or are they inside the powerhouse?"

"Yeah. That's exactly what I mean."

"If they brought them in the van, they would not have had much time to move them inside," said Brad.

"Unless there are four or five of them."

"There won't be more. Couldn't have gotten any more in there with Skye and Thea. I say three, tops." Brad sounded decisive.

Phoenix nodded. "Best scenario, even fewer and the

bomb's still in the van. Worst, four and they are setting the charge as we speak. Where are the damned cops? This is a job for special forces not Cherokee Indians."

"We can't just sit here and wait for them. We have to assume the worst scenario, son."

"We have to check the minivan?" Phoenix asked the question.

"Yep."

Phoenix looked at Brad. There was a weird half-grin on his face. He raised his eyebrows. Phoenix knew what it meant.

"You have the gun, I only have a bow and arrows. So you are going to cover me."

"Got it in one, son." Now he was grinning.

"Bloody hell! When this is over I'm going to buy a gun." Phoenix laughed.

He was about to step out from behind the hut and run to the powerhouse wall, which he would use as a shield en route to the parked van, when Brad held his shoulder.

"Gut feeling, there are only one or two of them. The amount of explosives needed to blow the dam would take a while to move. Caroline said they disappeared real quick."

"I hope your gut is right." Phoenix tapped the ample girth that Brad had acquired over the years.

"It is. Stay close to the wall all the way to the van. Duck under the windows. I am going to cover you from over there by the goats. I can get there behind those trees." He pointed at the line of deciduous growth that bordered the edge of the property in front of the fence. "What about them goats? Just kept on munching the grass with all that noise going on. That your influence, son?"

"Who knows?" Phoenix looked across at the goats. They were calm. Phoenix knew they were happy. One looked up at him and bleated once. He chuckled. "There's only one guy."

"How do you know that, son?"

Phoenix nodded at the goat. "He just told me."

"Thought you couldn't talk to the animals?"

"I can't, but maybe they can talk to me." He chuckled again. "Just kidding."

"Okay, not sure I believe you, but let's go kill this mother fuckin' son of a bitch. And if there happen to be any more, then we smoke them too."

"Yeah, okay, but be careful with that thing." Phoenix touched the old rifle. "Skye and I have to have twelve children, so I've been told."

"I'll try and miss your nuts."

"Just miss Skye."

"Okay, friend. Let's do it."

Phoenix ran to the side of the building and cautiously made his way towards the van.

*

Caroline gently removed the bullet out from Shadow's shoulder. Miraculously, it appeared to have missed everything that might fracture. "Well, old chap, I guess you've been lucky. Still, it was a small gun and you were a long way away."

Thea was lying with her head by Shadow, carefully listening to his breathing. Caroline broke the dog's serene vigil.

"Shit! I had to call the police." She fumbled for the cell phone in her jacket pocket. "Bugger! It's in the woods. Damn!" She had been concentrating on poor Shadow so much that she had completely forgotten Phoenix's last request. "You bloody fool," she admonished herself.

She looked at Shadow. He was going to be fine, but

she needed to suture up the gaping wound before it could get infected. Five more minutes, that is all she needed. She looked at Thea. There was total trust in her eyes. She couldn't let either of them down. Mowgli would never forgive her.

She threaded the needle. Surely there would be a phone in the gatehouse. Or one on the poor dead guard, or even the bastard she had killed.

She suddenly realised that she felt no remorse for what she had done. She would do it again in the blink of an eye.

She completed the first stitch and tied it off.

*

Skye's emotions were in turmoil. Had they killed Thea? She wanted to cry. Then she realised that whatever happened now the plot to blow up the dam was foiled. Their Cherokee lands were safe. She was instantly elated only to have her spirit crushed as she imagined what may have happened to her parents. She could see no reason why they would keep them alive once she had agreed to help them. As this latest despond took her, her mood swung again as she relived the slaying of the bastard who had orchestrated the whole nightmare. Was Thea alive? Where was Phoenix? She wanted to clasp her head in her hands, but she couldn't even do that. They were bound and nigh on useless to her cause.

She looked at the man pacing in front of her. Though thinking, he never took his eyes off her. That damned gun was always in his hand. She knew he could use it; he had almost hit Caroline with an improvised shot from nearly a hundred yards away. And anyway, it was a machine gun; anyone could use it if they could point it roughly in the right direction.

She hated him and she knew he hated her. From the moment they had taken them from their home, his lizard-like eyes had undressed her at every opportunity. His hands had wandered freely over her body whenever he had the chance. The lust had gone now, but the hatred in his eyes was still there.

She began to panic about Thea again. 'No, stop it, you idiot. We are winning. She is okay,' she told herself. She took some deep breaths in an attempt to regain her composure.

"What other ways are there out of this place?" Amir finally asked her.

"None," she said without thinking.

"You lying bitch." He marched over to her and struck her across the face yet again.

It was time for her to think straight. She took another deep breath. This creep was the only one who might know where her parents had been taken. The other man was dead, and the two dimwits had been instructed to take them somewhere. She fought the panic that was rising at the thought of what fate might have befallen her wonderful parents. If there was a chance they were still alive she needed him to tell her where they might be. Added to that, what purpose could her own demise have now that the dam was effectively saved? In all probability Phoenix or Brad might kill the creep before he could tell her where her folks were. The vision of Caroline decapitating the blond man with a stream of bullets filled her head. If she got to him first, she most definitely would kill him and her parents' whereabouts would remain a mystery.

She had to put Thea out of her mind and concentrate on what she could influence. She looked at the cretin in front of her. He was almost shaking with fear. Eventually she said, "We both have a problem."

Amir had no idea what she was talking about. He went to strike her again. It was action; it was all he could think to do.

"Wait," Skye said. She was calm; the impending blow did not bother her. "You need to get away before they kill you, like they killed your friend. The cops will be coming soon as well, and they will definitely shoot to kill, and there will be Special Forces. If you stay, you are a dead man walking."

Amir had already figured that much out.

"You need me to get you out of here before that happens." Skye stared at him. "Your cause is lost. This fight is over, but your life may not be. If I get you out of here, you must tell me where my parents are, even if you have already killed them." It was a slim chance, but it was Skye's only hope of finding them. She was sure that he would tell her what she wanted to hear, just to get her assistance.

Amir thought about her proposal. He knew that he needed her, if only as a hostage and a shield. But she could offer him more. What did he have to lose? If he offered her real hope she would be more willing to get them away from the powerhouse. He would kill her anyway when her usefulness was outlived.

"Okay, bitch. If you get me out of here, I will do even more. I will take you to them."

Skye knew it was a lie. He would kill her the second he was free. "That's not enough. I need to know where they are now. If you don't tell me, I will not help you. I am your only chance. If you kill me, you will surely die."

To Amir it made no difference if she knew the truth or not, she would not live long enough to act on it. "They are at your grandfather's place."

"What?" Skye was shocked. It was the last place she would have expected him to say. It was so fantastic a notion that initially she found it hard to accept as true, but the more she thought about it the more credible it became. These sick bastards never had any intentions of keeping them alive, but to drown them in the floodwaters of the mayhem they intended to create with their actions was sick enough to believe. It would be almost biblical in its dastardliness. There would be words in the Koran somewhere that their warped and twisted minds would find to justify their act.

"You bastards. You would have drowned them." She spat out at him, but then another thought took hold. "Oh no! Are they dead already?"

"Not as far as I am aware. My brother's brief was to secure them there and let Allah's wrath take them."

He was telling her the truth. She could see it in his eyes. There was hope. If she refused to help him now, he would surely kill her. If she helped him escape, the others were still out there and she stood a chance. He might be free, but he would be in Cherokee lands where the spirits that he would have harmed would hunt him down and kill him.

She stood up. "Let's go."

*

Phoenix made it to the main entrance door. He could see Brad lying prone in the woods near the goats. His rifle was pointing at the door and surrounding windows. It was only a short distance to the van. He lay on the ground and crawled commando-style to the rear of the vehicle. He reached up and twisted the handle and pulled open the door. Several boxes were stacked inside. Next to them was a smaller box. He reached in and opened it first. There was a simple mechanism, which he identified as the detonator and timer. There were several yards of wire and two nine-volt batteries. He opened one of the larger boxes and lifted out a slab of explosives wrapped in greaseproof paper.

He heaved a sigh of relief. Hopefully the overriding threat had been averted. However, it was possible there were more explosives that they had taken with them.

More confidently, he walked to the main entrance door and tried to open it. It was locked. He eased over to the window nearby and carefully looked into the hall. It was empty. He scanned the woods and areas around the powerhouse. It all looked quiet, so he gestured for Brad to join him.

"I think they must be inside, Brad. There is only one entrance and exit to the compound, through the gate, and they have not gone through it. The perimeter fence is high and covered with barbed wire. They would have needed wire cutters if they got out through the fence."

"Okay, son. What about the explosives?"

"The van is full of them."

"Thank God for that."

"They may have some, for all we know, but it certainly is not the load they had intended," added Phoenix.

"They are inside then?"

Phoenix nodded his agreement. "The door's locked."

"Any other way in?" asked Brad.

"Haven't a clue. There must be fire doors, but they will be locked too, at least from the outside. It was shut up overnight, nobody here until later according to the gateman."

"So, it's Skye, possibly some explosives and one man, according to the goat," suggested Brad.

"Best guess, yes. Hope the goat's right."

"There will be guns too, Caroline was on the wrong end of them," added Brad.

"I hadn't forgotten," said Phoenix.

"How quick can you load and fire that bow?"

"Longer than it takes to pull a trigger."

"Thought so, stay near me, son."

Brad smashed the window with his rifle butt and then tapped all the shards of glass onto the floor inside.

*

Caroline tied off the last suture as Shadow opened his eyes. Thea immediately licked them. Shadow's mouth half opened in what Caroline was convinced was a smile.

"Back with us, old boy," she said to the smiling dog. "You take it easy, and don't bother that wound. Thea look after him, I have to find a phone. Stay here."

Shadow wasn't going anywhere in a hurry, and if he wasn't neither was Thea.

Caroline ran to the gatehouse. She briefly looked down at the man who had killed the guard and hurt Shadow. He was unrecognisable. Only half of his head was still there.

She didn't linger, but entered the small cabin to search for a telephone. One sat perched in the middle of the table. It looked as old as the powerhouse. She picked up the receiver. Thank goodness, there was a dial tone. Her finger pressed the old chunky square buttons and she dialled 911.

A woman's voice answered. "This is the emergency services, how can I be of assistance?"

"We need the police. There has been a shooting and two people are dead. Others are still in danger," answered Caroline calmly. She could not help herself, she had to say it, "And if they had bloody well come when I warned them last night this may not have happened."

TWENTY-FOUR

There was a way out of the powerhouse that suited them perfectly. Since she had done the structural survey, Skye knew every nook and cranny of the building and its attached dam.

There were four exit doors from the old building. She did not intend to use any of them. They were perfectly reasonable doors, but all opened into the compound again. He would still be trapped, and a trapped animal could be dangerous. This one most certainly was. He would not act rationally, and although Skye had not witnessed any real religious fervour it must exist for him to have taken up jihad despite his lack of suitability for the position. She was sure that outside the constraints of the compound he would be less anxious, more predictable.

Other than through the gate there was one other way to get out. People entered and exited through the gate. The water entered and exited through the penstocks.

When it flowed down the tubes it would be lethal, but it only flowed when the sluices were opened. Right now they were closed.

She showed him along the corridor that led to the old iron cage whose pulleys and ropes would lower them down to the generators and turbines.

The cage was on the correct level and they stepped in. Amir looked bemused as Skye made a series of selections on coloured buttons and levers to set the elevator in motion. It clanked and groaned, then began its slow descent.

Skye stopped it one level down and got out. Amir followed with the gun at her back. She walked along another corridor and came to a halt by an old oak door.

"You will have to open it. I can't with my hands tied. Or you could untie me," she added hopefully.

He did not respond. He pushed her to one side as he slid the two deadlock bolts aside and pulled the large metal handle down.

Skye wondered if he would be vulnerable as he did it. But there was little she could do with her hands tied and he monitored her every move as he opened the door.

He dug her hard in the ribs and gestured for her to enter the cold damp tunnel that the opened door revealed.

"Where does this go?" he asked.

"The penstocks. You know what they are, don't you? That is where you would have put your bomb, had you not mislaid it." She could not resist the opportunity to mock him.

His reaction was predictable. Skye was getting fed up with being a punch bag. She decided she would hold her tongue in future.

It was freezing cold in the wet, puddle-strewn corridor that was cut through the rocks and concrete. "Turn that light on," she said.

Amir pulled the lever down on an ancient light switch. A series of dim and bare electric bulbs lit the cave-like scene. Skye led the way, not bothering to keep her feet dry. Eventually they came to the first pressure door, through which access could be gained to the first of the penstocks. It was hinged on one side and made of solid steel. Four metal wheels, one at each corner, screwed the sealed door tightly shut.

"You need to unscrew those, then pull the handle on the right. The door will swing open."

Amir set about the task. They were well lubricated and had obviously been opened regularly. He tried his best to keep an eye on Skye as he worked the wheels.

However, he had to face the door repeatedly as he released it from its watertight seat. As he did so, Sky wrote YONA with her foot in the damp residue of dust and soil that covered the floor.

The door creaked open and Amir looked inside. There was a vast concrete tunnel sloping downwards at an angle of about forty-five degrees. The dim light from the corridor barely illuminated the initial few feet of it. A trickle of water flowed rapidly down the middle.

"We have to go down there. At the bottom there is a huge turbine. We will be able to squeeze through the blades; I've seen them up close. We are going to get wet and if someone opens the sluices the turbines will make mincemeat of us." She added the last part to unnerve him.

She could see he was not anxious to get into the penstock.

"You go first," he said.

"I need my hands free to help steady myself on the way down."

"No way. Do you think I am mad?" He pointed his gun towards the opening into the penstock. "Get going. I will be right behind you."

Skye smiled inwardly. It would be pitch black in there. If she was quick, she might be able to get away, especially if he had a problem squeezing through the turbine blades. It was old and totally unsophisticated and relatively inefficient. The blades were ridiculously far apart, but he was bulkier than her and he had the gun to manoeuvre through as well. It might offer her a chance to escape, or better still, a chance to kill him.

*

Jamal pulled the cord on the outboard motor. It fired first time. Nawaz handed him the two Macy's bags that contained the bombs. Then he handed him two fishing rods.

He'd had a brilliant idea that the rods would help conceal their real purpose. Not that they had bothered to take them on any of the reconnaissance trips when others might have questioned their proximity to the dam. Now, he was pleased with his cunning.

Jamal looked at his watch. It was 10:50 am. 'Midday,' Mohammed had said. It would take ten minutes to place the explosives in the rotting concrete they had identified on a previous visit. And then they would have one hour to put as much distance as they could between themselves, Morgan Falls Dam and the onrushing flood that Amir's destruction of Buford Dam would precipitate.

He was looking forward to the glow he would feel as he watched the consequence of their actions on TV. It would be a stab in the heart of America, and a blow for Allah in his quest to show that he was the one true God. More importantly, to Nawaz, he could bask in the glory that his actions would bring him.

The small boat sped south towards the dam. As it did so, Nawaz checked the bags. He did not really understand how the mechanism worked that would explode the devices. Mohammed had said, 'Just connect the wires.' Then he had shown him which wire plugged into which. It was foolproof. They had different connectors, two to each bomb. Then he'd said, 'Press the red button on each timing device.' Once the second button was pressed, an hour later the devices would talk to each other with a wireless radio signal that would detonate the bombs simultaneously. Mohammad had set it up for them.

The lake was completely empty. Unobserved, they put the first bomb in he fissured concrete and pressed the red button. Jamal drove the boat a hundred yards to the second location. Nawaz connected the two wires on the second bomb and pressed the red button.

There were no body parts that could be buried. They were both instantly vaporised.

*

Further upstream in Suwannee, Skye's grandpa heard a dull thud. He instantly began to panic and frantically worked the wood against the plastic strap.

"Christ!" He shouted. "Is that it?"

Tristan, who had been trying his hardest to keep Missy conscious by any means he could, said, "What?"

"That bang."

Tristan had not heard anything. He said, "No, Gramps. The whole bloody earth would have shook with amount of explosives they needed to blow up Buford Dam. Believe me, we would know about it."

His heart slowed, but his efforts to get free did not. "How's Missy doin'?" he asked.

"Not good. She sounds very weak, but she's still awake," replied Tristan.

Missy heard them. "I'm fine, and I am still here if you'd like to talk to me directly, Pops," she said with as much authority as she could muster.

"Good, darlin', just stay that way. What did you get me for Christmas?" Gramps asked his brave and wonderful daughter.

*

Brad pointed the muzzle of his rifle through the smashed window and peered through. It looked clear. He nodded at Phoenix, who deftly climbed through. He reached back and gave Brad a helping hand through the gap.

Once inside, they carefully searched all the rooms using a technique they had seen cops do on the TV. It felt professional, but may have looked comical with one man clearing each room with a bow and arrow.

"They're not on this level," Phoenix whispered to Brad.

"Down then." Brad moved towards the old elevator.

"Wait." Phoenix grabbed his arm before Brad pressed the button to summon the cage.

He looked down the shaft. "It's just down one level. That is where they must have gotten out," he said.

Brad nodded and pressed the button. A symphony of cranks and groans brought the cage up to them. Once inside, Brad looked at the controls. "Jeez, how does this work?"

Phoenix looked at the levers and buttons. It was not immediately obvious. There were two levers and four buttons in a horizontal line, not vertical. It had to be the second or the third. He pressed the second. Nothing happened. He pulled down the first lever and it began to slowly descend, replaying the symphony. It carried on down but made no attempt to stop at the next level down. Phoenix pushed the third button. It continued to descend. He grabbed the second lever and the cage came to a crunching halt two feet below the floor level. They stepped up and onto the first level down.

Once again, they started to clear each room in turn. One door they opened gave access to a cave like tunnel. They cleared the rest of the rooms and returned to the damp tunnel.

A series of dim lights illuminated their way as they stepped through the door. Twenty yards into the tunnel they came across an opened pressure door that would not have looked out of place in a submarine. The dim light shone just a few feet into the void. There was a constant noise of running water and a cold draft emanating from inside the empty space. Phoenix leaned in and the noise of running water got louder.

He turned to Brad. "This must be where the water flows from the dam to the power generators. This door would never be left open normally. They must have gone this way."

"They did," Brad said, and then he pointed to the damp earth by his feet. A shoe had written YONA in the dirt.

Phoenix looked down.

"Are we going in after them, son?"

"No." Phoenix was thinking. "That shaft has to lead down to the river below. Once they are down there and out of the compound they could go in any direction. There is a better way."

Before Brad could say anything more, Phoenix was running back towards the elevator.

By the time Phoenix got back to the pick-up he was a hundred yards ahead of a puffing Brad. Thea greeted him first; she'd run to meet him. Not far behind her was Caroline.

"Have you got Skye?" she called to him as he approached.

"No, but we know where they have gone," answered Phoenix.

"I'm so sorry. I was slow to call the cops. I got carried away with Shadow, and…"

Before she could say anything else, Phoenix cut in, "Don't worry. How is he?" He ran to see his old chum.

Shadow was trying to stand up to greet him, but was still a little groggy.

"No, lie down, boy." Phoenix gently hugged his best

friend and inspected the bandages that Caroline had lovingly wrapped around the fresh bullet wound. "You'll do," he said as Shadow licked his face.

Caroline gave him a quick report of surgery. "He will be fine, Mowgli."

"Thanks, Caroline." Phoenix stepped forward and hugged her.

"Where are they?" she asked as he released her.

"They escaped through the penstocks down to the Chattahoochee. I need Thea to track Skye. We should pick her scent up where the water comes out after the turbines." Phoenix was excited.

Brad had finally caught up with him, but was unable to speak as he gasped for breath. Phoenix gave him no time to recover, "Grab Thea, she will track them down."

"Shall I come?" asked Caroline.

"No, stay with Shadow and wait for the cops. Tell them where we have gone."

"They will probably arrest me," she said.

"Yeah, they will, but you'll talk your way out of it." Phoenix smiled at her, and then he turned to Shadow. "Stay here and look after Caroline, okay?"

Shadow accepted his brief and lay back down in the rear of the truck.

Caroline watched as Phoenix and Thea ran down to the water's edge. Brad followed twenty yards behind. He still had not spoken.

*

Bert, the Flowery Branch cop, had been considering taking a ride out to Buford Dam for some time when the phone rang.

Bill, the desk guy for the day, had finally arrived and

295

picked up the receiver. "Flowery Branch Police Department, how can I help you?"

There followed a minute's silence as he took in what the caller was telling him. "Will do, ma'am," he said, and then hung up.

The look on his face told Bert that something was wrong. "What gives?" he asked.

"A shooting, two believed dead at Buford Dam. A British woman called it in."

"Shit!" Exclaimed Bert.

"It's worse than that. A bomb has exploded down on Morgan Falls Dam. The whole of fucking Georgia has been scrambled. Homeland Security, the Army, you name it. And we are the nearest cop shop. You are first response, Bert."

"Oh my God! Jack said some Brit nut-job had been calling all night about missing people and a terrorist threat. We've fucked up big time." He was already moving to the door and his Crown Vic that was parked outside.

"I'll call on the radio with any more info they give me. Go, man, Get down there. Gwinnet, Hall County, Cumming, they will all be there soon. The Feds will follow and Christ knows how many more agencies. There will people swarming all over this."

*

There was a steel handrail that travelled the length of the penstock. Skye knew it was there but failed to mention it to Amir. She had hoped he might slip and tumble down the steep and slippery slope. Without it, working in there would be impossible. The maintenance guys would attach a safety line to it that clamped hard round the railing, which allowed them to repair any lumps of concrete that may come adrift. Another, rusty bar, ran parallel to it about a foot higher. It was obsolete but no one had bothered to remove it. Higher on the curved surface were a series of safety rings at ten-yard intervals to which another line could be attached to their harnesses.

Unfortunately Amir was not as stupid as Skye had hoped. He located the rail immediately. He watched Skye as she used it to ease herself down, then followed suit.

The dim shaft of light that entered through the pressure door soon faded and they were in almost total darkness. If she'd had a free hand she might have been able to pull him away from the bar, but both hands were still bound together.

However, Amir was struggling too, his gun was now a hindrance to his own progress. He slipped on a couple of occasions, but managed to break his fall using the railing.

Skye was more sure-footed, but literally had to crab her way down whilst clinging to the bar with both hands.

At the bottom end light was breaking through the turbine blades. Skye could hear water rushing from another channel next to the turbines. It usually remained open so the river never actually stopped flowing and had only one sluice gate with no turbine. The water then flowed through a gorge cut into the rock before fanning out into a wide delta, where it slowed before resuming its natural flow south towards Atlanta.

It was through the gorge that they would most probably get wet. It might be possible to climb the canyon sides once they were through the turbine and out on the other side. She actually did not know. She hoped they would have to use the water to literally transport them through the gorge to the more natural river basin about one hundred yards further down stream. The man would have trouble keeping his gun dry. Not impossible,

297

because the ride would only take about forty seconds. From memory there were no hazards in the form of boulders or jagged rocks. The gorge had been man made and the flow of the Chattahoochee over the previous sixty years had smoothed the way.

She was about to slip through the blades when Amir shouted, "Stop. I will go first."

Perhaps he was not so stupid after all. Skye's plan had been to dive straight into the rushing water whilst he struggled through. By the time he got clear she had hoped to be free.

Navigating the turbines was relatively easy for her. Amir struggled a bit more, but managed better than she had hoped. On the other side he peered into the rushing water as they both stood on a ledge. The drop to the water level was only about three feet

"How deep is it?" he asked.

"Don't know. Pretty deep, I'd imagine."

When the whistle blew and the sluices were open the level would rise sixty feet up the side of the canyon. Right now she guessed it was maybe fifteen feet deep.

Amir looked at the side of the gorge to see if there was any way of avoiding the water. They were worn smooth. "Damn!" He uttered. He was not fond of the water and neither was he a particularly good swimmer. He looked at the Uzi in his hands and then at the water. He had a 9-mm handgun in his pocket that might work even if it was wet. If he tried to save the Uzi he would surely drown.

He was out of the compound and nearly completely free. He had no use for the girl anymore, and the gun was a liability. He would get rid of them both here and now.

Skye knew what was coming. Before he could even raise the Uzi from his hip, where he'd been holding it, she dived headfirst into the fast flowing river. Before she broke the surface of the water she took a deep breath. She was a good swimmer, but had no use of her arms. She heard two bursts of fire as she hit the water. Once beneath the surface she kicked hard to get as deep as she could. Projectiles sped past her, slowing in velocity as they left trails of small bubbles behind them. She kicked again to get deeper as the torrent took her. The bullets stopped. She figured she could hold her breath for a minute easily, by then she would be able to surface in the river proper. Once she had her bearings she could formulate her next move.

She felt the current slowing and the depth became shallower. She needed to breath. Just ten more seconds is all she wanted. Eventually the need for oxygen became unbearable and she broke the surface gasping greedily for air.

She spun round trying to get her bearings. The gorge was behind her, a wide slow flowing river stretched out in front of her. She kicked her legs beneath the water. Too deep she couldn't stand. With her hands stretched out in front of her she set out for the riverbank some fifty yards away. She kicked furiously in an attempt to put as much space as possible between herself and her pursuer.

Whether it was a quirk of fate or he was a good swimmer, she never knew, but somehow Amir appeared in front of her and off to one side. He too was gasping for air. In reality the current had just been kinder to him.

He saw Skye immediately and swam to the bank parallel to her. He had thrown the Uzi into the gorge before he dived in after her. With his hands available he could easily match her for pace. In fact, he reached the bank just before she did. He reached into his soaking wet jacket for the 9-mm. From his other pocket he pulled out a hunting knife. He stood and waited as Skye scrambled to her feet about twenty feet from him.

Both soaking wet, they stared at each other as the water that their clothes had absorbed sought to be reunited with the river that flowed around them. Skye knew she could not outrun him with her hands tied. She looked at the gun and the knife. She also knew that he would surely kill her unless she could give him a reason not to attack her.

The sound of police sirens saved her.

Amir watched a police vehicle approach the powerhouse and dam, which was now about half a mile away. He could hear others in the distance approaching from different directions. His head swivelled in an attempt to hear them all. His eyes filled with panic.

"You will never get away, unless I help you. I know these woods and this river like the back of my hand. They think you are inside, but it won't be long before they realise you escaped and then they will start to hunt you down." Skye knew she was pitching for her life. "I am your only hope."

Amir made a decision. "Which way?"

Skye did not answer but nodded a direction instead. She began to run through the tree-lined riverbank towards a trail that went south, away from the dam and towards her grandfather's home.

*

Phoenix could hear the first of the police vehicles approaching as he and Thea made their way to gorge. He realised that is where they would come out. He ran to the edge and peered down into the gorge where the water and penstocks exited the dam. There was nobody there. Then they charged down to the where the river widened.

He scanned the wide river where the water slowed from a torrent being spewed from the gorge. The scene was one of tranquillity, the peace being disturbed only by police sirens.

He had hoped to see two people in the water or a sign of them by the river's edge, but there was nothing. His eyes scanned the two riverbanks, a fifty-fifty chance. Nothing. They might have to swim across if Thea could not pick up Skye's scent on the side they were on.

He ran to the first point it would have been possible to get out of the water and said to Thea, as he held her collar and looked deep into her dark brown eyes, "Where's Skye, find Skye!"

Immediately Thea frantically started sniffing the riverbank. She zigzagged her way down stream. Phoenix followed repeating the command at regular intervals. They went two hundred yards then they doubled back. There was nothing.

Brad had caught them up, and the search had given him a chance to get his breath back.

"Thea can't pick up anything, Brad. You take this side. I know there are thousands of acres, but they will likely keep to the riverbank. Thea and I will swim across and search the other side, okay?"

"Sure, I've got it. Now get going, son," he replied.

Phoenix pulled off his jacket and shirt; they would just hinder him as he swam across the river. With his bow slung across his back, he ran into the water. Soon he was swimming to the other side. Thea trailed him by a few yards, like her mistress she could swim well. On the other side they went through the same process, dog sniffing and man encouraging. Seventy yards of detection work uncovered the scent Thea had been frenetically seeking. She stopped, circled the smell twice with her body, but her nose never left the source.

Phoenix looked down at the object Thea was showing so much interest in. A handkerchief lay on the mulch. It was soaking wet. Phoenix picked it up and sniffed it himself. There was no scent that he could decipher, but there was a letter S embroidered in one corner. Thea barked once and raced off into the woods.

"Clever girls," phoenix called after the dog as he began to run after Thea.

Brad heard the bark and knew its significance. He tried to keep pace with them and could see them appear intermittently between the trees on the far riverbank. Perhaps he could get a clear shot across the water if he needed to.

Man and dog ate up the ground in pursuit. They were in surroundings they knew, an environment they had hunted in before. In lands they had tried to defend before. They were Cherokee lands, their lands.

*

Caroline sat on the tailgate of the pick-up, stroking Shadow and waited for the first police car to arrive. Before it came to a halt near her she could hear several others approaching.

The cop got out of his car. He had his gun raised and pointed at Caroline.

"Oh, good God, man. Really? You have to be joking," she said in exasperation. In all honesty it was exactly what she had expected.

"Stand by the vehicle with your hands on the roof." The policeman did not lower the weapon.

Caroline sighed, but did as she was told. With a well-practised move he had her hands behind her back and the cuffs on her within seconds. He patted her down. Only when he was happy that she was not armed did he holster his own weapon.

"You call it in, ma'am?"

"Yes."

"You the same lady who called last night?"

"Yes."

"Where are the bodies?"

"By the gatehouse." Caroline nodded towards the barrier.

"Do you know who shot them?"

"Yes. The man without much of his head left shot the guard," answered Caroline.

"Who shot the other guy?"

"I did."

"Where is the weapon?"

"Next to Shadow." She nodded towards the gun that was still in the back of the truck.

"Is it loaded?"

"No, I emptied it into the bastard's head."

"Because he shot the guard?"

"No, because he shot our dog."

Bert couldn't fight back the smile.

"So, what is all this about terrorists?" he asked.

"You should have asked that last night."

It hit a nerve. "I know, ma'am. We're real sorry."

Caroline liked manners. Not many men she knew seemed able to say sorry. "Oh! Well, the good news is that they aren't going to blow up the bloody dam. All the explosives are in a minivan by the powerhouse entrance." She looked in the direction of the powerhouse. "There is something else. There is at least one other terrorist and he has my best friend hostage. They, or he, have taken her down the river, I think. My two colleagues are in pursuit." She couldn't help herself adding, "The two guys that stopped this bloody dam from being destroyed."

Bert stood dumbfounded at what he was hearing. He was snapped out of his stupor by three more police cars arriving. Four others were winding their way down the park driveway.

In the distance, Caroline could hear a helicopter

approaching. She looked up into the sky. Her gaze was broken by the cop asking, "Is the dog okay?"

She looked down to see the cop stroking Shadow; Shadow did not look uncomfortable with the accord. "Yes, yes he is. Thank you for asking," she replied. The cop had gone up in her estimation.

"I see you have bandaged him. I will get him to the animal hospital," he said.

"No need. The bullet is out and he is sewn up." Caroline saw the look of surprise on his face. "I'm a veterinary physician. I run the veterinary services for the Georgia parks," she offered by way of explanation.

Bert looked at the golden haired woman he had quite brutally cuffed. He took the keys from his belt and stepped behind her.

"What's your name?" he asked, as he unshackled her.

"Caroline," she said, as two more cops approached her.

A large black sedan stopped ten yards away. Two men in dark suits got out. The helicopter made any more conversation impossible as it approached to land on the grass nearby.

TWENTY-FIVE

Skye could hear Thea barking in the distance. She knew her bark anywhere. It was usually accompanied by bouncing and the unspoken, 'Throw it, throw it.' Her heart leapt. They were coming.

If her hands had been free she was sure that she could easily have put distance between herself and the creep. She was not really taking him anywhere. There was no planned escape route. She had just bought time so Yona could find her before the bastard killed her. She had managed to drop a handkerchief after she'd climbed out of the water that she hoped Thea or Yona might find. The barking told her that they had.

She deliberately slowed her pace even more. She did know the trails well and had walked them all dozens of times with Gramps. There were homes she could easily have taken him where he could have gained access to a vehicle. So she deliberately avoided any route that might make one visible. She looked behind her. He was ten feet back, with the hunting knife in one hand and the gun in the other. She deliberately stumbled to waste more time.

"Get up, bitch," he yelled.

Slowly, she got to her feet. Thea barked again. She was nearer, much nearer. She brushed the sodden leaves from her front.

"Move!" He shouted, and raised the gun in a threatening gesture.

She turned and continued along a trail that led back

to the water's edge. She noticed squirrels and deer watching her flight. A raccoon briefly matched her pace, as he followed through the undergrowth off to one side.

It all meant only one thing to her. Yona was near. She slowed some more.

*

On the far bank, Brad was losing ground. Occasionally he caught a glimpse of the white dog or Phoenix. He could hear her barking in excitement as she bounded through the woods. He simply did not have the fitness level necessary to keep up. He stopped and viewed his options. They were few. A trail led up the slope to his left towards higher ground. He may get a vantage point from higher up. He looked at the foliage on the nearly bare trees. Three dimensionally, trees were eighty percent air, but the trajectory of a bullet would meet one hundred percent of wood two dimensionally, with or without leaves. No, he needed to stay by the water. It was his best chance of getting off a shot.

The short rest had helped. He turned right, back to the trail that followed the river.

*

Once again the rain began to fall more heavily. Water was dripping down Skye's face and off the end of her nose. Some drops were running into her eyes. She raised her bound arms to wipe the water away. As she did so, her vision was temporarily blocked and her foot caught a protruding tree root that crossed the path. Her ankle turned and she went flying. Unable to properly break her fall with her hands, she slammed into another tree trunk that edged the trail. It temporarily knocked the wind out of her.

"Up!" The man screeched.

Skye tried to get up. The second she put her weight on her ankle it gave way. The tree trunk that had winded her broke her fall and offered support. She tried again. There was no strength in it at all. She thought her ankle was probably broken.

"I," she shook her head, "I can't, it's broken. I can't walk."

Amir stared at the half-drowned girl he had lusted after for so long. He'd had plans for her, but now she was useless to him. Despite her dishevelment she still looked beautiful. A strange malevolence took hold of him. His whole life had imploded. Everything he had ever been and could ever become had been destroyed in the previous hour. And this bloody whore had been central to his ruin. From the day he had first laid eyes on her it had all changed. He had a wife and children but cared nothing for them after he had seen her. He had become callous and hateful. He had observed his new persona, but did not care. All he had wanted was to possess her. It was the only thing that had motivated him through jihad and the atrocity he had attempted to commit. Now it was all over.

If he could not have her, he would make sure that no one else would. He raised the 9-mm handgun to shoulder height and pointed it at Skye. He took five steps to close the short distance to where the wounded beauty rested against the tree.

Skye looked at the man against whom she had been fighting for survival. Briefly, he stopped his advance. From a few feet away she could smell his breath as his heart raced. The lust she had not seen the last time she'd looked into his eyes had returned. His face was contorted between loathing and desire; his breathing was rapid, almost panting and as he squeezed the trigger.

There was a long pause as his finger took up the slack in the action. Skye's eyes challenged him. Her chin raised in the same defiant fashion it had all her life whenever she had been threatened or challenged.

Amir's face sneered back at her; a half-smile invaded his spiteful features as he closed the last few feet between them. His pupils dilated as his trigger finger beckoned to her, as it slowly continued to squeeze.

Skye had run out of time. She closed her eyes and thought of Yona. She did not see the flash of white get airborne and grab his arm in mid air, as if it were a Frisbee.

A loud crash echoed around the forest. Various animals scurried away from the devilish noise they associated with death. The bullet hit the tree trunk next to Skye's head.

Thea had taken the man's arm and gun with her, dragging him to the ground as she landed. The gun flew from his hand. Thea was on her feet again; the man's arm was still in her mouth. She dragged and shook it, killing her prey as she had a million Frisbees, but this time she was growling and snarling.

Amir tried to free himself from the rabid attacking dog. The dog's jaw was locked firmly round his arm. He struggled to release the hunting knife from its scabbard where he placed it.

Skye had rapidly assessed the new dynamic and saw what he was trying to do. She attempted to scramble the short distance to him before he could extricate the knife and attack Thea with it. She instantly fell to the ground and began to drag herself towards the grappling duo.

Horrified, she saw the knife appear in his hand. The blade was at least six inches long and would sever Thea's jugular artery with a simple sweep, or penetrate her heart with a single stab. "No! She screamed.

He raised the knife for the blow that would end Thea's life.

"No! Please, no," Skye pleaded with tears running down her cheeks.

Amir looked over at her. His eyes were filled with pure loathing.

A split second later his arm began its downward arc to execute the dog. Before it had travelled six inches the arrow slammed into his neck. Startled, he stopped. Three seconds later another arrow penetrated his heart.

Skye looked in the direction the arrow had come from. In the trees, twenty yards away, was Yona standing with another arrow already loaded. He was naked to the waist with his soaking wet, long, black hair trailing over his shoulders. His bare torso glistened with raindrops.

To Skye he had never looked more beautiful. She began to cry uncontrollably.

*

Within minutes flashing lights and a medley of uniformed men surrounded Caroline. City, county and state troopers all wanted a piece of her. Being the first on the scene, Bert had taken it upon himself to be her protector from the barrage of questions they all wanted to fire at her.

He recounted the story she had told him with regards to the terrorist, the guard and the dog.

As he did so two more helicopters arrived, Blackhawks, mean and menacing. Each one disgorged ten men fully armed and suited in Kevlar. Caroline noted the dagger on the troops insignia.

The guys in suits from the sedan had listened intently to Caroline's story. Only when Bert had finished did they take up the mantle. It was apparent to Caroline that they were going to take charge, and it was obvious that the troops were there at their behest. The Delta Force CO waited patiently for direction from the older of the two suits.

"HSA, ma'am," the silver-haired suit said, by way of introduction. He was fit and in his late forties. His whole appearance commanded respect. Caroline liked the cut of his jib.

"We are going to take it from here. You say the explosives are in the van?" He wanted confirmation.

"Yes. They never made it inside. I shot the first bugger. The second ran away. Well, kind of ran away. He took Skye as a hostage. They escaped down the Chattahoochee. Don't worry Phoenix went after them. He won't get far," she recounted with typical authority.

"Phoenix is?"

"Skye's lover and soul mate."

"Is the second perp armed?" asked the agent.

"Yes."

"What about Phoenix?"

"He has a bow and arrow." Caroline was beginning to enjoy the look on the agent's face.

"A what?"

"Bow and arrow, cowboys and Indians?" She looked questioningly at him. "Surely you know of the concept."

"Let me get this right. You shot a likely member of Al Qaeda six times and your friend is hunting the other one down with a bow and arrow." He found it hard to keep the shock out of his voice.

"Well he is a Cherokee Indian." Caroline could not resist it. "I think he's used it before, which is more than you can say for me and a gun."

The silver haired agent did not know what to say to the woman. Instead he turned to the Delta Force CO, who was grinning at the exchange. "Take ten men and secure the explosives, and then clear the powerhouse. Make sure there are no surprises in there. The rest sweep the river valley. Get the girl and Tonto. Take the perp alive if you can."

Caroline interrupted, "Skye's dog. Make sure Thea is okay. She was tracking them. Oh, and there is Brad too. Don't hurt Brad. He is kind of old. He will be some ways behind Tonto, as you called him. He has an old rifle, but he can't really use it very well."

The CO was outwardly laughing now. "Anything else we need to know, ma'am?"

"No." More seriously she added, "Yes there is. Sod the terrorist, bring my friends back alive."

The CO smiled. "We will, ma'am. Though, by the sounds of it your friends will probably not need our help."

"I hope not." She acknowledged his sincerity. "How come you guys got here so quickly?" she added.

The Homeland Security man answered, "There has already been an explosion at Morgan Falls Dam. We assumed terrorists. Various scenarios were considered after 9/11. Dams were one of them. Certain dams were high priority, the Hoover dam for instance. Buford was level two. Every dam on our list is getting a visit from security and police departments as we speak. In answer to your question, the guys were already on their way here the second Morgan Falls blew."

Caroline nodded. She was heartened that not all the authorities were imbeciles.

"Ma'am. Can I say that our country owes you and your friends a great debt? You have saved countless lives," the silver-haired man graciously said.

Caroline fought hard to curb her acerbic tongue. Instead of saying, it's not your bloody country, she said, "You're welcome."

The CO dispatched five men along each riverbank.

He took the others to see what carnage the British woman had wreaked.

Caroline turned to her new champion, Bert. "I don't know if you ever got, or read the reports of my calls last night, but there is more. Two other people were taken, Skye's parents. We have no idea where they are, or if they are alive. From what this gentleman says there must have been other terrorists to attack Morgan Falls Dam. It is only an assumption, but they may have been taken with those men."

Bert listened intently. He would never dismiss anything this woman said again. "We will look into that and get them back if we can, ma'am."

He went to his vehicle and called it in to dispatch. He returned to Caroline. "They are going to put out a BOLO for them and make enquiries with cops down at Morgan Falls. We are going to be all over this."

Caroline just looked at him.

*

Phoenix ran to Skye's side. He dropped to his knees and held her in his arms and allowed her to cry. Thea joined the pair of them and began to lick her tears. It was enough to stem the flow, and she slowly began to giggle.

"Oh, darling, I thought he was going to kill Thea. I thought the other man had already killed her. How is Shadow? Where is Shadow? Caroline, I saw her shoot him. Is she okay? Brad, I haven't seen Brad. Where is Brad?"

"Whoa, whoa, slow down. They are all fine, just fine," he said soothingly to the panic stricken Skye.

"Oh, thank God," she said, as he held herself tight to his chest. For the first time in hours she felt safe.

Phoenix kissed the top of her wet hair. He was as relieved as her.

As quickly as the calm had taken Skye, a sudden panic replaced it. She pulled away from him and looked up. "My parents. They took my parents to my grandfather's place. It's down the river."

"How far?" he asked.

"About another mile," she answered.

"It's further to go back, so we will go find them." Phoenix moved to stand up, but she pulled him back to her.

"I can't walk, darling. I think my ankle is broken."

"I'll go alone. This place will be crawling with rescue people soon, they will take you to hospital," suggested Phoenix.

"Call it in, the cops can get there quicker you," she suggested.

"I can't, my cell phone was in my jacket pocket. I threw it away." He was cross with himself.

"You don't know the way to Gramps. I can't explain, it's too complicated." She was beginning to panic again.

"No problem. I have my sat nav." With that he stood up and lifted her into his arms as if she were a small child. "Which way?"

Skye wrapped her arms around his neck. He began to jog in the direction she indicated with Thea at his side.

*

The Delta Force CO had returned from the powerhouse. He reported back to the HSA agent.

"All clear. Enough puff to do the job, without a doubt. You'll need two body bags. The old guard was killed with one clean hit. The terrorist will need DNA to identify him. He doesn't have a face anymore." He looked over to Caroline, who was busying herself with Shadow.

"Okay, Crime Scene is on their way. There will be quite a job to do here." The HSA guy said. "It turns out there are two more missing. The cop just told me; apparently the kidnapped girl's parents were taken too. The cops are looking." He looked over to Bert who was still talking to the golden haired woman. "Anything from your men down there?" He nodded to the river below them.

"Not yet." At that exact instant his earpiece burst into life.

A crackly voice said, "One dead, two arrows, one in his neck and another in his heart. No sign of the girl though, or her dog, or an Indian." The CO chuckled as his sergeant continued. "I reckon the Indian won. The dead guy's got a gun and a knife by his side. It looks over to me, sir."

"Keep looking, sergeant. Make sure they are okay. There is the old guy too." The CO smiled to himself.

"So, what's up?" the agent asked.

"Tonto got him."

"Fuck, would you believe it?" The agent was amazed. He was convinced they would need body bags for the Indian and the woman.

"Probably not, but now Tonto and the girl have disappeared."

"Jeez, this is the weirdest Christmas I have ever had. I…"

The CO put his hand up, as he strained to hear the voice in his ear. "Great. How is he? Good, bring him up."

Caroline had been listening to there conversations. "Is that Brad? Is he okay?"

"Yes, ma'am, he's fine. He says the other two went off down river."

314

Caroline smiled, and ruffled Shadow's ears.

*

Carrying Skye for a mile was harder than Phoenix had thought. The last part was uphill through some woods and over a lawn to an old wooden house. He was glad to put her down in a rocker that sat on the veranda that overlooked the river below.

He had managed to stay out of sight of the house until the last part. He whispered to Skye, "Was it your impression from what the guy told you that his buddies would be here?"

Skye did not bother to whisper back. "No, they were going to leave them here to drown."

Phoenix readied his bow anyway, and stepped into the open door by Skye. At first he was stealthy, checking for any unexpected welcome. Once he was happy that no terrorists were lurking in the shadows he shouted, "Missy, Tristan, where are you?" Then a second time, even louder, "Missy, Tristan."

He heard a muffled response. It was a male voice and one he did not recognise. However, he knew one word. BASEMENT.

He ran out to Skye. "Which is the door to the basement?"

"In the hall, by the old pine desk," she replied.

He rushed back in and located the door. A single lock with the key still in it barred his way. He turned the key, it opened first time and he pushed it open.

"There is a light switch by the door," the strange voice said.

Phoenix found it and flicked it on. He stood and stared down the stone steps to the damp cellar below.

"Christ!'

He could see Missy lying in a pool of blood, motionless. She was tethered to a wooden pillar. Next to her, similarly secured, lay Tristan. His leg was at an impossible angle. Broken. Phoenix had seen hundreds of animals with similar injuries.

Tristan raised his head as the light came on. He was conscious.

Wrapped around a third pillar was the man he assumed to be Gramps. He was still working to get his wrists free.

Phoenix took the stone steps two at a time. As he jumped from the last one, Gramps said, "Missy. She is the worst. She's been stabbed. Lost a lot of blood. Tristan has been keeping her awake, but she has just slipped off."

Three steps and Phoenix was by her side. He felt for a pulse. It was there, but it was weak.

"I need a knife, Gramps." It was the only form of address Phoenix had for the old man.

"In the draw under the workbench," he replied.

Phoenix found a Stanley knife. He quickly cut the plastic ties that bound Missy. He laid her gently on her side and investigated the wound. Like Shadow, it would all depend on how much internal damage the knife had caused.

He was on his feet again. He cut Gramps free. "I need dressings and disinfectant. More importantly, I need a phone."

Gramps answered, "Got them all. Come with me."

He tried to stand but staggered back to the floor. The lack of circulation in his old legs had taken its toll. Phoenix helped him up and steadied him with his arm around his waist whilst Gramps clung to him. He half-lifted him up the steps.

"The kitchen," Gramps said. "That door." Phoenix helped him cross the hallway. "In the cupboard," he

316

nodded to one by the rear door. "I'll call for an ambulance. Set me down there."

Phoenix put him on a chair by the telephone and watched as he began to dial. As Gramps gave the details of the horrific injuries his daughter and her husband had received, Phoenix gathered the supplies he needed.

Before he rushed back to the cellar, Phoenix looked at the old man.

"They are coming, and the police," Gramps said.

"Good, well done, sir. Your granddaughter is on the veranda in the rocker, Thea is with her. She has a broken ankle. She would love to see you. Don't tell her about her parents yet." Phoenix waited for a reaction.

The old man's face lit up. "She's alive?"

"Very." Phoenix grinned at him.

"Thank the Lord." Gramps was already making his way to the veranda.

Back in the basement, he said to Tristan, "I'll get to you in a minute, sir. Missy needs help first."

"Of course, save her, Phoenix. Please save her if you can."

Phoenix went to work on the still unconscious Missy. He cleaned and packed the wound and then waited.

Ten minutes later he heard the sirens approach. He was kneeling next to Missy, when he heard a paramedic say, "We'll take it from here, sir."

It was not until that point that he was able to see to Tristan, and then only briefly before the medics whisked them all away.

By now Skye had seen the extent of her family's injuries. She was horrified but, as always, practical. She was the last to get into the ambulance with her broken ankle. The medics already had Missy on a drip and were preparing the first bag of blood to transfuse her. Gramps had refused treatment until he reached the hospital.

A second ambulance was being sent for Tristan.

Moving him was going to prove difficult and Missy needed surgery as soon as possible.

"I'll wait with your dad," Phoenix said to her, as Skye was helped into the rear of the ambulance.

"Look after Thea, won't you?" She kissed him on the lips and stopped Thea from climbing into the ambulance with her.

As it drove away along the gravel drive, the detective next to him said, "Okay, would you like to explain to me one more time what the hell happened here?"

*

Caroline answered her cell. There was no caller ID. "Hello," she said gingerly.

"Lady Caroline, I presume."

"Mowgli. Where the hell are you? Bloody hell, man, half of Delta Force is looking for you." Privately her heart soared to hear his voice.

Phoenix chuckled. "Actually, I'm at Skye's grandpa's house."

"Where? What the hell are you doing there? Having afternoon tea?"

He chuckled again. "Not exactly. I need your help to look after a dog, a white dog."

It was Caroline's turn to laugh. "Okay, you know animals are my one weakness. Why do you need me to look after Thea?"

"Don't get excited, but I have to go to the hospital."

"What…?"

"Hang on. I'm fine. Skye has a broken ankle. Her dad has a broken leg and two dislocated shoulders and Gramps is badly cut up."

"How?"

"I'll explain everything when you get here. How is my best boy?" He thought it best to tell her about Missy when she arrived.

"Shadow is fine, just a bit lovesick. Best we reunite him with his bitch."

Phoenix laughed. "Yeah. Here is the address." He read it out. "The sat nav should get you here. I'll fill you in on what's happened when you arrive."

The detective offered to take Phoenix to the hospital. He declined, preferring to have Caroline bring Shadow. Once she had arrived she could stay with the dogs whilst he drove the pick-up to the hospital.

Whilst he waited he found a shirt of Gramps that nearly fitted him. He thought it best not to turn up half-naked.

He made a fresh pot of coffee and helped himself to a sandwich with some ingredients he found in the fridge. 'Not exactly Christmas lunch,' he thought. Regardless, it tasted good.

In the absence of any dog food, he made another for Thea and one for Caroline and Shadow when they arrived.

Fifteen minutes later there was a knock at the front door. He opened it and was greeted by a, now very awake, black ball of fur.

"Careful, boy. You shouldn't be jumping up." Phoenix eased Shadow to the floor, just as he spied Thea behind Phoenix wagging. Phoenix now forgotten, he and Thea disappeared into the house.

Caroline hugged him, trying not to get too emotional. Slowly she pushed him away and held his hands. "Are you really unhurt?" she asked with a motherly tone to her voice.

"Not a scratch." He was grinning.

"Good, at times…well, you know," she said, fighting back a tear still holding his hands.

"Come in, I've made you both a sandwich. I'll fill you in whilst you eat. I guess Thea will want another." He led the way to the kitchen. "Pour yourself some coffee."

As he prepared another sandwich for Thea, and of course a second for Shadow, he began. "First, they are all going to be fine. Just broken bones. Missy, however, has been stabbed. She is in a coma but I had a good look at her and did what I could. I honestly believe she will be fine too."

"Oh no. How?"

Phoenix related the little he had learned from Gramps. Then he explained what had happened during his pursuit of the terrorist and Skye. He explained the role Thea had played and why he had to carry Skye to her grandpa's.

"Well done, Thea," Caroline said to the dog that she was now tickling behind the ear.

Phoenix smiled inwardly. He had not expected any praise for his part in it. Neither did he want it.

After they had eaten, he said, "You okay here? I'll go and check up on them all."

"Yeah, send them all my love. Get along now." She shooed him out of the door.

TWENTY-SIX

Skye was sitting by her mother's bed when Phoenix walked into the hospital room. Her foot was encased in a large black boot. Two crutches were lying against the side of her chair. There was nobody in the bed.

"They said you were in Missy's room." Phoenix was a little alarmed to see the empty bed. He had expected to see Missy in it. He stepped over to Skye and kissed her. "How is she?" he enquired.

"They are still operating on her, and Daddy is in an operating theatre as well. They are having to put a metal plate and pins in his break," Skye said. She looked completely drained.

Phoenix noticed that she had not really answered his question. He waited.

Skye sensed his unspoken question. "Mum is in a bad way. They are having problems stopping the internal bleeding. Luckily no internal organs were lacerated. If they can stop the bleeding, they say she will be fine. The coagulants aren't working. They have already pumped several pints into her, so they have opened her up and are trying to stitch the internal wounds."

Phoenix took her hand to reassure her. "It often takes a while."

She smiled at him, a wan tired smile. As if changing the subject would make the horror of her mother's injury go away, she said, "We did it, didn't we? We saved our lands."

Phoenix realised that she could not feel quite the euphoria he did at their accomplishment with Missy being in a critical condition.

"Yes, Newadi, we did it. This time we won."

Skye could barely manage a smile. Surprisingly, she stood up. "Let's go and check if Daddy is out of surgery yet."

Before Phoenix could offer to get a wheelchair, she was out of the door swinging expertly on her crutches towards another part of the hospital. Phoenix rushed to keep up with her. "You've done this before," he said.

"Twice, both ankles, at different times. Apparently I am clumsy, " she said. This time with a happier smile on her face.

Phoenix smiled. Another, hitherto unknown, facet of his soul mate revealed.

Her mood lightened again when she found her father lying on his own hospital bed. One leg was plastered from ankle to thigh and both arms were in slings.

"Look at the state of you," Skye said, as she leaned forward to kiss him on the forehead.

Tristan looked at his daughter's boot. "It might look bad, but I'll never be as clumsy as you."

It actually made Skye laugh. More seriously, she asked, "How on earth did we both end up like this?"

Before he could answer a doctor entered the room. Without preamble, he said, "We have reason to be optimistic that your wife will be fine. The bleeding has stopped and she has gained consciousness. We will keep her in the ICU for a few hours and then she can recuperate in her own room. If all goes well, I see no reason why she can't go home within a week."

Skye dropped her crutches and hugged the doctor. All the strain of the previous twenty-four hours drained from her face. Turning to her father, she caught the boot on the leg of the chair and fell onto the bed laughing.

"See, clumsy." Tristan hugged his daughter.

"Daddy, I was so scared."

"No need, I fancy fate was on our side this time," Tristan said, as he kissed his daughter on the forehead.

Phoenix looked at the woman he was destined to spend his life with and the father-in-law who would play a role in his future. They were both old souls that he would enjoy being reacquainted with. Tristan caught him assessing the scene. He smiled at the man who had helped save their lives, and then he nodded an appreciation unseen by his daughter. Nothing more would ever need to be said.

A couple of days later, as the doctor had promised, Tristan and Skye were both at home again, and Missy would follow in a few days.

Those days had been spent answering questions from what appeared to be every agency in the country. Phoenix and Skye took the brunt of it, along with Caroline. Her shooting of Mohammed was dismissed as justifiable homicide, although the police report cited the guard and not Shadow as the catalyst for her actions. Needless to say, she strongly objected to the findings and insisted that Bert entered Shadow's name to the report. He acquiesced.

At the end of it all the authorities had a clear picture of what had occurred during the thirty-six hours running up to the terrorist attacks. The only part of the story that they seemed unable to get their heads around was the concept of the main protagonists' reincarnation, and the spiritual aspect of why they had been destined to confront the threat the terrorists posed. Some believed their story, however, the majority did not. It was not a problem to any of them that the boys in blue and the men in black generally dismissed Cherokee legend. They had expected it.

On the other hand, the press and media had a field day with it. Phoenix and the others did not want the

323

celebrity, but they couldn't avoid it. A source in the police force had given the reporters the story. They suspected Bert, who was now one of the few believers. And once the ball was rolling it was unstoppable.

Within days, headlines like, 'Cherokee Indians Foil Al Qaeda,' greeted them wherever they went. Within weeks, America had fallen in love with Skye and Phoenix. Lady Caroline, as she was now known to the world, had become a celebrity and appeared on chat shows and became the 'go to' voice on anything to do with animal welfare.

Phoenix hated it. The only upside he could see was that the State of Georgia poured a great deal of money into their work with the animals and promised Caroline that future funding would not be a problem. It was by way of a thank you for what they had done.

*

Skye noticed the first buds were beginning to bloom on the magnolia trees in the driveway. It was already hot after a late but short winter. She looked at the holes in the garage door where Caroline had honed her shooting skills and smiled. It was a smile that came with mixed emotions.

She was about to return the boot that had incarcerated her broken ankle to the hospital, and take her father to have a final X-ray taken to make sure the bone had healed sufficiently for the metal plate to be removed. He was already sitting inside his BMW with the keys in his hand for Skye to drive him.

Shadow, who was completely unaware that he had ever been hurt, trotted by Thea's side expecting to get into the car with Skye.

"Sorry, you two, not his time. You stay with Missy, we will be back shortly," Skye said to the dogs.

Reluctantly, they sat and watched her get into the car and pull out of the drive.

Sitting next to his daughter, Tristan said, "Okay, young lady, what's the matter?" He had sensed Skye's increasing melancholy over the past few days. "You've got your man, we are all well again, and you are being heralded as the saviour of the Cherokee Nation and you are a star. But you have a face as long as an armadillo." He smiled at his daughter who looked more radiant than he could ever remember despite her obvious moodiness. "Is it because Phoenix is working all the time?"

Skye laughed. "No, Daddy." She giggled again. "He is working to escape all the attention, and he is back every night. I'm getting enough of Yona, don't worry."

She loved the pained look on her father's face at the thought of what she had just implied. It cheered her up, and her mood swung once again.

"Mummy is looking great again, isn't she?" She wanted to change the subject.

"Yeah, she healed quicker than any of us once the hospital had sorted out the bleeding. The whole experience seems to have energised her. She won't leave…"

"Enough" Sky held her hand up to quieten her father. "Too much information."

Tristan laughed. "Truce?"

"Okay, no more embarrassing each other."

"Seriously, what is the matter, Skye?"

"Nothing really, Daddy. Well, actually there is, but it is nothing much and we will talk about it at the weekend."

Tristan looked at his daughter. She was happy again, so he said no more.

Other than to the authorities and to the press, when

pushed, they had hardly discussed what had happened between themselves. There had been traumatic aspects to it, especially for Tristan and Missy. They had all been offered counselling and all had refused, believing they did not need it. Their group had an incredible bond and they provided their own support network for any trauma that had been experienced. That said; Skye realised that there were things that they needed to discuss. Things she needed to be addressed.

To that end, she had arranged a special evening in Brad's Cherokee village, which had also benefitted from the State of Georgia, to get them all together.

She enlisted Lucy's help, Brad's wife, with the food and arrangements. Caroline, as always, was too busy to get involved in the minutiae of everyday life. Both she and Yona were too busy putting their newfound funding to good use for the four-footeds and the rest of the animal kingdom.

The weekend finally arrived and Skye was, in part, dreading it. The evening was warm, but Brad lit a fire in the pit anyway. Beer and burgers were handed round and conversation flowed for everyone but Skye. Shadow and Thea were lying curled up together on their blankets that Skye had tied together in a knot.

It was the first time either Missy or Tristan had been to the village. For Missy it felt like coming home. Tristan had long since lost his sceptical view of all things Cherokee, he too felt perfectly at home with them all in this homage to their ancestry.

Caroline and he had formed a separate alliance within the tribe, which Lucy had quite naturally joined. All three of them poked fun at the 'savages' they had grown to love. Caroline, in particular, had found a willing ally in Tristan and joked with him that they made odd Cherokee Indians with their Oxford English and weird table manners.

Skye did not really join in the frivolities, but sat back and studied her people, both English and Cherokee.

Phoenix kept an eye on her. A little concerned about her introversion. Like Tristan, he had questioned her about it and was also told that she would tell him this evening. There was a reason she had brought them all together and she was acting mysteriously. He waited.

Eventually he went and sat at her side. Neither spoke at first, they just watched the others chatting and laughing. He took her hand in his. "Newadi, we all love you, don't you think it's time to tell us what is troubling you so much?"

"Yes, darling, it is. I'm sorry I have been so moody." She took his cheek in her hand and kissed him lightly on the lips.

She gave him a second, more passionate kiss, and then let him go. She picked up a beer bottle and tapped it with a fork. "Hey, people, listen up."

Tristan winced at the Americanism. Caroline laughed at his reaction.

"There is something we need to discuss." It went quiet. All eyes were trained on Skye, but nobody spoke. "The legend," she added.

Phoenix knew exactly what was coming. The rest waited.

Skye continued, "The legend says that if we meet a violent or an inappropriate death we will be reincarnated," she paused, looking around the group, and then she continued, "Caroline has done some more research, and we now know that on at least two occasions a number of us met violent ends whilst we were defending our lands."

"But this time nobody died," Phoenix took it up.

"No," said Skye. "If we live out our natural lives this might be…"

"The last time," Phoenix finished her sentence.

There was complete silence.

"It makes me sad, that is all I wanted to say. I know it's silly, but I cannot bear the idea that we will not meet again." There was a tear in Skye's eye.

Phoenix held her. "No, Newadi, not sad and it's not silly. If the legend is true it makes you complete. It makes us all complete. Our spirits will live on in the spirit world as one."

"We haven't made it yet, kid," Caroline offered Skye as solace for her obvious unhappiness. "In fact, my Adahy wasn't here at all. That was pretty inappropriate." She smiled at her friend.

"Yeah, and who the hell is my soul mate? Sorry, Lucy, no offence, but you ain't no Cherokee, darlin'," added Brad.

"None taken, honey."

Brad's intervention triggered another question from Caroline, "In fact, Brad, who the hell were you in our past? We have to find out what your role was in all of this." She said, jokingly.

"I've been wondering that too, Caroline," said Phoenix. "And why does he call me SON every time he talks to me?"

Brad grinned, the idea appealed to him. The others laughed.

Now Skye was smiling too. She wiped the tear from her cheek.

"Talking about sons," she tapped her tummy, "that is why I've been so moody." She smiled at the faces staring at her. "We have to pick two names."

Phoenix dropped the bottle of beer he had been holding.

THE END

THE BENCH

Also available on Kindle

Another novel by N. G. Jones

The bench is Jacques's world. The place he visits each day with Buster, his beloved dog, to remember his remarkable life.

It was a life that took him from the Battle of Britain to the French Resistance, and later into a world of intrigue during the conflicts of Vietnam.

It was a life that witnessed tragedy and love, hurt, happiness and great humour. But a life he would not have changed, and one he lived to the full.

There were a number of incredible women who shaped that life and lived those adventures with him. Only one of there names is inscribed on the bench. That name he touches each day.

THE VOICE

Also available on Kindle

Another novel by N. G. Jones

Two teenagers are trapped beneath the ruins of a collapsed building. The result of a terrorist suicide bombing of the French barracks in Beirut, 1983.

They cannot see one another, but their voices keep each other alive for five days. Each voice beseeching and encouraging the other to survive the maelstrom they are incarcerated within.

A lifelong infatuation with each other's voice follows, and the search to hear that voice again and the person who owns it begins.

Their searches follow different paths through the Palestinian refugee camps of Lebanon, the genocide of Rwanda and to Afghanistan.

Relationships and tragedy guide those paths, but there is only goal.

AUTHOR

Nigel Jones began writing as a hobby to fill the quiet and unproductive early hours of the morning. Hours left void after the bars of Hong Kong, Singapore, New York and Cape Town closed. Hours the jet lag his career as an airline pilot suggested should be used more productively than watching early-hour TV reruns.

He has written seven books. Three of which are available through Amazon and Kindle.

Coming soon, other books include Publish and be Damned, a thriller with a core message that could change the world. It will be part of a trilogy, the second book is entitled World's End or Genesis, and the third is currently being crafted.

Another book is entitled February 29th. It is an epic tale of soul mates whose story begins in Kilkenny, with the first burning of a witch in Ireland, and concludes with a doctor and a pilot in present times.

Nigel is married to Sandi who is involved in the editing of all his books. They have a son called Ashley, who is a space scientist and whose job baffles his father.

If you would like to give feedback about The Bench, The Voice or The Lake please email: jonsn@hotmail.co.uk

10073280R00186

Printed in Great Britain
by Amazon.co.uk, Ltd.,
Marston Gate.